THE JEWISH KULTURBUND THEATRE COMPANY IN NAZI BERLIN

STUDIES IN THEATRE HISTORY AND CULTURE

EDITED BY THOMAS POSTLEWAIT

REBECCA ROVIT

The Jewish Kulturbund Theatre Company in Nazi Berlin

UNIVERSITY OF IOWA PRESS

IOWA CITY, IOWA

University of Iowa Press, Iowa City 52242

Printed in the United States of America

Design by Richard Hendel

www.uiowapress.org

The University of Iowa Press is a member of Green Press Initiative and is committed to preserving natural resources.

Printed on acid-free paper

Library of Congress Cataloging-in-Publication Data
Rovit, Rebecca.
The Jewish Kulturbund theatre company in Nazi Berlin / by Rebecca Rovit.
p. cm.—(Studies in theatre history and culture)
Includes bibliographical references and index.
ISBN-13: 978-1-60938-124-0 (pbk)
ISBN-10: 1-60938-124-6 (pbk)
1. Jewish theater—Germany—Berlin—History.
2. Judischer Kulturbund. 3. Jews—Germany—History—1933–1945. 4. Jews—Germany—Berlin—Intellectual life. 5. Berlin (Germany)—Ethnic relations.
I. Title.
PN3035.R68 2012
792.089′924043155—dc23 2012004394

For

HONEY WEISENFELD ROVIT

and

EARL ROVIT

CONTENTS

ACKNOWLEDGMENTS

This book is the result of more than a decade of research and travel that has taken me overseas to archives and interviews. I could not have written it without the help of many people and institutions. I remain indebted to the artists who are the subject of this study. I owe my gratitude first to the Kulturbund performers—and their relatives—who have shared with me the details of their lives in Nazi Berlin: Mascha Benya-Matz, Ruth Anselm-Herzog, Mira Rostovsky, Henry Bloch, Kurt Michaelis, and Hannah Kroner-Segal. I am obliged to Eva Wisten and Susanne Wisten-Weyl for their invaluable insight about their father and their generosity regarding his archival collections. And with the help of Dov Matz, Joan Durham (via Jackie Logan), and Dr. Ruth Gross (Pisarek), I gained access to family photographs and lore.

While researching and writing this study I benefited from the advice of colleagues and friends. I am grateful to Zdenka Fantlová and Max Rodrigues Garcia for all that they have taught me about creativity and survival. My work on the Kulturbund could not have been launched without the expert groundwork laid by the late Sybil M. Milton, Saul Friedländer, Alan Steinweis, Henryk M. Broder, the late Eike Geisel, and Volker Kühn.

I would like to acknowledge several people whose scholarship and friendship kept me company at times during the long and lonely process of writing the book: Sharon Gillerman, Alvin Goldfarb, the late Henry H. H. Remak, Eileen Julien, Anne Dutlinger, Guido Fackler, Pnina Rosenberg, and John London.

I have been fortunate to receive external funding for my study from several institutions. A grant from the American Council of Learned Societies (ACLS) allowed me to spend a research year in Berlin and London. I also received travel stipends from the Memorial Foundation for Jewish Culture and the American Philosophical Society to pursue my research abroad. The Advanced Center for Holocaust Studies at the United States Holocaust Memorial Museum granted me a two-week forum to try out my ideas in a summer workshop I led on Culture and the Holocaust. And a German Academic Exchange (DAAD) stipend afforded me extra time in archives overseas. Several people at archival institutions have given me access to extraordinary documents central to my research: the librarians at the Leo Baeck Institute, New

York; archivists Jürgen Wittneben, Stephan Dörschel, and Renate Rätz at the Stiftung der Akademie der Künste, Berlin, Robert-Koch-Platz; Jo Reilly, formerly of the Wiener Library, London; and David Marwell, director of the former Berlin Document Center. At the University of Kansas, I thank the College of Arts and Sciences and my chair, John Staniunas, for their support. The generous and timely book award from the Friends of the Hall Center for Humanities enabled me to publish many of the photographs in the book.

I extend my sincere appreciation to the staff at the University of Iowa Press for all of their assistance. Holly Carver, former director of the press, has been encouraging and always of a cheerful disposition. To my inspiring editor Tom Postlewait, I give my heartfelt thanks. His steadfast commitment to my book, his enthusiasm for my subject, his tireless reading, and, finally, his meticulous attention to every detail of my writing helped me to make this book its very best.

My deepest gratitude and love go to those who know me best: their presence and their belief in my ability to complete the book pushed me forward. I thank my dear Sarah, who has grown up amid this research, literally sitting among crumpled papers on my office floor. I am ever grateful to Robert Rohrschneider, my soulmate and most judicious partner, for his consistently keen insight. I have learned a great deal from the way that he pursues his own research with an admirable work ethic. My greatest debt is to my parents, to whom I dedicate this book. They have provided me with an incomparable model for creative and rigorous intellectual engagement. Their unwavering trust in my capacity to reach beyond my grasp to compile and to complete this study has given me great solace, confidence, and drive.

DRAMATIS PERSONAE

JEWISH KULTURBUND THEATRE IN BERLIN

Ruth Anselm (Condell; née Hentschke), dancer, cabaret actress, 1933–1938. Survived.

Dr. Julius Bab, drama critic, founding member and literary advisor to the theatre, 1933–1938. Survived.

Kurt Baumann, founding member of the Kulturbund and stage director, 1933–. Survived.

Mascha Benyakonsky, opera singer, 1936/1937–1938. Survived.

Alfred Berliner (Balthoff), actor, 1933–1941. Survived.

Martin Brandt, actor, 1933–1939. Survived.

Martin Brasch, lawyer, financial manager of theatre, member of executive board, 1939–1940. Did not survive.

Heinz Condell, head of scenography, set and costume designer, 1933–1938. Survived.

Max Ehrlich, actor, comedian, cabaret director, 1935–1939. Did not survive.

Herbert Freeden (Friedenthal), journalist, dramaturg, stage director, 1936–1938. Survived.

Herbert Grünbaum, actor, director. 1934–1939. Survived.

Walter Hertner (Herz), actor, 1934–1938. Survived.

Werner Hinzelmann, director of School Theatre, 1936–1938, actor, director of Jewish School Theatre troupe, active 1936–1941. Did not survive.

Dr. Leo Hirsch, drama critic and dramaturg for theatre, 1938–1941. Did not survive.

Fritz Jessner, stage director, 1934–1936. Survived.

Lilly Kann, actress, 1933–1939. Survived.

Hannah Kroner-Segal, dancer, choreographer, 1937–1939. Survived.

Ernst Lenart (also spelled Lennart; born Ernesto Levi), actor, 1933–1936. Survived.

Dr. Werner Levie, journalist and financial manager; managing director of Kulturbund and theatre, October 1938–August 1939. Did not survive.

Hanna Litten, set and costume designer, 1938–1941. Did not survive.

Kurt Michaelis, orchestra member, oboist, 1937–1941. Survived.

Steffi Ronau (Hinzelmann; née Rosenbaum), actress in school troupe, main stage, 1936–1941. Survived.

Mira Rostova (Rostovsky), actress, 1933–1934. Survived.

Jenny Schaffer-Bernstein, actress, 1933–1941. Did not survive.

Rudolf Schwarz, conductor of orchestra, 1933–1941. Survived.

Dr. Kurt Singer, managing and artistic director of Kulturbund theatre and opera, 1933–1938. Did not survive.

Ben Spanier, actor, 1933–1941, originally with Rhein-Ruhr Kulturbund. Did not survive.

Camilla Spira Eisner, cabaret actress, 1935–1938. Survived.

Kurt Süßmann, actor, 1938–1941. Did not survive.

Fritz Wisten, actor, head of acting division, stage director, managing artistic director of Kulturbund and theatre, 1939–1941. Survived.

JEWISH PRESS

Dr. Julius Brodnitz, editor, *C.-V.-Zeitung*, 1933–1936. Did not survive.

Arthur Eloesser, critic, *Die Jüdische Rundschau*, 1933–1938. Did not survive.

Leo Kreindler, editor-in-chief, *Jüdisches Nachrichtenblatt*, 1938–1942. Did not survive.

Dr. Hugo Lachmanski, drama critic, *C.-V.-Zeitung*, 1933–1938, *Jüdisches Nachrichtenblatt*, 1939–1943. Did not survive.

Kurt Pinthus, drama critic for *Der Schild*, 1933–1937. Survived.

Dr. Lutz Weltmann, critic for the *Jüdisch-Liberale Zeitung* and stage director of the Kulturbund's *Golden Chain*, 1936. Survived.

Robert Weltsch, editor, *Die Jüdische Rundschau*, 1933–1938. Survived.

Dr. Martha Wertheimer, journalist, *Israelitisches Familienblatt*. Did not survive.

NAZI OFFICIALS

Admiral Wilhelm Canaris, chief of military intelligence

Dr. Joseph Goebbels, minister of propaganda and enlightenment

SS-Reichsführer Reinhard Heydrich, chief of police

SS-Kommandant Hans Hinkel, director of Jewish cultural affairs and propaganda

SS-Officer Erich Kochanowski, head of propaganda division under Hinkel

Dr. Rainer Schlösser, *Reichsdramaturg* (chief dramaturg and censor of the Reich)

INTRODUCTION

OUSTED

On the evening of 1 October 1933 Gotthold Ephraim Lessing's classic eighteenth-century play about religious tolerance, *Nathan the Wise*, inaugurated an all-Jewish theatre on Berlin's Charlottenstraße. Just six months after the Reichstag voted to give Adolf Hitler dictatorial control of the German government, the subscription theatre emerged as part of a cultural organization known as the Kulturbund Deutscher Juden (Cultural Association of German Jews). Dr. Kurt Singer, the former director of Berlin's Municipal Opera, had negotiated the conditions for the Kulturbund with Ministry of Propaganda SS-Kommandant Hans Hinkel, the Nazi official assigned to Jewish cultural affairs. Singer ushered the theatre's first season into a new venue, signaling a cultural situation for Jews in Germany that would increasingly isolate them. As Singer welcomed the audience to the Berliner Theater, he called attention to the final scene of *Nathan*—an ending traditionally denoting harmony and the universality of religion. But when the curtain fell at the end of the premiere, Kurt Katsch as the Jewish merchant stood physically alone on the stage, with a pulpit and a menorah visible in his home. The director Karl Loewenberg had produced the last scene without translating Lessing's explicit stage directions into performance: no "all-around embrace" involving Nathan, the Sultan Saludin, and the Christian templar took place.

For more than a century Lessing's stage character Nathan had embodied the ideals of the German Enlightenment and featured the traits that the playwright valued in the philosopher and assimilated Jew Moses Mendelssohn, his close friend: humanism, tolerance, and an openness to world culture. Widely accepted among Jews and non-Jews in Germany as an exemplar of the cultural education known as *Bildung*, *Nathan the Wise* also represented German-Jewish interdependence to generations of German Jews, what Jeanette R. Malkin has referred to as a kind of "cultural shorthand": "the platform of Jewish aspirations for inclusion and acceptance in Germany."[1] But the Berlin Kulturbund's production of *Nathan* in 1933 did not portray Nathan as an assimilated Jew, whose ethnicity was either negligible or something to be forgiven. Instead Loewenberg's staging emphasized Nathan the Jew, showing him to be a compassionate man, albeit one whose exclusion from society was palpable. By underscoring the character's Jewish faith, the director inverted the illusory idea that Jews in 1933 were accepted in German society.

Hugo Lachmanski, the drama critic for the Jewish community's liberal-leaning *Centralverein Zeitung der deutschen Staatsbürger jüdischen Glaubens* (*C.-V.-Zeitung*), questioned the Kulturbund director's decision to stage the last scene with a sense of existential isolation. "Why did he [the director] leave Nathan . . . all alone like a man gone to pieces and staggering in solitude, so that one has to fear the worst for him?" he wrote, referring to the contrast between the way Lessing portrayed Nathan's character and the director's interpretation of the character's behavior.[2] A reviewer for the *Jüdische Rundschau* (the newspaper for Germany's Zionist Organization), however, believed that the premiere's altered ending commented on "Jewish fate" when the Muslim and Christian characters exited together and left "Nathan's lofty figure alone in the limelight, gloomy and solitary."[3] Impressed by the director's choice to offer audiences an apt representation of the Jew as isolated, the reviewer recalled Hans Hinkel's stipulation for permitting the Kulturbund in the first place. Hinkel had warned Singer only months before the premiere that the theatre was to be a "purely Jewish cultural affair."[4] The opportune timing of the Kulturbund's all-Jewish *Nathan* production two days after the Day of Atonement (Yom Kippur) allowed audience members to reflect upon the tangible reality of what "Jewish tragedy" meant historically and in the present.[5] The poignantly produced final scene drew attention to Nathan's Jewishness as he returned alone to his house and to his prayer stand.

This book chronicles the fate of the Berlin Kulturbund throughout its existence from 1933 to 1941. The Kulturbund's production of *Nathan* demonstrated a new reality for Jewish-born Germans. In the wake of Hitler's ascent to power, the government's large-scale *Gleichschaltung* (consolidation of authority) allowed the Nazis to control policy in all sectors of legal and public life in Germany. By March 1933 Goebbels's Reich Ministry of Propaganda and Enlightenment incorporated all of the arts within the Reich Chamber of Culture. The Chamber of Culture and its seven subsections effectively managed the arts in Germany. All theatre activities underwent a complete reorganization, culminating with Goebbels's appointment of Dr. Rainer Schlösser as *Reichsdramaturg* and the chief censor of play scripts for the Reich.[6] Through central planning and new policies, a concerted effort to oust Jews from the economic and public spheres ensued during the spring. Goebbels appointed Hans Hinkel, head of the Prussian Theatre Commission, to lead a purge of prominent Jewish artists and intellectuals from Germany's cultural institutions. With the later Reich Civil Service Law of April 1933 aimed to "restore a national professional civil service," all non-Aryans (Jews) were removed from their professional workplace.[7] The passage of new laws thus forbade Jewish artists in the Reich and its capital city to collaborate theatrically with their fellow German citizens. The Kulturbund Deutscher Juden (Cultural Association of German Jews) represented an artistic and organizational response to Germany's "racial" laws by a group of Jewish theatre artists.

When Kurt Singer (a colleague of his from the opera), Kurt Baumann, and the drama critic Julius Bab proposed the idea of an all-Jewish theatre to officials at the Reich Cultural Chamber in the summer of 1933, Goebbels delegated the chamber president, Otto Laubinger, to assess the plan's potential. Laubinger passed the decision to the Prussian Theatre Commission, where Hinkel responded with skepticism as to whether the Nazi ministry could control such an enterprise.[8] Yet Singer's good reputation with his former non-Jewish colleagues at the commission afforded him credibility. They favored his proposal to hire hundreds of unemployed Jews. Perhaps more importantly, Singer made it clear that the proposed cultural league would only be open to Jewish members.[9] On 6 July Hinkel—Goebbels's designated official for Jewish cultural affairs—approved the Jewish organization as long as its activities took place within "closed" quarters.

The story of the Kulturbund theatre reveals a vital tradition of theatre art, steeped in Weimar Germany and distinctly tied to German history and to Jewish culture.[10] The history of the theatre and its repertoire constitutes a testament to art-making under duress. Germany's racial laws of 1933 required all Jews in the performing arts to join the Kulturbund. Jews who wanted to attend cultural events as audience members also had to become members of the Kulturbund alliance. A network of all-Jewish cultural leagues and theatre ensembles extended from Berlin across Germany, coexisting for eight years with Nazi policies against Jews, before the Gestapo dissolved the theatre in 1941.

The Berlin Kulturbund and its theatre constituted the largest audience membership and the most extensive personnel of all the Jewish Kulturbund branches in Germany. The theatre included a main-stage acting ensemble, a troupe that cooperated with Jewish schools and performed for Jewish youth, a touring cabaret, an opera company, a full choir, an orchestra, and a film and lecture series. The main headquarters in the Reich's capital lent extra legitimacy to the Jewish theatre. By the middle of 1935 Berlin served as the official center for all local Jewish cultural agencies under the umbrella organization known as the Reichsverband der jüdischen Kulturbünde (Reich Association of Jewish Cultural Leagues). As director of the Berlin-based organization, Singer reported to the Ministry of Propaganda, specifically to Hinkel. As a result of his cooperation, Singer enabled the formation of regional and metropolitan Jewish cultural leagues in the Rhein/Ruhr region and the cities of Danzig and Breslau by late 1933 and Hamburg and Frankfurt in 1934. The Berlin Kulturbund, however, provided the subsidiary Kulturbund theatres with a template for how to operate and what to perform. Many of the actors employed by the Berlin Kulturbund also performed at the other Kulturbund theatres. The ancillary organizations shared the same concerns as the Berlin Kulturbund, from hiring unemployed artists to establishing programs for members of all ages and cooperating with local police.

The Kulturbund theatre's bylaws prescribed that only Jews could be members, attend cultural events, and review them in Jewish newspapers. The historical context in which the theatre emerged, however, created vexing questions about Jewish identity for the Kulturbund Jews. How did the cultural organization reflect its diverse Jewish community and at the same time abide by the Nazi racial laws that targeted Jews? Despite a minority Zionist contingent within Berlin, many members of the Jewish community saw themselves as "assimilated" Jews, more in touch with humanist, secular values and literary classics than with religious precepts of Judaism and East European or Hebrew-language drama.[11] The Nazi government, however, barred the Kulturbund from performing plays by non-Jewish Germans and Austrians. How did Singer and his two successors at the Kulturbund helm, Werner Levie and Fritz Wisten, balance the demands by the Nazi authorities with the differing conceptions on the function of art advocated by spokespeople and journalists associated with various Jewish community groups? By virtue of the "closed" nature of their theatre, Kulturbund artists had no choice but to present their separate theatrical and music programs as Jewish culture. As Nazi laws increasingly segregated Jews from German life and culture, the Kulturbund became their only safe place to participate in cultural events and to create art.

The theatre's administrative and creative directors under Singer found themselves repeatedly caught between the competing interests of their Nazi government overseers and their own Jewish community constituents. Pressure from the Zionists and from the assimilated Jews of the Centralverein about what plays to perform caused disagreement on the theatre repertoire and divided an already fractious community. This division manifested itself in a public debate in the Jewish press about the kind of culture that the Kulturbund could—and should—offer Jewish citizens in the new German Reich. The principal debate reflected contrasting viewpoints and began in the summer before the inaugural *Nathan* production. Newspaper editorialists responded to the theatre's emerging role in Jewish life. While one community critic might praise a play choice that a Nazi censor deemed unobjectionable (like Arthur Schnitzler's *Paracelsus* in 1934), that play could irritate another critic by not suitably reflecting "Jewish life." The debates influenced the Kulturbund's theatre repertoire and shaped the audience reception. Official censorship from the Ministry of Propaganda's Reich Chamber of Culture continually affected the repertoire, further modifying the theatre's role, while renewing tension between groups in Berlin's Jewish community.

The Kulturbund's name suggested precisely what it was: a cultural coalition peopled by German-Jewish artists and audience members. These Jews regarded themselves as Germans of Jewish origin. The majority of German Jews who had worked in the cultural sphere before 1933 had belonged to German cultural circles. They were bound by the German language to German audiences. Yet they had to join the Jewish community in Berlin before they could become Kulturbund members. Singer and his close associates—Bab as literary advisor, Baumann as director, Levie as administrator, and Wisten as actor—faced the daunting task of transforming a cultural association of Jews based only on a loose and varied sense of Jewish religious and cultural identity into an institution with a conscious communal identity.

The various labels enforced by the Nazi government on the Kulturbund—and on its members—reflect the organization's changing identity and its predicament in Nazi Germany. After the Nuremberg Laws passed in September 1935, Nazi authorities in Prussia ruled that the organization must officially change its name to emphasize its Jewishness. The Prussian court ruled against the term "German" in the Kulturbund's title, which eased the Nazi fear that Jews might create their own national minority in Germany. According to the court, Jews could be only Jews, not German, French, or Polish Jews.[12] Thus the association legally adopted the name "Jewish" Kulturbund in Germany. The emphasis on the league's Jewishness made clear the Nazi government's determination to separate Jews in Germany from German culture. A former Kulturbund artist acknowledged his shifting sense of identity: "Hitler made clear what we were. I saw myself as a Jewish not a German artist."[13]

The Kulturbund Jews found themselves subject to the new German reality as necessity and law defined their membership in a Jewish community and, by extension, redefined their culture. Laws mandated that all Kulturbund members carry picture identification cards stating that they were Jews "according to the laws of the Reich."[14] By 1938 all Jews had to carry supplementary cards (*Kennkarten*), identifying them as Jews. The Nazis would dictate in January 1939 that men adopt the middle name "Israel" and women the name "Sara." As one Berliner recalled, "[I]t's hard to understand how we could go on in our daily lives with a middle name that was not our own. As if it was normal."[15] Passports marked with "J" for "Jew" were issued shortly thereafter, followed by the Stars of David in autumn of 1941.

We cannot fully understand the Kulturbund theatre without considering the working relationship between the company's artistic director and Nazis who oversaw the institution, particularly in its early years. How did Singer and his dramaturg Bab establish the Kulturbund's theatre performance repertoire within the narrowing strictures dictated by authorities at the Ministry of Propaganda? As the cultural organization developed and established its repertoire, Singer pursued a tenuous alliance with Hinkel. The resulting decisions that Singer and his advisors made about the Jewish theatre exposed the fault-lines along which Nazi censors suppressed plays for being "assimilatory" to German life, not "Jewish" enough, or threateningly "too Jewish."

Schlösser directed Hinkel to ensure that Singer and his theatre staff would produce plays which specifically incorporated "Jewish" themes and characters. Hinkel not only sent Singer written directives but called the Kulturbund manager to his ministry office to enforce these directives. Even so, when Singer projected the Kulturbund's community role within Nazi Germany and the theatre programs he would offer audiences, he unconsciously drew on his cultural education and the theatrical tradition in Germany prior to 1933. This tradition included repertoires richly filled with world classics like Lessing's *Nathan the Wise*, a work that the stage director Loewenberg transformed for the all-Jewish theatre. The process by which Singer decided which play scripts to produce reveals the contradictions that ensued as a result of the interchange between negotiation and censorship with Ministry of Propaganda officials, within the Kulturbund theatre and its community, and in the Kulturbund branches that existed outside of Berlin.

Singer served as an intermediary between Jewish artists in the Kulturbund's regional centers and Hinkel. From his Berlin-Charlottenburg apartment in 1933 through 1934 and from the new theatre on Kommandantenstraße in central Berlin after autumn 1935, Singer directed the flow of manuscripts and permissions, issued warnings regarding those permissions, and booked touring performances to Jewish communities in Germany's provinces. Besides his alliance with Hinkel's office, Singer maintained ties with the centralized administrative organization in Berlin for Jews in Germany, the Reich Representation of German Jews (Reichsvertretung der deutschen Juden), which became part of the Reich Union of Jews in Germany (Reichsvereinigung der Juden in Deutschland) in 1939. The escalating bureaucratic incorporation of Kulturbund leagues into Nazi Germany's web of Jewish organizations facilitated the German government's control over the Kulturbund network and led to its dissolution in September 1941. Singer had emigrated from Germany by then, and the Kulturbund artistic directorship had passed to the theatre's administrative manager, journalist and economist Werner Levie, between October 1938 and 1939. Fritz Wisten took over as the Kulturbund's last artistic director from 1939 to 1941.

Singer and his staff wanted their cultural programs to convey a set of principled humanist values. The artistic director hoped to shape a theatre and music repertoire that reflected artistic openness in production. This meant featuring classics by authors like William Shakespeare, Henrik Ibsen, and Molière, as well as plays by lesser-known Jewish authors. To achieve this balance, however, Singer deliberated regularly with his personnel and with cultural leaders within Berlin's greater Jewish community. Despite his desire to uphold his artistic ideals, he often encountered conflict and contention. Given the many challenges to his theatre, Singer made compromises on the repertoire and contended with Nazi policies that grew more restrictive with each year. Nonetheless, Singer, his directors, and performers resisted the caricature of a Jewish theatre that officials from the Nazi Ministry of Propaganda more or less promoted. The Kulturbund members worked to create theatre art while Nazi law threatened their core belief in truth and the freedom of expression. Their seriousness of purpose and commitment to high standards of art remained at the core of their poignant struggle to maintain a theatre for Jews, even as the Nazi government increasingly singled out the Jewish community and its cultural network for extinction.

The Kulturbund theatre's beginnings in 1933 coincided with the initiation of a "cultural ghettoization," which gradually intensified as the Nazis deported Jews to physically enclosed ghetto and camp settings.[16] My study of the Berlin Kulturbund draws attention to the everyday life that the Kulturbund Jews continued to live despite the restrictive laws. I explain the details of the Kulturbund organization and its aims and show how the Kulturbund theatre operated within increasingly constraining conditions imposed by the Nazis. The Kulturbund arts community provided distraction, enlightenment, and hope, creating a full-fledged repertory theatre for which former participants and audience members have expressed gratitude. Cultural historians have questioned whether the Kulturbund was an institution that represented Jewish culture and high art or whether it was exploited by the Nazis for political purposes.[17] These questions mirror arguments made about theatrical and musical performance by victim-artists during the years associated with the Holocaust and the idea that cultural activity within the shadow of death and destruction was an anomalous and grotesque occurrence.

The Jewish Kulturbund in Germany, however, did not represent an isolated phenomenon in performance history between 1933 and 1945. An all-Jewish theatre developed in Amsterdam during the summer of 1941 under the former Kulturbund manager Werner Levie and cabaret artist Max Ehrlich. The Jewish theatre in Nazi-occupied Holland represented a situation more desperate than that of its German counterpart. At the Joodse Schouwburg in Amsterdam, Jewish theatre artists struggled to survive while the Nazi plan to eliminate them developed. On 12 July 1942 the Nazis converted the Schouwburg theatre into a deportation depot. From there they deported Jews to Westerbork, Theresienstadt, and Auschwitz-Birkenau. Even at transit and concentration camps, however, some artists organized cultural activities for authorized and clandestine venues.[18]

We must continually remind ourselves that those people who engaged in theatrical performances during the Third Reich, under the Nazi occupation, and in ghettos and camps could not know the full extent of what lay ahead for them. Nor did artists at the Kulturbund theatre and living day to day in Germany fathom how their lives would change in such a short time. They created theatre in the most difficult circumstances, within a political system that undermined their existence step by step. Yet their perseverance suggests the remarkable nature of human tenacity. As Victor Klemperer makes clear in his diaries, those who lived in the Nazi Reich day to day did not have the luxury of hindsight with which we now look at the years from 1933 to 1941; instead, they responded on a quotidian basis to the impediments imposed on their freedoms, seeking normalcy amid the downward spiral of events around them.[19]

My study of an extraordinary all-Jewish theatre inside Nazi Germany encompasses the complex interplay between history and human lives. By charting the path that the theatre company took to make art amid prejudice and censorship, I show how the artists compromised some of their ideals as they faced competing pressures from Nazi official policies and from within their community. In a dictatorship where laws targeted Jews and ousted them from the cultural sphere, the Kulturbund theatre represented an eight-year struggle in which artists attempted to maintain their livelihood and ethical commitment to their community under siege.

■ I have organized the book as a chronological narrative that describes the development of Berlin's Kulturbund theatre and its repertoire between 1933 and 1941. The theatre evolved within three historical phases of the Third Reich, each punctuated by debilitating legal directives against Jews which severely limited their civil liberties and well-being: the summer of 1933 to 1935 (from the Reichstag fire in February 1933 to the passage of the Nuremberg racial laws in September 1935); 1936 to 1938 (from the remilitarization of the Rhineland in March 1936 to the Summer Olympics of August 1936 and the Reichskristallnacht [Night of Broken Glass] of November 1938); and January 1939 to September 1943 (from the outbreak of World War II to the theatre's six-month closure and the first deportation of Jews from Germany's Baden-Palatine region in October 1940 to the dissolution of the Kulturbund and its aftermath). Each of the three sections is divided into chapters covering the period in which the theatre developed, from its establishment in 1933 through the autumn of 1941. The chapters focus on annual playing seasons, which typically ran from autumn to autumn.

This structure allows for a narrative of the theatre as it developed in response to historical events, including not only the actions of the Nazi government but also the intra-Jewish community debates that influenced repertoire choices. In this historical study of the Berlin-based Kulturbund, I examine its productions, leadership, and organizational decisions within the contexts of the psychological, social, political, and economic conditions. I draw on a wealth of primary source materials, including newspapers, production photographs, letters, memoirs, and archival materials from the Reich Ministry of Propaganda and Enlightenment. In addition, I conducted approximately twenty interviews between 1995 and 2010 with Jewish émigrés and former members of the Kulturbund. All of these sources have yielded clues about the plays and the historical production process and about people's personal dilemmas with their German Jewish identity. Published scripts used for Kulturbund productions proved especially valuable for my research, as did numerous scripts used at the Berlin Kulturbund by an actor or director, which contain original notations referring to line readings and script changes. Archival materials from the Ministry of Propaganda reveal censorship marks and commentary by Hinkel and his censors. Play reviews from contemporary Jewish newspapers and production photographs have allowed me to present as complete a picture as possible of Kulturbund repertoire choices and production methods. Finally, the reviews offer clues about the audience response to performances, while suggesting some of the potential risks that the plays may have represented for government censors.

To re-create the rich and contradictory historical narrative of this theatre, we must consider the difficult task of recording history that occurred within wartime. The ravages of World War II, emigration, and the deportation of many of the Kulturbund performers and eyewitnesses resulted in records destroyed and documents scattered across the world. It is essential to keep in mind the tightening of Nazi control over Berlin's Jewish community and its official newspapers when considering the debates in the Jewish community's newspapers about Jewish culture and the Kulturbund. After 9 November 1938 the Nazis banned the Jewish press temporarily, eventually authorizing one Jewish publication. The host of newspapers for Jewish readers dwindled to one official community newspaper, the *Jüdisches Nachrichtenblatt*, carefully supervised by the Nazi authorities and under the auspices of the Kulturbund itself.[20] By 1939 the Kulturbund monopolized not only the culture created in the Jewish community but also the reporting of that culture. Without the *Jüdisches Nachrichtenblatt*, however, virtually no public information would exist about the Kulturbund, which dominated the local news until 12 September 1941. Newspaper reviews by Jewish reporters and eyewitness reports offer historiographers a scintillating source of testimony. Although these memories may be filtered through time, the voices from the past offer us the lived experience of participant-witnesses, adding an unparalleled immediacy and sometimes contradicting the written record.[21]

"Part One: Inception and Identity in an All-Jewish Theatre in Nazi Berlin, 1933–1935" investigates the years during which Singer as the artistic manager and his colleagues conceived the idea of the Kulturbund. The three chapters cover the theatre's beginnings and its first two playing seasons. Chapter 1 begins immediately before Hitler took power and describes the people who established the goals and repertoire of the Kulturbund theatre during the summer of 1933. Chapter 2 introduces the first season (1933–1934) and examines the cultural debates on the theatre and censorship of the repertoire in the first year. I point to the inherent contradictions in the Kulturbund's struggle to represent its goals and identity while reflecting the demands of competing groups within the Jewish community. The campaign to produce a Jewish category of plays, uphold humanist values, and abide by Ministry of Propaganda restrictions caused the directors to produce a spate of plays with biblical themes related to Jewish history. Chapter 3 describes and contextualizes the Kulturbund's choice of plays in its second season (1934–1935), when the Nazis tightened their racial laws.

"Part Two: Dual Foundations of a Community Repertoire, 1935–1938" explores the Kulturbund's struggle to forge a repertoire after the passage of the 1935 Nuremberg Laws. The three chapters cover the playing seasons which led to the Reichskristallnacht in 1938. They show how Nazi policies affected the theatre and its players as pressure from Jewish community groups and from Hinkel pushed the Kulturbund to present "Jewish culture." Chapter 4 focuses on the 1935–1936 season, when the ongoing clash of intra-Jewish opinion and Nazi doctrine on the theatre continued. Chapter 5 considers the results of a 1936 conference that Hinkel organized for Kulturbund representatives on how to make the cultural programs exclusively Jewish. The conference took place after the Berlin Olympics, when the Nazi government encouraged emigration from Germany. During the 1936–1937 season and prior to his own emigration in 1938, Singer produced plays that featured Zionism amid a worsening social and political climate for Jews in Germany. Chapter 6 covers the 1937–1938 season, when Singer produced a contemporary play set in Palestine. Despite the systematic problem of censorship, he offset the repertoire's Jewish-themed plays with well-known classics by Ibsen (*Pillars of Society*) and Shakespeare (*Much Ado about Nothing*).

"Part Three: Appeasement and Unraveling, 1938–1943" encompasses the period after Singer's emigration, from autumn 1938 to autumn 1941, and the aftermath of the theatre through 1943. Chapter 7 covers the 1938–1939 playing season and the start of World War II. The theatre administration under Werner Levie experienced a tightening of restrictions. Yet, even as emigration drained the theatre company of personnel and audience members, directors staged adaptations from Mendele Moykher Sforim, Shakespeare, and J. B. Priestley. Chapter 8 examines the 1939–1940 playing season, including the closing of the theatre and the 1940 reopening, after Fritz Wisten assumed the leadership. He accommodated himself to a smaller theatre space and to renewed restrictions on the repertoire by Ministry of Propaganda officers. Chapter 9 looks at the final theatre season of the Kulturbund, October 1940 to September 1941, when the Nazis dissolved the theatre amid its production run of Ferenc Molnár's *The Play's the Thing*. The war, emigration, and increased Nazi censorship affected play choices, the performances, and the well-being of the performers. Even as Wisten decided which plays to produce, SS-Officer Erich Kochanowski, at the behest of Hinkel, initiated measures to dismantle the theatre. The immediate aftermath of the Kulturbund coincided with the government decree for all Jews to identify themselves by the Star of David. In the conclusion, I gauge the significance of the Kulturbund and suggest its legacy, while tracing the whereabouts of the theatre's main figures after 1945.

All translations from German are my own, unless otherwise specified. I refer to the theatre throughout as the "Jewish Kulturbund" or "Kulturbund."

In October 1940 a journalist for the only newspaper left to Jewish readers in Berlin described the Jewish Kulturbund as a "center of power" that could not be praised enough. On its potential legacy for theatre chronicles, Martha Sara Wertheimer wrote:

> If ever the history of the Jewish Kulturbund in Germany will be written—it deserves to be written—one will have to recognize a development of its purpose, which most markedly shows that this Jewish Kulturbund is alive; because only that which lives is able to evolve. . . . The Kulturbund has become a prominent educator, so much so that those educated have not been aware of the transformation.[22]

I wish to answer Wertheimer's poignant call for a history of the Kulturbund theatre in all of its vitality.

PART ONE

INCEPTION AND IDENTITY IN AN ALL-JEWISH THEATRE IN NAZI BERLIN

1933–1935

1 A CULTURAL COMMUNITY

THE JEWISH KULTURBUND THEATRE EMERGES

1933

At the end of the Weimar Republic, Berlin represented a cultural and intellectual epicenter. An influx of émigré writers and artists from central and eastern Europe had settled in the city after World War I and during the 1920s. Berlin's thriving theatre atmosphere attracted aspiring actors and playwrights.[1] And the city's renowned literary cafés emerged as a locus for the exchange of ideas and varying perspectives on avant-garde art and politics in what Shachar Pinsker has called the "complex negotiation between Jews and Gentiles, 'East' and 'West,' 'the local,' and the immigrant."[2] Even when Hitler's "Brown Shirts" shadowed German city streets during the 1930s, artists traveled to Berlin to study theatre, music, and dance, engaging in the vibrant literary and arts scene that marked the metropolis during the Weimar Republic's late years. Artistic opportunities abounded in Berlin for Germans and émigrés, men and women, as well as for Jews and non-Jews who lived there and worked together.[3]

In 1932 Ruth Hentschke Anselm was a twenty-three-year-old dancer and actress, who described her Jewish family as "assimilated" and politically engaged.[4] She grew up in Berlin's working-class district of Prenzlauer Berg, where artist and family friend Käthe Kollwitz drew her portrait. She studied acting as a teenager with Ilka Grüning, who directed one of the two leading acting schools in Berlin.[5] At about this time, Anselm met Helene Weigel, who was performing at the Schiffbauerdamm theatre. Anselm had performed in cabaret and opera for several years and was employed as a dancer at Berlin's Municipal Opera (Städtisches Oper Berlin), under the general direction of Kurt Singer. Anselm's cultural and political circle of friends also included Günther Weisenborn, Richard Huelsenbeck, Bertolt Brecht, and Hanns Eisler. When Anselm hosted her friends at home, she discussed the rise of fascism. Anselm warned them that a dictatorship was in the making; she already saw evidence at the opera theatre that Jews were being informed on and fired. According to her, even Brecht did not believe that the Nazis could hold onto power if they gained it.[6]

At the time when Anselm worked at the civic opera, twenty-two-year-old Mascha Benyakonsky was studying voice at Berlin's Stern Conservatory of Music. She had arrived in Berlin from her native Lithuania in 1931. Benyakonsky had been raised in a Zionist household in Virbalis, only about two miles from the Prussian border. She spoke Yiddish at home and Hebrew at school, in addition to Russian and German. Benyakonsky dreamed of a singing career. When Hitler took power in 1933, she stayed in Berlin, tutoring Hebrew within Berlin's Zionist circles. She described a liberating sense of limbo during early 1933: "There were many artists in Berlin. . . . I'd never met people like that before . . . personally I felt wonderful. We were young. . . . Jews would sit in outdoor cafés in the afternoons and at night where non-Jews were, get beaten up, and yet go out again the next day. No one knew how long the Nazi dictatorship would last." Benyakonsky claimed that people did not believe that it could.[7] She was not yet directly affected by Nazi law. As a foreign music student, she supplemented her income through her increasing number of Hebrew students. She often went to the opera and cultivated close friendships with well-known artists, including the Jewish-born poet and émigré Mascha Kaléko.[8]

Anti-Jewish cultural policy by the Nazi government swiftly emerged, however, simultaneously with increasing street violence toward Berlin's Jewish residents and citizens by the SA (Hitler's Sicherheitsansatz). In spring 1933, as part of the *Gleichschaltung* (coordination) of the arts, Hans Hinkel successfully initiated the removal of Jews from Germany's cultural institutions. Born in the Rhineland in 1901, Hinkel rose quickly within the ranks of the Nazi Party in Munich during the 1920s. Within ten years, the skilled organizer and propagandist had become the press chief for the Berlin district Nazi Party. His close association with Goebbels enabled him to launch a Berlin-based Kampfbund (Combat League) for German Culture. The Combat League then merged with the Nazi Party to promote a culture free of Jewish influence.

Organized attacks on Jewish economic interests soon followed, leading to a systematic expulsion of Jews from the arts and academe. The Nazi boy-

I. Hans Hinkel, no date. Bundesarchiv, former Berlin Document Center, photographer unknown, courtesy Alan Steinweis.

cott against Jewish-run shops on 1 April 1933 gave way to the Law for the Restoration of the Professional Civil Service on 7 April. This decree eliminated Jews from all government employment. The so-called Aryan paragraph 3.1 identified Jews as non-Aryans: "civil servants who are not of Aryan descent are to be retired." This detail barred Jews from working at public cultural institutions like Berlin's Municipal Opera. Anselm and several of her colleagues at the opera, including her fiancé, Heinz Condell, lost their positions and joined their former artistic director, Kurt Singer, in unemployment.[9]

Singer, born in Berndt, West Prussia, in 1885 as the son of a rabbi, garnered respect in German national circles. He served Germany in World War I and received the Iron Cross for his service as a military doctor. Yet he did not qualify for the Civil Service Law exemption for war veterans. After the war he merged his interests in medicine and music and conducted a physician's

2. Dr. Kurt Singer, no date. Akademie der Künste, Berlin, JKB 20.53.001, photographer unknown, courtesy Akademie der Künste.

choral group and orchestra in Berlin. In addition to working as music editor for the Social Democratic Party newspaper *Vorwärts!* (Forward) he advanced his reputation in music at the Municipal Opera. Between 1927 and 1930 he served as deputy artistic director under the composer Heinz Tietjen. From 1930 to 1931 Singer took over the opera's management. He taught at the Berliner Hochschule zu Musik between 1923 and 1932 and directed Johann Strauss's *Wiener Blut* (Viennese Spirit) at the Berlin State Opera (1932), before the Nazis forced him from work by spring 1933.

In May 1933, under the advice of the progressive civic leader Rabbi Dr. Leo Baeck, Singer worked with two colleagues to establish a venue for Jewish performing artists who had no work, no retirement funds, and no plans to leave Germany. Kurt Baumann was one of Singer's production assistants from the opera who had lost his job. The twenty-six-year-old stage director drafted a prospectus detailing the Jewish Kulturbund organization and its theatre. Baumann knew that they could rely on his distant relative and Singer's good friend Julius Bab (born in 1880), whose expertise in drama criticism made him an invaluable resource for planning a cultural organization. For twenty years, Bab worked in Berlin as a critic for the *Schaubühne* and its successor magazine, the *Weltbühne*. He wrote plays and was a longtime lecturer at Humboldt University. Despite Bab's service to the German nation during World War I, like Singer, his Jewish birth cost him his job when the Nazis banned the *Weltbühne* in 1933.

According to Baumann, Bab's initial response to the plan for a Jewish cultural organization was "Are we allowed?"[10] Bab, however, devoted himself to finding a way to reengage those Jews who had been disenfranchised. Ruth Anselm recalled early discussions she had with her former colleagues about a league for unemployed Jewish artists: "We were sitting around with Julius Bab, talking about doing something for the Jews who had been thrown out."[11] Although Anselm would later criticize Singer for collaboration with the Nazis, in 1933 she knew that she wanted to be part of such a venue from the start. She could work as a dancer, choreographer, and actress. Many of her friends in the theatre had lost their jobs, including her fiancé, Heinz Condell, a set designer for the Municipal Opera who had trained under Max Reinhardt. Anselm knew several unemployed performers who would join a new cultural organization.[12]

Nazi law had impinged on the professional aspirations of Jewish-born artists in Berlin, including aspiring actress Anselm and Mascha Benyakonsky (Benya-Matz), the singer from across the German border. Anselm's German heritage did not protect her from the law or save her job at the theatre. Ironically, Benyakonsky's status as a Jew and foreign artist required her to have a work permit, as she indicated: "Just because of my Yiddish and Hebrew repertoire, I was given the permit especially willingly. I was a persona grata to the Nazis."[13] Both women found work at the Kulturbund for Jews in Germany.[14]

The two former Kulturbund artists represent opposing backgrounds: the Jewish-born German for whom German culture defined her sense of self, and the East European Jew, versed in Yiddish and Hebrew folklore. Anselm did not practice Judaism, while Benyakonsky believed strongly in traditional Jewish practice. One woman undertook resistance activities against the Nazi regime, while the other participated in Zionist organization meetings. Besides working at the theatre, Anselm belonged to the leftist underground movement in Berlin, helping people to leave Germany. She sometimes slept outdoors in park sandboxes before reporting to the theatre in the mornings. No one at the Kulturbund knew about her double life.[15] Eventually the Gestapo arrested her. "I played the role of my life—the Idiot," she recalled, describing how she dissembled under interrogation lights before her release. "I always thought that I could save Germany," she remembered. She wanted to prevent the Nazis from ruining her country. But Anselm was lucky to have saved herself in the end.[16]

Normally these two women would have little in common except for a love of the arts. But their lives intersected because they were performers in Berlin during the 1930s—and they were born Jewish.[17] Anselm saw herself as a political player and an actress: "I was never afraid; on the contrary . . . I always had the feeling that I was fighting for something and doing something good for people."[18] Although Benyakonsky identified herself as an *Ostjude* and a singer with a beautiful voice, it was her audition of classical arias in French and Italian that ultimately secured her position with the all-Jewish Kulturbund opera.[19]

The differences between the women represent a major predicament within the Kulturbund. These two performers personify what many members of Berlin's Jewish community and its theatre organization (the audience and the performers) struggled with as they acknowledged their identity as Jews in the Third Reich and the role of the Jewish theatre in their lives. Significantly, Anselm's and Benyakonsky's different backgrounds and family histories emphasize the paradox of the theatre for the Kulturbund Jews: the majority of the artists, like Anselm, Singer, Bab, and Baumann, believed that their organization and its theatre would have to reflect their European heritage and their Jewish culture. Benyakonsky, however, belonged to Berlin's minority Zionist community. Their philosophy advocated a Jewish cultural separatism which mirrored the basic ideas on art proposed by such Nazis as Hinkel but diverged from Singer's views.[20] This predicament reflected the sociocultural character of Berlin Jewry before Hitler's rise to power. Not only did government policy after the Nazi takeover accentuate the differences between Jew and Gentile in Germany, but differences between groups within the Jewish community became more sharply defined, renewing existing tensions from the preceding century.

Throughout the nineteenth century Jews in Germany strove for equality and acculturated German customs. Even after their emancipation in 1871, however, Jewish-born Germans could not hold high posts in state-run institutions. Despite their prosperity in German society at the turn of the twentieth century, many middle-class Jews were self-employed entrepreneurs with jobs in commerce and trade. During the Weimar Republic, the trend continued as Jews settled on independent occupations in law, medicine, and the arts.[21] Jewish integration into German social affairs grew, and intermarriage "was at an all-time high" by 1929.[22] As more German Jews opted for a secular religious affiliation, membership in the Zionist Organization significantly dropped. At the same time, a renaissance of secular Jewish culture occurred, spurred by Zionists who promoted emigration to Palestine. In their search to define a religious community and to transmit knowledge about Judaism, philosopher Martin Buber and Rabbi Leo Baeck (members of the Kulturbund advisory council in 1933) participated in the Jewish revival.[23]

Prior to the Third Reich, a process of "dissimilation"—a differentiating of oneself as being separate—evolved within Jewish communities in Germany as numbers of Jews reassessed their position in society and their sense of themselves as both Germans and Jews in Germany.[24] Jews in Germany had long considered themselves to be German citizens of the "Israelite" or "mosaic" faith. Yet many Jews underwent baptism or converted to Christianity to gain full acceptance in German society.[25] Jews had contributed to German culture for centuries. But writers who presented Jewish issues disguised them to make them neutral. Jews opted not to stress their Jewishness in German culture. Jewishness had not been emancipated along with the Jews.[26]

Jews remained a "recognizable subgroup" within German society. As cultural historians have noted, Jews in Germany did gain partial entry into non-

Jewish society, but their "entry remained incomplete, and thus problematic."[27] Various German social clubs and associations not only excluded Jews from joining but prevented them from organizing beyond the local level. Precisely because of their partial entry into the Gentile society, Jews developed communal identities within the Jewish communities while at the same time aspiring to membership in German society at large. This is the dilemma that the Jews of the Kulturbund faced when the Nazis excluded them from German society and its cultural sphere. Of the 525,000 Jews in Germany in January 1933, one-third of them lived in Berlin.[28]

Generally speaking, the artists associated with the Berlin Kulturbund's inception—Singer, Baumann, and Bab—as well as the first artists recruited to work on the theatre—Anselm and Condell—had been educated according to the liberal traditions of the Weimar era; they saw themselves for the most part as political liberals or Social Democrats. At an early age, many German-born Jews had been exposed at school to the humanist concepts of *Bildung* and *Sittlichkeit* (morals and manners).[29] They identified with being German by birth, culture, and language. A former Kulturbund musician who knew Singer's family suggested that Singer's acculturated family members—as well as his own—were "barely practicing Jews." At the same time, Kurt Michaelis conceded that for some of the artists, while feeling German was "in all of us, having lived as Germans for many generations . . . we always felt as Jews."[30] While he could not judge personally whether Singer embraced his Judaism, he said: "I know that his family did, and I have no reason to doubt that he felt as Jewish as others, me included."[31] The founding artists of the Kulturbund strongly recognized their double roots of German and Jew—being part of a society and at the same time apart from it, especially after 1933. To complicate matters, the prospect of a Jewish cultural association would have to include all Jews, regardless of their religious, ideological, and cultural background.

Singer and his closest advisors Baumann and Bab articulated their ideas for the all-Jewish theatre during the late spring and early summer of 1933. They did not know whether the Nazi government would permit them to proceed with their plan. Despite the ongoing uncertainty about the theatre, however, the men estimated the budget, considered the personnel needs, and discussed the repertoire that they could offer. Even before the Nazis officially approved the theatre, Bab recruited performers from Germany's most illustrious stages to the Kulturbund. Some of these actors, like Fritz Wisten, actively sought engagements.

Word of a new cultural enterprise for Jews reached Wisten (born Moritz Weinstein in Vienna in 1890) shortly after Stuttgart's Württemburgisches Landestheater dismissed him in the purge of Jewish artists from German stages. Wisten had performed for twelve years at Vienna's Burgtheater under Max Paulsen and at Berlin's Residenztheater alongside Fritz Kortner. His versatile acting range included roles such as Johann Wolfgang von Goethe's Mephisto and Christian Grabbe's Napoleon as well as Richard III and Oedipus. Wisten worked with Emmy Remolt in Stuttgart and performed there with Emmy Sonnemann Köstlin (who became Hermann Göring's second wife). After losing his job, Wisten contacted Bab: "I heard from Emmy Remolt of your intention to found a Jewish theatre in Berlin. I may understand in this, your desire to bring together the now-unused Jewish workforce within the framework of a German-speaking enterprise. I am skeptical only about the question of whether such an undertaking will be authorized, given the momentary attitude of the authorities."[32] Bab immediately confirmed that the cultural league of Jews had been established with permission pending from "higher authorities," as he put it, "not improbable." After all, Bab wrote to Wisten in May 1933, "On principle, the authorities want nothing other than to build a new 'Ghetto,' and that is unfortunately and necessarily the starting point of the enterprise."[33]

Bab anticipated that official government approval for the Kulturbund would follow a community public relations campaign planned for later in the summer. He told Wisten that he hoped the actor would contribute to a theatre of "high quality" that would "garner respect in non-Jewish circles."[34] By the end of May the arrangements for the theatre had progressed to negotiations with the "authorities." Bab voiced confidence in securing a theatre contract for Wisten, with the caveat that wages likely would be meager.[35] Singer and Baumann meanwhile completed a detailed proposal for the Kulturbund theatre, which was sent in June to the police and to various high-ranking officials within the Ministry of Propaganda, including Otto Laubinger, the president of the Theatre Chamber.

Singer and Baumann proposed that the "German-Jewish Cultural Association" operate within Berlin's Jewish community, which numbered approximately 81,000 active members in June 1933. In principle, the organization would employ only Jewish artists and staff members. They suggested two ensembles of approximately fifteen members each: one theatre troupe and one opera ensemble. Each ensemble would include up to three prominent actors or singers. The organization would initially hire artists by 1 August for a quarter of a year, but on renewable contracts. The directors also recommended that the cultural organization employ a choir of twelve singers and a chamber orchestra of twenty-five musicians. With Bab's assistance, Singer and Baumann devised a repertoire plan based on six basic categories of play scripts and libretti: "German and classic" scripts; "foreign" plays; "Jewish" plays; "opera"; "Singspiel" (folk plays); and special events, including concerts and lectures.[36]

In their June 1933 proposal, Singer and Baumann recommended that the theatre repertoire include German playwrights of stature: Friedrich Schiller (*William Tell*, *Cabal and Love*), Johann Wolfgang von Goethe (*Egmont*, *Goetz von Berlichingen*, *Faust I*), Heinrich von Kleist (*The Broken Jug*), Christian Grabbe (*Scherz, Satyre, Don Juan and Faust*), Georg Büchner (*Wozzek*), Gerhard Hauptmann (*The Weavers*, *The Beaver Coat*), the satirist Carl Sternheim (*Bürgel Schippel*), Franz Werfel (*Juarez and Maximilian*), and Franz Wedekind (*Franziska*, *Pandora's Box*). Sternheim and Werfel were the only Jewish-born writers among the recommended "German and classic" writers. The classic plays proposed for their stage included works by William Shakespeare (*A Midsummer Night's Dream*, *The Merchant of Venice*), August Strindberg (*The Dance of Death*), and Henrik Ibsen (*Ghosts*, *Peer Gynt*).[37]

The proposed "foreign" play category included plays in languages other than German by European authors, regardless of whether they were Jews by birth. Within this category, Baumann and Bab recommended playwrights Luigi Pirandello (*Six Characters in Search of an Author*) and Carlo Goldoni as well as Leo Tolstoy (*And the Light Shineth in Darkness*), Maxim Gorky (*The Lower Depths*), and Eugene O'Neill (*The Emperor Jones*). The initial list sent to Ministry of Propaganda officials included plays by non-Germans within their proposed "Jewish" category: Sholem Asch (*Uncle Moses*) and the Austrian-born Hermann Bahr (*The Concert*), for example. The Jewish German-language writers whose names appeared on the list were Arthur Schnitzler, Klabund (pseudonym for Alfred Henschke), and Richard Beer-Hofmann.

Singer and Baumann made proposals for annual and monthly costs for the organization and its central theatre; the organizational structure; advertising, technical, and personnel issues; the physical space requirements for the theatre; and the intended repertoire. They based their budgetary estimates on the number of tax-paying Jewish Germans in Berlin who frequented the theatre each month. The plan required approximately 12,000 to 15,000 members to join the organization and attend the theatre twice a month at a monthly membership fee of 2.50 Reichsmark. This necessitated a modern theatre space that could seat 1,300 people. The membership price, which included a free cultural newsletter (the *Monatsblätter*), allowed members to attend approximately three events a month, including one theatre or opera production, one orchestral concert, and one lecture. The theatre would offer a premiere every two weeks. Theatregoers would receive their seat assignments through a lottery system. The seats were all the same price. Members could draw their tickets from three divisions of seating possibilities before each performance to avoid getting back seats each time. This assured every member a good seat at every third performance.

The idea of an all-Jewish theatre prompted discussion within the Reich Cultural Chamber. Ministry of Propaganda officials recognized Singer's distinguished record of service in the arts before 1933. In mid-June Goebbels personally enlisted Laubinger to ask Hinkel to evaluate the viability of Singer's theatre plan. Hinkel, as the newly appointed Prussian minister of culture, however, immediately rejected the idea of the theatre. He justified his opposition to the Jewish cultural league by pointing to the "possibilities of destructive tendencies" within such an enterprise as too great to maintain oversight.[38] Ironically, the Kulturbund theatre owed its existence to the Nazi government. The government patronage of the Jewish-run theatre resulted only from Singer's persistent negotiations with Hinkel, who had overseen Singer's expulsion from the opera.[39] Throughout the month of June Singer persevered in his attempts to persuade Hinkel to consider his proposal. In doing so, Singer relied on influential former colleagues like the Baron von Holthoff, an aristocrat who belonged to the Prussian Theatre Commission. The baron wrote to Hinkel, championing Singer's "lofty" goal to engage two hundred to three hundred unemployed Jewish artists in an enterprise that the esteemed non-Jewish conductor Wilhelm Furtwängler condoned. At the end of June Singer requested a personal meeting with Hinkel to discuss the organization. Singer repeated that the Kulturbund would "only permit Jewish members" to attend events and assured the commissar that his plan involved "completely closed performances" for Jews only. He also assured Hinkel that the events would not be advertised in the press. All advertising must be left solely to the subscription newsletter for members.[40]

Hinkel granted Singer a face-to-face meeting on 6 July 1933, when the Kulturbund founder addressed what he referred to as the "urgency of the situation and the emergency faced by [Jewish] artists." On that day Hinkel approved the Jewish organization, as long as its activities took place within "closed" quarters. Hinkel thus permitted the Kulturbund theatre to be not only "tolerated, but protected," as Bab wrote to Fritz Wisten the following day, now that the theatre was "90% certain."[41] Despite Singer's initial triumph in securing permission for the theatre, Hinkel hammered out the preconditions for the organization. His dictates provided the basic tenets of the Kulturbund's bylaws: the organization's all-Jewish status, its rules for operation, the makeup of the executive board, and the Kulturbund's function within Berlin's Jewish community. The first statute declared the organization's primary goal, as promoted by Singer: "The purpose of the Kulturbund is to cultivate the artistic and scholarly interests of the Jewish population and provide work to benefit unemployed Jewish artists and scholars. To fulfill this purpose, the Kulturbund will organize for its members above all theatre performances and concerts, lectures, and art exhibitions, whose artistic and scholarly share will be attended fundamentally by Jews."[42]

In mid-July Hitler seized full control of Germany when he banned multiple political parties. At approximately the same time, on 15 July, Hinkel forbade "The Cultural Association of German Jews" to add the year "1933" to its name. Singer agreed to this amendment and to Hinkel's five basic terms for the organization. First, only Jews were permitted to be members of the theatre association, which would require all members to receive a photo identification card. Second, no ticket sales would be allowed at the box office. Third, all programming choices would be subject to approval by the Prussian Theatre Commission, with programs submitted for review at least one month in advance. Fourth, each member would pay the same monthly fees without a supplement for separate events. Finally, the only press-related venue for advertising or "propaganda" would be newspapers within the Jewish community.[43]

Singer and Bab advertised the Kulturbund as a social institution to provide a cohesive cultural community for disenfranchised Jews. To take care of the general administrative matters, Singer hired Dr. Werner Levie to be the secretary for the Kulturbund. The Dutch-born Levie had studied German, economics, and theatre in Berlin, where he worked as a journalist for Ullstein Verlag. Levie was a dedicated Zionist with a keen sense for business. Operating from Singer's private apartment at 56 Mommenstraße in a makeshift office staffed by five people, the operation grew to twelve workers by late September.[44] Public announcements for the Kulturbund honorary committee listed among its members well-known figures in German Jewish society: Rabbi Leo Baeck; the novelist Jacob Wassermann; Arthur Eloesser, the art and drama critic for the Zionist newspaper; and the painter Max

Liebermann. Besides Bab as the dramaturg and Baumann as a stage director, appointees to the administrative executive committee board included representatives from the largest Jewish self-help and welfare organizations in Germany: the Reich Representation of German Jews, the Zionist Organization, and the Central Association for German Citizens of the Jewish Faith, as well as the Jewish Women's League and League for Jewish Veterans. By including representatives from powerful Jewish organizations on the executive board, Singer could not make unilateral decisions. In addition, he needed financial sponsorship.

When Singer appealed to the Jewish community to support the Kulturbund during the summer of 1933, he found himself at the forefront of several debates in Berlin's Jewish community, which reinforced differing viewpoints on the "Jewish Question" (*Judenfrage*) and the Kulturbund's ideal role, given the government's anti-Jewish stance. Spokespeople for the central organizations waged the debates in newspapers affiliated with their groups. Jewish Berliners had long read a variety of German-language Jewish newspapers which reflected the political interests of those who considered themselves Zionists, assimilationists, nationalists, or liberals.[45] Families normally read one of four major German-language Jewish newspapers. The oldest political newspaper was the Zionist Organization's *Jüdische Rundschau* (established in 1901), which appeared twice a week. Its main competitor, the weekly *C.-V.-Zeitung* (established in 1922), had the largest circulation in Berlin. It represented assimilated German citizens of the Jewish faith (Centralverein deutscher Staatsbürger jüdischen Glaubens). The *Schild* (established in 1921) was affiliated with the national organization of Jewish combat veterans. Only the Hamburg-based *Israelitisches Familienblatt* was privately owned and ideologically independent.[46]

Community newspaper editors in 1933 amplified the basic issues that affected the Jewish public in Hitler's Germany. What social mission suited an all-Jewish organization during a time when government policy forced Jews to the margins of German society? Did Singer's proposed theatre have a specifically Jewish cultural or political duty to the community, as the *Jüdische Rundschau* editorial staff claimed? Or, as the more liberal proponents recommended in the *C.-V.-Zeitung*, should the theatre repertoire provide Jewish citizens with a worldview that extended beyond their new cultural ghetto?

The *Jüdische Rundschau* adopted a position on the Kulturbund that seemed similar to Hinkel's public position. Editor-in-chief Robert Weltsch encouraged the Kulturbund directors to reflect Jewish life in their programs. This meant shaping a repertoire that included East European authors, translated from their original Yiddish language. Berlin's Jewish community, however, consisted of a majority of citizens like Singer and Anselm who rejected Zionist ideas of Jewish nationalism and cultural separatism. Singer promoted the artistic traditions that he had supported before Hitler came to power. He and his colleagues objected principally to an artistic agenda that would disproportionately pad the theatrical repertoire with unfamiliar East European literary models. They also opposed ideologically motivated program choices that underscored so-called national Jewish concerns over aesthetic principles.

The Kulturbund produced an additional incentive for the Zionist Organization to continue its ongoing ideological battle (begun in the 1890s) with the Centralverein der deutscher Staatsbürger jüdischen Glaubens (Central Association for German Citizens of the Jewish Faith). Founded to combat anti-Semitism in Germany, the Centralverein (C.-V.) promoted a separate Jewish identity. Unlike the Zionist call for a cultural separatism in Germany and a political link to Palestine, however, the Centralverein emphasized its proponents' German heritage.[47] New restrictions on Jewish life in 1933 reinforced the community newspapers' biases, particularly the Centralverein's focus on German culture and the Zionist attention to Jewish culture in the Diaspora.

At the Nazi Ministry of Propaganda Hinkel was under orders to ensure that the emerging Kulturbund theatre emphasized its "Jewishness." Singer recognized the need for the organization to feature artistic programs relevant to contemporary Jewish life. Yet he and his administrative staff, as well as the expanding creative team, planned to host lectures on secular subjects and to produce plays by dramatists with no Jewish link at all. Baumann and Bab actively programmed this duality into the Kulturbund's proposed theatre repertoire. Lectures on Hayyim Bialik and stage adaptations of stories by Sholem Aleichem would reflect the Jewish literary legacy that belonged to the secular revival encouraged by Buber. But the notion that the East Europeans represented the genuine Jews only further separated the East European Jew from the German Jew.[48] The estrangement of one kind of Jew from the other played itself out in Berlin's Jewish community as Singer encouraged a repertoire grounded in the West European tradition. Kulturbund members knew this tradition far better than the heritage deemed "authentic," based on imported Hebrew and Yiddish literary traditions.

Performers and writers could not dissociate themselves from the German language; nor could they eradicate the powerful influences of Goethe, Schiller, and Kleist, who in part had shaped their art. Musicians depended on music by Johann Sebastian Bach, Franz Schubert, and Ludwig van Beethoven as crucial musical models within their repertoires. The politics of Hitler's new regime, however, laid further emphasis on the Jews' complex relationship to German society: both belonging and "not belonging." The government's anti-Jewish policies exposed the tenuous bond that many Jews had established with their community and its organizations.

The Kulturbund artists adopted a practical viewpoint toward their theatre. They regarded their association with the theatre as economically advantageous, allowing them to expand their repertoire and give them more stage-time. Mira Rostova (Rostovsky), a Russian-born actress who performed in the theatre, emphasized that "the Kulturbund was not a political thing." She viewed her theatre engagement as necessary, after being "pushed out" of mainstream theatre. She saw her mandatory membership in the Jewish community merely as her entry to the acting ensemble. It never occurred to her that this new institution restricted its access to Jews. As she made clear, in the 1930s "even the hat-makers had unions."[49] Nonetheless, the Nazi government politicized the Kulturbund from its beginning by enforcing ethnic policies that squelched the spirit of inclusion for anyone who was not born Jewish.

Singer suggested in the Kulturbund theatre's first year that actors eventually might have to be retrained to perform plays from eastern Europe with a specifically Jewish milieu. Kulturbund actors, however, have disagreed about whether this was necessary or whether it ever occurred. Rostova believed that playing a Jewish role was no different than playing someone royal. One merely played the role within the world of the play, whatever world that was.[50] Nor did Ruth Anselm prepare in a special way to play Jewish roles. She did not experience a religious transformation of "feeling more Jewish" after playing Jewish characters; nor could she remember whether Singer instituted classes to train performers in Jewish roles.[51] According to Benyakonsky, a built-in bias against the plays imported from the far-away Jewish East existed. As she put it, "German Jews in general looked down on the East European Jew [*Ostjude*]."[52]

The designated head of scenography for the theatre, Heinz Condell, however, found new artistic models from the East inspiring for the work he could bring to the Kulturbund. He was intrigued by foreign, stylized modes of theatre performance and design influenced by the Habimah Theatre, a mode that he found "original, expressive, and un-European" in form, which "greatly excited" him as "a 'Jewish' theatrical style."[53] The new stage design evolved for practical reasons. Given the political and cultural climate in 1933, the Jewish theatre would have to work "more economically and more intellectually" than subsidized state theatres and opera houses like the municipal opera had. For this reason, Condell hoped to elicit a "spartan style" of stage design for the Kulturbund.[54] Yet he aimed to create stage pictures that evoked a Jewish milieu.

In late July 1933 Singer used the *C.-V.-Zeitung* to recruit Kulturbund members. He appealed to his fellow Berliners in an open letter: "You German Jews: you may not destroy what the authorities have permitted us to build! In the Kulturbund, we no longer want to separate Zionist and non-Zionist. We wish to reach out our hand to all."[55] Thousands of Jewish Berliners attended a series of public relations events for the Kulturbund at city synagogues in late July. The events featured orchestral music performances, prominent speakers, and recitation for prospective members.

Hinkel and Singer finalized their negotiations for the Kulturbund on 3 August, when Hinkel approved a revised draft of Singer's operational plan. Hinkel required revisions, including stricter control of membership status. Family memberships for the organization would be allowed only if direct familial links existed. Hinkel's explicit approval for the Kulturbund, however, led Singer, Baumann, and Bab to expand their membership drive. Singer also gained local police permission for "closed" performances for Jews only, and Hinkel authorized Singer temporarily to lease the Berliner Theater on Charlottenstraße for the first performance. Bab continued to court actors for the ensemble and in August formally offered Fritz Wisten the role of the Dervish for the *Nathan* production, promising him a contract by the end of the month. It was "fairly certain" that the theatre would open with *Nathan*, he told the actor.[56] A theatre company was being assembled step by step. But the Jewish community had still not embraced the proposition of the Kulturbund.

Evolving debates within Berlin's Jewish community revealed a public deeply divided about the future role of the all-Jewish organization. The editors of the *Jüdische Rundschau* pursued an animated exchange with Singer, especially about opening his theatre with Lessing's play. In late July a writer for the newspaper asked: "Why *Nathan the Wise*?" He took umbrage at Bab's public remarks about the long history of Jewish life and cultural production in Germany. "It would be an insincere pretense to believe that Jews in 1933 could represent the Germanic tribes of thousands of years past," he wrote, advocating that Jews in the "new Germany" look to the future and not to its past. "We want to see how we come to terms with today's privation of Jews. We must show Jewish viewpoints, but some [people] are not keen on seeming too Jewish. We national Jews do not prefer inferior products by Jews to the work of great authors; but we must recognize that we Jews are part of the assimilation-dialectic that assumed Jewish participation in a non-Jewish environment." Now that the German state thwarted Jewish cultural participation with non-Jews, the journalist concluded that the *Nathan* production "must not spin a world of illusions for German Jews." Accordingly, he advised the directors to make the upcoming premiere "an artistic act and not motivated by politics."[57]

Singer responded to the criticism by denying that politics motivated his choice of a play linked to Germany's emancipation of Jews. Singer saw *Nathan the Wise* as "timeless in its theatrical and human language of the soul" and absolutely suitable for the Kulturbund premiere. "If the Jew wanted to triumph over the artist," Singer offered, "then liturgy and Hasidic folksong would be the theme of musical production. True art is international."[58] Polemics did not belong at the Kulturbund, he emphasized. Singer believed that Kulturbund programs could address important social, ethical, and artistic tasks, not politics. He defined the purpose of the Kulturbund according to these tasks.

First, the organization would employ Jewish artists who had lost their jobs. The Kulturbund would then imbue in future members (especially youths) cultural and religious values for better times, including a "prideful sense of themselves as Jews." Singer believed in the Kulturbund as an artistic site for knowledge and recognition, where theatre art would mirror life. Just because "emergency and crisis . . . welded Jews together," the director did not see that the theatre should be a locus for the "confessional Jew" versus the "renegade Jew." Instead, Singer called on all German Jews to join the new cultural enterprise, regardless of their view of Judaism: "We [Jews] must work together here. One league. One community. One desire. One religion. Aren't we in accord?" The *Rundschau* editorship responded to Singer by agreeing with him in principle. But if Jewish artists could perceive art without falling back into the "old assimilationist Judaism," it would only amount to a necessary change in attitude, not a change in artistic content, the journalist concluded. He conceded that the Kulturbund need not limit that content to Jewish art production. But "a self-aware Judaism must be the basis for all action."[59]

Singer's defense of the *Nathan* premiere in late August, before the event was even scheduled, aptly underscores the artistic director's commitment, however idealistic, to world-class art with an enduring appeal. The Zionist-bent journalist criticized the Kulturbund's choice of *Nathan* because Singer never addressed the need for Jewish artists consciously to become more self-aware. This would require them to adopt a Jewish mode of perception. Singer had different views. He believed instead that art creation and performance could synthesize—and transcend—the cultural politics of being German and being a Jew. Singer's repertoire outline for Ministry of Propaganda officials showed his plan to stage dramatic classics while reflecting a spirit of Jewish humanism. The proposed play categories ("German and classic," "foreign," and "Jewish") incorporated titles by writers central to traditional European theatre repertories prior to 1933. Notably, the draft submitted to the Nazi authorities did not include Lessing's name among the list of German-language authors under the "German and classics" category. Did Singer independently determine the choice of Lessing's *Nathan* for the premiere? Or did Hinkel prompt the opening production of Lessing's play about a Jewish merchant as a way to promote his magnanimous role in creating the Reich's only all-Jewish theatre?

On 1 September Hinkel assured the Gestapo that the Kulturbund's all-Jewish performances in "closed quarters" would "keep in check Jewish influence." An exact autumn date for the inaugural performance still had not been set; nor had Singer determined the length of the *Nathan* run once it began. Hinkel, however, anticipated concerns that local officials might have about a Jewish theatre. He made it clear to the police representative that confining Jews in their own theatre would prevent any "liberal camouflage, which leads to subverting our unique culture."[60] Hinkel had a new domain within which to expand his political authority.

In mid-September 1933 Singer finally scheduled the theatre's production of *Nathan the Wise* for 1 October to coincide with the Jewish High Holidays. But just days before the premiere, Singer chose the *C.-V.-Zeitung* to explain his cultural mission to the public once again. It is likely that at this early stage the artistic director thought that he could find common ground with the Nazis. He adhered to his belief in the vital bond between Jewish identity and the cultural work that lay ahead: "As German Jews, it is clear that we emphasize more than ever our link to Jewry. We will incorporate Jewish creation for drama and music. . . . That we are committed to and bound to the culture of German thinkers and artists need not be emphasized. A compromise then? Yes! Out of firm, unyielding, and finely understood conviction."[61] Singer described an organization in progress that would develop step by step. Singer, Baumann, and Bab had grouped plays in categories that they believed represented a serious repertoire that could appeal to a diverse audience membership. They readied their list of ideal play recommendations even before Hinkel authorized the theatre. The Jewish administrators nonetheless selected titles of plays that belonged to first-rate repertory theatres.

By autumn of 1933 Goebbels had appointed Rainer Schlösser to lead the Theatre Chamber and be the main censor for the German stage.[62] Born in Weimar as the son of a professor of literature, Schlösser's own ideological training was highly political as the cultural-political editor for the *Völkischer Beobachter* (People's Observer). Hinkel reported to Schlösser to discuss what plays and operas would be permitted at the Kulturbund. In light of the government's racial laws, Schlösser forbade the performance of all plays written by Jewish writers on the German stage. Conversely, for the new Jewish stage, Hinkel barred the Kulturbund from featuring German-language plays written by non-Jews. With the exception of Lessing's *Nathan* as the inaugural production, Hinkel prevented productions of plays by Schiller, Goethe, and Kleist, authors whom Goebbels endorsed for the German stage. Accordingly, the Kulturbund could not stage plays by Hauptmann, Grabbe, Büchner, or Wedekind. Just as Schiller, Goethe, and Kleist emphasized Germanic heroism in their work, dramas by Strindberg and Ibsen's *Peer Gynt* were thought to portray Nordic ideals. Such dramas were systematically forbidden for the Jewish stage, as was Shakespeare's *The Merchant of Venice*. After the first Kulturbund production in 1933, the more generous Jewish merchant Nathan also lost his place on the Jewish stage.[63]

By mid-September 1933, however, rehearsals for *Nathan the Wise* were underway as Singer's company-in-progress prepared for its October debut. The Kulturbund's praiseworthy function for the Jewish community remained undisputed. Administrative secretary Levie referred to the organization and its theatre as a vital social institution that had already employed over two hundred talented but unemployed Jews.[64] Kurt Singer served as the chief administrator and the artistic director of the whole enterprise. Under him were administrative and creative directors for opera (Joseph Rosenstock), stage technology (Hans Sondheimer), and scenography (Heinz Condell).

Kurt Baumann and Julius Bab would oversee all of the artistic aspects related to directing, dramaturgy, and the lecture series, except for the concert division, which Singer led as musical conductor. The administrative offices, headed by Hans Sander and Levie, included office staff for membership and publicity.

Even while he focused on promoting his new theatre and preparing for its first opening night, Singer had to look beyond the first production toward the first season. Hinkel required potential manuscripts in advance. Singer hoped to follow the *Nathan* production with *The Marriage of Figaro*. He also anticipated a premiere of Emil Bernard (Cohn)'s *God's Hunt* (*Jagd Gottes*) as the first Jewish play for the season. Singer submitted this play by a German-born rabbi about a Jewish community under siege to Hinkel mid-month. Hinkel forwarded the play to Schlösser for review, with a reminder about the Kulturbund's status: "The events of the 'KDJ' [Kulturbund Deutscher Juden] take place exclusively with Jewish actors and lecturers in closed performances for exclusively Jewish audiences."[65] Hinkel reinforced this point in subsequent newspaper interviews on the imminent Jewish cultural efforts. Two days before the Kulturbund's official opening, Hinkel lauded "these Jews [who] did not leave Germany to spread cruel anti-German propaganda." He had authorized the new enterprise, he told a Nazi news venue, to give Jews who "have lived in Germany so long, the chance for their own cultural work; but they may not appear publicly."[66]

Besides establishing his control over the Jewish enterprise, Hinkel's remarks suggested his expectation of an emerging "Jewish quality" in the Kulturbund's work. The Jewish community's Zionist response to Hinkel's preview of the Kulturbund, however, interpreted that "Jewish quality" differently from the Nazi party line. The German state had already pushed the Jews from mainstream cultural and economic life. "The Jews still hover between peoples [Germans and Jews], leading to a progressive deterioration. This is why Jews must follow with an active process of dissimilation," a journalist cautioned. By looking to the future (and Palestine), Jews could create something positive from a negative situation.[67] The recurring idea of dissimilation as a positive process for Jews reemerged in the public domain. If German Jews differentiated themselves from other Germans, they could transform themselves and develop a distinct Jewish character. The German Zionists, as deeply attached as they were to Germany, saw the Kulturbund programs as the start of a transformative process toward a new Jewish identity.

Similarly, in the days leading to the inaugural production, the board for the Reich Representation of German Jews issued a public statement, hoping that "the suffering of these days" would cause German Jewry to "regenerate its essence in a new way."[68] Singer once more asserted his idea for the cultural organization, again turning to the *C.-V.-Zeitung* to project the role he saw for German Jewry with the emerging Kulturbund. He described how the theatre had gained legitimacy over the previous months. But to move forward, he emphasized, "[a] primary condition [to founding the organization] was to keep politics out of the methods and content of our work. Further, it must be stressed that the Kulturbund cannot concern itself with Jewish interpolitical opportunities. We want to, we must, we will remain apolitical and above politics."[69] Perhaps Singer was naïve enough to think that he could avoid politics. But he had chosen the political newspaper with the largest circulation to address his audience as he sought middle ground from which to launch his theatre.

During the summer the Zionist newspaper editors' ongoing concern was that Bab and Singer preferred not to "seem too Jewish" in their public statements or in their play selections for the theatre. *Rundschau* journalists had pointed repeatedly to Singer's unfortunate choice of *Nathan* as the premiere production, branding it a politically motivated decision. Singer also unexpectedly faced difficulties, however, when he promoted plays by Jewish authors on Jewish themes. Not long before the *Nathan* premiere, Singer's choice of *God's Hunt* for the theatre encountered resistance from Reich Ministry officials. On order of the *Reichsdramaturg*, Hinkel rejected the play. The Jewish press never knew about Singer's efforts to stage a play about a Jewish community in peril. They only saw that the new Jewish theatre featured *Nathan the Wise* on the stage.

Singer and Baumann's recommended category of "Jewish" plays proved to be the most problem-ridden group of plays in their Kulturbund repertoire. No specific Jewish culture existed separately in the German-Jewish sphere inhabited by Kulturbund Jews. Jews had worked in Germany long enough to integrate German language and culture into their lives. Jewish-themed drama never developed in Germany. A Yiddish-language repertoire existed primarily in eastern Europe and in the United States. Authors such as Ossip Dymov, Sholem Aleichem, and Halper Leivick, for example, offered regionalized portraits of the Ostjuden and life in eastern European shtetls. The majority of the assimilated Kulturbund artists and audiences, however, were unfamiliar with the lives dramatized in these plays, even in German translation. Singer, Baumann, and Bab would have to introduce Jewish culture to German Jewish audiences. This required them to distinguish traits of Jewish culture and then reflect those characteristics in theatre programs.

Even before the theatre officially opened, Nazi censorship undercut the Kulturbund repertoire choices, as theatre directors compromised some of their program objectives. Singer yielded to Nazi government policies which directly affected his aesthetic decisions on the repertoire. Schlösser and Hinkel banned submissions of plays whose content too closely incorporated German culture. Hinkel's own regulations ought to have hindered Lessing's play from its all-Jewish production. But Hinkel permitted the premiere. Perhaps the play's Jewish protagonist and obvious compassion for Jews made it an unworthy choice for the German stage. It is also true, however, that the censors still did not have guidelines as to how to censor plays for the Kulturbund theatre.

Given the unprecedented situation of a separate Jewish theatre in Germany, Singer and his creative team had to reassess the artistic style of a text in performance. How would the merchant Nathan sound and behave onstage? What might the stage director ask of the designer? Would the play depict the values of identity and group solidarity that Jewish journalists expected? Although Singer communicated openly with Berlin's leading Jewish community newspapers about the theatre's aims and repertoire choices, Zionist spokespeople and their counterparts at the Centralverein tried to influence his decisions by using the press to advance their ideological agendas.

When the Kulturbund prepared for the theatre's first production, Goebbels consolidated control over cultural affairs by creating the Chamber of Culture in September 1933. He appointed Schlösser as chief administrator and censor for the Theatre Chamber. Hinkel oversaw Jewish cultural affairs. The idea for a Jewish theatre had developed in Jewish circles, however, before Kurt Singer approached Hinkel. Goebbels ultimately approved the Kulturbund for German Jews after he made the rules clear: only Jews could be members, attend performances, and review the performances in the Jewish press. Schlösser and Hinkel authorized *Nathan the Wise* to be the first production of the all-Jewish theatre.

2 UPROOTED

THE KULTURBUND AND THE FIRST PLAYING SEASON

1933-1934

The theatre curtain opened on a scene with a "Palestinian style of architecture and palm trees in the background" for the inaugural production of *Nathan the Wise*.[1] The Kulturbund premiere of 1 October 1933 coincided with the end of the High Holidays; and for the audience members celebrating the Jewish year 5694 the performance marked a sobering start to their cultural life in Hitler's regime. Kurt Katsch (born Isser Katz in Grodno) performed the title role. Describing his participation on the Kulturbund stage as a religious mission that he had to fulfill, he would later recall the "weeping" spectators after his first performance: "I felt myself to be more like a priest than an actor," he wrote in his memoir.[2] Before 1933 the actor performed with the State Theatre in Frankfurt am Main and with Max Reinhardt's troupe. Julius Bab as deputy director of the Kulturbund drama division had recruited Katsch to join the ensemble's thirty-five actors and singers. The cast members for the *Nathan* production included actors from theatres in Königsberg (Lilly Kann as Daja), Dresden (Jenny Schaffer as Sittah), Kiel and Berlin (Ernst Lenart as the templar), and Stuttgart (Fritz Wisten as the Dervish). Karl Loewenberg, formerly of Frankfurt's Neues Theater, directed the production. Heinz Condell designed the costumes and the settings. Arthur Sondheimer was the technical director.

Hinkel and Singer, the true architects of the Kulturbund and its premiere, sat in the audience. Earlier on that October Sunday an article in the *Frankfurter Zeitung* previewed the Kulturbund enterprise and publicized Hinkel's role in founding the theatre. Goebbels probably knew that he could use the liberal-leaning newspaper to spread his propaganda. His Ministry of Propaganda therefore had refrained from completely controlling the contents of the estab-

3. Set by Heinz Condell for *Nathan the Wise*, 1 October 1933. Akademie der Künste, Berlin, JKB 20.53.309, photographer unknown.

lished Frankfurt newspaper. The article's author recognized Hinkel's magnanimous gesture toward Jews who had lost their jobs. By authorizing the theatre, he wrote, Hinkel allowed "many unemployed Jewish artists to find opportunities to earn their living." Hinkel had told the reporter about the special conditions for the Jewish theatre. The ensemble of the "private theatre," Hinkel explained, consisted of "non-Aryan and foreign artists who performed non-Aryan authors according to the appropriate Aryan laws."[3] The *Frankfurter Zeitung* did not report the title of the Kulturbund premiere. Nor did German or outside journalists attend the Lessing play that evening. Only Jewish reporters could verify that the play performed was written by a German who was not a Jew.

Hinkel, however, scored an immediate political victory with his remarks about the Kulturbund. He received credit from colleagues in Berlin and abroad for preserving Germany's cultural sphere for Aryans: "You have loaded a difficult, very difficult responsibility on yourself, reformed an astounding principle, that is, expelled the Jewish element from the arts," an admiring friend wrote Hinkel on the day of the premiere.[4] Despite the obvious political significance of Hinkel's comments, Singer insisted that the all-Jewish theatre would remain politically neutral. The Kulturbund directors did not present their first production as a political event. But the cultural politics of opening with *Nathan the Wise* could not be ignored.

Nathan the Wise stresses the ability of three world religions—and their representatives—to coexist harmoniously. The accounts of the staged production at the Kulturbund, however, show that the stage director presented Nathan to the audience as an ostracized "other." In Loewenberg's interpretation, Katsch as Nathan appeared as a "dissimilated" Jew—no longer part of the group of religions, but alone as a Jew.[5]

The theatre was packed for the opening night performance. The company actors and staff sat among the audience, greatly excited by the event and moved by Kurt Singer's welcome to the audience. The orchestra seating area offered a picture reminiscent of premieres in Reinhardt's time, according to Herbert Friedenthal (later Freeden), a journalist who attended the production. The difference was that the invitations for the Kulturbund premiere had urgently asked Kulturbund members to avoid driving in front of the theatre and to make sure that their "appearance, dress, and attitude" at the theatre reflected the fact that they represented a community in "an emergency situation."[6]

Some of the stagehands were not experienced technicians, and they showed their nervousness. To the apparent horror of experienced artists in the audience like Ruth Anselm, instead of raising the curtain completely they lowered it.[7] Before the curtain rose, the audience heard the music of a Hasidic melody. Spectators like Friedenthal who knew Lessing's play well had to suspend their expectations about the character of Nathan. As the performance began, audience members saw Condell's evocatively designed exotic cityscape with two houses onstage. Katsch as Nathan returned home humming a Hasidic tune. The visible symbols of Judaism—a menorah and a Star of David—adorned his house. The silent Nathan bent over his prayer stand and incanted his first words as the Hebrew blessing "baruch haba" (blessed is he who comes).[8] Besides Katsch, among the ensemble's new actors were Käte Foerder and Ernst Lenart as the young Recha and the templar; Lilly Kann as Daja; and the talented Jenny Schaffer as Sittah, sister to the Sultan Saludin, played by Martin Brandt. Fritz Wisten infused his first Kulturbund role as the Dervish with abandon. The director presented the play in its entirety, without cuts. Loewenberg, however, reinterpreted

Lessing's ideal of religious harmony and changed the ending to suggest a tragic tone. Katsch played the role with a prophetic quality, accepting his Jewish destiny with pride. In a startling way, the production captured in its final stage image the enforced isolation of German Jews in Nazi society. The physical snapshot of the solitary onstage Jew gave Kulturbund audiences an image for further debate on the theatre's duty to its community.

The production unleashed a flurry of criticism and praise in the press during the first week of October. Hugo Lachmanski of the *C.-V.-Zeitung* lauded Lessing's message of tolerance for fellow humans. The Jewish theatre "could not have chosen a more appropriate work to inaugurate the house than Lessing's master poem," he wrote, referring to the play as the "crown of German intellectual culture."[9] But the Zionist *Rundschau* attacked Singer's play choice as a travesty; after all, Lessing grounded his play in the eighteenth-century spirit of Jewish emancipation. Ascribing political and ideological motives to Singer, a reviewer concluded that in the present times "to use *Nathan* as a 'song of tolerance' is not doing Jews a service."[10] The journalist commended the director, however, for aptly positioning the pious merchant alone at the play's end.

The premiere sparked intense discussion among Zionist groups surrounding *Rundschau* editor Weltsch. If Jews could not present German culture, what was the "pure Jewish culture" in Germany that Hinkel expected of the theatre? The debate among these *Rundschau* journalists and their counterparts at the *C.-V.-Zeitung* pivoted on whether or not the Kulturbund ghettoized its culture along with its members. While Singer conceded that Jews in Berlin were being physically separated, he did not see Jewish culture as enclosed. He believed in a German Jewish theatre that included "specifically Jewish creation" and "the culture of German intellectual and art traditions."[11] He maintained that in spirit the Kulturbund would transcend ghettoization with a repertoire of world classics. Lessing's Nathan embodied emancipated Judaism in a humanist guise. Yet Singer acknowledged after the premiere production that public debates on the place of Jewish culture in Germany had begun in earnest: "Here the Zionist, here the revisionist, here the German Jew."[12] He already faced opposition from Hinkel to producing plays whose universality made them indistinguishable from German plays.

Singer and Bab proceeded to plan the first playing season during the two-week *Nathan* run. During this time Hinkel approved *The Marriage of Figaro* for performance; the Kulturbund began rehearsals in October. Yet the artistic team did not know where and when the scheduled performances of the opera would take place. The Kulturbund needed a permanent theatre. Singer urged Hinkel to support the leasing of a permanent theatre space. But Hinkel rejected his requests to move the Jewish theatre into the esteemed Lessing Theater, Deutsches Theater, or Theater am Schiffbauerdamm.[13] Hinkel argued that Aryan actors would lose their jobs if the Jewish troupe took over a German theatre space. Singer used this opportunity to ask for an expansion of cultural leagues for Jews across Germany.[14] He assumed that if Hinkel agreed to permit a network of active Kulturbund theatres for Jews only, he would more willingly approve a legitimate theatre space in Berlin as the central theatre hub.

Singer and his staff thus worried about the longevity of the Kulturbund and the regularity of its performances. Fritz Wisten still commuted from Stuttgart to Berlin to perform in *Nathan the Wise*. Despite this period of uncertainty, however, Singer scheduled repeat runs of *Nathan* for 30 and 31 October and 1 November 1933 in the Berliner Theater. Bab wrote to Wisten in October 1933: "Where we will play *Figaro* after that [*Nathan*], we still do not know, nor where we will continue to play. The situation is indescribably intricate and difficult."[15] Nor did the theatre directors and actors know what Hinkel would permit them to perform after *Figaro*. The theatre's general secretary and manager, Levie, had reminded Hinkel of a month-old request to produce the Jewish-themed *God's Hunt*: "We would be very grateful, highly esteemed State Commissar, to receive your permission very soon," he wrote, adding that rehearsals for the play would begin soon.[16] What Levie did not know was that *Reichsdramaturg* Schlösser had already forbidden the Jewish play.

Hinkel gave no reason for the ban. Instead he warned Singer against mixing Judaism with German culture. By the end of 1933 it became clear to the Jewish community artists that Schlösser and Hinkel would reject all attempts by the Jews to incorporate German culture in any form into their theatre programs and publications. They also forbade the publication of an article on Jewish art in Germany and its influence. Nor would the ministry tolerate Levie's request in October to hire unemployed German musicians as substitute players for the Kulturbund orchestra. Jewish and German musicians could no longer perform together even temporarily.

Hinkel publicly championed the Jewish theatre's separate cultural sphere and its potential repertoire choices. Why would the *Reichsdramaturg* object to Kulturbund performances of *God's Hunt*, a play about Jews and written by a Jew? Schlösser set out his specific concerns about Jewish actors performing the play. When Schlösser's report arrived on Hinkel's desk in late October, its contents guided him on how to evaluate potential play texts for the all-Jewish theatre:

> Very honorable Herr Staatskommissar!
>
> Having examined the drama *God's Hunt* by Emil Bernhard, I hasten to inform you that the performance by the Kulturbund of German Jews does not appear to me to be very opportune. The whole thing is a kind of "solace of Judaism," a kind of "restorative" for Jews. In itself, the play is not tendentious and would be harmless if one had played it during the last Reich. The Third Reich, however, has recognized Judaism in its imminent danger, thus making the matter appear quite objectionable, especially since the play's background is a Russian rabble of soldiers that mistreats Jewry. One can imagine with whom the suggested Cossacks will be identified.
>
> Heil Hitler![17]

The play "*takes place in a Jewish village high in the Carpathian mountains, of a forgotten name and forgotten time*" inside an ancient synagogue. The Jewish community waits behind locked doors, hiding from the Cossacks. A redeemer-like figure in the play sacrifices himself as a martyr to the Cossacks.[18] Schlösser's description of the play's "restorative" effect on Jews likely referred to a focus on Jewish community cohesion, which he thought could engender a renewed Jewish spirit in spectators.

Hinkel expected the Kulturbund theatre to produce Jewish-themed plays; but he censored even those plays because of their messages about a triumphant Jewish collective. By suppressing plays like *God's Hunt* from the theatre's first season, Hinkel compelled Kulturbund stage directors to produce plays that conveyed a Jewish cultural quality but did not appear to be resistant to German society. Nor should the play content portray Germans in a negative way. The Ministry of Propaganda's cautionary viewpoint and its censorship of potential Jewish stage material undercut those voices in the Jewish community that pushed for a strongly Jewish slant in Kulturbund theatre programs. The *Jüdische Rundschau* and its readers promoted plays precisely in the mode of *God's Hunt*. In contrast, the assimilated Jewish citizens represented by papers like the *C.-V.-Zeitung* advocated dramas that did not necessarily feature Jewish characters. The principal lines for public dissension among community organizations emerged sharply during autumn 1933 as Singer and Bab considered what to produce in the first season. Would the Kulturbund theatre be a Jewish-run league for culture in Germany or would it espouse Jewish culture within the German Reich?

The largest subsidies generously given to the theatre came from the Jewish community and the Central Committee for Jewish Assistance and Welfare. Singer thus resolved to feature works with Jewish themes in the first season. His thwarted attempt to produce *God's Hunt* indicates the precarious position he occupied as he negotiated with Hinkel. At the same time, Singer presented himself to the Jewish public as the theatre spokesperson. Journalists thus reviewed and discussed the artistic director's ostensible motives for his programming choices. But they never knew the full details and complications of his dealings with Hinkel. Singer submitted play titles, manuscripts, and librettos weeks and even months in advance. For example, Singer did not receive Hinkel's rejection of *God's Hunt* until five weeks after submitting the play manuscript for review. This time lapse prompted Singer on subsequent occasions to submit three to four scripts at a time to schedule the playing season more efficiently.

Schlösser's assessment of the Jewish play reveals his role in establishing guidelines for censors to evaluate Kulturbund play texts. Hinkel and his staff examined most of the scripts that Singer submitted for review. Above all, Hinkel believed that the play's content must not be distinguishable as part of Germanic culture. Schlösser's report established an additional unwritten rule that the plays must be distinctly Jewish—without appearing too Jewish. Hinkel's office staff and censors, "Stehr," "Blank," and "Fräulein Framm," had little to no training in the arts.[19] They judged the merits of plays based on their personal loyalty to the Reich's "national revolution" rather than on cultural and stylistic principles.[20]

Hinkel, however, made serendipitous decisions for Singer about the Kulturbund's repertoire during the first season. He permitted play productions which contradicted the very precepts that he advocated for the Kulturbund theatre. Perhaps his inconsistent decisions stemmed from Schlösser's imperfect guidelines on how to censor the Jewish theatre. The government's decisions on permissible plays lacked consistency, especially given that the Kulturbund was supposed to limit itself to plays that promoted Jewish culture. For instance, for a December 1933 production, Hinkel approved Friedrich Hebbel's *Judith* as a substitute for *God's Hunt*, which Schlösser had censored because of its "tendentious" parallels to the Third Reich. Although Hebbel was a non-Jewish German writer, Hinkel authorized the play, apparently because it portrays an ancient Jewish woman who saved her fellow Jews from their enemy.[21] But Singer then postponed *Judith* for technical reasons. Adding to the confusion, the government rejected I. L. Peretz's *The Golden Chain*, probably because its main character is an overzealous rabbi who seeks to suspend the Sabbath. That same month (November), however, Hinkel permitted Singer to stage Wolfgang Amadeus Mozart's *The Marriage of Figaro*, although the lead character revels in his ability to outsmart his master. Could the opera's social criticism be interpreted as a restorative parallel for the Jews' second-class standing in German society? Or did Hinkel approve the comic opera because Mozart's librettist Lorenzo da Ponte was a Jew? Hinkel and his censors may simply have been learning how to censor texts and used different criteria for opera libretti. He did refine the principles for play suppression over time as he evaluated more scripts and received firmer guidelines from Schlösser.

In November 1933 Singer successfully secured the Berliner Theater for the first season. This facilitated the organization's needs for additional office and storage space. With a growing membership that would reach 20,000 in 1934, the organization encompassed significant numbers of workers from clerical staff to technicians, printers, carpenters, painters, and performers. The Kulturbund expanded beyond the theatre, setting up a scene shop at the end of Charlottenstraße in Jordan's, a former department store. Condell and his assistants used a large hall as a workshop where they constructed scenery, designed props, and kept materials. The theatre building itself housed the costume shop, practice rooms, and the administrative offices. One office belonged to Singer and his secretary, and another was the central administrative hub where Werner Levie served as an intermediary between the theatre and the membership office, located in the nearby Kochstraße. Levie dealt with the financial side of the theatre: paying salaries, monthly rent, and utility costs; raising honoraria for guest artists; and often deciding performance rights and royalty issues. If Levie and his manager Hans Zander took care of these duties, Singer, Bab, and Baumann (in 1933) could focus in their meetings on artistic and creative decisions about repertoire and performance.[22]

One such decision ensued as Singer and Bab struggled to find a suitable script for the Jewish play slot. After his unsuccessful attempt to stage *God's Hunt*, Singer understood that he might fare better by featuring a play about Jews only, without non-Jewish characters. Accordingly, in November he tried to reverse Hinkel's initial rejection of Peretz's three-act "drama

4. Behind the scenes: the Kulturbund Theatre Box Office, no date. Akademie der Künste, Berlin, FWA 20.63.18, photographer unknown.

of the Hasidic family," assuring him that the theatre never "wished to perform all three acts, rather only the first act by itself as a complete, balladic poem." In the first act of *The Golden Chain*, Singer explained, "the relationship of Jews to the non-Jewish world is not touched on. Instead, a pure inner-Jewish tragedy is present."[23] The tragedy involved the ostracism of a daughter when she married an outsider to the Hasidic community. "Please take note that I CANNOT agree even to a performance of only the first act of *The Golden Chain*," Hinkel warned Singer.[24] In the first act the charismatic rabbi prays for an "eternal Sabbath" to bring about redemption, chanting: "The world should go to ruin! But we, joyous Sabbath-celebrating Jews, free from rejoicing for absolution, stomp over the rubble."[25] Perhaps it was this proclamation of passion by a Jewish religious leader that led Hinkel to censor any overt onstage portrayal of Jewish dominance at the Kulturbund.[26]

Although the Kulturbund artistic director and his production assistants failed to stage a Jewish drama in December 1933, they produced *Othello* as a substitute for *Judith*, starring Katsch as Othello, with Fritz Wisten as Iago. Ironically, on German stages, the Nazis interpreted Othello as a light-colored Moor to avoid the appearance of racism. The Kulturbund production in a translation by Julius Bab (with Elisabeth Levy) marked the theatre's attempt to stage a play without any specific connection to religion or to nationality. Consequently, Shakespeare's tragedy of the jealous Moor expressed elemental human passion. Condell's scenic assistant Walter Auerbach designed a "deliberately economical" set, architectonically reminiscent of Leopold Jessner's productions with its raised platform, flanked by columned buildings. The minimalist quality of the set allowed viewers to concentrate on the action and the intensity of the acting. Several of the actors from the *Nathan* production performed again. Besides Katsch, Käte Foerder played Desdemona with a soft tenderness. Lilly Kann played Emilia. And Wisten's personification of evil intelligence was evidently convincing enough to assure the rising star of leading roles in the future and the highest wages in the ensemble for his artistic output.[27]

Singer also submitted Arthur Schnitzler's *Paracelsus*, which did not emphasize an overtly Jewish milieu. Hinkel approved the one-act after one of his censors reported: "No objections to a performance of this 'intellectual albeit a bit too artistically' constructed one-act by the Viennese Jew . . . an absolutely great opportunity to 'milk the brain' and give our 'Jewish friends' some fun."[28] Singer and Bab decided to produce *Paracelsus* along with the theatre's first Yiddish-language import in translation, Semyon Yuschewitsch's *Sonkin and the Jackpot* (*Sonkin und der Haupttreffer*).

In January 1934 a new stage director joined the theatre as head of the directing division and directed the double bill in February. Fritz Jessner (1889–1946) was a cousin of the director Leopold Jessner and the former artistic director of the Königsberg Schauspielhaus. After working with Max Reinhardt's ensemble, he came to the Berlin Kulturbund, where he led the Department of Acting.[29] Bab, officially in charge of the Dramaturgy Division, called the *Sonkin* production "a modest start" to stage a well-known Jewish author's play from the previous century. He attributed the Galician comedy's charm not so much to a Jewish interest in content but specifically to the Jewish milieu of the Russian shtetl.[30] But Bab objected to a solitary Jewish focus by the theatre, even while he applauded the league's function as a "help organization" for Jewish artists. He clarified the league's aim for Kulturbund audiences: "We do not wish to establish a new ghetto; we want our work to preserve for German Jews a living connection to Western culture, to which they have been connected for centuries."[31] Bab believed that the play about the sixteenth-century alchemist Paracelsus represented a familiar culture. The play integrated ideas of Freudian psychology (hypnotism and dreams) with kabbalism.

While Bab argued for the Kulturbund to choose plays which represented a European dramatic heritage, some Jewish community authors criticized this approach. One such critic, Ludwig Davidsohn, vented his disappointment at the Kulturbund's repertoire choices because of a general lack of Jewish content. He particularly faulted the *Sonkin* production because it did not reflect the Jewish situation. Nor did it make a play Jewish if characters were named Abraham and Moses, he protested in the *Jüdisch-Liberale Zeitung*.[32] Although all the political newspapers analyzed the situation of Jews in Germany according to different religious and political criteria, they shared a deep attachment to Germany and a common view of Judaism as an "intellectual direction and a source of moral strength."[33]

Thus the drama critic who registered his dismay at Singer's choice of *Sonkin* protested a missed chance to engage audiences with examples of Jewish pride and ethical substance. This kind of criticism spurred Singer to join a public debate that ensued between the *Jüdisch-Liberale Zeitung* and the more independent-minded *Israelitisches Familienblatt* about the Kulturbund and its community role.[34] The liberal newspaper called for a German theatre for Jews, while the *Familienblatt* asked that the plays exude a specific Jewish spirit. "Every few evenings for months I sat together with my dramaturg Bab to consider our repertoire for the next few months," Singer wrote, describing his frustration and his difficulty choosing plays. "Now the acting ensemble director Dr. Jessner has joined us for more intensive discussion, with pitiful results regarding plays by Jews and with Jewish content."[35] Singer pointed to the poor economic conditions that restricted the theatre's technical production capability and the budget. These limitations further complicated the production of many works by modern Jewish dramatists.

The heated debate among newspaper spokespeople appeared to be theoretically detached from the reality of Singer's situation. The artistic director accommodated himself to Nazi government restrictions and to the growing pressure to produce plays about Jews. Even while editors faulted the Kulturbund for "ignoring" Jewish culture in Kulturbund productions, the theatre produced Franz Grillparzer's fragment *Esther* as part of a special program of several kinds of presentations.[36] The biblical Book of Esther tells the story of Purim—the victory of ancient Jews in Babylon under the reign of King

Ahasuerus of Persia.[37] Fritz Jessner staged *Esther* as the centerpiece of an evening program for Purim. He featured Grillparzer's fragment between popular opera waltzes played by the symphony orchestra (under Singer) and a dance pantomime set to Mozart's *Eine Kleine Nachtmusik*, with Ruth Anselm in a ballet solo.[38]

Leni Steinberg portrayed Esther in her first meeting with the king (Fritz Wisten) as strong and unafraid to voice her opinions to her sovereign, who confides in her that his wife does not love him.[39] Esther, willing to be considered as a potential bride for the king, acknowledges aloud that a Jew would be an unfit match. Her cousin and guardian Mordecai worries that one word from Esther to the king about her true heritage as a Jew will result in her being spurned. Grillparzer's fragment ends after Esther gives the king a letter from Mordecai, warning that Queen Vashti and her steward are planning an attack. Jessner limited the action to Esther's decision to accept the king's offer. No final meeting took place between the king and Esther about Vashti's plan for vengeance.[40]

The newspaper debate over the Kulturbund repertoire intensified during the spring of 1934 after *Sonkin* and *Paracelsus* and Grillparzer's *Esther*. Jessner also staged a three and a half hour production of Ibsen's *Wild Duck* (*Die Wildente*) in March 1934 with Wisten in the main role (Hjalmar Ekdal) and the former Gustaf Gründgens student Mira Rostova as Hedwig. Although some newspapers defended the Kulturbund's commitment to world culture, others complained that so far the productions had little or nothing to do with Jews. The disagreements multiplied. Some editors ignorant of the Nazi mandates argued that no play should be forbidden, because German Jews shared a common heritage with Germans. But Weltsch of the *Jüdische Rundschau* insisted upon the need for plays with Jewish themes and characters. This campaign, however, came under attack as political "propaganda for the Zionist party," as a more liberal-leaning Jewish newspaper proclaimed. Rejecting the label "ghetto theatre" and decrying the "one-sidedness" of an all-Jewish repertoire, the paper called for a German theatre for Jews.[41] In an effort to find a middle position, the editors of the *Israelitisches Familienblatt* suggested on 15 March 1934 that the productions should "radiate Jewish passion," even when a play was not written by a Jew.[42] This proposal, although well intended, was little more than an idealistic sentiment.

Singer struggled to establish a repertoire that pleased all community factions. He found himself caught between those community organizations and their journalists sympathetic to his repertoire choices and theatre critics who demanded explanations for his decisions. Many people in the community did not understand the nature of the restrictions he faced. "Don't the plays we performed—*Nathan*, *Esther* [Grillparzer], *Sonkin*—have something to do with Jewish being, the Jewish way of sensing the world, and Jewish yearning?" Singer demanded when pressed to stage plays with "valuable and effective Jewish themes" for Jewish audiences.[43] His sentiment raised questions which shaped the public discussion about the theatre's spring repertoire. Given the present circumstances for German Jews, could Jewish authors even create a forum in which to depict their situation? Should the Kulturbund perform plays about Jews but written by non-Jews? Was a "Jewish" play one with a Jewish milieu or a Jewish character, like *Esther* in Grillparzer's play or Shylock in Shakespeare's *The Merchant of Venice*? No indigenous Jewish literary tradition existed in Germany. Perhaps Jewish writers in Germany would write "topical" plays for the Kulturbund, one journalist suggested. In the meantime, he concluded, foreign plays by Jews could be translated into German.[44]

Singer recognized that it was impossible to fulfill his critics' demands to concentrate right away on "specifically Jewish-cultural work." It was hardly possible to take actors and musicians out of the "centuries-old tradition they had learned on German stages" over the past decades. Singer saw the Kulturbund as an ensemble of actors "who believed in collective work, not stardom."[45] Nor did he have available Jewish theatre material for a repertoire. He could count only five plays of the fifty recommended by Jewish critics with stage-worthy qualities. But those plays could not be staged because the theatre lacked sufficient technical and lighting equipment or the staff could not appease audience factions in the community or the Nazi authorities had excluded them.

Singer challenged his skeptics on the question of what constituted Jewish culture: "There is no such a thing as a Jewish opera. No one complains and is resentful when the Palestinian opera plays Verdi. But one wants to close out the 'world-embracing' spirit of Figaro. Why?" he asked. He and his artistic team tried to develop a distinctive production style for the theatre repertoire that would convey "[w]hat is real and true, noble, and human—what is spiritual and moral as an idea, a word, the sound and scenes of Jewish people of the German language, resonating aesthetically in the souls of German-speaking Jewish listeners."[46] Singer's eloquent vision remained elusive. Perhaps he deceived himself about his ability to put this ideal into practice, given the restrictions that he faced. Before he could establish a characteristic acting style for the theatre, he would have to compromise on a repertoire that fit into the narrowing parameters set by the Nazis.

Bab's fellow literary advisor for the theatre and the lecture division, Lutz Weltmann, offered concrete examples of what a German-Jewish repertoire with "its own face" might look like. Weltmann, who worked for the *Israelitisches Familienblatt* as a drama critic, urged the Kulturbund to adopt biblically themed plays by Jewish German-language writers to celebrate the Jewish spirit and holidays.[47] The problem was that living Jewish playwrights did not always grant Singer the playing rights to stage their work. In April, for example, Singer requested permission to produce Richard Beer-Hofmann's biblical dramatization *Jacob's Dream*. Hinkel authorized the play in early May. Beer-Hofmann had already denied the Kulturbund the rights to his plays months before. Once again he refused to authorize *Jacob's Dream*.[48]

Three kinds of plays emerged within the Kulturbund's "Jewish" play category during the 1933–1934 season and more pointedly during the 1934–1935 season. First, it included dramas set in biblical times which portrayed familiar scenes from the Old Testament, like Grillparzer's *Esther* or *Jacob's Dream*. Second were contemporary Jewish-themed plays from the German-Jewish milieu, like the banned *God's Hunt* or imported plays from eastern Europe or Palestine such as *Sonkin*, which portrayed life in a Russian-Jewish shtetl. In the third type of Jewish play, the theme and use of symbolism transcended a particular time and place: such plays might also express a Jewish mysticism, specifically a symbolic redeemer-like figure or message of renewal for Jews. The script for *God's Hunt* featured a symbolic figure in a protagonist who died as a scapegoat for the besieged community.

Community critics and those inside the theatre like Singer shared a common belief that Jewish artists must dissociate themselves from pre-1933 Berlin theatre. This presented them with a dilemma, because their commitment to the theatrical tradition of the Weimar Republic lay rooted in their German-Jewish identity. Many of the artists joined the Kulturbund because of social and political circumstances. They no longer belonged to the cultural networks that they had taken for granted a year earlier. Anselm, Condell, Wisten, Jessner, and other ensemble members rallied behind Singer's plans for the theatre. Wisten prepared a statement on behalf of his fellow artists in April, demanding solidarity from the press. The artists acknowledged their membership in an "emergency association" (of Jews) due to political circumstances. These conditions necessitated material and artistic sacrifice. Ensemble members asked journalists to apply new standards for criticism to offer constructive support for "the struggling theatre in its plight." Wisten and his colleagues sought understanding from the press; they asked the Jewish media to give them time to evolve, because, the artists declared, "Inner disputes and the threatening echo from the non-Jewish press greatly damaged the material condition of the Kulturbund."[49]

Jewish newspaper editors thus pledged to work together with the Kulturbund to nurture Jewish culture. Nevertheless, throughout 1934 the Kulturbund was beset by a mix of criticism and praise for the trend toward dissimilation among Jews. Using the remarks of a reporter for the Nazi *Völkischer Beobachter*, a journalist for the Zionist paper led the charge against assimilation. He wrote: "We cannot make the Jews different or make them Jewish. That is their task. We can only watch out so that this German-Jewish confusion does not recur. . . . That is what the Aryan laws are for."[50] The Jewish *Rundschau* reporter accepted the Nazi suggestion that Jews must actively differentiate themselves from the surrounding "majority," which he believed the "avowed assimilationists" at the Kulturbund failed to do when they produced *Nathan the Wise* with a "helpless lack of taste." The writer may have deluded himself about the Nazi aims. His logic suggested that—as a result of laws that excluded Jews from German affairs—Jews could shape the inner contours of their condition of differentness or dissimilation.[51]

In contrast, Jews from the Centralverein rejected the idea of cultural dissimilation. They favored a Jewish "regeneration"—a renaissance that would develop from the German-Jewish experience and its culture.[52] The Kulturbund artistic team believed that dissimilation would only evolve outwardly for Jews as Germany set up additional legal hurdles forcibly to separate them from German culture. The editors for the *C.-V.-Zeitung* agreed. They proclaimed that as Jewish Germans "[we] should assimilate ourselves to German culture, dissimilate ourselves, however, from the dominant idea of race. The national [Zionist] Jews in Germany dissimilate themselves from German culture but assimilate their idea according to dominating perspectives on race. Something cannot be right—but by whom and to what extent?"[53] The divide between the Zionist Germans and the assimilated Jews reveals a fractious community that could not agree on their relationship to one another. This complicated identity situation created an ongoing tension for the Kulturbund leadership as Singer plotted a course through the swells of political and religious resistance to his theatre agenda.

The cultural work ahead required Kulturbund Jews to reorient themselves to the new conditions under Hitler. In May 1934 a law defined their membership in a Jewish community and by extension redefined their theatre's cultural direction. The German "reality" had determined everything just a few years earlier. Present circumstances for Jews in Germany, however, necessitated new strategies, not falling back on old ones and living an illusory life. The artists had to accept the new reality of working only among Jews. But because Germany in the 1920s and early 1930s lacked a closed Jewish culture, the "Jewish stage" would have to draw on the repertoire from other closed Jewish "systems" or traditions like those belonging to the Jewish Diaspora. The community organizations had reached a tenuous consensus to support the Kulturbund theatre's commitment to Jewish culture, but critics still debated what "Jewish culture" meant and whether the repertoire choices of the first season adequately reflected that culture.[54]

Lutz Weltmann appealed directly to Singer to stage plays in the second season which specifically affected Jews and presented the historical spirit of the times. He believed that it was imperative to look at what was happening outside of the theatre and to establish an "onstage" relationship to the real-life events unfolding in Berlin, even when the "boundaries between the plays and the environment that created them had been breached."[55] The political and cultural restrictions on Jews in Nazi Berlin made it all the more necessary for the repertoire to expose the societal rupture that Kulturbund Jews experienced. To pretend that the earth was not "shaking" outside of the Kulturbund theatre was "inexcusable," wrote a drama critic.[56] And yet a glance at the repertoire choices of late spring and summer 1934 shows that the repertoire evaded any attempt to evoke the spirit of the times. Only the opening night of Jessner's production of Shakespeare's *As You Like It* (*Wie Ihr wollt*) in May 1934 alluded to the times. The performance was dedicated to the Central Committee for Jewish Assistance and Social Improvement. The president of the Reich Representation of German Jews, Leo Baeck, addressed the audience about their situation and tied it to Shakespeare's view of humanity. His speech provided audience members with spiritual guidelines before they watched a production that balanced the sentimental with the burlesque. Cabaret and film actress Rosa Valetti joined the troupe as a guest during the summer, transforming the theatre temporarily into something like summer stock for an illusory month or two.[57] She performed in and co-directed productions of Noel Coward's *Weekend*, Arthur Schnitzler's *In the Play of Summer Breezes* (*Im Spiel der Sommerlufte*, 1929), Bruno Frank's *A Storm over Patsy* (*Sturm im Wasserglas*, 1930), and a dance pantomime.

Singer took to heart the advice of his critics and submitted scripts to

Hinkel for the next season that resonated with the times while adhering to his restrictions. But Weltmann had identified a problem inherent to the Jewish community that affected its cultural production. The all-Jewish theatre by its very isolation had no choice but to proceed as a completely "closed" theatre. The editorial board for Berlin's "newspaper of the whole [Jewish] community" analyzed the problem that the Kulturbund faced:

> No other art is like that of the theatre—bound to the whole life of a community. . . . Without an all-encompassing and established culture there can be no theatre true to type; and just as no other art can be artificially developed, the theatre cannot reveal a unique life without a connection to a "closed" culture [*geschlossene Kultur*]. In this context, if one should ask today whether there is already a Jewish theatre and Jewish plays for this theatre, then every unbiased observer must unrestrictedly deny this question. Because here in Germany there has been no closed Jewish culture before now, a Jewish stage in any real sense cannot exist.[58]

The Kulturbund drew on past theatrical tradition, incorporated the members' Jewish heritage, and reinforced community bonds. But those members saw themselves as mostly assimilated or in a cultural sense German. The Kulturbund Jews lacked a connection to an established repertoire or material with which to create any kind of Jewish stage.

If we agree that theatre as an art form relies on a connection to a "closed culture" (or a self-reflexive system) to develop its own spirit and its own repertoire, we must also assume that "Jewish" plays must be written within such a system. They should not be borrowed from elsewhere—in this case, from eastern Europe. Singer and his inner circle knew that the Kulturbund must become a new kind of theatre whose productions could offer audiences plays that revealed historical circumstances. So too would drama critics require a new model for reviewing Kulturbund productions.

Hinkel demanded that Singer take into account current politics as he considered which plays to schedule for the theatre's upcoming playing season, 1934–1935. "It goes without saying that the performances may not allude at all to any political or cultural things in Germany," Hinkel warned Singer during the summer of 1934.[59] Singer decided to include in the season repertoire biblically themed dramatizations by German Jews. His choice to produce Beer-Hofmann's Jacob drama, however, would have to wait until the playwright granted the performing rights. In the meantime Singer requested permission from Hinkel in September for a "preperformance" of Stefan Zweig's *Jeremiah* for "charity purposes."[60] Hinkel promptly authorized Singer to mount the production in October 1934 provided that Singer "as usual . . . take into consideration exactly the conditions [for authorization] already known to you."[61] Singer reassured Hinkel that "of course we have been painstakingly scrutinizing all of our texts in advance."[62]

Hinkel had already approved Hebbel's *Judith* and Beer-Hoffman's *Jacob's Dream*. These modern renditions of biblical stories appealed to theatre audiences before 1933, as had Grillparzer's *Esther*. Hinkel and his censors could accept dramatizations of Jewish history and Jewish characters as "Jewish" plays because the playwrights used sources from Hebrew biblical literature. Although two of these plays were written by non-Jewish authors, the plays shared with the *Esther* fragment characteristics which Jewish community critics had deemed desirable. They had argued the benefits of staging German-language plays with strong Jewish characters and themes of universal appeal. It would appear that Singer was putting together a repertoire season that would please everyone. In the meantime Singer conceded to Hinkel's warnings about what not to produce.

Having received instruction from Schlösser on how to evaluate the plays for the Jewish theatre, Hinkel suppressed the publication of literary articles which referred to Jewish spiritual strength and repeatedly barred plays with content that championed divine influence. Schlösser's warning against staging *God's Hunt* in 1933 had led him to recognize the potential rallying power of scenes that might be interpreted as "solace" for Jews or perceived as unflattering to the Reich. In the forbidden *God's Hunt* script, a group of characters represented their faith and an outsider character sacrificed himself for his fellow Jews. The play's unified Jewish community symbolized redemption and, by extension, the Christian notion of a redeemer. When Hinkel reviewed the first act of Peretz's *The Golden Chain*, in which the rabbi appealed for the Messiah, he knew what to censor and banned the play.

For the imminent 1934–1935 playing season, Singer resolved to achieve a successful staging of a "Jewish play." His decision to open the new playing season with Zweig's biblical *Jeremiah* (*Jeremias*) satisfied all the critics, because the play's author was a German Jew; his poignant play about the Hebrew prophet depicted a vital episode in Jewish history; and its appeal to audiences had special meaning in Hitler's Reich. Hinkel also approved the choice. Fritz Jessner would direct the production to coincide with the Jewish High Holidays of 1934.

3 GROUNDED

ESTABLISHING A REPERTOIRE

1934–1935

At the Kulturbund benefit performance of Stefan Zweig's *Jeremiah* (*Jeremias*) on 7 October 1934, the audience listened to preperformance remarks by Zionist Organization spokesman Siegfried Moses and the president of the Centralverein, Julius Brodnitz, as they addressed the unique situation for Jews in Germany one and a half years after Hitler's takeover. The Sunday evening performance reinforced a new campaign by the Reich Committee for German Jewry to promote Jewish self-help organizations.[1] The play about the biblical prophet resounded with parallels to Berlin's current Jewish community. Still reeling from what he called a "deep shock," Brodnitz cautioned Jews to "answer to the duties of the present, after everything had collapsed" in the world as they knew it.[2] Pointing to the significance of the Kulturbund for the times, the guest speakers tapped into the positive message of *Jeremiah*. Zweig had set his play within Jewish history during the Babylonian siege of Jerusalem. Despite Jeremiah's premonitions of destruction, he asked his people not to rebel against the usurpers. At the end of the play the Jews united in their resolve to rebuild their destroyed city.

Brodnitz used Zweig's play as a springboard to describe to fellow community members the Kulturbund's obligation to Jewish citizenry in 1934: to provide economic assistance, creative uplift, and opportunities for the future. He reminded those assembled of the Kulturbund's role in improving life for Jews under Nazi rule: "It mattered to the 100,000 who wanted to stay in Germany [after 1933], to ease the transition; it mattered that we could mitigate the privation of the day," he told the crowded auditorium. Listing the cultural benefits for the community, he said that "it mattered" not to lose "great artistic and intellectual forces in our community;

and it mattered that we nurture our youth, who must not lose the ability to smile."[3]

The *Jeremiah* premiere launched the 1934–1935 playing season with gravitas. At the debut performance, the audience reveled in the mass spectacle of an "Oratorium" that Fritz Jessner achieved by means of living tableaux.[4] He successfully orchestrated multiple crowd scenes to heighten the effect of Jeremiah's influence on the people of Jerusalem. Because the play required an especially large cast of actors to portray the masses, Singer had hired an extra fifty-six unemployed Jewish actors for the production. He saw a chance to prolong the improved social conditions for the artists by planning a *Jeremiah* tour to Breslau just weeks after the premiere. But Hinkel did not permit the tour. Singer urged him to reconsider, because the tour could benefit the extra performers by boosting their "modest earnings."[5] With a tour, Singer reasoned, the Kulturbund could also extend its reach to Jewish communities beyond Berlin. Hinkel refused to change his mind, however; such a large group of traveling Jewish actors from Berlin would require close supervision on tour and in Breslau. He could not guarantee such control outside of his jurisdiction.

The Berlin production of *Jeremiah*, starring Fritz Wisten, was the first performance at the Kulturbund theatre of a German-language play written by a Jew with a biblical theme. Zweig had adapted his nine-scene play from the Book of the Prophet Jeremiah and the Lamentations of Jeremiah. The play's ninth scene, "The Everlasting Road," best signified the playwright's message that Jews would unite in a fearless, indomitable community when an enemy laid siege to their homeland. But Zweig's depiction of Jeremiah's hope for Jewish emancipation mirrored a theme present in scripts that Hinkel had already banned at the Kulturbund—the idea of achieving spiritual purification through suffering. Despite their forced exodus, the Jews in Zweig's play looked toward the future, determined to restore their broken lives and their temples. This notion appealed to many Berlin Jews as they faced the uncertainties of Jewish life in 1934.

Yet Hinkel rejected crucial parts of Zweig's play, stipulating that Singer and Jessner significantly revise their production script before the play could be performed. Hinkel's main objections followed a pattern of censorship that Schlösser had developed a year earlier, when Singer submitted scripts featuring charismatic Jewish leaders like Jeremiah. The process by which the Kulturbund artistic manager and the head of the theatre's directing unit (Jessner) altered Zweig's script for production provided them with a template for staging other biblical-historical scripts that Hinkel principally authorized. Central to his preconditions for a production of *Jeremiah*, Hinkel insisted on emending any dialogue that expressed Jewish resistance to a perceived enemy. He thus forbade the performance of play passages where Jeremiah explicitly called on fellow citizens to remain strong, proud Israelites. In preparation for the October performance, Jessner worked from a much-truncated production script of Zweig's original, omitting three-quarters of the play's final scene 9 in performance. As written by Zweig, the prophet's appeal to his people culminated in this last scene as Jeremiah urged his followers to draw on their inner resources and their belief that Jerusalem would prevail. When Jessner adapted the play script to the Kulturbund stage, he preserved the basic line of action but altered and deleted the crucial scenes which Hinkel and his censors might have interpreted as seditious. In production, these script changes consequently weakened the play's overall message of deliverance, diminishing Jeremiah's role as a Jewish redeemer.

The Kulturbund audience, however, witnessed the process by which Zweig's title character became a prophet. As the curtain rose on the opening scene of *Jeremiah*, Wisten as Jeremiah staggered onto the stage, gasping from foreboding visions. God had anointed him; but Jeremiah could not yet comprehend the magnitude of this choice. Jeremiah's mother, Rebecca (Lilly Kann), appeared, prompting him to question his sanity or whether he was ordained by God to fulfill a mission. "I follow my own path," he told his mother after she banished him for spreading premonitions of doom in the city. The second scene showed Jeremiah's resolve to reveal God's will. Only one young follower, Baruch (Walter Hertner), recognized Jeremiah's potential greatness and pledged to save Jerusalem from destruction. Those assembled in the Berliner Theater watched the play's first scenes as originally scripted by Zweig: Jeremiah's worst fears and visions materialized, and the Israelites saw their city plagued by disaster.

The onstage action heightened as soldiers in Jerusalem stood ready to defend their city from an attack. Although Zweig began this scene with a debate on the necessity of war in Jerusalem, audience members familiar with the play did not hear the debate. As written by Zweig, one Jewish sentry referred to the traitorous foes as "our enemies, and it is our duty to hate them." The second sentry's response ambiguously suggested that the warring side had as valid a reason for fighting as they did. He then questioned the meaning of war and admitted that he had no reason to hate what he did not know.[6] Jessner omitted the entire provocative exchange from performance.

Instead the director opened the scene late in the action (at least a quarter into the scene as originally written) with a nighttime entrance by King Zedekiah (Ben Spanier), refusing to take Jeremiah's advice to surrender to the enemy, Nebuchadnezzar. Jessner produced a simpler line of stage action by avoiding Jeremiah's entrance with his disciple Baruch. Had Jessner staged this scene as the playwright had written it, the Kulturbund audience would have witnessed Jeremiah's recognition of his inability to avert the disaster he foresaw.[7] Under Jessner's direction, however, Wisten evidently underplayed Jeremiah's self-doubt. Jessner also reduced the emotional effect of Jeremiah's reunion with his dying mother (scene 5).[8] By paring down the scene in production, Jessner deprived the audience of Zweig's emotionally charged dialogue, in which Jeremiah lied to his mother about the disastrous reality.

Jessner did direct Wisten to incorporate anguish into his performance. The audience witnessed Jeremiah's self-contempt as Wisten showed the character's struggle with his lonely mission.[9] Jessner translated Zweig's descriptions of the prophet's use of sudden "furious exclamations" and frenzied cadences into stage action when Jeremiah persuaded his people to join his cause in the play's middle scenes (6–8). Hugo Lachmanski found that Wisten convincingly showed the prophet's struggle with "inner demons."[10] In Zweig's written script, Jeremiah succumbed to God's will and the consequences for his homeland—siege.[11] Jessner avoided staging action that overtly compared Jeremiah's suffering with that of Jesus in Zweig's script. Thus he did not present Zweig's powerful imagery in the scene (7), where Jeremiah responded to calls for his death with his arms stretched out "as if on the cross."[12] Rather, the director dramatized in production only the main plot line of suffering Jews who lost their city but regained pride in their destiny. Jessner's production muted even the theatrical expression of this dramatic arc, because he cut the bulk of the play's final ninth scene and transposed the sequence of the remaining action within that scene.

In this way, Jessner's *Jeremiah* diluted the essence of Zweig's text in production. The director shortened the overall length considerably by significantly revising the final action. He simplified the plot, reduced the stage effect of Jeremiah's influence on his followers, and weakened the prophet's mission and his leadership when he spurred the mass exodus from Jerusalem. Jessner sped up the action and the prophet's call for citizens to sacrifice their homeland but to trust in God.[13] The director then cut to a stage image so that the audience saw Jeremiah with "arms outstretched" at the top of the stage set's wide stairway to the temple, urging his followers to leave the city. Jessner left intact a chorus of exultant voices, reflecting on their liberation by Moses.[14] But he collapsed Zweig's ensuing choral praise for liberation and instead focused on Jeremiah's push toward exodus. The production retained Jeremiah's words to the masses, which likely would have struck the Kulturbund audience as apt for the times: "Again and again have we been yoked to the plough, enslaved; God has helped to free us from exile."[15]

Similarly, in 1934 the word *Führer* (leader) was synonymous with Hitler. The Kulturbund production avoided all use of this word, which recurred in the last scene's dialogue between the prophet and his followers. Jessner also omitted from performance the questions from the disciples about their fate and Jeremiah's ominous words on the eternal nature of Jewish suffering.[16] Hinkel probably had mandated such a directorial decision to lessen the emotional effect of the wanderers' choral ode to suffering in exile. Yet Hinkel probably condoned the production's implied call of the wanderers to reclaim Palestine as a homeland.[17]

Hinkel permitted Kulturbund administrators and dramaturgical assistants Julius Bab and Leo Hirsch to retain dialogue about a return to Palestine, but he consistently censored Zweig's scripted call for Jewish community resistance. The playwright had portrayed the Jews as unfazed by their Chaldean challengers. And historically the Jews embodied spiritual opposition to those conquering tribes. The Kulturbund production avoided explicit stage action related to the overt references to Jewish resistance expressed in Zweig's script. Jessner omitted from performance all dialogue among the Chaldeans that discussed Jewish strength in migration, including the play's final lines about the Jews:

> THE CHALDEAN: See how they are walking to meet the sun. His light shines on their foreheads, and they themselves shine with the strength of the sun. Mighty must their God be.
>
> THE CHALDEAN GENERAL: Their God? Have we not broken down his altars? Have we not conquered him?
>
> THE CHALDEAN: Who can conquer the invisible? Men we can slay, but their God who lives in them we cannot slay. A nation can be controlled by force; its spirit, never.[18]

Despite the absence of this significant ending, Jessner's production captured the Jews' triumphant exodus. He translated the gist of those forbidden words into movement on the Kulturbund stage. Arthur Eloesser, a Kulturbund lecturer and the drama critic for the Zionist newspaper, praised Jessner's use of the *Sprechchor* (speaking choir) technique in a sensory symphony: Jessner staged the mass exodus in "an excited atmosphere of dancing fanaticism," to the sound of a harp, triangle, drums, and the half-chanting, half-speaking choir.[19] Onstage Zweig's Jews sustained a victorious spirit. Yet an appeal to spiritual strength and community among Kulturbund Jews gave Hinkel provocation enough to ensure that such ideas would not reappear in a public forum.

Just days after the charity performance, Singer forwarded to Hinkel excerpts from *Jeremiah*'s final scene along with an analysis written by Julius Bab. But Hinkel prevented the publication of the essay, precisely because Bab identified an unyielding spiritual strength within the Jewish soul as the play's message. Objecting strongly to this suggestion, Hinkel underlined two main ideas in the essay as unacceptable, which also coalesced in the play's censored ninth scene.[20] First, Bab attributed to the character Jeremiah the recognition that "*the message and meaning of Judaism lies not in the external deployment of force, but rather in the permeation of inner religious strength*." Second, Bab linked Jeremiah's desperate recognition of his fate to the historic destiny of all Jews. Bab concluded that this destiny led the prophet to grasp the "*indestructible meaning of Judaism, that his affirmation of God bears with it great suffering*."[21] Consequently Hinkel ordered Singer to exclude these passages, because they appeared to promote a "Jewish" spiritual power that challenged Christianity. He subsequently repressed references to Jeremiah's empathy for the suffering of others and rejected analogies in the text between Zweig's prophet Jeremiah and the Christian savior.[22] Hinkel likely demanded that all statements about the play should be in accord with Jessner's production script.

The censorship of the *Jeremiah* script and its one Kulturbund production demonstrated Singer's problem establishing a repertoire that would satisfy Hinkel and reach the stage yet still transmit a playwright's work meaningfully to an audience. After Hinkel blocked further performances of *Jeremiah*, Singer organized touring lectures and recitations by actors that integrated excerpts from Zweig's play. Hinkel condoned such small-scale venues outside of Berlin, because they were easier to supervise than were large groups of traveling actors. For Singer, these recitations served to edify and entertain Jewish audiences in regions without a Kulturbund organization. Only weeks after the October performance of *Jeremiah*, for example, Hinkel approved a publicity lecture of the play for the Frankfurt am Main–based Kulturbund branch.[23] Hinkel also authorized Lilly Kann (Rebecca) to tour the play's fifth scene as a lecture-recitation to Rostock, Lübeck, Gustrow, and Schwerin. This coincided with a dramatic reading of the play's final chorus of wandering Jews.[24] Although Hinkel permitted occasional recitations from *Jeremiah* outside of Berlin, he forbade actors to incorporate monologues on Jewish suffering with references to an invisible Jewish God.[25] At the same time, all of these programs appear to have retained Zweig's final image of the Jews' historic exodus: "An unending throng of people then march out of the city and through the ages."[26]

The Kulturbund production of *Jeremiah* and all play-related lectures reminded audience members of their own situation under dictatorship. Goebbels's promotion of the "Aryan" doctrine of "Blut und Boden" (blood and soil) among non-Jewish Germans caused conflict within the Jewish community. The racist ideology excluded German citizens of Jewish birth, because it was based on ethnicity and ensured that citizens of German blood and descent rightfully occupied German territory. Religious Jewish leaders voiced opposition to what they saw as a cultural apartheid resulting from the new German laws that curtailed Jews' rights. One could not "undo" the past 150 years after being incorporated into civilization, a prominent rabbi named Löwenstamm declared. Yet he conceded the reality of the situation for Jews in Germany, admitting that Jews must accept their Jewish culture, because "creating culture requires us to thoroughly study and come to terms with our own [culture] and the unknown or foreign."[27]

Singer, Bab, and Werner Levie recognized that they must distinguish the Kulturbund's cultural programs from the familiar German culture. At the same time, Singer and other figures in the community continued to view the enforced and "closed" nature of their theatre—for Jews only—as contradictory to their kinship with German culture as Jewish-born Germans. Consequently the administrative staff tried to maintain a connection to the artistic world outside of the Jewish community, even while shaping an artistic program within the new "emergency community" of Jews. They adamantly adhered to the precepts of the West European humanist tradition, which informed their German Jewish heritage, despite Hinkel's ban on producing non-Jewish German playwrights. But Singer and his colleagues knew that to move the Kulturbund forward and preserve it, the organization's division heads from acting (Fritz Wisten), directing (Fritz Jessner), and drama (Julius Bab) had to infuse a Jewish sense of life into theatre programs. They wanted to communicate to all age-sectors of the audiences something of Jewish history, philosophy, and biblical literature. But they faced the ongoing challenge of integrating Jewish concepts into their programming.

Singer decided to appeal to the younger generation of theatregoers by developing a lecture series, which would prepare young spectators for theatre productions like *Jeremiah*. In spring 1934 Singer already had instigated special performances of plays such as Hugo von Hofmannsthal's *Death and the Fool* for invited groups of schoolchildren. Hinkel then readily granted Singer's request for school pupils to attend an opera performance of Bedřich Smetana's *The Bartered Bride*, as long as Singer "guaranteed that only Jewish pupils will be granted admission."[28] Singer resolved to attract Jewish teenagers and young adults to the theatre on a regular basis. He would cultivate young audiences through literary programs and Jewish-themed plays to promote Jewish identity and solidarity within the youth community. By seeking ways to engage the younger generation in Kulturbund events, Singer and leaders of newly formed Jewish Kulturbund branches like Rhein-Ruhr (March 1934) singled out those impressionable young citizens, who represented the future of the Jewish community. At the central Berlin Kulturbund theatre, Singer expanded Wisten's pedagogical duties to supervise technical speech work with the emerging generation of young actors.[29]

As vital as it was to train the youngest actors of the troupe and to add youth members to the cultural organization, Singer wanted to retain members from the older generations, who were more rooted in German traditions. During November 1934 the Berlin Kulturbund produced two German standard works: Beethoven's *Fidelio* and Goethe's *The Siblings* (*Die Geschwister*). Perhaps Hinkel overlooked an opportunity to block works by German masters by permitting Goethe's one-act play in a double-bill with a one-act by Molière, *The Learned Ladies* (*Die gelehrten Frauen*). Nor did local Gestapo officers initially object to the all-Jewish production of a Goethe play.

Ironically, it was the Jewish Eloesser who publicly derided the choice of a Goethe play—on the grounds of artistic merit: "If one cannot cast three out of three roles, then one should not put on the play—least of all when it is by Goethe."[30] In swift succession, a propaganda chief for the Nazi Party in Berlin registered a complaint about the audacity Jews showed by producing German classics, while "tactlessly" referring to "our wonderful Beethoven" and Goethe's *Iphigenia at Aulis* as an appropriate choice for a Kulturbund performance. "It is even more tactless," the propagandist continued, "when the Jewish Kulturbund performs *Fidelio* with an entirely Jewish cast of singers.

What do Beethoven and Goethe have in common with the Jews anyway?"[31] Someone in the party forwarded the complaint to Hinkel, who must have admonished Singer not to repeat the performance. Kulturbund Jews no longer performed Beethoven or Goethe after November 1934.[32]

Hinkel could not personally scrutinize in advance all of the literary material of the many Kulturbund-related publications and play productions. By early 1935 he routinely sent Singer warnings to accept "full responsibility" for any texts proposed for the Berlin theatre and for other Kulturbund branches, including texts which were under review for lectures. In shifting a supervisory responsibility to Singer, Hinkel was training Singer to precensor the material before actually submitting it for review.[33] Yet by delegating oversight to Singer on programming decisions, Hinkel inevitably ceded some control to the Kulturbund staff on a number of repertoire decisions. In January 1935 Hinkel condoned a production of Robert Neuner's *The Lifelong Child (Das lebenslängliche Kind)*. The blacklisted writer Erich Kästner used the alias "Robert Neuner" precisely to bypass the censor. But Hinkel did not know this, and it took three months for Schlösser to reverse the decision and ban the Neuner play. In March he forbade Neuner's publisher to grant the playing rights to the Kulturbund, effectively blocking the production.[34] The arbitrary manner in which Hinkel revoked his permission exposed his own ignorance of Jewish authors and their pseudonyms. It also reflected the fluidity of Schlösser's rules for the Jewish theatre, which Hinkel followed and executed depending on the circumstances at the time.

The February 1935 production of Richard Beer-Hofmann's biblical drama *Jacob's Dream: A Prologue (Jaákobs Traum: Ein Vorspiel)* illustrated some of the challenges that Singer faced when he produced plays with Jewish content. Despite Hinkel's authorization of a premiere, Beer-Hofmann himself delayed the performance date by nine months after twice denying the Kulturbund the production rights. The playwright offered no reason for his early refusals to grant the Kulturbund a performance. While he supported the Zionist cause, he opposed an ethnocentric nationalism and emigration to Palestine. He believed instead that Jewish life could exist in the Diaspora. Given this viewpoint, Beer-Hofmann may well have been against an all-Jewish production of his play.[35] Yet he eventually permitted the theatre to stage his work, which Hinkel reauthorized in late January 1935 as a benefit event for Jewish old-age homes.[36] When Singer received permission to produce the play, he promptly submitted to Hinkel a supplementary preface, written especially for the February performance. A narrator would recite introductory words by Leo Hirsch before the play's "dream text" (act II), Singer assured Hinkel.[37]

Despite its two-part structure, *Jacob's Dream* constituted a separate play in itself and merged three categories of the Jewish-themed plays that evolved within the Kulturbund repertoire. First, Beer-Hofmann had written a biblically infused German-language play. Second, he chose a title character from the Old Testament whose mythic heroism revealed Jewish historical and moral values. Finally, regardless of their religious beliefs, contemporary audience members could readily identify with the work's universal theme, which transcended its biblical time and place. Beer-Hofmann originally wrote *Jacob's Dream* (first performed in 1919) as a prologue to his trilogy on King David. Originating from two biblical episodes of Genesis, *Jacob's Dream* dramatized how Jacob attained the name "Israel" to lead future generations of Jews. Beer-Hofmann set up the conflict between the two brothers, Jacob and Edom (Esau), after Jacob received the parental blessing which rightfully belonged to his brother (act I, Beersheba). As the "Chosen One" of the Almighty, Jacob personified the wandering Jew who cast his lot with God on the mountain of Beth-El (act II). Act I thus prepared the spectator for the painful confrontation between the brothers in act II. The second act culminated in Jacob's vision and overnight conversion to "he who struggled with God, Yisroel."[38]

Singer had scheduled the sole performance of *Jacob's Dream* as a self-help event on behalf of the elderly in the Jewish community. On 5 February 1935 prominent community leaders from the Zionist Association and Centralverein joined the predominantly elderly audience in the Berliner Theater for the celebratory evening performance.[39] After Hirsch's introductory remarks and an adagio by Johann Sebastian Bach, the play began.[40] Under Jessner's direction, the audience watched the play's three scenes of the first act flow into Jacob's night vision, the core of act II. Jessner had cast several of the same actors who had performed in *Jeremiah*, including Walter Hertner as Jacob and Wisten as the archangel Samael. Once more Lilly Kann played a mother (Rebecca). Opposite Hertner as Jacob, the youthful Herbert Grünbaum played the spurned Edom. Heinz Condell's set design featured a prominent gauze curtain at center stage to mark the transition between the earthly realm of the first act and the ethereal realm of the second act. Lighting effects alternated dim and glaring spotlights on Jacob as the archangels descended on Beth-El to spur Jacob's transformation.[41] Jessner's choice to stage Jacob's vision behind the transparent curtain modified the movements of the performers and enhanced the dream mood of this scene.

Hirsch's supplementary "prologue" may have affected the play's reception even more than the technical stage effects, however, because it established a new context in which to view the character of Jacob and his effect on ancient Jewry. Addressing the audience directly, Liselotte Collin delivered Hirsch's verse to introduce the program. She distinguished the young "dreamer" Jacob from those pragmatic seniors assembled, "for whom this play unfold[ed]."[42] The narrator spoke of the aging process and Jacob's real-life difficulties with his wife and children. Stressing Jacob's idealism in act II, the actress cautioned the audience: "You only see the young Jacob." But, she continued, the audience would neither observe hunger nor be privy to the fears that Jacob may have felt as an old man. In present times of hardship, the narrator reminded her listeners, many elderly people could identify with such need. Jessner used the preperformance remarks as a pragmatic thank-you to the community leaders who assisted the aged. With the prologue, the director linked the play's action to present times while influencing audience expectations about the protagonist before he appeared onstage:

I am here for just a short time	Ich komme auf einen Sprung
to thank all of those and in memory of	zum Dank und zur Erinnerung,
those who have helped us	an alle, die uns hilfreich sind,
to give the elderly bread and refuge	die Brot und Zuflucht für die Alten
and, God willing, will keep it up.	besorgen und, so Gott will, halten.
Then Jacob is also young once more	Dann ist auch Jaakob wieder jung
and dreams and lives—	und träumt und lebt—
the play begins.	das Spiel beginnt.[43]

Hirsch's simple rhyme scheme contrasted sharply with Beer-Hofmann's eloquent verse. The new words suggested that Jacob would face a normal aging process. But in his original text Beer-Hofmann portrayed Jacob only as a young man who struggled toward his destiny, ready to take on the pain of his people, the Jews. The "dream text" dramatized Jacob's acceptance of his fate as God's messenger. In his vision, archangels told Jacob that his descendants would wander the world and as a result experience faith, hope, and suffering.[44]

Jacob's dream sequence in act II made up the crux of Beer-Hofmann's drama. Had Singer insisted that the introduction precede only this sequence as he initially informed Hinkel, the new verse placement between the two acts would have undermined the dramatic effect of Jacob's conversion on the audience.[45]

The reviewers did not mention that Jessner adjusted the tone and radically altered the staged text just as he had pared down the *Jeremiah* script for production. Leo Hirsch's added prelude to *Jacob's Dream* may have weakened the power of Jacob's religious conversion. As it was, critics commended the play's Jewish message in the "wonderful" dream sequence where Jacob received his God-given mission: "This production accepts German Jewry in a . . . daily changing tragedy of destiny—leading to a rebirth of religious, historical values," Lachmanski wrote.[46] Further, Eloesser lauded Grünbaum (Edom) for his brute physicality and "heavy wildness" in act II, when the slighted brother charged at Jacob with a bow and knife.[47] In the play's first scenes, Edom lashed out at his mother, vowing to cede all earthly pleasure for his brother's blood.[48] These scenes set up the eventual confrontation between the brothers in the second act, where Jacob tried to regain Edom's trust. Whether the actors expressed Beer-Hofmann's lofty ideals adequately in performance remains unclear. Dr. Otto Hirsch, an occasional Kulturbund lecturer, wrote to Singer that the production was flawed, because only Wisten achieved the oratorical skills necessary to express the conflict between brothers and between Jacob and God's angels.[49] And Lachmanski admitted that not even Hertner (Jacob), an "extraordinarily talented, young actor," could elongate or enunciate secondary syllables in the verse, which weakened the force of the words.[50] As a result, the vital fraternal encounter on Beth-El may have lost some of its intensity in performance. This, in turn, would have diluted Beer-Hofmann's lyrical message about Jewish spiritual and historic fate.

Based on the reviews, the Berlin production included the meeting between the two brothers. Beer-Hofmann originally scripted the scene so that Jacob cut his arm, drew blood, and spilled it in the dirt to mix with his brother's blood. The symbolic act allowed them to transcend their dividedness to seal their blood brotherhood ("Brüderschaft") with a drink (lines 965–973). Hinkel probably vetoed the symbolic drink because the rite too directly resembled German fraternal bonding rituals. Even without the onstage communal drink, Singer produced a play in early 1935 that featured a man's transformation into a spiritual leader of Jews. Only months later a change in government procedures would censor future Kulturbund stage versions of *Jacob's Dream* because of the play's assimilatory nature. Beer-Hofmann's modern take on Jacob, father of the Israelites, who tricked Edom out of his birthright, risked too closely allegorizing the German and Jewish "brothers" in Germany.[51] Accordingly, Hinkel informed Singer that the scripted blood rite between brothers must be struck from the *Jacob* text for a production at the Hamburg Kulturbund branch. Hinkel ultimately allowed the production, but its premiere, ironically, coincided with the adoption of the Nuremberg racial laws.[52] By mid-September 1935 Hinkel would demand additional changes to scripts already approved, as in the case of Beer-Hofmann's script, which had been revised before the Berlin performance.[53] He eventually banned all productions and public recitations of *Jacob*, in particular of the second act.[54]

An overall process of managerial reorganization occurred at the Kulturbund theatre during the seven months following the Berlin production of *Jacob* as a result of Germany's racial laws. In April 1935 government regulations decreed that the cultural organization must be newly registered under the name "Jewish Kulturbund Berlin E.V. [*sic*]." The encompassing term included a growing network of all-Jewish cultural associations across the Reich. It proved difficult, however, to coordinate the management of disparate satellite theatres and orchestras from the Berlin-based Ministry of Propaganda and the Reich Representation of German Jews. In 1935 Goebbels authorized Hinkel to establish a central umbrella organization that would be managed by one executive committee.

Known as the Reich Association of Jewish Cultural Leagues in Germany (Reichsverband der Jüdischen Kulturbünde in Deutschland), the umbrella organization incorporated all theatrical and musical production by Jews in the Reich. Seventeen men from regional Jewish Kulturbund branches and Berlin's main headquarters composed the executive board. Eight of these committee members also served on the board of directors, which supervised all business operations in the Kulturbund enterprise. Hinkel designated Singer as the general manager and artistic director of all Kulturbund alliances. Werner Levie was promoted to general secretary of the organization. Because he was a foreigner from a country with diplomatic ties to Germany (Holland), Levie's status may actually have facilitated his relationship with Hinkel. No apparent undercurrent of personal conflict existed between the two men. Alice Levie remembered that her husband "could go relatively speaking without danger into the cave of the lion, which is to say, to Hinkel. My husband got along very well with Hinkel; there was no friction."[55] Unlike the complex connection that Hinkel and Singer shared as German citizens, Levie's non-German background afforded him cultural distance from his supervisor. This may have aided Levie's control of the Kulturbund's operational affairs, which progressed smoothly during the mid-1930s.

By late April 1935 Hinkel entrusted Levie with administrative authority of the cultural organization, while granting Singer additional supervisory responsibilities. Levie managed budgetary requests and membership drives. Singer quickly became the official liaison for communications between the regional Kulturbund theatres and Hinkel and by extension with the Ministry of Propaganda. Singer passed on all requests from other Kulturbund managing directors for cultural programming from Berlin. His intervention did not ensure that plays approved by Hinkel for the Berlin theatre could be produced at subsidiary Kulturbund branches.[56] Nonetheless, Hinkel often granted Singer's requests when the Kulturbund required permissions or the playing rights for a performance. This occurred when Hinkel willingly intervened on Singer's behalf for an April production of George Bernard Shaw's *Candida*. Fischer Publishing would only release the rights to foreign plays if the Reich Theatre Chamber approved. Hinkel settled the issue with Schlösser, who then resolved the issue with the publisher. It is true that Hinkel also imposed limits on some of Singer's bolder requests for assistance. When he asked to take the orchestra abroad for four weeks during the summer of 1935, Hinkel rejected this request on the same grounds on which he had forbidden large-scale tours of actors outside of Berlin a year earlier. Would Singer "take responsibility for each utterance and action by approximately 40 members of the orchestra abroad?" Hinkel asked. Singer backed down and canceled the tour outright.[57]

Behind the scenes at his Berlin theatre, Singer adeptly juggled the demands placed on him by his players as well as by his patrons. He arbitrated potential disagreements that arose among his artists. For instance, a personality clash emerged between Fritz Wisten and Jessner, which affected the casting for the *Candida* production. The independent-minded actor had bristled under his colleague's direction during January rehearsals for Luigi Pirandello's *Six Characters in Search of an Author*, because Wisten (the Father) did not attend a blocking rehearsal. The tension erupted between the men when Jessner told the actor to "shut up." Wisten, who had agreed to play Morell in *Candida*, refused to participate because of Jessner's "pub talk."[58] Singer had to recast the lead role and resolve the rift between his colleagues. He placated Wisten by giving him more artistic responsibility, including the training of young actors. Wisten did not perform under Jessner again until October 1935. But Singer also asked the actor to direct a comedy by Molnár that was scheduled for the summer.[59]

In April 1935 Hinkel authorized the Kulturbund to substitute a stage adaptation of Georg Hermann's *Jettchen Gebert* for the comedy by Kästner (alias Neuner) that had been vetoed.[60] Despite its focus on a German Jewish family in Berlin during the 1840s, Hinkel agreed to the production as long as it avoided any discussion that too clearly accepted assimilation that might therefore offend Germans. *Jettchen Gebert* lent itself well to the 1935 Kulturbund stage, because many of the audience members could identify with the characters and the play's milieu. The audiences understood issues such as Jews converting to Christianity, Jewish family rituals, and liaisons between young Jewish women and Christian men. The play's plotline depicted a recognizable plight: Jettchen's love for the Gentile Dr. Kössling greatly dismayed her uncles. Despite the family's assimilated status, Jettchen's uncles pressure her to marry a distant cousin of lower-class *Ostjude* status. But Jettchen and Dr. Kössling vow to maintain their love. At the end of the play, Jettchen throws flower petals out of the window on her wedding day. She does not appear for her wedding ceremony. The play's final scene takes place after the thwarted wedding, when the bride's absence suggests her possible suicide. An aunt of the groom-to-be delivers the play's last line: "I really only wanted the best," she tells Jettchen's uncle.[61] With its focus on a young woman, Kulturbund educators hoped that the play would appeal to all age groups.

It had become an ongoing priority to win over youth audiences at the Kulturbund. By June 1935 educators Kurt Baumann and Friedrich Brodnitz intensified their efforts to broaden the membership base by recruiting younger audiences. Baumann exposed the uneven demographics of the theatre membership just before the *Jettchen* premiere:

> The current season's repertoire program is aimed at a generation of people whose age is between 45 and 65. . . . This number constitutes the overwhelming majority of those already affiliated with the Kulturbund. It

is understandable, then, that young people between 15 years and 35 years of age can hardly derive vital stimulation from experiencing Kulturbund performances.[62]

Targeting the young and the old within the community, Jessner's own stage adaptation of Berlin native Hermann's *Jettchen* premiered in July 1935.

Jessner's production unfolded in five scenes against the backdrop of Condell's set design, which replicated the Biedermeier era. Ruth Reimer played the title role opposite Walter Hertner's Dr. Kössling. Jessner cast Hertner's romantic rival, Herbert Grünbaum, as Jettchen's East European cousin. The actors addressed their characters' awareness of the problems intrinsic to their German and Jewish identity. The family patriarch Jason Gebert, for example, referred to family heritage: "And besides, our family is *proud* [actor's underlining] that we are esteemed and respected here as Jews. If my father had baptized us as we were counseled to do, then perhaps our name would be 'von' Gebert and . . . we would be government officers or counsels."[63] Many in the Kulturbund audience could connect personally with such a statement. But a Jew in Germany in 1935 could not voice onstage the line's second part, which referred to Jews in government posts. Jessner had advised the actor cast as Jason to "break off" in mid-sentence. Jessner also kept intact a scene where the uncles addressed the dilemma of Jettchen marrying outside the Jewish faith. One uncle warned her to end her liaison with an outsider (and non-Jew): "No one will marry into this family."[64]

The *Jettchen* production offered Kulturbund audiences a portrait of a Jewish family in Berlin which reflected aspects of their own lives: Jettchen's assimilated background, her social status and relationships, and the well-heeled neighborhood of Charlottenburg, which was home to many Kulturbund members. Jessner's production script retained most of the text's language, except for changing the word "pastor" to "rabbi" and a deleted reference to "the evangelical church newspaper."[65] Given the play's subject matter, it may seem curious that Hinkel did not further censor the content. The production, however, emphasized the impossibility of Jettchen's out-of-faith marriage. What amounted to her moral transgression resulted in punishment, because the final scene alluded to her possible suicide.

Jettchen's uncles pushed her to marry her East European cousin. The onstage debate among the Gebert men echoed a pertinent and familiar discussion within contemporary Berlin Jewry about resisting intermarriage and thereby the dissolution of Jewishness. This idea significantly underscored a common belief among assimilated Jews in preserving Jewishness through marriage. Recalling the past era as one in which the "Jewish Question" belonged to Jewish circles, the reviewer Hermann Sinsheimer wrote that discussions of "the Jewish Question" were omnipresent in 1935, especially "outside of Jewish circles."[66] A reviewer for the *Frauenbund* paper referred to the significant photo album–like scenes (as staged) that revealed the dramatic details of the familiar Gebert family life. The audience identified with the German-Jewish milieu onstage; but the reviewer warned against drawing trivial conclusions about "our contemporary problems." She faulted Jessner for directing actors in too "Jewish" a speech intonation that led to caricature.[67] The *Jettchen* production may have lent itself to melodrama. Hertner as Dr. Kössling apparently overplayed the unhappy lover. "Hertner loves the Tremolo," wrote Sinsheimer.[68] He also felt that the acting and the inherently dramatic plot suffered at the expense of the scenic achievements.

Singer promoted Jewish programming among all demographic groups in the community.[69] By attracting new members with repertoire choices which reflected community concerns and appealed to citizens' sense of communal belonging, Singer hoped to widen attendance at the Berlin Kulturbund theatre. *Jettchen Gebert* appealed to the assimilated Jews in the audience as well as to religiously conservative Jews. Yet even while Singer and his staff debated how best to function artistically within their new "emergency community," they pledged to maintain a connection to the world outside of that community. In August Singer produced Ferenc Molnár's popular comedy *The Play's the Thing* (known as *The Play in the Castle* [*Spiel im Schloß*]) in keeping with his plan to offer light entertainment during the summer months. But as late summer 1935 turned to autumn in Berlin, the theatre staged a Jewish play that focused on more topical concerns: an immigrant Hasid in New York. Ossip Dymov's *Bronx Express: A Dream Play in 3 Acts* (*Bronx Express: Ein Traumspiel*) highlighted the dangers of assimilation in the diasporic United States. Jessner's production premiered on 1 September 1935 at roughly the same time that lawyers for Hitler's regime were drafting the Nuremberg racial laws. The Gestapo soon banned the play after ten performances.[70] But Hinkel gave no reason for the ban.

Dymov's play presented an orthodox protagonist, Khatskl Hungershtolts (Hungerproud), played by Sigmund Nunberg, caught between two disparate worlds with different values. The play begins with Hungerproud aboard the Bronx Express subway surrounded by advertising slogans. After Hungerproud falls asleep over his Yiddish-language newspaper, the popular advertising figures Mr. Wrigley, Aunt Jemima, Baby Nestlé, and a cigarette girl inhabit his dream world. The play focuses on this dream world, in which Hungerproud works on Wall Street and earns a lot of money. He figures out a "get rich" plan to persuade Wall Street's millionaires that they can increase their profits by working on the holiest day of the Jewish year. As he puts it, the best way to "Americanize Jews" would be to "pay the Jews double, triple, ten times. They'll work Yom Kippur too."[71] Yet Hungerproud's "high life" haunts his dream, for he has betrayed his family, his values, and his Judaism. The play shows a man's struggle to maintain piety in a new world rife with consumer enticements like cigarette girls, chewing gum, and work on High Holidays. Condell's stage represented the character's split focus and dilemma in an expressionist dreamscape with tilted New York skyscrapers and an austere Bronx bedroom.

The Kulturbund production of *Bronx Express* provided a counterpoint to the production of *Jettchen*. Both plays reflected timely concerns for Berlin's Jewish community, whose members struggled with the question of identity and belonging. In 1935 the Berlin Kulturbund theatre staff catered to community demands for a repertoire that presented audiences with recognizable scenarios. Singer had produced two plays in close succession which tackled the prickly topic of assimilation among Jews at home and abroad. *Jettchen Gebert* may have appealed more to Centralverein Jews, while the Dymov script and production could attract Zionist-oriented audience members. These two play productions from the so-called Jewish category resonated with moral messages for audiences: Jews, whether German citizens or East European immigrants, were obliged to adhere to family tradition and avoid secular (or non-Jewish) temptation. The productions adopted a didactic vantage point that may have mitigated Hinkel's growing preoccupation that the Kulturbund Jews would produce plays whose content too closely assimilated German culture.

In a letter to Singer dated 29 June 1935, Hinkel reiterated the Nazi Party's program to prevent all Jewish influences from infiltrating German "pure culture." No aspects of German culture should pervade the repertoire of the new Jewish stage. To this end, Hinkel periodically warned Singer that even the mention of German and Jewish identity or culture in a sentence would be viewed as an overture to assimilation, a word that had become a pejorative in Nazi Germany. Any reference or image in any Kulturbund-related text could be perceived as an attempt to merge German culture with non-Aryan culture. Hinkel made it quite clear that overstepping the established boundaries would immediately result in curtailing the organization's activities.[72] Nonetheless, as much as Hinkel tried to prevent the Kulturbund from producing material written by non-Jewish German authors or assimilationist in content, it was inherently problematic, as is evident in Hinkel's apparent carelessness in permitting the Kulturbund to perform Goethe's one-act play. It remains intriguing that in the summer before the Nazis passed the 1935 Nuremberg racial laws Hinkel allowed Singer to produce *Jettchen Gebert*, a play that featured Jewish characters and addressed themes of assimilation and intermarriage between Jews and Gentiles. Despite the careful steps that the Nazis imposed on the Kulturbund to keep Jewish culture distinct from German culture, the process was fraught with ambiguity. While accommodating his repertoire choices to Hinkel's demands, Singer may have figured out contradictions in Nazi cultural policy, allowing him to produce plays which did not neatly fit in either a Jewish or a German category; some of these plays, like *Jettchen* and, thematically, like *Bronx Express*, actually merged those artificial categories.

Singer cautiously cultivated what remained his most important collaborative association: his relationship with Hinkel. Singer knew that to ensure the livelihood of the Kulturbund and its theatre he had to work with Hinkel. The director thus engaged in a partnership that resembled a careful two-step dance. For Hinkel, self-interest played a role in his sponsorship of Singer's theatre. Hinkel's cooperation with Singer afforded him some prestige within Nazi Party circles. His alliance with Singer served a public relations purpose in that he could claim that he had created a separate cultural venue for the Jewish artists and kept German culture pure of Jewish influence. On a micro-level the two men had to hammer out the day-to-day details of the theatre, while abiding by the changing government laws regarding Jews in Germany.

Singer and Hinkel regularly corresponded as often as every two days and sometimes more than once a day, with Singer sending permission requests and Hinkel either formally approving or denying them. The men also met face to face, in meetings requested by Singer or called by Hinkel, sometimes just a day ahead.[73] They even socialized informally for drinks and discussion.[74] Hinkel admired Singer as a cultured man and musicologist who had established his reputation in Berlin well before 1933. Spurred partly by his sense of himself as a cultured man, Hinkel maintained a proprietary stake in the Kulturbund's progress. His presence at the Kulturbund always contained a supervisory aspect. Even so, he apparently enjoyed the evenings out at the theatre, where he occupied his own box across from the proscenium stage. His wife regularly attended theatre events with him, as did his theatre-obsessed chauffeur and as many as six or seven guests.[75] For his part, Singer promoted his relationship with Hinkel. He was fully aware that he had to give Hinkel an incentive to encourage the theatre's longevity. Singer thus made sure that Hinkel had a chance to see the productions, even sending him theatre tickets to premieres like Verdi's *Nabucco*, for which he himself conducted the music.[76]

The men's alliance incorporated more than the reciprocity of securing theatre tickets or a box at the theatre. Singer depended on Hinkel to find a permanent theatre space for the Kulturbund. When Singer could not renew the lease for the Berliner Theater in the winter of 1935, he immediately approached Hinkel about leasing another theatre. The search to replace the "dilapidated" Berliner Theater lasted throughout the summer. Singer took the initiative and identified several theatres as potential homes. Hinkel initially had no objection to the Theater des Westens in Charlottenburg, yet he unconditionally ruled out the Lessing Theater, which he apparently identified as a "German" house.[77] Curiously, the Lessing Theater had long been associated with popular Jewish actor managers such as Oskar Blumenthal and Carl Meinhardt. By May 1935 Singer was unable to lease a theatre. He suggested the vacant theatre at Nollendorfplatz (manager Rudolf Bernauer had emigrated to England), but the task of securing a new home for the all-Jewish troupe remained complicated. The Reich Chamber of Culture and its *Reichsdramaturg* preferred to house German acting troupes in empty theatres, not Jewish artists. Nor did Schlösser want to displace German actors with Jewish ones or permit Jews to use German theatre spaces.

In July 1935 Singer encountered resistance when he tried to lease the vacant Wallner-Theater as a last resort. He entreated Hinkel for assistance, conveying the urgency of the matter: "If this project also fails, I see no way to preserve the Jewish Kulturbund Theatre in Berlin."[78] Hinkel rejected the Wallner-Theater. This rejection is puzzling because Viennese and German Jews such as Franz Wallner, Otto Brahm, and Victor Barnowsky had managed the Wallner-Theater, which had featured Theodor Herzl's first dramas. Not until 5 August 1935 did Hinkel's intervention allow Singer to lease a theatre, previously known as the Herrnfeld Theater, for the Kulturbund's third season.[79] Hinkel could expedite the business transaction, because the theatre, known as the Theater in the Kommandantenstraße, was unquestionably affiliated with Jewish managers and artists.[80]

During the season of 1934–1935 Singer solidified his artistic inclination to develop a repertoire that reflected the many faces of his Jewish community. Even as the Nazis modified the scheme for what constituted German culture and what belonged to Jewish art, the theatre had featured foreign imports, some of which had no overt Jewish content at all. Yet the management team ensured that the audience could attend performances of plays by Jews like the biblically themed German-language *Jeremiah* and *Jacob's Dream*. These productions illustrate the challenges posed by Schlösser and Hinkel's censorship of Jewish stage material and how Singer and his artistic team subsequently went about staging that material. The productions of *Jettchen Gebert* and *Bronx Express* show how Singer, Levie, and their artistic team effectively addressed Hinkel's demand to counter any overt mixing of German and Jewish culture onstage. The two productions in 1935 sharpened the plays' inherent didacticism about acculturation, a problem that Germans of Jewish descent increasingly faced whether they stayed in Nazi Germany or sought a new life outside of Germany.

As the Nazi government developed the Nuremberg Laws, Goebbels decreed mandatory membership in the Reich Association of Jewish Cultural Leagues for Jews in Germany who engaged in cultural affairs. Thus the Ministry of Propaganda could better monitor Jews in the Reich and consolidate their cultural output. By mid-September 1935 six hundred thousand members belonged to the centralized Kulturbund network, now extending to regions well beyond Berlin.[81] Singer kept public relations with Hinkel cordial enough to cater to his demands and provide Kulturbund audiences with as varied a repertoire as possible. In a surprising start to the new season, Singer planned to open the next season with a play by a non-Jewish German classic writer: Friedrich Hebbel's biblical dramatization of *Judith*. The production coincided with the new Jewish year, despite worsening conditions for Jews in Germany and the cultural biases against their creativity.

PART TWO
DUAL FOUNDATIONS OF A COMMUNITY REPERTOIRE
1935–1938

4 SOLIDARITY

A NAME CHANGE FOR A NEW THEATRE

1935–1936

On 8 August 1935 Hitler halted anti-Jewish demonstrations and assaults on individual German Jews in Berlin. The increased level of anti-Semitic violence during the summer was hurting the public image of the Nazi Party. To appease those party members who encouraged a policy of public harassment of Jews, Hitler and his legal advisors were already drafting stringent laws on how Jews in Germany could be treated. The Reich chancellor planned to introduce the laws at the Nazi Party rally in Nuremberg the following month. In advance of the laws, Hitler's ministers, their clerks, and local police forces across Germany began to issue anti-Semitic measures. These actions affected the Kulturbund during that rainy August, when Berlin's police chief warned Singer that he faced "coercive reprisals" if he failed to change the inclusive title for the collective organizations of the Kulturbund. "Despite my objection to the designation 'Cultural League of *German* Jews,'" the police chief cautioned, the association had yet to change its name. Singer had four weeks to eliminate the German designation from his association's title.[1]

Singer knew that Hinkel and Nazi authorities in Prussia had discussed the legality of the Kulturbund name a year earlier. The Prussian court had concluded in 1934 that Jews could only be Jews, not German, French, or Polish Jews—a ruling which temporarily eased the Nazi fear of an emergent Jewish national minority in Germany.[2] Although the court case pushed German Jewish artists to amend their status, Singer had not formally changed the association's name. Kulturbund members accepted the organization's label as legitimate, Singer told Hinkel when he appealed for assistance in spring 1935. Singer did not state the obvious reason for protesting the name change: simply put, German Jews identified themselves with the doubled noun of their organization's designation. But Hinkel refused to intercede on Singer's behalf in the legal process. He believed that Jewish artists embodied their own "cultural league" within Germany.[3] The emphasis on the organization's Jewishness reinforced the Nazis' resolve to separate Jews in Germany from German culture. After the Nuremberg Laws passed in September 1935, the government enforced the league's official name change to the "Jewish Kulturbund in Germany."

The Nuremberg Laws included two vital decrees based on "race" and culture. First, the Reich Citizen Law instituted procedures which divided the citizenry into nationals and foreign citizens. Non-Aryans like Jews became secondary citizens with fewer civic rights than Aryan or "pure" Germans. Second, the Law for the Protection of German Blood and Honor forbade intermarriage and extramarital sexual relationships between Germans and Jews. These laws immediately affected Berlin's Jewish community members and their Kulturbund. Singer reluctantly acceded to the law, which determined the location of the new theatre he leased. In September 1935 Singer and his staff changed their theatre location along with their theatre name. Their office move took them farther away from Berlin's theatre center on Charlottenstraße to a theatre at 57 Kommandantenstraße that bordered the Jewish quarter (the Scheunenviertel). The 800-seat Herrnfeld Theater had been a venue of Jewish popular "jargon" theatre for decades.[4]

The start of the third playing season marked a caesura in the lives of the Kulturbund Jews. The impact of the official racial laws on Jewish life constricted their freedom outside of the theatre, adding extra solemnity to the occasion of the High Holidays. The new theatre location forced many to travel across the city to a space roughly one-third smaller than their old theatre. The Kulturbund takeover of the theatre house in the Mitte district was more than just a change of venue for the organization; it also further isolated the Jews physically.

On 2 October 1935 Singer inaugurated the Kulturbund's new theatre space with Friedrich Hebbel's biblical *Judith*.[5] Even though the author was a German non-Jew, Hinkel had originally authorized a Kulturbund production of Hebbel's play in 1934. Singer delayed the production for a year and a half due to technical difficulties. Schlösser and Hinkel categorized Hebbel as a Nordic writer, whose plays, while censored for too many Christian elements, were performed throughout the Third Reich. Only *Judith* remained off-limits.

5. Theatre on the Kommandantenstraße, 1935. Akademie der Künste, Berlin, FWA 74/86/1906, photograph by Arno Kikoler.

Although the play had been highly popular in repertory during the Weimar Republic, after 1933 Schlösser banned the play from German theatres because of its controversial Jewish heroine.

The inaugural *Judith* premiere and its subject matter provided a commentary on Jewish history with new import for the Kulturbund audience. The early Jewish Book of Judith was not an original part of the Old Testament; it was translated into Greek as part of the Septuagint and relegated to the "hidden" scriptures known as the Apocrypha.[6] Judith, like Esther, saves her fellow Jews from death and destruction; she charms, seduces, and decapitates Holofernes, the army general for King Nebuchadnezzar, to prevent an attack on her home city of Bethulien. Hebbel's dramatization of the story heightened the legend's sensationalism of enticement, betrayal, and murder. In his characterization of the beautiful Jew (the Hebrew meaning of Judith is "Jewish woman"), the playwright created a tragic heroine. The play opens as Holofernes demands from a high priest a sacrifice on the altar of a mighty God. Holofernes is a ruthless but pensive warrior. So accustomed is he to his unchallenged authority that he wants an enemy to oppose him.[7]

Holofernes carries out Nebuchadnezzar's commands, but he has contempt for the king and doubts his claim to be the sole "God." Thus begins Hebbel's play in earnest, when Holofernes hears of this "people of crazies," who keep to themselves and worship a God so great that no one dares to pronounce his name. So fearless are these Hebrews that they will not surrender to his army. He then journeys to Bethulien and boasts: "Too bad that I must destroy that which I admire."[8] The play shifts to Judith, a widowed virgin, who has transcended her physical nature to embrace God. In the third act she decides that she can seduce and destroy Holofernes to save her people. As she invokes her duty to God, preparing to use her beauty for a deadly purpose, the townspeople believe that they must surrender to Holofernes to protect themselves.[9]

The riveting onstage seduction and murder scene of the fifth and final act projects desire and hatred. Holofernes is gluttonous and awed by his power. Judith is strong, contemptuous, and sensual, as she seduces Holofernes and cuts off his head. Evoking the Euripides drama *The Bacchae*, Hebbel's play ends sensationally as Judith parades onstage with the head of Holofernes on a stake. With Judith's last words to her maidservant, she prays for mercy and a barren womb.[10]

Addressing the audience before the performance, Singer associated the Kulturbund and its mission with the sacredness of Yom Kippur. He promised audience members that their new theatre would become a "true temple of art."[11] Singer often referred to the league's mission in terms of his commitment to reach Jewish audiences with serious, high-quality theatrical productions. A reviewer for the opening production praised Singer for his pledge to shape a Jewish style of art which would resonate with "our Jewish present."[12] The Greek-inspired elements in Hebbel's play script lent themselves to a straightforward and economical production style. Given the new spatial and budgetary constraints, the production team for *Judith* opted for a minimalist stage design and technique. Condell created a stage environment with several acting areas, including an onstage wailing wall. His designs incorporated a streamlined look with the characters clad in robes, evoking biblical times. From a practical standpoint, Jessner's *Judith* required minimal stage technology.

Jessner had already offered audiences his stage versions of *Esther*, *Jeremiah*, and *Jacob's Dream*. For his production of *Judith*, he relied on the ensemble's considerable talent, casting Gerda Klein-Weissmann (Queen Vashti in *Esther*) as the fiery Judith. Fritz Wisten played the mute and blind prophet Daniel, who rejects the idea of submitting to the enemy. Holofernes was played by Hans Hinrich. Jessner had shown a talent for creating massed stage tableaux in *Jeremiah* and once more effectively orchestrated crowd scenes, this time on a smaller scale. The Kulturbund's new theatre interior was significantly smaller than the league's former theatre, which had seated 1,400. With a smaller theatre, Singer and Bab believed that they could create a more intimate theatre experience for the audience and instill in theatregoers that feeling of community which provides solace in the face of adversity.[13]

The production accounts in October 1935 suggest that the Kulturbund ensemble staged *Judith* without highlighting its parallels to contemporary politics. Significantly, reviewers agreed that the theatre's auditorium and stage allowed for a "modest, unpretentious" style that reflected the Kulturbund's purpose.[14] The reviewers focused on issues of stagecraft and character development in their critiques rather than on politics. They commended the success of the production, especially praising the designer's use of the stage.[15] Hugo Lachmanski wrote that Jessner used crowds well, despite the limited "spatial conditions." But the reviewer believed that Condell's "spartan" setting detracted from the plot's intensity.[16] The costumes distracted another critic, who may have expected more local color. Lutz Weltmann wrote off the main character's costume as too contemporary, in fact "impossible, reminiscent of a modern evening gown, complete with modern stockings underneath."[17] Despite her emotional appeal as an actress, Klein-Weissmann got mixed reviews for her portrayal of the passionate Judith. Weltmann deemed her performance "cold, with too much uniformity" when she delivered her lines.[18] According to Eloesser, however, the actress developed in stature and purpose, particularly in her final scenes with Hinrich (Holofernes), who performed with "extraordinary" oratory skill. When Weissmann as Judith raised the sword above the sleeping general, her "fiery resolve" intensified.[19]

Jessner evidently preserved the core of Hebbel's drama. Reviewers suggest that the Kulturbund ensemble may have mitigated the analogy of Jews under siege. Yet the suggestion that Judith was portrayed as too contemporary makes us wonder whether the production team tried to make a visual statement about the present times. After all, the Kulturbund audience witnessed the onstage murder of a usurping enemy by a woman dressed in almost contemporary fashion. Underlying Hebbel's story is the plot's kernel: Judith's vengeance on Holofernes for trying to take over her homeland.

The *Judith* production is an example of Singer's choice to establish the Kulturbund's new sanctuary with a deceptively simple play based on a biblical story. Yet the play also depicts how a Jewish woman from the "people of crazies" prevailed over military might. The audience could nurture their Jewish solidarity and revenge fantasies against despots, because Hebbel's play embodied unmistakable, even ironic, parallels to the times. In addition to the play's thematic emphasis on Jewish community, Judith engaged in a sexual relationship with a non-Jewish aggressor and enemy and became idealized for her actions. The fact that Hinkel permitted the Jewish league to produce the play by a revered German non-Jew points to the ongoing ambiguity within his own directives for the theatre, even after the Nuremberg Laws. According to the racial laws passed by the government, any second-class Jew who undertook any of Judith's actions glorified in the play would severely have transgressed the law. Under a theatrical lens, however, the Kulturbund's *Judith* revealed universal traits such as defiance, loyalty, and betrayal and a high-drama seduction scene under the guise of a biblical legend.

After *Judith* Singer ensured that audiences could continue to attend plays by non-Jewish writers whose subject matter had nothing to do with biblical times. As late autumn 1935 turned wintry and Hanukkah approached, Kulturbund artists offered their fellow community members lighthearted entertainment at sites outside of their new theatre. The Kulturbund established a cabaret in Charlottenburg's Café Leon, featuring performance revues approximately every six weeks. On a small stage Max Ehrlich served as master of ceremonies for skits. Piano music pleased the guests, and sometimes Ruth Anselm danced Spanish and Russian dances against colorful backdrops painted by her husband. To help those in need, these artists also participated in a winter benefit performance (Winterhilfe) on 7 December at the Bach-Saal on Lützowstraße, where they performed music by Jacques Offenbach.

The one-time benefit performance coincided with the Kulturbund production of Shaw's *You Never Can Tell* (1899) at the theatre on Kommandantenstraße. Eloesser wondered why the Kulturbund would perform this particular comedy, which Shaw termed one of his "plays pleasant." Could it be because of the imminent Festival of Lights and the need to brighten the dark days with a light-spirited comedy?[20] The landscape for Jews in parts of Europe looked ominous indeed: anti-Semitic riots were taking place in Poland and Romania, and the Gestapo had recently banned the use of pseudonyms for all artists at the Kulturbund.[21] Walter Hertner (who had played Jacob in *Jacob's Dream*) took back his birth name of Herz when he starred in Shaw's comedy as the romantic lead, the dentist Valentin. The Berlin-born Herz had trained at the acting studio of Berthold Viertel and Selka Steuermann-Viertel. Before he joined the Kulturbund at thirty-three, he had performed at Dresden's Albert-Theater and under Victor Barnowsky at the Lessing Theater.

Set at a British seaside resort, Shaw's play begins in Valentin's office, where the young Dolly Clandon (Ellen Moses) has sought treatment for a bad tooth. She is vacationing with her mother, the formidable Mrs. Clandon (played by Lilly Kann), her twin brother (Ernst Lenart), and her elder sister, Gloria (Ruth Mannheimer). Amid "playful" set designs, light banter and mistaken identities spur the plot to resolution, reuniting the Clandons with their missing father after eighteen years.

Hinkel had arranged with the Fischer Verlag for the German translation rights of Shaw's plays with the Kulturbund production of *Candida*.[22] At the same time, the Ministry of Propaganda saw Shaw as an Irish anti-imperialist with views in line with the Nazi cause. Goebbels and Schlösser approved productions of Shaw for German theatres, despite his socialist sympathies and his rebuke of anti-Semitism. Ironically, Shaw's German translator, Siegfried Trebitsch, was an Austrian Jew. Schlösser had banned his writing. The ministry, however, circumvented royalty agreements by coordinating direct payments only to Shaw and not to his translator, thus permitting performances in German theatres.[23] Translations of foreign, non-Jewish playwrights like Shaw presented new problems for Nazi censors who determined objectionable subject matter. For living authors like Shaw, censors considered the writers' attitude toward the Nazi state and whether they held German-friendly views.[24] Shaw numbered among his influences some writers like Arthur Schopenhauer, Friedrich Nietzsche, and Henrik Ibsen who were esteemed by the Nazis. The Kulturbund nonetheless staged Shaw's light comedy.

Fritz Wisten got the chance to direct Shaw's witty play. Wisten had already impressed audiences and critics by his versatile acting skills. Now he garnered praise for eliciting from his actors their best performances to date.[25] His production adhered to the censor's orders by ridding the play text of references to Western philosophy and pluralism in government and muting Shaw's social critique and any suggestion of assimilation. He deleted seemingly innocent references from the text which evoked stereotypical Jewish or Germanic traits, such as substituting "Krösus" (the god of money) for

"Jew" when Valentin likens his landlord to a rich Jew. Wisten also omitted a line about "clear-headed" ("hellköpfig") children, perhaps because the word ambiguously translates to light (blond) and mentally astute.[26]

Even while the Nazi academic response to Shavian philosophy was on the whole positive, Wisten's production demonstrated how censorship could deprive the stage of a forum for political discussion. Wisten treated Shaw's use of repartee with caution. He omitted all references to Charles Darwin, John Stuart Mill, Aldous Huxley, and Herbert Spencer on women's rights and other democratic ideas. Wisten also left out provocative exchanges about societal values. In act II, for example, Mrs. Clandon reunites unexpectedly with her friend McComas (played by Martin Brandt). McComas enumerates Clandon's public speeches on political equality. Wisten struck from the performance the long list of topics: a woman's right to equality, a university degree, a profession, and the vote, and a married woman's right to her own property. Wisten further muted the political tone of discourse by eliminating the following exchange on socialism entirely from his production:

> MCCOMAS: I call myself what I am: a Philosophic Radical, standing for liberty and the rights of the individual, as I learnt to do from my master Herbert Spencer. . . . I'm out of everything because I've refused to bow the knee to Socialism.
>
> MRS. CLANDON: (*shocked*). Socialism.
>
> MCCOMAS: Yes: Socialism. That's what Miss Gloria will be up to her ears in before the end of the month if you let her loose here.
>
> MRS. CLANDON: (*emphatically*). But I can prove to her that Socialism is a fallacy.
>
> MCCOMAS: (*touchingly*). It is by proving that, Mrs. Clandon, that I have lost all my young disciples. . . . We're old fashioned: the world thinks it has left us behind. There is only one place in all England where your opinions would still pass as advanced.
>
> MRS. CLANDON: (*scornfully unconvinced*). The Church, perhaps?
>
> MCCOMAS: No, the theatre.[27]

The audience never heard Shaw's criticism of late nineteenth-century British society and political ideology.

Hinkel consistently censured all philosophical debate on freedom and equality. Thus Wisten reworked Shaw's play to avoid any potential political misunderstandings; in the process, he diluted Shaw's social provocation by removing a key exchange between Mrs. Clandon and her daughter's suitor, Valentin, about military production. Valentin compares the buildup of heavy artillery to the "battle of the sexes," suggesting a clever social critique. "You build a ship proof against the best gun known: somebody makes a better gun and sinks your ship. You build a heavier ship, proof against that gun: somebody makes a heavier gun and sinks you again. . . . Well, the duel of sex is just like that."[28] But in the German military context of December 1935 any onstage references to ships, guns, and armor plates would bring to mind Hitler's recent flouting of international peace treaties like the Treaty of Versailles. European countries had signed the pact to keep the size of German military in check. Hitler, however, had defied the treaty terms, reinstituted conscription, and transformed what had been a relatively small Reichswehr into the full-fledged Wehrmacht—a three-pronged army, navy, and air force. Hinkel probably instructed Singer to sacrifice Shaw's turn of phrasing on the "duel of sex" to avoid onstage allusions to the German military expansion. As much as Singer and Wisten may have tried to retain Shaw's core ideas, the compromises they had to make to produce the comedy may well have undercut the playwright's and, by extension, Mrs. Clandon's "humanitarian" concerns.

In the spirit of Hanukkah 1935, Singer also emphasized the charitable when he sponsored two performances of a feel-good musical event in December. A group of the theatre's cabaret artists and musicians participated in Nicolai Elijaschoff's pastiche of Jewish-themed vignettes which embraced his East European heritage and interspersed skits on Palestinian life. With its focus on Jewish ritual and atmosphere, the festive benefit "A Photo Album of East Europe and Palestine" paved the way for the theatre's German-language production of Peretz Hirschbein's pastoral *Green Fields*.

Hirschbein, like Ossip Dymov, belonged to a second generation of émigré Yiddish-language playwrights, influenced by I. L. Peretz and Sholem Aleichem. The Kulturbund dramaturg Leo Hirsch translated the Yiddish-language play into High German for the Berlin premiere on 1 February 1936. *Green Fields* (*Grüne Felder*) presents two neighboring families and the details of their life on the land.[29] The daughter of one family marries the son of the other, after she overcomes her father's resistance to the match. A young man from "outside" the community arrives in the village. A teacher and scholar of the Talmud, he marries the daughter of the other family. His influence does not disturb the family idyll; instead the stranger enriches the characters' lives, bringing Jewish education into their home.

Jessner directed *Green Fields*, whose bucolic quality might ideally allow audiences to imagine community cohesion among Jews. The play invokes nostalgia for Jewish rustic life. Jessner cast Elijaschoff as the itinerant scholar and Herbert Grünbaum as the romantic lead, a modern man of the earth. Ellen Moses and Gina Friedmann played the young lovers, with Ruth Anselm as an understudy. For the stage settings, Condell relied on local color and lighting to show the characters' milieu. His designs incorporated the peasant garb of the shtetl and highlighted the Jewish home's *Gemütlichkeit* (coziness).[30]

The designer presented the folk play "in an uncomplicated manner," with a mix of "cheerfulness and poignancy," according to Lachmanski.[31] He noted that audiences showed enthusiasm for the Jewish folk onstage who had mezzuzahs on their door and referred to the Torah. As the tutor, Elijaschoff and the seasoned Lilly Kann and Jenny Schaffer-Bernstein played their roles as the peasant mothers to perfection. But the production reportedly lacked the richness of the Yiddish original, because the other characters did not reflect their environment. Instead of emphasizing their rustic characteristics, the actresses who played the daughters overplayed the role of urban coquettes. Perhaps Jessner's larger directorial challenge was dealing with Hirsch's difficulty in transferring the "colorful idiom of Yiddish to modern High German." Jessner instructed his actors to stress "specific Jewish speech patterns and the melody of overenunciated speech."[32] But this sounded affected, according to Lachmanski.

In February 1936 outside reality seeped into the theatrical sphere as Hinkel aborted the play's production run before Jessner could improve the performance work. On the same day that Lachmanski's production review appeared, Hinkel not only closed down the production but forbade all further programming in the German Reich on the direct orders of Goebbels.[33] Hinkel permitted the theatre staff to prepare for productions already in progress but froze future programming requests. *Green Fields* did not resume its run until two years later, when the Kulturbund Youth Stage troupe restaged the play under the direction of the actor Herbert Grünbaum.

Germany played host to the Fourth Winter Olympic Games in Garmisch-Partenkirchen in Bavaria beginning on 6 February 1936. During the weeks prior to the games the government instituted an ordinance to promote the veneer of peace and soon thereafter passed another law to crack down on German citizenry. First, the government orchestrated a pause in anti-Jewish harassment. The SS and local police removed anti-Jewish slogans from public places in Bavaria. The government then passed the Gestapo Law on 10 February 1936, giving the secret police operational freedom without the need for judicial oversight. The police could detain citizens, arrest them, and enforce the law at will. The Ministry of Propaganda projected a public image of a unified country that respected the international spirit of the games. But only days after the Olympics ended on 16 February, the Nazi government denied Jewish citizens the vote in Reichstag elections. Goebbels also called for the end of the religious press in Germany, although the Jewish newspapers continued to operate and were seemingly exempt from the official decree.

The Ministry of Propaganda's halt to Kulturbund activities may have been linked to Hitler's plan to remilitarize the Rhineland. In defiance of established European peace treaties, German military troops reoccupied the French border zone on 7 March 1936. When Hinkel lifted the performance ban in mid-March, Singer calculated that the lengthy "involuntary performance pause" had lasted for thirty-eight days. This stalled the theatre's previously scheduled production of *Antigone*.[34] Hinkel probably approved the Sophocles drama well before the February ban. Rehearsals for Jessner's production took place throughout the month. Singer announced to the actors that they would produce *Antigone* right away as planned; the play premiered on Sunday, 15 March 1936, the day Hinkel officially ended the moratorium. Two weeks later German voters supported abandoning the Treaty of Versailles with 98.6 percent of the vote. Singer's decision to resume production of *Antigone*—in double performances if need be—suggests his shrewdness in finding ways to work around Hinkel's dictates to promote the theatre's best interests. The *Antigone* production shows Singer's resolve to keep in repertory theatre of high aesthetic quality with social relevance for the times.[35] Hinkel and his censors at the Ministry of Propaganda may have been so preoccupied with affairs of the Reich that they did not pay close attention when approving the Sophocles play for the Kulturbund.

The play pits Antigone's individual freedom against her responsibility to her family and to the greater state, represented by her uncle, King Creon of Thebes. The play also examines the role of the state and its allegiance to the gods. Fifth-century Athenians generally supported their city-state and their leader loyally, much as a typical Nazi sympathizer in Berlin would during the 1930s. Given the German obsession with blood laws and a strong state, the Sophocles tragedy remained popular in German theatres during the Nazi regime. Greek drama was viewed as vital background for German theatre classics. Yet Hinkel authorized the play for the Kulturbund.

Jewish theatregoers in Berlin in 1936 could have made clear analogies to a tyrannical government, empathizing with Antigone's defiance of state law for a higher unwritten law and accepting a death sentence for her actions. The Kulturbund production of *Antigone* reveals that considerable improvisation and even arbitrariness existed within the censor's office about the playwrights and the texts permitted for the Jewish stage.

On the night of the *Antigone* premiere, a musical concert featuring Christoph Glück's *Iphigenia Overture* preceded the Kulturbund performance. Johannes Rosenmüller's Sonata in E Minor for Strings and Bach's Fourth Brandenburg Concerto followed.[36] Under Fritz Jessner's direction, audiences could consider social issues in a drama whose universality and seriousness of purpose even made it suitable to be performed on Hitler's birthday on 15 April that year.[37] For the production, Condell transformed part of the auditorium into a "sunken orchestra" with steps to the stage, approximating the ancient Greek theatre. Many of the actors entered and exited through the orchestra seating area to reach the stage.[38]

Jessner's cast included some of the ensemble's top actors. Wisten played Creon, and Gerda Klein-Weissmann, who had shown her dramatic capabilities as Hebbel's Judith, played Antigone. Walter Herz, known for his romantic leads, played Haemon. The director reduced the Theban chorus to ten male elders. As a Max Reinhardt protégé, Jessner not only experimented with transforming the physical space between actor and audience; he adopted the declamatory technique of the *Sprechchor* for the chorus to express the community's political will, relying on a modality between song and speech to intone the verse.[39] The chorus members chanted their lines alone and in unison, accompanied by lighting effects and underlying sounds, including "ancient-sounding" music composed for the production.[40] Although the Nazi *Thingspiel* spectacles of 1933 used this rhetorical form to promote a national folk community, by 1936 the Nazis had banned the *Sprechchor* from German stages because of its liturgical and Marxist origins.[41] Hinkel probably did not know that the Jewish actors would use the performance technique once associated with national propagandist art. Or he did not care about its use as long as Aryan actors kept it off German stages.

For his script Jessner used a translation by a nineteenth-century scholar, Georg Thudichum, which Lachmanski considered a poor translation choice; according to him, even Jessner could not "polish up" the script or rid it of its dustiness to convey the play's ideas.[42] But Jessner revised the antiquated language to make the verse flow smoothly and condensed the script, changing and deleting passages which might have been considered seditious if performed.[43] Surprisingly, however, the production retained words which had become loaded terms in Nazi parlance, like "Führer," "Vaterland," and "Vaterstadt." In Creon's first exchange with the chorus, for instance, the director kept intact the king's self-reference as "Führer" when he voiced his "awesome task of setting the city's course" to maintain security, deeming a leader who "refuses to adopt the soundest policies" worthless. Jessner also retained the binary of friend ("Freund") and foe ("Feind"):

> Whoever places a friend
> above the good of his own country [*Vaterland*] is nothing . . .
> nor could I ever make that man a friend of mine
> who menaces our country. Remember this,
> our country [*Vaterstadt*] is our safety.[44]

Hinkel and his censors would interpret any voiced threat to the city-state and leader as disloyal, so Jessner consistently chose to avoid references which insinuated defiance of the state. Early in the play Creon lashes out at the chorus and sentry, who inform him of an attempt to bury Polyneices. In production Jessner cut Creon's response: "Exactly when did you last see the gods celebrating traitors?"[45] While the director tweaked the Kulturbund production to direct Creon's suspicions toward disgruntled dark forces within his regime, Jessner sidestepped language that suggested overt conspiracy. The Kulturbund's Creon thus skipped references to citizens throwing off the "yoke" of submission to their king, as indicated:

> No, from the first there were certain citizens
> who could hardly stand the spirit of my regime,
> grumbling against me [in the dark, heads together,
> tossing wildly, never keeping their necks beneath
> the yoke, loyally submitting to their king].
> These are the instigators, I'm convinced—
> they've perverted my own guard, bribed them
> to do their work.[46]

Nor did Wisten as Creon address the corrupting power of bribery or refer to defying the law.[47]

Jessner streamlined his stage production to spotlight Creon more than

Antigone, pare down chorus commentary, and transpose the king's moment of recognition to the end of the play. In the original Sophocles play, Creon's self-discovery occurs after viewing his dead son. In production Jessner moved Creon's speech on the agony of life and justice later in the action to the moment when he sees his dead wife. The two suicides compound Creon's grief: he blames himself for his son's death then hears of Eurydice's death.[48] Jessner presented the audience with an increasingly anguished king for whom retribution had been swift:

> CREON: Oh I've learned
> through blood and tears! Then, it was then,
> when the god came down and struck me—
> . . . Oh, the agony,
> the heartbreaking agony of our lives![49]

The director's delay of the king's self-discovery focuses the audience's emotional response on the arc of Creon's fall from grace instead of on his recognition.

Reviewers, however, critiqued the Kulturbund production in terms of general artistic principles and performance, although one critic brought up the ethics of Antigone's "unwritten right" to bury her brother within Jewish law.[50] Perhaps reviewers were so familiar with the play that they responded instinctively to the play's core conflict between moral judgment and moderation despite Jessner's numerous text revisions and transpositions. Antigone acts on her own free will, although a family curse may predetermine her actions. Caught between their fated blood bond and their contradictory wills, Creon condemns Antigone to death and faces retribution for violating divine law.

Jessner's production illustrates his caution in staging subject matter which had reverberating moral and political implications for the times. For example, he carefully preserved but truncated vital exchanges between Creon and Haemon, which highlight the dangers of public criticism of a sovereign. In a pivotal scene, Creon and his son argue about the role of ruler to the state and father to son; their quarrel leads to Haemon's death with his entombed bride. Jessner softened Haemon's original criticism of his father considerably and eliminated all of Creon's references to breeding sons to side with him against all state enemies:

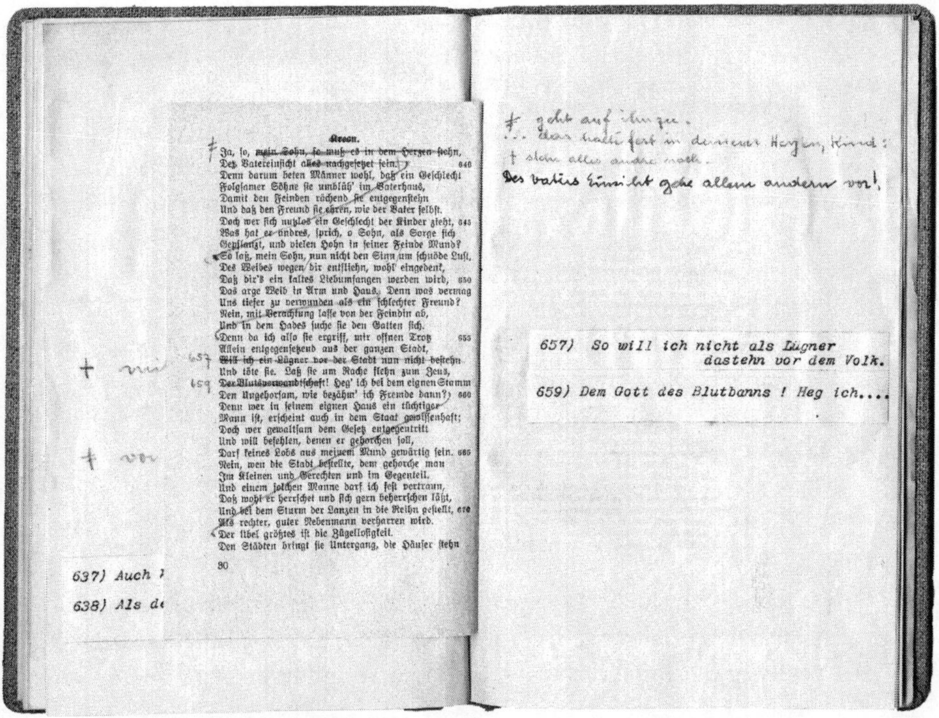

6. Sophocles, *Antigone*, Wisten rolebook for Creon (blood jurisdiction passage), spring 1936. Akademie der Künste, Berlin, FWA 8°-27.264.30, photograph by Akademie der Künste.

> CREON: That's what a man prays for: to produce good sons—
> households full of them, dutiful and attentive,
> so they can pay his enemy back with interest
> and match the respect their father shows his friend.[51]

The censors may have feared that empathy for the would-be breeder-king onstage could encourage Jewish theatregoers to breed their own blood-related resistance to a perceived enemy. In an apparent attempt to prevent just such a miscommunication, Jessner made a particularly interesting word change within Creon's scornful speech about killing Antigone.

The original script has Antigone beg mercy from Zeus, "who defends all bonds of kindred blood." But Jessner replaced the term signifying a hereditary blood relationship, "Blutverwandschaft," with the political and legal term for blood jurisdiction, "Blutbann," when referring to the power of Zeus. The substitution politicized Creon's words as well as Zeus; but it would also have appeased Hinkel by ridding the speech of a biological reference to blood lineage.[52] This verse usually precedes Creon's speech—entirely absent from the Kulturbund performance—stating that a man who controls his household and rules his city-state well must be obeyed, no matter what:

> Staunch in the storm of spears he'll stand his ground,
> a loyal, unflinching comrade at your side.
> But whoever steps out of line, violates the laws
> or presumes to hand out orders to his superiors,
> he'll win no praise from me. But that man
> the city places in authority, his orders
> must be obeyed, large and small,
> right and wrong.[53]

Jessner heightened the onstage effect of a king's sovereignty for his audiences. He bolstered this effect by softening Haemon's criticism of his father, also omitting the Sophocles metaphor of a too tightly steered ship and its destruction:

> HAEMON: Bend or break. The same when a man is sailing:
> haul your sheets too taut, never give an inch,
> you'll capsize, go the rest of the voyage
> keel up and the rowing-benches under.[54]

Nor did Jessner draw out Haemon's plea to his father to yield to change. Jessner's script revisions suggest the potential repercussions of such provocative verse in spring 1936:

> CREON: Am I to rule this land for others—or myself?
> HAEMON: It's no city at all, owned by one man alone.
> CREON: What? The city is the king's—that's the law!
> HAEMON: What a splendid king you'd make of a desert island—
> you and you alone.[55]

It would have been too inflammatory, indeed dangerous, to permit on any stage in Nazi Germany the image of a strong leader ruling a desert island.

Haemon's accusations of his father's injustice could be perceived as public censure of a leader. Initially, it appeared that Jessner omitted Haemon's scornful reference to a state ruled by one man alone, but evidence shows that the line was reinstated in altered form: "It's no longer a city at all, owned by one man alone." Haemon's reference to Creon as a "splendid king" of a desert island, however, remained absent from the performance. Jessner also ensured that his production muted Haemon's claims that Creon had "offended justice" and "trampled the honors of the gods," thereby committing crimes against humanity.[56] Without Haemon's reasoned critique of his father's rule, the Kulturbund's Creon appeared resolute and unbending onstage. But did the production effectively portray the vision of Sophocles in artistic terms?

As Creon, Wisten garnered almost unanimous praise for his oratory.[57] Lachmanski wrote that Wisten enacted the tragic figure with depth and purpose.[58] Eloesser even suggested that the production ought to be called *Creon* instead of *Antigone* because of the actor's strong performance; he criticized Wisten for overhumanizing Creon, resulting in a less than mythic portrayal.[59] Hermann Sinsheimer saw in Wisten's performance an "artistic restlessness" which bordered on the artificial and detracted from his delivery of the verse.[60] Kurt Pinthus faulted the actor for psychologizing his role more than necessary, which resulted in "nervous effects" such as too much fiddling with his red cloak. Such stage business, Pinthus felt, led Wisten to play tragic scenes instead of enacting a "tragic vision."[61] Reviewers more or less agreed that the entrances from the audience reduced the distancing effect that the overall style of Sophocles demanded. The actor playing Tiresias (Martin Chassel) evidently stopped directly in front of the first row of audience members. This spatial intimacy undercut the actor's portrayal of the blind seer; one reviewer considered him not mythic enough in stature, dress, and voice or in articulating his vision.[62]

Jessner generally demanded a stylized mode of acting, and speech delivery was especially difficult for the younger actors to execute. Arthur Eloesser questioned the director's objectives, suggesting that action would follow the words if the language of Sophocles was graphically powerful. He felt that the chorus sounded muffled, while the other actors' modern, "distinct" vocal quality made it difficult to understand their words.[63] Pinthus faulted the Messenger (Martin Brandt) for appearing "too unhappy," motivated more by emotion than by the words, and said that his "excited" mode of speech undermined the message about the dead lovers.[64] Sinsheimer concluded that all of the actors relied too much on a nuanced modern vocalization in their performances, except perhaps for Wisten and Jenny Schaffer-Bernstein as Eurydice.[65] By all accounts, Klein-Weissmann's performance was considered more sentimental than decisive. Eloesser sensed that hatred motivated her performance more than love, making her ready to decapitate a second tyrant (after Holofernes).[66] Her performance and Wisten's performance as Creon may have been squeezed between the effects of stylized oratory and externalized psychological realism.

Wisten's blocking cues indeed suggest a tendency to enact his role by relying on affective attitudes and simple movements that indicated emotion. He "angrily turns away" (line 699) when Haemon praises Antigone's defiant and heroic act and whispers, moans, hides his face, and "sinks down over the prompter's box" when Tiresias refers to the arrows of fate which will target the king's heart. "You'll never escape / their burning, searing force," the prophet tells Creon.[67] Kulturbund audiences reportedly were not put off by such emotive acting; they responded favorably to the *Antigone* production. They appeared to be uplifted and "shattered" at the same time.[68] Their response in effect mirrored the onstage response of the chorus, which functions as an ideal audience outside of the action but emotionally engaged in it.

The question remains why Hinkel would permit the Kulturbund to present the play in the first place. Was it a careless oversight on the part of the censors? Or did they simply call for text revisions based on their ideology? According to their guidelines for drama, the Nazis would have encouraged the depiction of a strong leader on the German stage. The Nazi censor would first rid a play text of passages that criticized the government or its leader. Haemon's criticism of his father in *Antigone* weakens the king's stature. For the same censors who scrutinized texts for a Jewish theatre, a second phase in the censorship process emerged: Jews were viewed as a separate race. Any references which appeared offensive to government leaders or partial to democratic ideals had to be eliminated to avoid provoking recognition or protest among theatregoers.[69] Hinkel likely knew that the closed nature of the Kulturbund performance allowed the play's provocative themes of individual moral choice and justice to be kept in check.

After the resumption of cultural programs in spring 1936, Hinkel's control widened as theatre employees and audience members adapted to new restrictions. The ban on stage names undercut the actors' artistic freedom. Ordinances required audience members attending events to show a photo identification Kulturbund membership card or an identification card issued by the Reich Association of Jews (Reichsverband der Juden), the so-called R-Karte.[70] As summer set in, the debate about programming persisted at the Kulturbund; the core dilemma, regardless of how it was framed, remained virtually unchanged and unresolved in its third year. As Singer asked in June 1936, "Are we a Jewish league for culture or a league for Jewish culture?"[71] His public query reflected the league's problematic status and its recent name change to the Jewish Kulturbund. Forced to be an artistic collective, the Kulturbund defined its identity by its exclusion from the German cultural mainstream. Nonetheless, the *Jüdische Allgemeine Zeitung* and the *Familienblatt* leveled criticism against what they saw as Singer's flawed adherence to isolating a "cultural historical" problem instead of a "theatre" or dramaturgical issue. Singer's repertoire, community newspaper editorialists wrote, continued—even imitated—the pre-1933 bourgeois German theatre repertoire, albeit with more restricted means and lower artistic standards.[72]

As they had advocated two years before, Jewish editorial writers still championed a theatre whose repertoire would reflect the Jewish situation of the 1930s instead of one based on play scripts without relevance to Jews.[73] Critics challenged Kulturbund administrators to create a "pro-Jewish" theatre art movement that was not a political Jewish stage but a theatre that was "lebendig-jüdisch" (actively lived Jewish).[74] Most significantly, these critics believed that the Kulturbund's success would depend on whether its central concept was "specific" and its profile as a Jewish theatre "unambiguous." The "Jewish-specific" emphasis must ensure that the repertoire responded to the times and to its audiences.[75] While Jessner's *Antigone* production set up a meaningful social and political parallel to the times, the play had not reassured community critics of its "Jewish-specific" status.

The Jewish theatre in Germany had to develop in what was now considered an "un-Jewish" language—German; this reinforced a central linguistic problem, intrinsically linked to dramaturgical weaknesses in the performance repertoire. Unlike the natural cultural communities developing in the Hebrew-language community in Palestine and Yiddish-speaking East Europe, the Kulturbund emerged only because its artists and audiences were identified as Jewish and therefore un-German. Their rootedness in the German language and culture had created a paradox which stymied the development of a new repertoire of play scripts. The short-lived production of *Green Fields* suggested that translated scripts from Yiddish failed onstage partly due to linguistic limitations. One way of surmounting the difficulty with language, it seems, was the promotion of a new style of acting, play-writing, and design which would ideally develop from a "studio" collective of artists, in the tradition of Reinhardt or the Habimah Theatre.[76] Could the theatre repertoire be grounded in the Jewish situation of the times, instead of incorporating the work of dramatists who had "assimilated to non-Jewish surroundings"?[77] At the heart of the question is an argument mounted—and legitimized—over time by Berlin's small but influential Zionist group. The *Rundschau* journalists had concluded that community youth would benefit most from such a theatre rooted in a singularity of spirit and initiative; this was the group that Kulturbund educators had recently pledged to engage with a program for young audiences.

These journalistic currents determined the general direction of the cultural debate about the Kulturbund theatre's existence in 1936. During the summer the demands on Singer from the Jewish community and from Hinkel did not compete as much as they converged, at least temporarily. With the approach of the Olympic Games, summer 1936 may be viewed as a pivotal point in the Nazi government's portrayal of the Kulturbund to the outside world. Hinkel himself set the national stage policy for what he deemed a necessary "cultural cleansing" in Germany: he published his views in "Jews Can Lead Their Own Life" in the *Berliner Illustrierte* (Berlin Illustrated). As long as the Jews did not concern themselves with "a direct or indirect influence of German cultural life in any of its forms," Hinkel declared, they would be tolerated at the Kulturbund.[78] A recurrent criticism of the Kulturbund reverberated among such Nazi propagandist descriptions of the theatre. Hinkel put it this way: "They [Jews] experienced the tough consequences of the so-called assimilation, saw how so few of their poets, composers, or playwrights limited themselves to Jewish problems or motives without making concessions to non-Jews."[79] The only option open to Jewish artists was to work honestly within the narrowing parameters that the Nazi Ministry of Propaganda offered them.

As Germany prepared to host the Summer Olympics in Berlin from 1 to 16 August, Hinkel announced plans for a three-day conference from 5 to 7 September 1936 on the Kulturbund's goals, pushing the agenda of Jewish culture to the forefront for Singer's attention. When Germany hosted the Winter Olympic Games in February, the Ministry of Propaganda suspended all cultural performances by Jews. Five months later, however, when German nationalist newspapers referred to the Kulturbund, they portrayed themselves as magnanimous hosts to foreigners (and "foreign elements"). For the opening of the Games on 1 August local police had removed anti-Semitic posters and banners. As during the Winter Games, citizens refrained from persecuting Jews. Jewish athletes even participated in the games as a show of the international tolerance that the Nazis stage-managed for two weeks.

The Ministry of Propaganda also temporarily loosened the restrictions on non-Jewish visitors to the Kulturbund as well as Jewish visitors to other theatres.[80] Hinkel regularly brought guests into his personal theatre loge on Kommandantenstraße. But now he permitted several international journalists and German editors to accompany him to a Kulturbund performance of Molnár's 1935 comedy *A Great Love* (*Große Liebe*; premiere on 3 August 1936). After a visit to the play, journalists for the *Berliner Daily News*, *Berliner Zeitung*, and *Morgenpost* coordinated their praise of the Jews' efforts to develop their culture outside of the German (or Aryan) mainstream "under Zionist leadership."[81] Using matter-of-fact language, one columnist lauded the Jews for their cultural cocoon. Jewish audiences, the journalist informed readers, applauded generously at performances.[82] As Hinkel claimed, Jews could feel good to be among fellow Jews in the Kulturbund, allowing their culture to develop "unencumbered by the outside culture."[83] In truth, an "outside" censor had tweaked the Molnár script for content before the performance.[84] Condell had designed costumes depicting ladies in the height of fashion, "modeled on Parisian style."[85]

Prior to the September conference for the associated Kulturbund organizations, Singer and his staff identified "problems of Jewish Art." Werner Levie outlined several vital areas for discussion which related to Hinkel's established repertoire guidelines. The overarching topic was the general conundrum of what constituted "Jewish" theatre. Levie hoped to specify how the Kulturbund might connect its work within the Reich to Jewish theatre outside of Germany. After assessing the current programming, the Kulturbund could consider adding new plays to the repertoire.[86] Finding appropriate texts for performance perhaps remained one of the most challenging tasks. The lack of rootedness in a language and culture separate from German had created an artistic void for the Jews, especially the actors. Kulturbund performers would need new training methods. These measures could lead to strategies for educating audiences.

The Nazi public relations machine churned out propaganda in late August 1936, which commended the German government for its attention to the plight of Jewish artists who could no longer practice their craft, as one journalist posited: "Were the German government as hate-filled and inhumane as it often has been suggested abroad, then the government would not have bothered with these citizens of Jewish origin. But because the cleansing of German cultural life ensued for purely objective reasons . . . Hinkel along with Dr. Goebbels strove to offer Jewish artists an existential possibility [for work] that relies on their own nationality [Volkstum]." Berlin's prominent Zionist Rabbi Joachim Prinz would suggest publicly at the upcoming 1936 cultural conference that as the Kulturbund adjusted to its responsibility to promote Jewish culture—what National Socialists called "jüdisch-volkisch" (Jewish folklike)—that culture must incorporate a "national-pedagogical meaning."[87]

5 DIDACTICISM

FALSE MESSIAHS

1936–1937

The main assembly hall of the Josef-Lehmann school off Berlin's Kurfürstendamm echoed with the rich tones of a Felix Mendelssohn chorale. It was Saturday evening, 5 September 1936. On a raised podium, the Kulturbund chorus performed under the direction of Berthold Sander for a broad spectrum of Jewish Berlin. Representatives from the Reich Association of Jewish Cultural Leagues and its affiliates gathered for Hinkel's conference on Jewish culture.[1] During the day the school on Joachimsthalerstraße served Jewish children who had been expelled from local German schools. On this late summer evening in September, however, Kurt Singer issued a pedagogical challenge for delegates from the Jewish press, women's groups, the Zionist Organization, and the Centralverein: over the next years, he told them, the Jewish cultural leagues would unite in their goal to create a "Jewish essence" in their theatre.[2]

Singer addressed the conference guests and praised their unity of purpose. As he saw it, ultimately "no disagreement existed between the Zionist and non-Zionist desires" for Kulturbund programs. Magnanimously singling out Hinkel, Singer observed that the Kulturbund had been subject to state control and protection since 1933; the *Reichskulturwalter*'s presence at the weekend conference reinforced the significance of the proceedings. Singer acknowledged Jewish cooperation across many organizations. He then invoked the bravery of Jews living in British Palestine. Their cause gained urgency with the summer revolt of Arabs against Jewish immigration to Palestine.[3]

Participants at the Berlin conference would work together in committees to focus on the problem of making the theatre repertoire Jewish. Singer reminded his listeners of the Kulturbund's performance history of plays with Jewish themes: some had been successful like *Jeremiah*, while others never made it to the stage. It was not economically tenable, he said, to create a theatre with a solely Jewish purpose. Yet he proposed a threefold plan for the theatre's immediate future that accounted for the problems that Jews faced in Germany. The theatre would preserve plays of an international culture; produce plays of Jewish origin no longer performed in Germany; and embrace the task of translating Jewish literature, originally works written in Hebrew and Yiddish.[4]

The audience responded favorably to Singer's remarks. But the evening's second speaker received especially strong applause for his presentation. Joachim Prinz, a thirty-four-year-old rabbi and dynamic orator, had a doctorate in philosophy in addition to his rabbinical training. Raised in an assimilated German family in Singer's birthplace of Oppeln, Prinz nonetheless aligned himself with Zionist organizations. When he arrived in Berlin in the late 1920s, he warned standing-room-only crowds about anti-Semitic influences in Germany and easily won young followers for his Zionist cause. At the 1936 conference Prinz addressed the role of the Kulturbund theatre in view of the threat to Jewish cultural life in Germany.

Prinz called on the Kulturbund to make actors the "pedagogical Masters of Judaism," using the stage as their pulpit. No Jewish language existed for Jews in Germany, so no works had a specific "Jewish" nature. Therefore Prinz told his audience that the actors must develop a positive connection to Jewish life outside of Germany, in eastern Europe and in Palestine, and convey that onstage. The choice of repertoire material, accordingly, could embody a "national-pedagogical" meaning and "lead Jews from the periphery of Jewish life to the center of that life."[5] Prinz concluded that the actors must develop their relationship to a text and to their "completeness" as Jews. Prinz's message appealed to Hinkel, whose own agenda for the Jewish theatre relied on a full separation of Jews from German culture.

Hinkel had made his opinions on the Kulturbund known before the conference, specifically his core idea that the theatre should emphasize Jewish-themed plays. Jewish newspapers incorporated his views into the conference discussion points proposed by theatre employees like Werner Levie, a dedicated Zionist. The day before the conference began, the *Jüdische Rundschau* published Levie's ideas on the repertoire's Jewish content. Levie focused on the actor as an intermediary between dramatic text and audience. He advised educating the artistic team on the foundations of Jewish philosophy and the study of significant eras within Jewish history. Actors did not receive special training for the 1934 production of Zweig's *Jeremiah*. But if the theatre was going to produce Yiddish- and Hebrew-language plays, Levie argued that stage directors needed linguistically accurate adaptations and must ensure the actors' familiarity with Jewish history, politics, and even religious concepts such as the Messiah.[6]

Levie's view of actor training reflected a plan already under discussion: a Hebrew-language studio for actors.[7] More immediately practical, however, would be the production of Hebrew and Yiddish plays in German. With both the Nazis and the Kulturbund focusing on Jewish culture, Hinkel had reexamined the script for I. L. Peretz's drama of a Hasidic family, *The Golden Chain* (*Die goldene Kette*), which he had banned in 1933, and authorized its production to coincide with the conference on Jewish culture.[8] Fritz Wisten had taken on a more active role in actor training at the theatre. He too participated in the conference's Theatre Commission and offered ideas for the Jewish actor based on his own role preparation as a miracle rabbi in the play by Peretz. In the Yiddish-language original, the play's "chain" signified an unbreakable chain of religious faith begun by Baal Shem Tov and maintained over successive generations of rabbis.

Participants broke into spontaneous applause when Wisten described a physical role preparation through which assimilated German Jewish actors could breathe life into the unfamiliar world of Hasidism. He encouraged an acting style that could motivate actors to perform with "plasticity" or three-dimensionally. In Wisten's view an emphasis on actors' movement as "loose in a dancelike way" was as important as speech training. He argued that an actor who enacted a role physically, as if by second nature, would adapt to an internal process of preparing a role psychologically and attitudinally. Wisten suggested that Jewish actors should use their artistry to "erect a new building." Before acquiring the proper internal and physical attributes in role preparation, however, the actors must master their real-life role as Jews. Wisten felt that it was his duty to train the emerging generation of actors to undergo an internal transformation, recovering a Jewish identity and attitude. Only after this personal preparation could actors acquire the internal and physical abilities to make a Jewish role into an "inner reality" immersed in an orthodox lifestyle and spirit. Actor training for *The Golden Chain* production must incorporate the concepts of messianism and the religious ecstasy described in the Kabbalah.[9] A prepared actor had to spiritualize the world of the play before rehearsals began. Then the actor could mediate Jewish cultural values to fellow Jews. The theatre commission approved Wisten's ideas on actor training as well as the idea of an archive staffed by specialists in Hebrew and Yiddish to familiarize actors with Jewish content.[10]

The Golden Chain production represented a new phase in the Kulturbund's preparation of Jewish-themed plays in which Wisten's ideas for the actor appear to have been realized in production. The production also signified a change in Hinkel's relationship with Singer and his Kulturbund staff in their mutual goal to produce Jewish art. Initially Hinkel objected to Peretz's play in autumn 1933 (see chapter 2). The "inner-Jewish" problems of the Hasidim had sufficiently alarmed him to ban the play for three years. In 1936, however, Hinkel permitted *The Golden Chain* to exemplify Jewish culture. As the distress of Jewish citizens in Germany heightened by autumn of 1936, Peretz's play displayed a world where rabbis reveled in an ecstatic spirit to heal their community.

The Kulturbund premiere took place during the transition to the new Jewish year, during the first week of September, instilling renewed purpose in the community. The Kulturbund hired one its lecturers and literary advisors, Lutz Weltmann, to direct the production. Weltmann's production marked a transition of personnel within the creative production team. Fritz Jessner had left the theatre and Germany in the summer of 1936 to lead the State Theatre in Bern, Switzerland. His departure left vacant the head position of the Acting and Directing Division. Wisten was the natural choice for the position, but Bab needed the actor to perform and to train other actors. With Weltmann and Wisten leading the creative team, however, the production of *Golden Chain* bridged the theatre's old style of producing Jewish-themed drama with new stage techniques to help artists scenically and atmospherically conceptualize material that dealt with mysticism. Jessner had orchestrated frozen stage pictures and poses in production and emphasized speech work over plasticity in movement. But for his production Weltmann substantially revised a German translation of the original script and rewrote sections of the play to emphasize symbolic elements in his staging. This allowed him to convey a physically charged quality in production. To simplify the plotline for the audience, his artistic team consulted the Yiddish-language original, which included realistic scenes that had been omitted by the German translator.[11]

Weltmann had worked as a published drama critic and a dramaturg with the Lessing Theater. For his production of Peretz's play, he substantially revised the first act, where the patriarch Rabbi Shlomo (Wisten) refuses to perform the ritual prayer of Havdalah that breaks the weekly Sabbath in order to prolong it eternally. To orient the audience to the unfamiliar material, Weltmann added a prologue and directed the technical crew to create an "otherworldly" mood with music and lighting when the curtain opened on the rabbi's house:

> Sabbath = an unending melody.
>
> [Then] light, falling on the table with burned-down candles, then on the window, then on the tree branch, *then light on Abraham* [a Hasid].
>
> Branch begins to move, before the entrance of Lemech, Rich Hasid, Young Hasid. Music breaks off.
>
> Enter one by one from stage-left.[12]

Weltmann's supplementary prologue presented villagers who spoke about "lost" business, because no transition had been made from the Sabbath to the work week. They attributed the community problems to a newcomer:

> RICH HASID: One says that a young doctor has come to town.
> LEMECH: May his name be wiped out!
> YOUNG HASID: They say he's a magician. He can make it rain and snow indoors![13]

The Hasids declared the outsider's presence to be "the devil . . . at work," responsible for bewitching their rabbi:

> LEMECH: Here he sits alone in the dark of night, and struggles against all evil.
> YOUNG HASID: In mortal danger.
> RICH HASID: They say he is sick, not quite right in the head.
> LEMECH: Who knows whether witchcraft is not behind all of this.[14]

Before the first act officially began, Weltmann had implicated the play's outsider (an assimilated non-Hasidic Jew) as the cause of the rabbi's erratic behavior.

The director also staged the first act to accentuate the ominous effect of the suspended Sabbath on village life. Technical effects included the projection of dark shadows looming outside the stage window and gaining mass as the folk gather onstage. Outside a snowstorm began, leading to Shlomo's

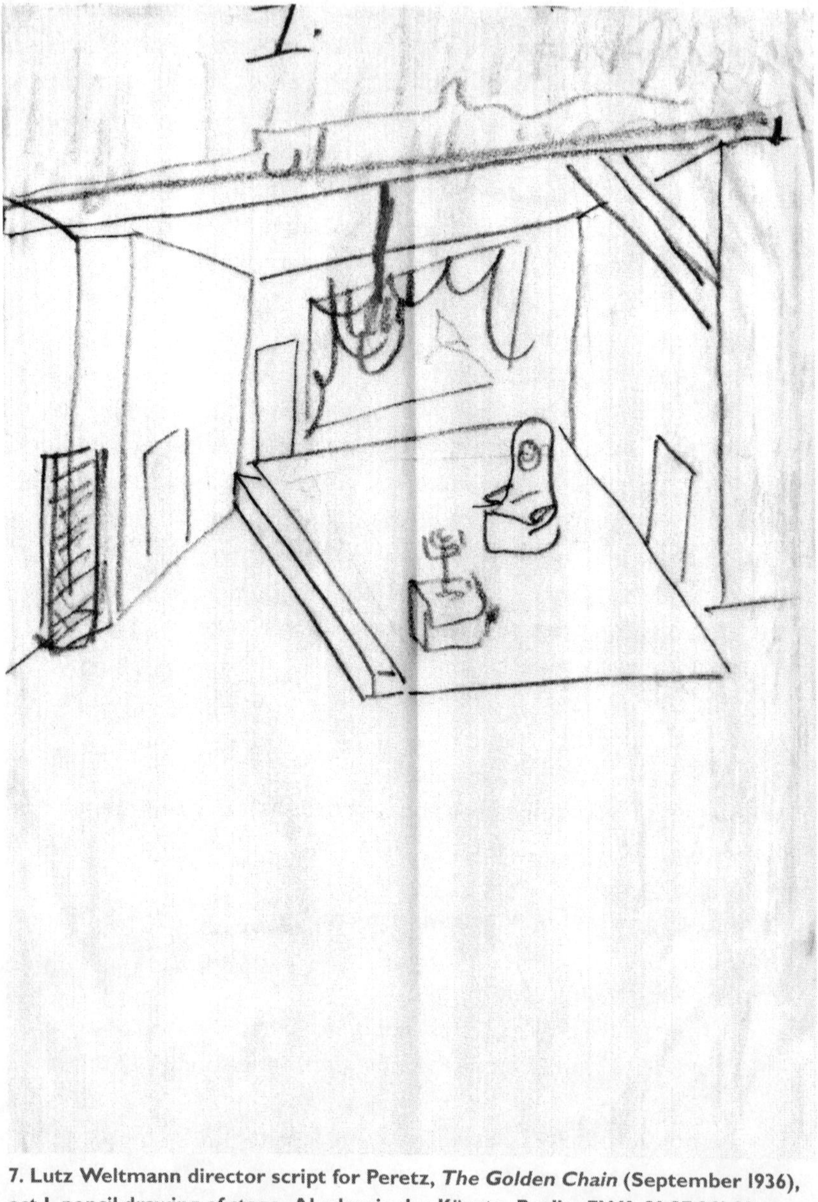

7. Lutz Weltmann director script for Peretz, *The Golden Chain* (September 1936), act I, pencil drawing of stage. Akademie der Künste, Berlin, FWA 8°-27.261.02, photograph by Akademie der Künste.

entrance. Weltmann arranged for "bright light" to accompany the rabbi's entrance, while "[m]usic chimes the chandelier motif," and the "shadow of people darken the light."[15] This was the moment when the audience first saw Wisten, pale and clothed in white, with a white beard and black *kippah* on his head. With "eyes . . . large and rapt—shining," the actor turned to face the audience and the crowd at the open door, announcing: "Sholom will not make the Havdalah!"[16]

The Hasidic prayer recited before the Havdalah ceremony typically invokes protection for Jews, but Wisten as the enraptured rabbi refused to recite the prayer, which separates the Sabbath from an ordinary day. Weltmann emphasized the play's conflict with an onstage storm, to externalize the rabbi's unnatural demand for an unending Sabbath.[17] The message that the audience received was Shlomo's call for Jews to trample the "rubble of the world" in their eternal Sabbath-mode. They would be "great, proud Jews, singing and dancing up to Him!" he proclaimed. Under Weltmann's direction, Sholomo's remarks led to a crescendolike moment where the staged indoor and outdoor scenes merged, unleashing wildness. Inside his home, the rabbi led a frenzied dance, while the audience saw a raging snowstorm outside the window.

Wisten followed the director's stage directions, re-creating an ecstatic feeling that "begins in the fingertips, and gradually affects the entire body. Abraham places himself protectively in front of the rabbi; the old men make a circle around him. Ecstasy gradually takes hold of them all. . . . The dance is snakelike around the rabbi. Miriam stops clapping to take Shlomo's hand." During the dance, the stage crew coordinated the audiovisuals of the melody of the chandelier with light projections from reflective colored prisms.[18]

The Baal Shem Tov (Rabbi Israel ben Eliezer) believed that religious song and joyous dance would lead followers to experience an elevation of their souls that heralded the coming of the Messiah. As the storm strengthened outside the stage window, Shlomo's dance and his chant from the Song of Songs provided a dramatic snapshot of this concept.[19] The production thus tweaked the biblical relationship between Creator and the Created. Shlomo's attempts to preserve the Sabbath transform him into a creator, challenging the concept of an Ultimate Creator. When a congregant ends the Sabbath and welcomes the week, Shlomo loses the ability to redeem the world's "soul" and collapses.

Shlomo's son, grandson, and great-grandson succeed him as holy rabbis, perpetuating the dynastic order of Hasidic life. In act II Herbert Grünbaum as Moshe becomes the next link to prepare for the Havdalah. Then comes Pinchus (Sigmund Nunberg), and finally Jonathan (played by Walter Herz). When Shlomo's great-granddaughter Leah (Gerda Klein-Weissmann) flees her father's home with the outsider Dr. Bergmann, her flight into the non-Hasidic world threatens family stability and tradition. Her return and her plea for help in the play's final act, however, restore the generational cycle. Moshe "puts on his tallis" (prayer shawl) and calls on his forefathers and the Baal Shem Tov for help.[20] As staged at the Kulturbund, the play's last act takes place in the rabbi's room, with a Beth-Hamidrash (pulpit) for sacred study.[21] The action depicted the triumph of an intact "chain" of Hasidism under Jonathan, who is seen as a holy rabbi. Weltman directed Herz as Jonathan to express doubt with the new last line, "I? Rabbi!" while audience members saw a "glowing Star of David" on the visible Torah ark before the final curtain.[22]

Reviewers commended the director for risking a production of the play. The subject matter could have estranged audience members and challenged actors unacquainted with the Hasidic milieu. A critic from the middle-of-the-road *Israelitisches Familienblatt* wrote that putting actors in the "exciting darkness of a mystical world" was an undertaking well worth praise.[23] Lachmanski pointed positively to the underlying romantic current in the production, commending the actors, especially Wisten, for exhibiting strong emotionalism through an effective show of religious fervor.[24] Eloesser also praised Wisten's energy in revealing the play's spirit through dance and song.[25] Wisten realized onstage the "dancelike" acting style that he had advocated for actors at the recent conference. Eloesser, who was familiar with the play, observed how the first act impressed spectators powerfully as "lyrical outbursts of single voices and choral echoes" swelled into "an ecstatic state." The critic felt that the first act could stand alone, because it encapsulated the "catastrophe."[26]

Singer had tried in vain three years earlier to convince Hinkel of the completeness of the first act, but Hinkel had reconsidered his aims for the Jewish theatre. He now permitted, perhaps even encouraged, non-Jewish German critics to review certain productions, including *The Golden Chain*. One critic suggested what might have caused Hinkel's initial ban of the play, particularly the first act. Shlomo's repeated defiance that "the World will be redeemed!" presumes the world's destruction before its deliverance. When men recite Havdalah, sinners whose souls were temporarily freed of their torment on the Sabbath begin their agony on earth again.[27] The German reviewer cautioned readers about the "strange play's Jewish nationalist dream for political dominance." He warned that the realization of the dream as "Judobolshevism" in Europe could easily endanger Germany.[28] This reaction illustrates the narrowing parameters for Singer and his creative production staff when choosing plays for the repertoire, even when those plays portrayed a Jewish milieu.

The repertoire increasingly reflected a didactic strategy by Kulturbund administrators like Levie and educators who familiarized audiences with writers from the Diaspora. At a time when "assimilation" had become a pejorative word for Jews, outside influences could be deemed dangerous to community cohesiveness. The shtetl milieu of the plays provided an exotic locale onstage, while conveying the message to live by one's own set of religious and cultural principles in one's own community. Singer, Bab, and Levie decided to produce more plays from Yiddish and Hebrew sources. Hinkel's acquiescence to this goal enabled the Kulturbund's dramaturgical staff to produce a translation from Hebrew of Nathan Bistritzky's play *Sabbatai Zevi* about the historical "false Messiah."[29]

Not quite two months after *The Golden Chain* production, the German-language premiere of *Sabbatai Zevi* on 3 November 1936 ran for twenty-one performances. The 1931 play centered on the seventeenth-century "false Messiah" and his role in the reparation of the Jewish and world communities. As director of the Department of Youth and Propaganda for the Jewish National Fund, Bistritzky actively promoted Zionist education in Jewish Palestine. His interest in history and political change led him to Sabbatai Zevi, regarded by some as a savior.

The Sabbatian messianic movement grew around the Turkish-born Sabbatai Zevi (1626–1676), whose idealized persona satisfied a communal desire for a redemptive liberation, long predicted by kabbalists. The historical Sabbatai Zevi cultivated his mission as the messianic leader. His chief supporter, the self-proclaimed prophet Nathan of Gaza, believed in the redemptive harmony of existence (*tikkun*), but only the Messiah could complete this process as an intermediary between worshippers and God.[30] Sabbatian messianism thus required a divine "messenger" with suprahuman powers—identified as Sabbatai Zevi—to transcend evil (impenetrable by individual human beings) and save the universe.[31] Although Bistritzky's play dealt with a figure from the Ottoman Empire, the idea of a Messiah was rooted in biblical history; "Mashiah" means "anointed one." Prophets like Jeremiah associated a transformation of life for Israelites with an extraordinary leader who would release them from servitude and restore justice.[32] After the Jews were expelled from Spain in the fifteenth century, some communities embraced kabbalist mysticism over rationalist philosophy. It was in this context that ideas for messianic redemption and reparation (*tikkun*) developed.[33]

Why would a theatre community with so many assimilated members choose to produce a play based on a seventeenth-century prophet of messianism? As an idea, messianism corresponds to a "deeply rooted yearning for redemption arising from a profound dissatisfaction with the real world when judged against religious teachings about perfection and the power of God." Messianic movements like the one around Sabbatai Zevi have been associated with a "crisis cult" when people feel that their culture no longer "works."[34] Bistritzky's play opens with a prologue, set in a synagogue in Smyrna in 1648, where a twenty-two-year-old mystic speaks the forbidden full name of God (YHWH). The young man then proclaims himself the "Messiah." Act I begins eighteen years later with Sabbatai Zevi claiming to be the Messiah. The ensuing acts follow the charismatic leader's life and his unmasking as a pretender and apostate. Perhaps Kulturbund audiences would find the popular cult around Sabbatai Zevi appealing and draw solace from the hope for better times and a transcendence of crisis.

Singer had not yet appointed a permanent head for acting and directing. Bab asked one of his lecturers and dramaturgical aides, Otto Bernstein (the husband of actress Jenny Schaffer), to direct the Kulturbund production. Realizing that audiences (and performers) might have difficulty understanding the play's obscure historical and philosophical background, Bab and Bernstein arranged educational events to enlighten the cast and audiences about the play's metaphysical and political context.[35] Twenty actors played multiple roles, except for the title character, played by Hans-Karl Rosenberg. Other main roles included Wisten as Reb Nechemya and Alfred Berliner as the sultan. Because the play's scripted action swept liberally across time and space, Condell incorporated projections and montage effects into his stage design. This enabled the artistic team to show the many scene changes from the Middle East to the ghettos of eastern Europe.[36]

Curiously, Hinkel approved a German-language adaptation of Bistritzky's play for the Kulturbund stage. The play's translator faced censorship even when he described the complex translation process of *Sabbatai Zevi*. So provocative was the subject matter of a real-life Messiah figure, it seems, that even the translator's report on his linguistic conversions got ensnared by Hinkel's government censor.[37] Meier Broser, the translator, aimed

8. Fritz Wisten as Reb Nechemya in Bistritzky's *Sabbatai Zevi*, November 1936. Akademie der Künste, Berlin, FWA 20.63.245, photograph by Anni Kühn.

at a proper balance of words and sentences in translation; as he provocatively stated, one must "look to the right at the Hebrew poet; looking to the left to the *German-Jewish person, for whom the scale measuring the degree of combined German and Jewish components still varies.*"[38] Just the mention of German and Jew in one sentence provoked the censor. This compounded the translator's dilemma, which was twofold. He had to translate the script into German to avoid linguistic choices which the censor could interpret as subversive. The translator then had to render the play's bewildering content accessible to the largely assimilated German audience, unversed in the history of the Kabbalah. Linguistically, it may seem an exercise in futility for the Hebrew-to-German translator to render a play into German only to purge the script of references merging "Germanness" with the text's inherent Jewishness.

In crafting his translation of *Sabbatai Zevi*, Broser tried to simulate Bistritzky's writing style, in which the spoken language stemmed from the characters' historical situation. A specific sentence cadence, vocabulary, and particular quotations defined each character. Crucial to his task, however, was the integration of the "quotation treasure troves" in the original. Characters cite material from the Bible, Talmud, Kabbalah, rabbinical literature, and liturgical poetry. Because Jews from different countries (Spanish, Turkish, Egyptian, and Polish Jews) appear in the drama, their linguistic singularity characterized their voices. The Hebrew of the Polish Jews, for example, showed traces of Yiddish, which had to be rendered through translated German dialect. Bistritzky also used Aramaic words when referring to "mystic-kabbalistic thresholds," to suggest how the non-Jews spoke. Broser believed that this "stylistic symphony" could barely be translated into a modern European language, given the "equally weighted" linguistic layers merged with Hebrew. But he accentuated differences within the German language in his translation.

The play's language relied heavily on multilingual layers of speech, requiring a fusion of Hebrew and German. For Bernstein's production, Broser left intact first names or "liturgical terms" which the German Jewish audience would understand. He kept kabbalistic terms originally in Aramaic in the production script and added German equivalents. Despite his desire to render the text in "beautiful German," he opted for a "lesser beautiful German" to fit the play's characters. He followed the Hebrew original by differentiating language nuances within each character through vocabulary and rhythm.[39] The complex link between language and content in the play made it difficult for the Kulturbund to promote Bernstein's production.

During the three-week production run of Bistritzky's play, Hinkel censored an event that was to inform audiences about the play. Max Nussbaum's lecture "Who Was Sabbatai Zevi?" scheduled for 18 November 1936 may never have taken place.[40] Nussbaum had already enlightened Kulturbund audiences about Hasidism in preparation for *The Golden Chain*. Now he prepared to teach audiences about the historical significance of messianism as a "balm for all the wounds of time." But Hinkel objected to Nussbaum's lecture, confiscating the lecture notes because the speaker wanted to explain the Messiah's role in political terms: "If one believed that the Messiah as national redeemer brings the Jews to their land—if one believes further that the Messiah brings the Jews together as a people, delivering them from abroad—then one logically ceases to be an object and changes back into a historic subject." This idea by Nussbaum led to his main argument, which Hinkel found even more offensive. Nussbaum believed that all human hopes for Jewish and cosmic deliverance led to messianism: "*If one senses* the advent of redemption, and one believes that this is *not only for the Jews, but for the whole world, then one has messianized the world; (and then one may speak again to the world, for now it will hear)*."[41] Although Nussbaum situated his words in the seventeenth century, a public explanation of Jewish messianism in 1936 as a world event had dangerous ramifications for Hinkel and his censors.

In practical terms, a theatre production of Bistritzky's play risked amplifying the idea of messianism. Nonetheless, Bernstein's production ran beyond 18 November (the date of Nussbaum's banned talk). Broser's translation of the complex material received mixed reviews. "We may not look at or judge his [Bistritzky's] play 'with Western eyes'; because it is a naïve and primitively worked play," written for and performed by "simple workers," Kurt Pinthus wrote about the production, which lasted until almost midnight.[42] Despite its length, however, other reviewers observed that the production engaged audiences. While they might have been initially skeptical about the play's content, they longed to see depictions of Jewish "misery," Martha Wertheimer of the *Israelitisches Familienblatt* reported after the premiere performance. She added that the audience "understood the language of these characters . . . their plight and their desire for deliverance" and empathized with the stage characters.[43]

Bernstein's Kulturbund production exposed the linguistic and cultural pitfalls that emerged when translating a Hebrew play into German and transferring controversial subject matter like messianism onto the Jewish stage. German censorship quickly suppressed language and content before

Jewish audiences could see the production. In portraying Sabbatai Zevi as a demagogue, Bistritzky's play focused on the followers who await the restoration of Israel. This focus suggests why audiences could view the false Messiah as the real one.[44] Eloesser referred to the Kulturbund's "touching" tableau of onstage characters as crucial to the play.[45] Wertheimer, however, criticized the absence of the masses onstage: they receded into the background whenever a main character came forward. Without the visible *Volk*, the play lost its pulse, she observed, describing the populace as "greedy for deliverance, the blind believers who yearn for the Holy land, and those who are eternally hopeful, throwing their arms up in the air, screaming, and dancing."[46]

The difference in opinion on the stage director's portrayal of the masses may have depended on the reviewers' responses to the designer's use of color and light.[47] Pinthus judged the production "exciting with colorful scenes and stage effects," making the sparse stage appear larger.[48] Eloesser described the stage setting as a backdrop that could have come from *Caligari*, "operalike" in its presentation of the "concerted sound of people's voices." He compared the semidarkness of the Lemberg Ghetto to a Rembrandt group portrait. Squeezed together on one side of the stage were the rabbis who rejected the idea of Messiah; on the other side of the stage ghetto residents gathered in ecstatic tribute to the Messiah.[49]

The play's central third act opened with the Lemberg Jews awaiting the Messiah, where "*Light shines from all the houses; the doors are open. One hears the sounds of preparations to leave Lemberg, interrupted by ecstatic song.*"[50] Celebrants gathered outside their homes, crowding around the ghetto peddler, who told them how Jerusalem would be rebuilt for all Jews.[51] The onstage arrival of the purported Messiah, however, may have disappointed the audience. Hans-Karl Rosenberg as Sabbatai Zevi was too young to play the part convincingly. Good-looking as he was, several reviewers claimed that that he failed to characterize the necessary "demonic personality." His performance did not strike critics as credible enough to make a false Messiah seem real.[52]

While Kulturbund audiences in November 1936 watched Bistritzky's Messiah be revealed as an imposter, in real life the Nazi government had just joined Benito Mussolini in officially recognizing Francisco Franco's dictatorship in Spain. Goebbels's Ministry of Propaganda then cracked down on the German press on 27 November, banning journalists from publishing art and literary critiques. So entwined were politics and the arts that the critics were only allowed to write descriptive reviews.[53] Yet Kulturbund audiences still enjoyed the relative freedom of reading art criticism in their separate press. Jewish newspapers also regularly featured reports about the Middle East, where the general Arab strike had ended by late autumn. Tenuous relations between Arabs and Jews simmered through the end of the year. The German Emigrant Association in Palestine in Jerusalem prodded the German consul to increase emigration in December. Zionists in Germany set the same goal, one that the Nazi government championed more and more.

As 1936 edged to a close, the Kulturbund's mission to expand membership and its Jewish-themed programs peaked. An auxiliary touring youth group theatre or *Schultheater* was formed.[54] Some actors from the Kulturbund cabaret troupe and the ensemble joined the youth theatre to offer children monthly play productions. The Theatre of Jewish Schools (under Werner Hinzelmann) worked with schoolteachers to coordinate a play list with the classroom curriculum.[55] Besides presenting audiences with staples such as Shakespeare's *As You Like It* (October 1936), the youth theatre presented Dymov's East European fairy tale *Jusik* (November 1936). The Jewish community continued its push to enlighten audiences about Judaism and Palestine at the Kulturbund with religious programs, Hebrew classes, and puppet shows.[56] Werner Hinzelmann and Steffi Hinzelmann (née Rosenbaum; stage name Ronau) used hand puppets to introduce topics like emigration that children might be experiencing at home, as in *Kasper Emigrates* (1936) and *Kasper and the Magic Lamp* (1937). Werner Levie hired the former cultural director of Germany's Zionist Association to bolster the "Jewish direction" of the theatre repertoire. Herbert Freeden (born Friedenthal) thus began his work at the Kulturbund in 1936 as a director's assistant to the acting ensemble. He worked to establish a didactic politicized path for the repertoire, identifying Jewish values and settings.

Singer, meanwhile, proceeded with his double-pronged approach to the theatre repertoire, alternating productions of didactic Jewish-themed plays with Shakespearean comedy and European farce. The reception of Shakespeare perhaps best reveals the blatant inconsistency between Nazi Germany's official guidelines on aesthetic criticism and Goebbels's policy for the Kulturbund. Shakespeare's popularity in Nazi Germany remained unparalleled. He was even more significant than Ibsen, whom Germans revered as a Nordic compatriot. Goebbels promoted translations of Shakespeare by August Wilhelm von Schlegel and Dorothea Tieck as truer than the original sources themselves.[57] Yet he—and by extension Schlösser and Hinkel—permitted the Kulturbund to perform Shakespeare's comedies in

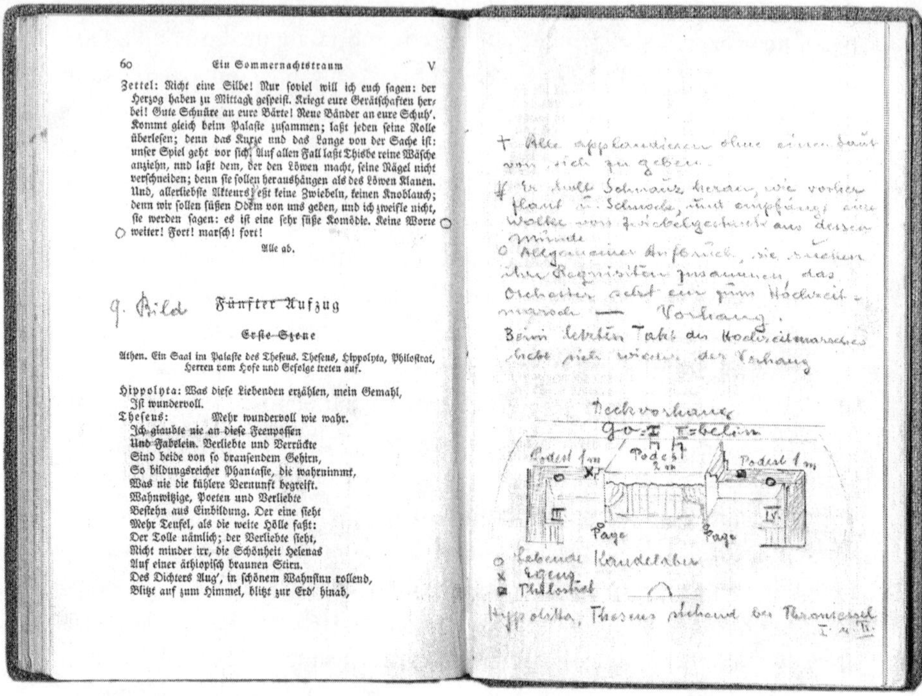

9. Wisten director's script for Shakespeare, *A Midsummer Night's Dream*, December 1936. Akademie der Künste, Berlin, FWA, 8°-27-272-60, photograph by Akademie der Künste.

the same translations used for the German stage. In 1936, ironically, the Kulturbund produced *A Midsummer Night's Dream*, a play in which characters escape to the forest and find a sanctuary from society. The production's popularity reinforced the Kulturbund's commitment to a European, non-Jewish theatre repertory.

Audiences attended the production of Shakespeare's play in higher numbers than they did for the Jewish-themed plays. Twenty-five performances of *A Midsummer Night's Dream* (*Ein Sommernachtstraum*) in von Schlegel's translation played throughout December 1936.[58] Among seven theatrical events between fall 1936 and April 1937, Singer registered the highest rate of attendance for *A Midsummer Night's Dream* at 14,914, while attendance for *Sabbatai Zevi* a month earlier had only been 12,908.[59] The esoteric themes of messianism could not compete with the more familiar comic tropes of Shakespeare. Dreams and illusion, disguise and playacting, love and the fairies' magic distinguish the liberating spirit of *A Midsummer Night's Dream*. The action moves

10. Shakespeare, *A Midsummer Night's Dream*, December 1936: Ruth Anselm as Hermia on right. Akademie der Künste, Berlin, FWA 0074/86/20_25, photograph by Abraham Pisarek, courtesy Ruth Gross.

from the city to the forest and from unrequited to reconciled love, reinforced by a triple wedding at the end of the play.

Singer recruited Fritz Wisten as stage director for the production. Rehearsals ran from 5 to 20 November for the 2 December 1936 premiere.[60] Wisten retained the incidental music composed by Felix Mendelssohn, which Singer rearranged for the orchestra. Condell's minimalist and modernist setting was in keeping with the limitations on his budget. A plastic tree and a painted backcloth with a cloud cover depicted the forest. Downstage left, two small hills and a tree trunk provided space for the lovers. Wisten applied the acting training methods which he so successfully employed for *The Golden Chain* to the non-Jewish repertoire. His focus on the actors' plasticity of movement and speech was evident in the performances, especially Shakespeare's mechanicals and Ruth Anselm's performance as Hermia.[61]

Wisten transformed the play's five acts into nine scenes with a "break" before the eighth scene, where the mechanicals prepare their "lamentable comedy and cruel death of Pyramus and Thisbe" for the duke's nuptials.

Wisten paid careful attention to the metatheatrical subplot of the play-within-the-play. He cast two of the Kulturbund's well-known comedians, Willy Prager and Alfred Berliner (Balthoff), to play the carpenter Peter Quince (Squenz) and Bottom the Weaver (Zettel). Wisten tapped into his actors' comic skills, plotting their stage business and physical humor.[62] For example, in the second scene, set in the woods, Quince distributed the play's roles and described the play for his acting crew, including Bottom. When cast as Pyramus, Bottom (Berliner) was dismissive about playing a lover. He then emoted as a tyrant, his "chief humor" (line 25), engaged in horseplay, and bumped into Snout and Starveling.[63]

Wisten's attention to his actors' flair for comedy showed his versatility as an actor-director. When performing Jewish-themed plays, he engaged Jewish actors comfortably with the material; but he also gave his fellow actors access to non-Jewish classics, leading them to link movement and speech and in the case of *A Midsummer Night's Dream* to capture Shakespeare's comic timing and quick repartee. This was evident, for example, when the craftsmen performed the play within the play (scene 9). The Kulturbund curtain rose on Quince's hut (scene 8), where the players awaited Bottom. Wisten used stage equipment that could easily be wheeled off the stage to allow for a speedy transition to the ninth scene. The actors engaged in physical stage business as they readied themselves for the following scene: "They gather their props; the orchestra sets up the Wedding March—Curtain. At the last measure of the Wedding March, the curtain rises again" on the scene at the palace of Duke Theseus.[64]

A Midsummer Night's Dream remained the fourth most popular Shakespeare play in German theatres during the Reich. But while Goebbels's ban on criticism in the German press limited its exposure to the non-Jewish public, Kulturbund audiences read reviews which commended Wisten's direction of Shakespeare. Wisten directed seasoned actors like Berliner to improvise freely and used a "firm but elastic hand" in his close work with the young actors.[65] Eloesser especially praised Anselm's animated performance as Hermia, which lent rhythm and plasticity to Shakespeare's verse.[66] The director also ensured that the play's characteristic song and dance ended the evening, after which Puck bid farewell.[67]

In February 1937 Goebbels ordered Hinkel to tighten his control over copyright issues and the Jewish Kulturbund, including direct payments to foreign authors or publishers.[68] Translations of non-Aryan playwrights generally could present problems for those Nazi censors who determined objectionable subject matter. Hinkel and his supervisors at the Ministry of Propaganda gave Singer leeway to produce Shakespearean comedy and plays by foreign authors, especially if a Jewish link to the author existed through a translator or publisher. Hinkel thus approved a production of Sidney Kingsley's *Men in White* that was published in German by an émigré publisher (George Marton). The Jewish connection may have helped Singer to obtain playing rights without extra cost for the January 1937 production.[69]

Hinkel also permitted the early February 1937 performance of two one-acts by Hugo von Hofmannsthal and Rabindranath Tagore just prior to revoking the rights for foreign works at the theatre. When the Austrian writer Joseph Roth referred to the Kulturbund in 1937 as Berlin's "officially sanctioned centerpiece of the new ghetto," he did not mention that the Kulturbund had already produced a play by Hofmannsthal, a fellow countryman and Jew.[70] Roth instead criticized German Jews for cravenly accepting their plight: "This Kulturbund . . . is nothing more or less than an unwarranted concession on the part of the Jews to the barbarous theories of National Socialism. Its basis is not the assumption—accepted by so many Jews today—that they are a separate race, but the implicit admission that they are an inferior one."[71] Addressing the cultural discrimination that Jews faced, he concluded: "Whereas no one would have dreamed of forbidding some Tibetan, Caucasian, or Japanese Kulturbund to perform Goethe or Beethoven, the Jewish Kulturbund is not allowed to do so."[72] Roth understood the reluctance of Berlin's Jews to depart Germany. His outsider status, however, prevented him from understanding the compromises that Singer had to make to keep the theatre running.

Singer knew perfectly well, as he put it, that a "larger portion" of Berlin's Jewish population refused to join the Kulturbund on principle because they would not be "ghettoized" or commit themselves to specific subscription policies. In 1937, for example, as many as 12,000 Jewish families in Berlin refrained from joining the Kulturbund.[73] Yet despite the concessions that Singer made to Nazi policy, the portion of the Jewish population that did join the cultural league could use theatre temporarily to transcend the daily strictures that restricted Jews. Actors could mask their accommodation to the Nazis, what Roth called their "cravenness." By performing great works of art, they could believe, while on the stage and behind the scenes, that no constraints were imposed on them. Audiences could enjoy the liberating spirit of Shakespeare in Schlegel's translation. By going to see plays by European playwrights of repute, they might justify being freer than they actually were. Audiences might also find in the plays parallels and allegorical situations onstage that reflected their own lives. At the same time, they could attend plays which transported them to the exotic realms of Persia and India, as in Hofmannsthal's *Marriage of Sobeide* (1897) and Tagore's *Post Office* (1914).

Wisten directed the double-bill which dramatized the inner life of characters and their urge for freedom. In Hofmannsthal's one-act, a wealthy merchant releases his unhappy bride Sobeide from the confines of her marriage on their wedding night; yet the next morning Sobeide escapes another unrequited love by jumping to her death.[74] The play ends with the young woman's suicide and her merchant-husband's grief. In *The Post Office*, the dying boy Amal may "on no account" be let outside, on his physician's orders. Amal only communicates with passersby through a large window near his bed. The play title refers to the king's post office, visible outside Amal's window. Amal awaits a letter from the king. He tells the king's watchman, who passes by, "I am here where they have left me—I never move a bit. . . . Oh, I do wish to fly with time to that land of which no one knows anything."[75] The watchman informs the boy that a gong lets people know that "time waits for none, but goes on forever," suggesting that the gong signals death. Death liberates Amal from the confinement of his illness and room.

Wisten began the Kulturbund production with the Hofmannsthal one-act, adding a prologue and an epilogue. Dressed in Oriental costume, a flautist played in front of a curtain. To enhance the nighttime and indoor action in *Sobeide*, the designer focused spots of cool blue and yellow light on the young actress (not quite twenty) who played the bride (Anneliese Töpfer) as she expressed a fear of being pulled toward a golden, glistening place beyond the shadows.[76] The plays juxtaposed images of enclosure and flight. Wisten deleted Sobeide's final words to her husband: "Our soul lives within us like a caged bird. When the cage is smashed, it [the soul] will be free."[77] In *The Post Office*, however, the dying boy Amal (played by Erika Praetorius) spent most of act I at a large picture window, which ran parallel upstage nearly the entire length of the stage, or in bed downstage right during the second act.[78] During the second act the window remained shut. Wisten added a gong sound at the end of the play to change Tagore's ambiguous ending about whether the boy was sleeping or had died. Wisten's production invited audiences to enter the lyrical world of the plays, venturing far from the Berlin present into a universal, emotionalized fantasy.

Reviewers interpreted the evening differently. Kurt Pinthus reported that the Tagore production enchanted the audience with its warm, soft lights and colors. He felt that the stage ambience with a visible landscape beyond the window offered a glimpse into a fairy tale as characters passed by the open window.[79] Wertheimer, however, faulted Wisten for focusing on oratory over action, which thwarted the Kulturbund audience's response, especially in *Sobeide*.[80] Pinthus admitted that the underlying atmosphere of foreboding, heavy shadows, and melancholy in Hofmannsthal's play unnerved the audience.[81] Only death saved the main characters from suffering, freeing their souls and extending their memory to the mourners. The reviewers' response to the two plays suggests that audiences in 1937 preferred a fantasy world, removed enough from their own to liberate them from their worries. Shakespeare's comedy drew many more theatregoers than attended Hofmannsthal's and Tagore's plays, with their focus on death. Singer reported that 12,116 theatregoers attended the Hofmannsthal and Tagore evening. This was almost on a par with attendance for *Sabbatai Zevi* three months before. The theatre's didactic take on Jewish history did not appeal to members as much as secular comedy. But the dramaturgical staff continued to offer Jewish-themed plays.

As spring approached, Wisten chose Sholem Aleichem's *Der Haupttreffer* (The Big Win) to fill the Jewish play slot. Translated by Meier Broser and retitled *Amcha*, the comedy set in the shtetl turns on the fortunes of a poor tailor whose life changes radically upon winning the lottery.[82] *Amcha* premiered on 5 April 1937 and ran for nineteen performances. The translator faced linguistic problems with the script similar to those he had experienced when translating Bistritzky's play. Broser began with Yiddish and Hebrew texts and then translated the play into German dialect, slang, and Yiddish. He wanted to guide actors in "seem[ing] Jewish, without being limited by an exaggerated 'yiddeling'" or being forced to exaggerate Jewish vocal intonations and speech patterns.[83] Broser's strategy relied on language nuances to indicate class difference and character pretensions: for example, he presented the Europeanized educated Russian-speaking characters of the play with a careful dialect-free High German. Wisten and his actors used the language to draw out the play's comic and milieu-related context. Scenically, Condell further enhanced the characters' milieu with his designs, using local color and stage effects to reflect economic status. Thus when the poor tailor's fortunes turned good, a multisided painted prism suggested a fairytale ambience.[84]

Critics weighed in on *Amcha*'s language experiment, praising the sounds of the "ostjüdisch," although Eloesser judged the High German dialect too removed from the play's Jewish roots to portray the intrinsic folk character of the villagers.[85] Former Kulturbund performers have corroborated the ambivalence with which Kulturbund directors treated Jewish-themed plays and their content. Ruth Anselm (whose last Jewish role had been in the short run of Hirschbein's *Green Fields* in 1936) claimed that Wisten made no special efforts to coach actors in impersonating Jewish characters. Mascha Benyakonsky reiterated this claim. The Kulturbund staff had rejected her expertise in Hebrew and Yiddish folklore when she first approached the Kulturbund in 1935–1936. After her audition in 1937 for the opera with an aria in French, the Kulturbund hired her "almost on the spot." The day after her audition the soprano secured the role of Norina in Gaetano Donizetti's *Don Pasquale*.[86] Her engagement with the opera and its West European bias, however, did not preclude her passion for East European Jewish music. She sang liturgical music for house concerts outside of the Kulturbund. Nor did she change her Zionist convictions because of her new roles at the Kulturbund.

Kulturbund members could follow the current political turmoil in Palestine in their weekly newspapers. After Arab attacks on Jewish settlements in 1936 and ensuing strikes, the British Mandate of Palestine squelched the unrest. As the summer approached, the mandate prepared to release the results of an official inquiry into the conflict by the Palestine Royal Commission.[87] On 7 July 1937 Lord Robert Peel issued the Peel Report recommendations for land partition in Palestine for Arabs and for Jews. The directors and staff in Berlin incorporated into Kulturbund programming as much thematic material about Palestine as Hinkel would authorize. But theatregoers preferred relaxation to edification during the summertime, according to Singer.[88]

Singer continually reflected on his theatre in progress, weighing the advantages and the realities of the need to appease one group while conceding to the demands of another. He also appealed to the preferences of his audiences. During the same period when Kulturbund actors performed *The Golden Chain*, *Sabbatai Zevi*, and *Amcha*, they performed plays by authors whose work belonged to the literary tradition that Singer valued. Ironically, Goebbels and Schlösser had expressed a proprietary claim to the same models of world literature—foreign dramatists of stature, for whom the "German mind" must remain open: classical Greek dramatists, Shakespeare, Shaw, Molière, and Ibsen.[89] Alongside plays about Jewish life, insulated from threatening forces, classics characterized the Kulturbund playing season of 1936–1937, with comedies by Shakespeare and Molière, Kingsley's *Men in White* (1937), and one-acts by Hofmannsthal and Tagore (1937). Singer also scheduled plays by writers such as contemporary Hungarian Jews Ladislaus Bus-Fekete, Ferenc Molnár, Ladislaus Fodor, and Emmerich Kálmán in the summer of 1937. Comedies like Bus-Fekete's *Jean* (June 1937) and Henri Bernstein's *Hope* (July 1937) satirized the bourgeoisie.[90]

Cheerful theatre visions marked the Kulturbund repertoire during the summer months, when Britain's newly elected prime minister shaped Britain's policies for the Mandate of Palestine and international relations with Germany. As the British mapped out a separate Jewish state in the Middle East, Neville Chamberlain crafted a foreign policy to appease Germany that would permit Hitler to expand his power to foreign countries. In August 1937 Zionists in Europe rejected the Peel Report Plan of Land Partition, as did Arab Palestinians. Meanwhile the Kulturbund Jews confronted the realities of the worsening situation in Germany. Should they leave or stay in a country whose leadership betrayed its citizens? Was Joseph Roth fair to indict the Kulturbund's purpose as a craven acquiescence to the will of the Nazis? Did the Kulturbund theatre only amount to being an "officially sanctioned centerpiece of the new ghetto"? Such a charge could only be made from the sidelines. Certainly some Kulturbund Jews deluded themselves, while others compromised their ideals by adapting to the dictates that ruled their lives. It was not the phenomenon of the Kulturbund that was abnormal but the circumstances, affecting thousands of Berliners who tried to lead their lives in an abnormal situation. As the community readied itself for the new Jewish year of 5698, the Kulturbund would stage a play about an esteemed community leader unmasked as a self-serving opportunist. The theatre's production of Ibsen's *Pillars of Society* would highlight the destructive effects of a leader's deception on public life.

6 PROTECTION

COMMUNITY VALUES

1937-1938

The sound of the shofar announced the High Holidays of 1937, accompanied by a call for new members to join Berlin's Kulturbund and its theatre. Arthur Eloesser urged his *Rundschau* readership to support the cultural organization. He invoked a sense of "Jewish obligation and honor" in his appeal for communal participation. For, as he noted, the theatre represented a "social and spiritual healing factor of incomparable power." He praised Singer for his achievements over the past four years. Although the Kulturbund was not a "public assistance institution," Eloesser insisted that its service to the community had kept the lives of hundreds of people intact. Importantly, middle-aged Jewish citizens had retained their jobs and been able to raise their families. This demographic group needed more economic aid than the younger generation. The young would wander, the journalist reminded his readers.[1] For the Kulturbund members who stayed in Germany despite the precarious times, Singer's decision to close the theatre's fourth playing season with Henrik Ibsen's *Pillars of Society* (*Die Stützen der Gesellschaft*) gave audiences a chance to reflect on moral and social concerns that preoccupied them in their lives.

Ibsen's play about a hypocritical community leader premiered on 4 September 1937, one day after Eloesser had appealed to the community on behalf of the Kulturbund. *Pillars of Society* ran for twenty-three performances. The successful businessman Karsten Bernick represents a "pillar" of his community in the play. His business deals benefit the community, including his newest venture, a coastal railway that connects to a fertile area of land. But Bernick purchased property in that area before publicly announcing

11. Ibsen, *Pillars of Society*, September 1937. Akademie der Künste, Berlin, FWA 20.63.274, photograph by Abraham Pisarek, courtesy Ruth Gross.

his railway plans. He also bought the silence of his business partners, other "pillars" of the community.

Bernick's impeccable moral and civil record is based on a web of deception. His brother-in-law Johan took the blame for Bernick's youthful indiscretions (adultery and alleged embezzlement) before emigrating to America. Bernick married for money (Johan's sister Betty) and not for love (Johan's stepsister, Lona Hessel). After Johan and Lona return home fifteen years later, Bernick's secrets are exposed, leading to the unraveling of the plot—and Bernick's reputation. Bernick tries to cover up the secrets. He has no qualms about sending an unseaworthy ship to sea before it is repaired. In a plot twist, Johan has decided to return to America on that very ship. Bernick's son has stowed away on the ship (which never leaves port). With the help of Lona Hessel, Bernick experiences a "conversion" of spirit and in the final act addresses community members to rectify his actions.

Fritz Wisten returned to the Kulturbund stage in the role of Consul Bernick under the direction of his fellow-actor Herbert Grünbaum. Grünbaum had joined the ensemble in 1934 with twelve years of stage and screen experience. Assembling a strong cast, Grünbaum gave Jenny Schaffer-Bernstein the role of Betty; Lilly Kann played Bernick's former love, Lona Hessel. The newcomer Fritz Melchior took the role of Johan, while Anneliese Töpfer (Hofmannsthal's Sobeide) was cast as the young woman he wishes to marry. The cast also featured Alfred Berliner as a cousin and Martin Brandt as the schoolmaster Rorlund. Condell's set design showed that Bernick's work world infiltrated his living domain. The audience could see part of the consul's study on the side of the main set's garden room. Bernick's familial sphere and his professional realm thus coexisted spatially. This staging choice showed how Bernick's two worlds collided, especially after Johan and Lona Hessel return home.

Grünbaum struck the final line from his production of *Pillars of Society*; in fact, much of the play's final exchange between Bernick and Hessel was not performed. Hessel directed the final line to Bernick: "[T]he spirit of truth and the spirit of freedom—*those* are the pillars of society."[2] The omission of the play's last line is telling. No democracy or justice can exist without truth and freedom. Bernick's community never rested on the foundations of truth and freedom. Hinkel could not let the Kulturbund show onstage the blatant hypocrisy of a community leader. Yet the play's subtext made it clear that Bernick deceived his followers, even his wife. The Kulturbund production retained allusions to the consul's duplicity, but Grünbaum accommodated himself to the basic guidelines for censorship, excising many of Bernick's key speeches. The major cuts to the original script suggest that the production evaded significant moral issues.

Wisten as Bernick avoided lengthy onstage explanations for his past transgressions.[3] Further, Grünbaum edited the third and fourth acts so that the audience did not learn the full lie upon which Bernick had built his career and community service. These omissions rendered the Kulturbund's Bernick guarded and less introspective than Ibsen's character. In the third act, after Johan demanded that his name be cleared of slander, Bernick did not respond as Ibsen had written: "I need every scrap of moral credibility. That's why I *can't* speak out. . . . Wouldn't I stand revealed as the man who saved himself by an untruth, and who for fifteen years let the untruth take root and grow without the least effort to counter it?"[4] The audience never heard Bernick's anxious words about his impending ruin; nor did they know his fear of exposure for investing in the railway venture. In the Kulturbund's staging of the play Bernick did not take responsibility for his actions. By cutting passages related to Bernick's self-doubt, the stage director may have censored the text so much that he denied audiences the core significance of Ibsen's play.

The Kulturbund performances of *Pillars of Society* took place around Yom Kippur. The play about a leader who publicly admits his faults and tries to amend his behavior would be especially meaningful for audiences during the Days of Awe. Yet Grünbaum's production avoided Bernick's onstage pangs of conscience in the pivotal third act: Wisten's Bernick did not speak the lines which registered his unease about his past actions until it was clear that his son had decided to follow Johan to America. Perhaps the most noteworthy omission in production was the stage director's choice to cut a lengthy exchange between Rorlund (Martin Brandt) and Bernick in which the consul, "quite pale and upset," voices doubt about having ordered the American ship to sea. Hoping to ease his conscience, Bernick asks the schoolmaster, "What if a man stood on the brink of a tremendous undertaking that could make an improvement in thousands of lives—and it required the sacrifice of one, single individual?"[5] Concealing the source of his unease about the ship, Bernick refers to his railroad deal and poses hypothetical situations to defend a project for the common good, even if a life may be lost. Grünbaum presumably instructed Wisten to skip the scene that exposed Bernick's gnawing conscience.

According to reviews, audiences reportedly enjoyed the thrill of Ibsen's "well-made" play, which was imbued with psychology.[6] But Lutz Weltmann pointed to one crucial scene that had been deleted in the Kulturbund production. He conceded that the scene was irrelevant and too long, but for him and for those who knew the play the scene's structural significance was vital to the play's composition. The excised scene represented a "missing weight which naturally led to the denouement or unraveling of the plot."[7] Grünbaum would not have eliminated such a pivotal scene in the protagonist's development for aesthetic reasons. The omission of this scene from performance undercut the effect of Bernick's remorse and self-revelation, including his public admission of guilt in the play's last act. These changes in production are reminiscent of how Jessner staged *Antigone*, rendering Creon a stronger king than the play text suggested. Similarly, Wisten portrayed Bernick as a stronger leader than Ibsen originally scripted. Had Singer and his creative team unwittingly become complicit in Hinkel's plan to deprive Jewish audiences of the moral contradictions in human behavior?

Hinkel had already found any onstage discussion of sacrificing one's life for the common good unsuitable. He censored thematic patterns of martyrdom or messianism several times for the Jewish stage: in *God's Hunt*, *Jeremiah*, *The Golden Chain*, and *Sabbatai Zevi*.[8] The dilemma of a sacrifice for the community-at-large in *Pillars of Society* may have led Jewish audiences to draw undesired parallels to their place in German society, especially given insistent calls to resolve the "Jewish Question." Hinkel would have known that *Pillars of Society* and *An Enemy of the People* were among the Ibsen plays staged by German theatres for propaganda purposes.[9] Bernick's contrition scene in act III probably never played for Kulturbund audiences, thus neutralizing the play's message.

The production by the Jewish theatre also softened Ibsen's inherent social criticism. The director reworked the scene in the fourth act where Bernick receives gifts from the townspeople for his railroad venture. In the original script Bernick admits to his duplicitous role in the railway operation and acknowledges guilt for Johan's crimes. But Wisten's Bernick kept his public admission of wrongdoing to a bare minimum. Grünbaum also transposed lines from one act to another, which reinforced Bernick's role as a leader.[10] His words specified that only he could develop the coastal land. He justified the sale this way: "As they stand now, those properties are just about worthless to their different owners; they were sold off for relatively little. If one waited till the branch line [railroad] was public knowledge, the owners would have inflated the prices out of all reason."[11] The Kulturbund thus emphasized Bernick's "home-grown" business acumen, but the director ensured that the consul did not utter lines which linked business with foreigners and by extension with Jews. Grünbaum understandably had deleted the consul's line "In this country generally, it's only families from foreign countries who have a knack for big business."[12]

In 1937 any discussion of property acquisition and the value of land on a Jewish stage would have been viewed in the context of "Aryanization." From 1933 through November 1938 the Nazis issued a series of property-related measures to take over Jewish businesses.[13] The revisions in the Kulturbund script concerning Bernick's land deals suggest that censors did not want the Jewish audience to misperceive what constituted "lawful" property ownership. At the same time, censors may have demanded the removal of lines that evoked common Nazi suspicions about Jews. Rorlund's excised line about the railway as a useful transport system is especially ominous in hindsight: "The railroad potentially could prove a way by which we could expose ourselves to corrupting elements from without, but it could prove a way of ridding ourselves of them as well. And, as it is, we can hardly keep ourselves free of such undesirable elements."[14] With whom might the Jews identify those "undesirable elements" during that autumn of 1937? These sentiments echo Rorlund's overt intolerance about foreigners in general: on the Kulturbund stage, his character did not refer to the American ship crew as "scum of the earth"; nor did the director retain Rorlund's hostile reference to keeping the community "pure" or the chilling analogy between weeds and human beings in his early moral musings to a party of village women in the first act: "No denying, of course, that weeds grow among our good grain as well, but we strive in good faith to root them out the best we can."[15]

The Kulturbund produced Ibsen's play throughout the month of September 1937. During this time land and its ownership became a politicized topic in Germany and abroad. The government prepared for a systematic takeover of Jewish property on German soil. The Reich chief of police Heinrich Himmler issued a September order that any detained Jews could be released from custody if they emigrated. During the production run of *Pillars of Society*, the active membership of artists in the Berlin theatre actually decreased to 1,763 members from 2,493 the year before. As a chief administrator for the theatre, Werner Levie compiled the sinking numbers and attributed this drop to a strong trend in emigration from Germany to other countries, including Palestine.[16] Although the season's final production of *Pillars of Society* avoided explicit allusions to the times, theatregoers who knew Ibsen's play may have inferred parallels between a community leader who whitewashed the truth and their betrayal by their government.

During 1937–1938 Kulturbund programs pointedly exposed audiences to the Jewish world outside of Nazi Germany while emigration to Jewish Palestine increased. Newspaper series featured weekly stories on life in new countries, and advertisements for travel agencies appeared in the theatre's printed flyers and programs. A Zionist lobby for Kulturbund Jews became a serious part of the organization. Singer launched the fifth season with a play from the Jewish category. A new production of Halper Leivick's *The Golem (Der Golem)* premiered on 9 October 1937. Before the curtain rose on the play's first scene, audiences viewed a short film promoting the *Jüdische Rundschau*. The film used "impressive music" and scenes of daily life in Palestine to promote Jewish life there.[17]

How does one enact characters with supernatural powers convincingly for an audience? For *The Golem*, Wisten resumed the role of director, adeptly moving from his role as Bernick to reacquaint the actors with ways to convey Jewish mysticism from eastern Europe to Kulturbund audiences. In his staging of *The Golem*, Wisten focused on the legendary rabbi Loew (played by Herbert Grünbaum), who breathed life into a Golem—a lump of clay—to create a Protector for the Jews of Prague and their land. The Golem gains spiritual energy from the Hebrew alphabet. Kabbalah-practicing rabbis like Loew were known by the Hebrew acronym MaHaRaL (Our Teacher Rabbi Judah Loeb). They could instill a Golem's life force by inserting God's secret name or the word "truth" under the creature's tongue or onto its forehead.[18]

The legend of a Golem as servant or savior was revitalized in the 1920s, when Leivick wrote his Yiddish version of the medieval folktale.[19] According to folklore, the rabbi created a Golem to prevent pogroms related to the libel that Jews used Christian children's blood in their Passover matzoh. Leivick set his play in the seventeenth century, where his Golem character, Yossele (Joseph), proves inadequate as a Messiah figure, becoming destructive to the community that it was supposed to protect.

Wisten used Leo Hirsch's adaptation of Leivick's eight-scene play, which focused on the rabbi and not on the Golem character. The Kulturbund artistic team used Leivick's episodic form with seven scenes entitled "Clay," "Walls," "Darkness," "Beggars," "Unsummoned," "Revelations," and "The Last Mission."[20] In the play's pivotal fourth scene ("Beggars") at the ruins of the "Fünferturm" (Fifth Tower), the Maharal has ordered the Golem to sleep among the poor, sick, and crazy Jews of Prague. Two "wandering paupers" arrive: an old beggar called Elijah the Prophet and a young man in rags (Leivick describes him as "THE MESSIAH"). The old beggar's arrival signals the significance of his companion, the "unsummoned one" of the fifth scene. But the rabbi sends the men away and delays a redemptive restoration for the Jews.[21]

The mood builds ominously in the play's last scenes as the rabbi's wife and granddaughter seek him among the ruins. The Golem finds his master and begs not to be forsaken. The final scene, "The Last Mission," takes place in a synagogue anteroom on the Sabbath. Desperate for the Maharal's attention, Yossel goes on a rampage, destroying everything in sight. When he returns, he reports that he spilled "Jewish blood."[22] The rabbi has overestimated his control over the Golem and decides to take back his life. The Maharal then recognizes that he has defied God by seeking reparation (*tikkun*) through force (the Golem). Burying his face on the lectern where Sabbath candles burn, he laments "my insignificance, my massive sin? . . . my sin against all Jews?"[23] The rabbi commands Yossel to rest eternally.

In production, Wisten cut Leivick's seventh scene, "In the Cave," and used an alternate script that reversed the order of Leivick's last two scenes.[24] Leivick's original "In the Cave" scene features cave spirits, a vengeful Jew-hating priest named Thaddeus, the Messiah, and a Christ-like figure (the "Man with the Cross") in a clash about redemptive power. The Maharal orders the Golem to fulfill his mission, even while the Golem tries to halt it. The Kulturbund production, however, concluded with the seventh scene in the synagogue, where the rabbi tells the Golem to lie down, stretch out, close his eyes, and "return to peace."[25]

A foreboding atmosphere pervaded the production from the start. The veteran actor Siegfried Urias played the Golem to Grünbaum's Maharal. Both wore exaggerated masklike makeup. Especially striking was the Golem, whom Leivick describes as "*powerfully built—a giant. Large eyes. There is something heavy and dull about them and at the same time something childlike.*" His "Golem-like" expression is a "stiff, frozen smile at nothing."[26] The Maharal passes Yossel off to the townspeople as a stranger whose physical force makes him a useful laborer, but the villagers fear the hulking creature. Condell's stage settings evoked an ominous ambiance.[27] Rudolf Schwarz composed musical motifs to suggest the giant's movements and an "eerie even threatening" atmosphere. Lighting effects created semidarkness, highlighted by gray dawns and dusks and shadows.[28] Walter Herz played the Messiah opposite his frequent stage partner Grünbaum (as the Maharal). But the stage focus remained on the Maharal.

The production's strong points with reviewers appeared to be related to the stage atmosphere. Eloesser viewed the production as a "Gesamtkunstwerk" (synthesis of the arts) where lighting depicted scenes of misery and suffering, heightening the mood of the ghetto: "The sun shines rarely here; daylight has little to do with this play," he wrote.[29] But Wisten's objective to elicit a similar response of ambiguity from his performers may have fallen short. *The Golem* lacked "kavanah" on the part of the actors, wrote Martha Wertheimer in the *Israelitisches Familienblatt*. "Kavanah," Hebrew for "intention," refers to focused energy. Most of the actors in the production, she suggested, appeared to be estranged from the play's Jewish material, as were the audience members she sat among.[30]

The play's esoteric world may have remained emotionally off-limits to spectators, for whom the kabbalistic practices and references to legend did not resonate. In theory the play ought to have appealed more to its audiences. The exotic premise made sense: as long as the Golem's mission remained incomplete, the Messiah's coming would be premature. The Maharal had told the beggars that the Messiah was not to be summoned:

MAHARAL: Why did you have to bring him here
To let him see the face of death and danger?
What can he do for us? What should he do?
The world has not exhausted yet
Its store of cruelty, on us.[31]

The world was not ready for reparation, least of all one mystically engendered by a miracle rabbi. Kulturbund audiences had already seen this theme dramatized in *The Golden Chain* through the actions of the protagonist. They may have watched Bistritzky's take on the false mysticism and messianic ardor in *Sabbatai Zevi*. Like Jeremiah, whose predictions of bloodshed went unheeded, the young Messiah onstage in *The Golem* felt dread and entreated his companion to shield him from his visions:

YOUNG BEGGAR: Silence me. Make dumb my tongue.
Close my eyes and shut off sight.
Terror like a pall has fallen:
Fears of pogroms, Pesach night.[32]

This dramatic onstage moment in 1937 presaged the increasing horrors of the months ahead. Yet the Kulturbund *Golem* production ended without resolution. The Golem's unpredictability had rendered it a poor defense for Jewry. The imperfect creature could never become a national deliverer. Although the play ran for twenty-four performances, the muted response of Kulturbund members in the auditorium may not have met the expectations of Wisten and his team.

With his next production a month later, Wisten appealed to an audience more eager for cheerful comedy than for the weightiness of Leiwick's drama. He directed Eugène Scribe's farce *Duel of Love* (*Zweikampf der Liebe*), which had nothing to do with Jews. Spectators, preoccupied with how to manage their daily lives, were not seeking miraculous salvation. Laughter helped them. According to one *Rundschau* critic, audience members at *Duel of Love* were reportedly grateful to leave their worries behind and "enjoy an hour of true delight and relaxation" at the theatre.[33] Perhaps the reporter overemphasized the escapist pleasure of theatregoing in response to censorship.

As winter of 1937 approached, however, Kulturbund Jews had more choices for their cultural enjoyment and instruction. The Kulturbund executive committee negotiated the leasing of a large hall in the building directly next door to the main theatre. The Kulturbund-Hall opened in late November, giving Singer a versatile performance space to house Max Ehrlich's cabaret troupe. The former ballroom on the third floor at 58–59 Kommandantenstraße seated seven hundred and featured a wide podium for concerts and a stage twenty-one feet deep. At a music-filled matinee before Hanukkah that marked the official opening on 28 November, Singer served as master of ceremonies.

The Kulturbund School troupe had been offering young audiences theatre performances on a regular basis. In late November 1937 Hinzelmann's players staged the Jewish fable *The Pojaz*. Georg Hirschfeld adapted the novel by Karl Emil Franzos for the Youth Theatre. The Rhein-Ruhr Kulturbund had toured the production throughout the Rhineland during January 1937.[34] Now school audiences in Berlin could watch the play about a young orthodox Jew in nineteenth-century Galicia, who feels like an "outsider" even "inside" his shtetl. Sender wants to be an actor and leaves his shtetl to be in the theatre. The shtetl inhabitants call Sender the "Pojaz," one who makes a fool of himself for being different. Sender's quest to be different, however, results in his contracting tuberculosis. Before his death, he finds solace and reconciliation in his community.

The play opens in the village of Barnow, where a touring theatre director discovers that Sender may have potential as an actor. He must "learn German" first, the language of theatre in Galician cities. Being a Jew is not enough for Sender. He wants to be a "man of the world," as he calls it, a "Bocher" (bigshot). He struggles with his sense of Jewishness, despite his religious dress and phylacteries (*tefillin*).[35] After he secretly learns German, his rabbi curses him for it. In a plot twist, Sender wins the lottery, causing the villagers to behave differently toward him. He laments having learned German: "There is but one language! There is only Yiddish! There is only Barnow!"[36]

A subplot concerns the Rebbe's decision that the boy should marry. Two potential brides enter Sender's short life, German-speaking Malke from Czernowitz, and Jütte, the matchmaker's daughter. When Malke flees Barnow, she inspires Sender to follow. As he prepares to leave the shtetl, Sender sheds his caftan: "Now I am modern. Now I won't stand out in Czernowitz. But above all, the *payes* betray everything. [He takes the scissors and almost enraged, cuts off his sidelocks.] Away with them."[37] Although Sender dispenses with the external signs of his orthodoxy, he remains caught between his orthodoxy and his artistic vocation.

Traveling to Czernowitz, Sender finds the director, offers a frenzied recitation from *Hamlet*, and sinks "almost lifeless into a chair."[38] The dying Sender atones for his sins: "My father was a poor Schnorrer [beggar], but I am a pious Kaddish." Sender mourns, but he will be mourned with the Kaddish prayer. The play ends with the blessing "Shma Yisroel" (Hear O Israel) and the lighting of two candles.[39]

Georg Jacobsohn directed the Berlin production of *The Pojaz*, featuring Werner Hinzelmann as the rabbi and his wife, Steffi Ronau, as Jütte, with Werner Bukofzer as the teenager in "a caftan and sidelocks." Jacobsohn followed the production script: "The sidelocks do not really suit him; he gives the outward impression that he is only playing at being the Barnow Jew. Even his caftan has something artificial about it."[40] The staging juxtaposed the "joyless" world of the *Ostjude* "realistically" with the dream world of the theatre and Czernowitz. The young audience evidently came away from the performance with a better understanding of the conflict between generations. According to reviews, the teenagers responded with excitement to the "eternal tragedy of being Jewish."[41]

The Youth Theatre production highlighted the dangers of assimilation and outside influence. The play offered its audiences a distinct pedagogical message: do not forsake your Jewish roots, emphasized by the last image of lighted candles and the Hebrew prayer. Symbolically, Sender returned to his community to die and to come to terms with his origins. The play's message about the hazards of assimilation mirrored the message that Goebbels expected Schlösser and Hinkel to reinforce when they censored scripts for the Jewish stage. *The Pojaz* production showed that the threat to the community came from the protagonist's urge to leave. But the young Kulturbund audience also could identify with the teenager's rebellious yearning for freedom.[42]

While youth audiences learned about Jewish history, comedies also played throughout the 1937–1938 season. Shakespeare's *Much Ado about Nothing* (*Viel Lärm um nichts*) entertained theatregoers twenty-three times in January 1938. Wisten made sure that his production played without allusions that Hinkel could interpret as assimilatory. In the run of legal measures defining who was a pure German, Jews were identified as foreigners. Thus Wisten left out a courtier's witty observation about Benedict's whim for disguise: "a Dutch-man today, a French-man tomorrow; or in the shape of two countries at once, as a German from the waist down . . . and a Spaniard from the hip upward."[43] Such a reference to a German's sexual prowess and mixed lineage would have been considered offensive. The Jews did not have a country of their own. Any suggestion that a Jew could also be German was too risky to utter aloud, even from the mouth of a Jewish actor playing Shakespeare's Italian Don Pedro.

Hinkel clearly supported Jewish separatism, but he rejected a politically charged Jewish nationalism within Germany. The call for political emancipation among Jews had become well established by the 1930s. An increasing number of intellectuals had developed an interest in restoring a political entity in Zion.[44] By 1938 Werner Levie had already investigated the possibility of using the Kulturbund as a model for an orchestral enterprise in Palestine. Kulturbund directors and staff incorporated into their theatre programs as much thematic material about Palestine as Hinkel's office would authorize. Hinkel made it clear to Singer that the Kulturbund film series would be used primarily to disseminate information about Palestine. The films ought to encourage emigration among Jews, portray "Palestinian culture," or portray only "pure Jewish characters, played by Jewish actors."[45] These precepts applied to the theatre as well. Yet inconsistencies continued to mark the censorship process.

Wisten's February production of Ladislaus Bus-Fekete's *Cape of Good Hope* (*Kap der guten Hoffnung*) offered audiences an entertaining non-Jewish look at love, bankruptcy, and Vienna. As with the *Much Ado about Nothing* production, the censors insisted on cutting references that seemed assimilatory. Nor could the Jewish actors use humor that depicted Germans unfavorably. Omitted from Wisten's production of Bus-Fekete's play, interestingly, was the protagonist Felix's exchange with a business director, who touts his company's accident insurance. Given Nazi extortion practices in business and the intimidation of Jews, bank director Felix's retort would have been especially cheeky had it been permitted: "When a business burns down, who strives to prove that it was the owner who set it on fire, you, only you."[46] Bus-Fekete's Felix also spoke a Viennese dialect. The dialect remained more or less intact on the Kulturbund stage, although a line about a mixed-breed dog ("Foxmischling") was suppressed before production.[47]

On 11 March 1938, as the Wehrmacht moved to take over Austria, Singer directed Adolphe Adam's opera *If I Were King* (*Wenn ich König wäre*) at the Kulturbund. A simple fisherman in Goa saves a beautiful princess from drowning and dreams that he is king for a day. Fantasy and reality merge when the king brings the sleeping man to the palace. Thus ensues a romance between the princess and her savior, who live happily ever after. A reviewer praised the director for a delightful evening of moving and carefree music: "Singer wove a magic carpet from the colors and images onstage, achieving the illusion of a massive undertaking with his orchestration of details."[48] Mascha Benyakonsky sang the role of Princess Némea, and Ruth Anselm danced against lavish decor designed by her husband, Heinz Condell. The feel-good fairy tale unfolded in Berlin during evenings in March as the Nazis in Vienna pushed 170,000 Jews into a situation as desperate as the one their Berlin counterparts faced. After Kurt von Schusshnigg conceded to German military force, Goebbels could tout the results of a mock plebiscite. On 10 April 99 percent of Austrians voted "yes" to join the German Reich.

Emigration took on great urgency during spring 1938 in Germany. After the record number of 8,000 Jews emigrated to Palestine from August 1937 to March 1938, Palestine's high commissioner severely lowered the quotas for the period from April to September. Only 3,000 new emigrants from Germany would be permitted entry, with the highest numbers allotted for those with independent financial resources, workers, and students.[49] Kulturbund staff personnel scheduled more lecture events on emigration. The theatre repertoire also fostered the expediency of resettlement in Palestine. Herbert Freeden got permission to translate and adapt for the stage Shulamith Batdori's contemporary Hebrew-language *The Trial* (*Das Gericht*), about the burgeoning Zionist state.

Freeden recalled his surprise that the censors permitted the production. He had initially found the play ineffective: it was too long and largely irrelevant to a Jewish audience in Berlin. But after he reworked the script for its world premiere in May 1938, he judged the play a total success—and it played to full houses for one month. Freeden conceded long after the event: "It was the first and the last time at the Kulturbund that we performed subject matter related to current events. Events in Palestine were central to Jewish interest at the time; and we succeeded in creating a realistic picture of these timely events."[50] Agricultural resettlement by Jews in Palestine had steadily increased through the 1920s and early 1930s. Batdori wrote her "Palestine play from the year 1936" on a kibbutz amid the unrest between

Arabs and Jews. She set her play against that backdrop as Arabs attacked Jewish settlements and the British forces tried to restore order. With British troop reinforcements, the momentum of Zionist activity had lessened. By the time Freeden readied the play for its 1938 production at the Kulturbund, the Peel Commission Report had instigated controversy and conflict in Palestine about partitioning the land.[51]

The Trial portrays the struggle of the Arabs, the Jews, and the British. The action develops in two time frames. First is the compressed time frame of one night, 23 July 1936, when Arabs set fire to a wooded area near a settlement and Jews take up a defense of the area. Second is action that breaks linear time, going backward and forward. The omniscient narrator addresses the audience and interacts with the characters: a Jewish settler (Chaim), an Arab policeman (Mahmud-Ali), and a British soldier (Tom Lucky). The middle scenes play as flashbacks, where the Narrator summons the dead characters to show what led to their deaths in Palestine. The play ends with the sons of the dead men onstage, representing the hope and future of Palestine.

Freeden spoke at a Sunday matinee program, "Living Palestine," that preceded *The Trial* premiere on 8 May 1938. He compared the life of Jews in the Diaspora to an existence always in the "spotlight." His presentation concluded that art's task was to improve people.[52] The ideas expressed in Batdori's play represented for him the beginning of a Jewish reality, in which Jews could flourish. Incorporating poetry recitation and music with an "Oriental" timbre, the program affirmed support for Zionist settlements in Palestine. The opera chorale performed. Benyakonsky sang a Hebrew love song and a Yemenite dance melody. And Herbert Grünbaum, cast as a "pioneer," recited poetry by Rachel Bluwstein and Hayyim Bialik in German and Hebrew.

The speakers and performers invited the audience to participate in a new world of hope and promise. Upon entering the theatre, audience members filed through the theatre lobby, adorned with photographs of Palestinian landscapes. As they took their seats in the auditorium, they saw that a trench had been constructed before the curtain, to the left of the orchestra. To the right, steps led downward. In his opening remarks, Singer told those assembled that their proximity to the actors would draw the audience into the action.[53] Condell's stage settings combined film projections of Palestine as the background along with the freestanding wooden barracks of a Jewish settlement. The mix of three-dimensional constructions with film footage enhanced the atmosphere and made the Palestinian landscape seem real.

Near the barracks and the trench, theatregoers could see a barbed wire fence and a forest.

Fritz Wisten directed the play in six scenes. He also played the Narrator. The cast included Alfred Berliner as Chaim; Gina Friedmann, Martin Brandt, Ruth Anselm, and Herbert Grünbaum as settlers; Hans-Karl Rosenberg (Sabbatai Zevi) as Tom Lucky and Jenny Schaffer-Bernstein as his mother (in a flashback scene); and Alfred Lichtenstein as Mahmud-Ali. Wisten wove together in documentary style the stage snapshots of the daily fears and dangers of the Palestinian reality. The play began within a framing scene where a huge radio opened to reveal the broadcast room of the radio station. The Narrator's voice on the radio reported the violence of that July day in 1936 and news of strengthened regiments and Arab armies at large: "A police station has just been attacked. An armed and shooting group of Arabs has disappeared near the settlement of Ramat Haamakim."[54] Some armed men sit in the barracks around a radio. It is clear that a siege is underway: rockets could be launched, and the men wait to defend their land. Bad news of fire attacks comes through on the telephone. Shots ring out, and the scene opens in a glaring red light focused on settlers' Trench Number 8.

This scene established the contemporary problem for Jews in the Diaspora, as actors Rosenberg (Tom Lucky) and Berliner (Chaim) debated why the Jews were building settlements:

> TOM: Why? Life was not good for you over there?
>
> CHAIM: No, life for the Jews isn't good anywhere; because they have no home.
>
> TOM: And here?
>
> CHAIM: We are building a home here.
>
> TOM: But things are not going well for you here. The Arabs are attacking you. They say that the land belongs to them. And they are taking the land away from you.
>
> CHAIM: There is enough [land] here, for *us* and for *them*.[55]

Chaim and Tom and the Arab policeman are killed shortly after this scene.

As the Narrator, Wisten presented background information on Palestine and acted as arbiter for the three men, facilitating their public admission of guilt in the Palestinian unrest. He interrogated them about the dilemma facing the three factions in Palestine. The Narrator stood at the side of the stage and addressed the audience: "Are you alone? It's a good thing that we can speak without witnesses. Just so no one disturbs us, I will close this curtain."[56] He reopened the black curtain to restart the action. Then in the middle scenes he called on the dead to relive for the audience the portion of their lives which led to their deaths.

Wisten used special lighting effects to signal the flashback sequences. When he opened the curtain on the Arab's home, Mahmud-Ali reenacted the day before the battle that killed him. The audience witnessed the Arab point of view as Mahmud-Ali sought to avenge the killing of Arabs by Jews. The Narrator rewound the action seven years for the scene with Tom Lucky, when a recruitment advertisement for the British Army led him to the Middle East. Then the Narrator pushed time ahead to 1933. The newly arrived settler Chaim, sick with malaria, showed his dream of replenishing Palestinian land with Jews.[57] The actors relied on soft and accentuated vocal patterns and facial work to relay the sense of another time and place for the flashback scenes. In the final scene at Trench Number 8, red light reflected three corpses. As the dead were taken away, the next generation appeared: Gideon, Mustapha, and Bill Lucky.

Reviewers agreed that the play's content moved the audience and had meaning for them. But Weltmann believed that the Narrator detracted from the production's aesthetic quality.[58] The play framed an ethical discussion among the dead men on whether they were responsible for one another's death. They died for what their worlds symbolized: life (settler), order (soldier), and Allah (policeman). Their comments in the interrogation scene led to their exoneration before the audience. The play's open-endedness left the audience to ponder how the next generation of Arabs, Jews, and colonialists would shape the future of Palestine.

Weltmann linked the play's last words, "The future belongs to our youth," to the unresolved dilemma "in the historical tragedy of Palestine that makes the Peel Report so unsettling."[59] The Peel inquiry covered many months of discord. After the commission released the results in spring 1938, anti-Semitism increased across Europe and the British restricted immigration for Jews to Palestine. Even avid Zionists could no longer expect Palestine to absorb the new floods of emigrants from Europe. As is evident in the new commission's quotas for 1938, the number of Jews permitted into Palestine shrank.[60]

Given the hindsight that Kulturbund audiences had in 1938 about the actual turmoil in Palestine in 1936, *The Trial* provided a somber look at a significant problem for Jews and their struggle for independence in Palestine when the British and the Arabs rejected the Peel Report recommendations for land partition. Subsequent calls for separate zones for Jews, Arabs, and the British also came to naught. The Kulturbund Jews could not transcend time like the Narrator in Batdori's play. They could not know that the quest for political unity for Jews in Palestine would wait until 1948. Their "non-ending applause" at *The Trial*—and their praise for the actors—showed that the reality of present-day Palestine deeply affected them as they "stood like a wall in the orchestra at the end of the play, stunned" by what they had witnessed.[61]

The promise of hope for Berlin's Jews still existed into the summer of 1938. Obstacles increasingly hindered their path toward achieving release, however, at home and abroad. After *The Trial*'s success, Batdori contacted Wisten to thank him for producing her play.[62] Yet Hinkel's new series of general performance bans that summer and in the fall of 1938 thwarted further correspondence. Hinkel banned all performances by Jews across Germany from 18 to 27 June except those at Berlin's Kulturbund. A decrease in Kulturbund membership forced Singer to reduce his actors' summer salaries.[63] He managed to produce light comedies by Georges Courteline (July 1938) and Ladislaus Fodor (August). But new laws curtailing Jewish involvement in German society affected the rest of the fifth playing season, 1937–1938. As autumn of 1938 neared, the Nazis mandated extra identification measures for Jews. They were required to register themselves—and all of their property—with the government authorities.[64]

The fifth playing season at the Kulturbund closed in September 1938 with another play by Ibsen, *Ghosts* (*Gespenster*). The leadership's decision to produce Ibsen two years in a row allowed the theatre to showcase its commitment to high-caliber drama that distinctly revealed the community's European heritage. Yet Julius Bab's choice to stage a second tragedy by Ibsen a year after *Pillars of Society* also reflected an increasing bleakness that enveloped the community. The play showed the inexorable unraveling of a family secret: Osvald Alving's inherited venereal disease. Bab revised the script to make the language more colloquial and to heighten the pathos for Wisten's production, starring Walter Herz as Oswald and Jenny Schaffer-Bernstein as Mrs. Alving. The play's grim content juxtaposed the suffocating darkness of destiny and Oswald's yearning for light, space, and freedom.

The physical setting reinforced a feeling of claustrophobia in the production. In all three acts, one room with the partially visible outdoors showed "steady rain," "thick mist," and darkness. "The sun—the sun," calls Osvald in the play's last lines as he sits motionless and blank-eyed, succumbing to his fate and to blindness.[65] While Leo Hirsch thought the play a worthwhile choice for the Kulturbund repertoire, a reviewer for the *Rundschau* found *Ghosts* too depressing for the times: "We need solace and relaxation. That's the function of theatre in this phase of our lives. This failed. The [play's] battle of ideas absorbed almost all of the energy."[66] Singer recognized that the press generally applauded the production; but the majority of the audience "rejected the play's tragic tendencies."[67] Metaphorically speaking, syphilis as an inescapable scourge brings to mind the way the Nazis determined inherited "race." The charting of the Nuremberg Laws and the validation of a state-instituted anti-Semitism provided an eerie backdrop for the Kulturbund production of *Ghosts*.

Singer announced a new public relations campaign with publicity events in September. He hoped to expand the Kulturbund by 1,000 to 1,500 new members. The organization's membership had decreased by 4,000 members in one year. This meant that actors would have to settle for last-minute contracts and reduced wages for the sixth playing season.[68] Members of Singer's creative staff had begun to take leaves of absence. The chief designer, Heinz Condell, left on a six-week trip to the United States in mid-September. His wife, Ruth Anselm, did not accompany him. She awaited a visa for emigration to the United States. According to her, when she told Singer of her plan to emigrate, he asked her to leave the Kulturbund because someone with her viewpoint did not belong there. But perhaps Singer found out about her work for the resistance during 1937–1938. After her arrest by the Gestapo, Anselm's work at the Kulturbund may have become a liability for Singer. Her last acting role at the Kulturbund was in *The Trial*.[69]

For those left among Kulturbund audiences, solace lay in the promise of emigration to a new land. One of the scheduled publicity events to attract new members was an opera about Palestine, *The Pioneers* (*He Chalutz*). Chemjo Vinaver directed Jacob Weinberg's opera, starring Mascha Benyakonsky. Benyakonsky recalled the event at a Berlin synagogue as a "concert . . . in German except that I sang the aria from 'Song of Songs' in Hebrew with the orchestra."[70] A reviewer praised the "inner passion" of her voice, pointing to the "magnificence of a cantilena that we sense as Jewish."[71] Audience members were encouraged to join the pioneers of Palestine and join the Kulturbund. Would-be émigrés also enjoyed a theatrical snapshot of Palestine by attending the opera.

In Germany the outlook for peace appeared bleak. By mid-September

Hitler's Nuremberg Rally speech signaled his plan to grant Germans in the Sudetenland self-determination. While European leaders tried to avoid a confrontation with Hitler, German troops plundered Jewish and Czech shops in the Sudetenland. By the month's end Neville Chamberlain and Édouard Daladier appeased Hitler by signing onto the Munich Agreement, which gave Hitler control of the Sudetenland region. The Nazi takeover of Czech land coincided with the High Holidays in 1938 and with the last opera that Singer would direct for the Kulturbund.

On 1 October 1938, the day of the premiere for Verdi's *Rigoletto*, Singer commemorated five years of theatre since the first *Nathan* production.[72] He reminded his artistic staff: "We have made difficult years bearable through work and success; we have assuaged a lot of suffering and want by keeping our artistic standards high. . . . We ourselves have achieved . . . a sense of self in the artistic, the human, and in the Jewish realms. It has not been in vain."[73] In mid-October Singer left Berlin for a six- to seven-week information trip to the United States, where he embarked on a university lecture tour. A lawyer for the administrative council approved Werner Levie to be acting artistic manager of the Kulturbund during Singer's absence. Wisten continued to lead the Acting and Directing Division. Just before Singer left for America, Wisten begged him not to forsake his "second child," the Kulturbund, which needed strong guidance. Singer knew that his cultural enterprise faced insurmountable risks in Nazi Germany. Part of his reason for going abroad was to see whether he could find a sponsor for the Kulturbund organization and its artists. His idea to transfer the whole enterprise to American soil, however, fell on deaf ears.

In 1938 Kurt Singer emphasized his ongoing "compromise" for the Kulturbund to offer "instructive" theatre art that affected the "Jewish heart." This specific Jewish art would be defined by its ability to convey a "feeling of home, anchored in the language of the play." But Singer also voiced his commitment to a theatre whose core humanist values transcended religious faith, which was not exclusive to plays written by Jews that centered on their plight. He indicated the Kulturbund's success in "gathering audiences around us, artists among us, and instilling a feeling in us without thinking of this as simply an experiment—without pulling away from the literary and dialectical bond to a century of culture."[74]

Singer conceded that the theatre produced by the Kulturbund through 1938 was necessarily the "middle road." Yet by choosing to make concessions to others about the programs that the organization offered, the artistic leader maintained a balance of vital universal ideals and kept the support of liberal, assimilationist, and Zionist Jews. He put it this way: "We built a temple for the stage and for music next to the temple of religion we achieved good standing in upholding truth, beauty, art, faith, community, and stayed true . . . to God. We have understood the signs of the times without letting them take us by surprise."[75] Nazi storm troopers and their government-endorsed pogrom, however, would temporarily interrupt all activities at the Berlin theatre.

Singer was still in the United States in early November when the events of Reichskristallnacht not only took Jews across Germany by surprise but shook them to the core. He began his journey homeward even though people advised him to stay in the United States. He resolved to return to his Kulturbund to be there in "the hour of greatest need." Determined not to leave the Kulturbund in the lurch, he decided that he could not remain "a private citizen on safe ground."[76] But by the time his ship docked in Rotterdam, he realized with a crushing recognition that the Kulturbund could not last. He could not see how in the short term Jewish actors, musicians, and artists would be able to build an ensemble of quality. Torn between his commitment to the organization that he founded in his beloved country and his anguish about whether he could save the Kulturbund from imminent decline, Singer decided to stay in the Netherlands. Life inside and outside the theatre would never be the same after he left the Kulturbund and Germany.

PART THREE
APPEASEMENT AND UNRAVELING
1938–1943

7 ASSAULT

THE VISE TIGHTENS

1938–1939

Jewish religious and cultural life suffered once again on 27 October 1938 when Hans Hinkel issued an official ban that affected the Kulturbund: "I hereby forbid *immediately through and including 26 November 1938* all Jewish events taking place under the auspices of the Reich Association of Jewish Kulturbunds. . . . Solely exempt from the ban are all *theatre* performances of the Reich Association of Jewish Cultural Leagues."[1] The news of the general ban reached Werner Levie, who served as acting artistic manager during Singer's absence. Final performances of *Rigoletto* and of Max Ehrlich's cabaret revue *Mixed Cocktail* proceeded as scheduled. Rehearsals for the new season's first play also went forward as planned. Merton (Horace Emerton) Hodge's light comedy *The Wind and the Rain* (*Regen und Wind*) was scheduled to open on 2 November 1938.

The cheery romance under Wisten's direction temporarily transported audiences to a Scottish university town.[2] Hodge's play follows several medical students as they mature, face professional examinations, and fall in love. The action spans roughly five years, the time that it takes for the protagonist to pass his medical examinations. The cast featured Lilly Kann, Alfred Berliner, Walter Herz, and Ruth Mannheimer as well as Elfriede Borodkin, hired from the Hamburg Kulturbund, and twenty-four-year-old Berthold (Bert) Segall, who had performed in *The Trial*. Even while several actors awaited exit visas to emigrate, they prepared for a production run with projected performances for 6, 7, 10, and 12 November.[3]

The Nazi government had expelled between 15,000 and 17,000 Polish Jews from Germany on 28 October 1938. Among those expelled were the parents of Herschel Grynspan, who would shoot minister Ernst vom Rath on Sunday, 7 November 1938. On the morning of 8 November the international media first reported the assassination of the German diplomat in Paris.[4] Herbert Freeden and Fritz Wisten were conducting morning rehearsals at the Berlin Kulturbund for a German version of Mendele Moykher Sforim's Yiddish-language *Benjamin . . . wohin?* (*Where To, Benjamin?*). Wisten interrupted the first scene run-through to take a telephone call from Levie. Levie had just received a telegraphed order from the Reich Ministry that all cultural activity must come to a standstill. As a follow-up, Hinkel informed Levie: "I have (1) notified all Kulturbund branches that with immediate effect the publication of the *Kulturbundblätter* is forbidden until further notice. (2) I have with immediate effect canceled all of the presently running events for this evening in the Jewish Kulturbund branches within the Reich-district; and I have informed them that the events are forbidden, until further notice."[5] Wisten immediately sent everyone home.

The news of vom Rath's death propelled a series of actions culminating in the Reichskristallnacht. Mascha Benyakonsky saw the Nazis smash windows of Jewish shops on the Kurfürstendamm while passersby watched. No one protested or stole anything. The Gestapo rounded up Jewish men at night and arrested them. On the evening of 9 November the government-endorsed pogrom against Jews and their property began in earnest. Bert Segall, who played the protagonist in *The Wind and the Rain*, went into hiding for several days, as did some of his fellow artists.[6] The Gestapo detained Wisten and other actors on 10 November and sent them to the Sachsenhausen camp under "protective custody."[7]

On 14 November Hinkel lifted the ban on Jewish cultural events, ordering the Berlin Kulturbund to resume performances and rehearsals as soon as possible. His directive could hardly go into effect, however, as long as Wisten stayed under arrest.[8] Hinkel negotiated with Levie, requesting a list of Kulturbund artist-detainees in order to secure their speedy release.[9] The following day Wisten returned from the camp with his head shaven and a severe case of pneumonia. Segall had avoided arrest. Upon returning home, he received a signed letter from Hinkel that identified him as an "active" member of the Kulturbund theatre. The letter effectively granted him protection, directing him to reappear at the theatre for rehearsals. It took almost two weeks, however, for Wisten to recover from his ordeal and return to the theatre.

The Kristallnacht pogroms shattered the ideal of a healthy organic theatre art for Jews in Germany. The membership of the Berlin Kulturbund dwindled from 17,500 members at the start of the 1937–1938 playing season to 13,500 members at the beginning of the 1938–1939 season. By early November that number shrank to 12,500 members. The material situation for the Jews had so worsened that the organization's executive committee reduced the membership fees from Reichsmark 2.85 to 1.85, and those fees would only be collected for theatre productions; voluntary donations of Reichsmark .075 were suggested per concert.[10] Meanwhile the race to emigrate further depleted the membership rosters as well as the number of musicians and actors. The theatre and opera ensemble had lost many significant artists: in addition to Singer's absence, Heinz Condell had left Berlin permanently—but not with his wife. He had written Levie from abroad that he would not be returning to the Kulturbund. Nor did Anselm work at the theatre anymore. Benyakonsky was en route for the United States. Despite the weakening of the theatre's artistic staff, Hinkel expected the Kulturbund theatre to continue its performances.

Although Hinkel's protection may well have been in place, Hodge's *The Wind and the Rain* played to an almost empty house when performances resumed on 22 November 1938.[11] Technical director Hans Sondheimer had replaced Condell as set and sound designer. Wisten orchestrated the production details to produce an intimate chamber play and streamlined the plot to highlight the relationships between characters.[12] But the aftermath of Kristallnacht had severely altered the mood at the Kulturbund. Morale remained low at the theatre. Singer was in the Netherlands. What Levie called a "material crisis," especially with Singer's absence and the departure of others, left those still employed with a deepening sense of uncertainty and anxiety. No one knew whether they would build the theatre up or close it down.[13] The Ministry of Propaganda decreed that the *Jüdisches Nachrichtenblatt* would be the only sanctioned newspaper for Jews. Its first issue appeared on 23 November 1938, announcing the "Reich Association of Jewish Cultural Leagues' resumption of its activities." In order to secure a complete roster of all existing artists, the Reich Association requested all active Kulturbund artists to register again.[14] A new phase in the Kulturbund theatre had begun.

Hinkel meanwhile asked Levie to persuade Singer to return to Germany and to the helm of the Kulturbund. He took the unusual step of dispatching Levie to Amsterdam on 24 November to convince Singer of his duty to the theatre. But three days of talks between the small Kulturbund delegation and Singer came to naught. From his self-imposed exile, Singer informed Hinkel of his disillusionment about a renewed Jewish cultural life in Germany.[15] He saw no possibility of maintaining a quality cultural enterprise, he told the theatre's Jewish leadership in December. "I could not . . . lift what is sinking," he wrote to his former colleagues, explaining his decision first to return from the United States then to stay in the Netherlands. He could only be "a partner in sorrow, not a leader. Maybe you all can right the sinking ship."[16] In fact, Singer felt that "liquidation" was the best answer for the Kulturbund in Germany now that its artistic and economic future was "equal to zero."[17]

Upon Levie's return to Berlin, Hinkel officially appointed him as general manager of the Kulturbund in Germany and made it clear that "the Kulturbund work must continue."[18] Despite his publicly announced belief that his theatre plan could no longer succeed, Singer believed that the Kulturbund's current administrative team could carry on a semblance of what he had begun there. If Wisten led the acting and directing division, Bab kept the lecture department active, Rudolf Schwarz and Berthold Sander directed music, and Sondheimer supervised the scenic and technical work of the theatre, Singer considered himself well replaced, he informed his colleagues.[19] During the time Levie served as the Kulturbund's artistic manager (November 1938–August 1939), he and Fritz Wisten, who would replace him in 1939, tried to maintain their original objective for the theatre.

Even before Kristallnacht, Wisten, assisted by Freeden, had prepared a production script for the first Jewish-themed production of the season, *Where To, Benjamin?* It premiered on 15 December. Hermann Sinsheimer adapted the play script from the work of Mendele Moykher Sforim.[20] Sinsheimer devised a framing prologue and epilogue for the play, in which a book salesman (Mendele) and his companion Senderle reenact their story of the Third Benjamin. The peddlers become characters in their story-within-a-story as Benjamin seeks the ten lost tribes of Israel. Benjamin and Senderle thus travel through Russian villages with satirical names like Parasitingen (Parasite-Village) and Dummdorf (Dumbtown). There they encounter adventure in a local market, in a dream, and among soldiers in the tsarist army. The epilogue caps their return as itinerant peddlers, seeking the Messiah.

Wisten transferred the East European Jewish play to the Kulturbund stage, which Sondheimer had adorned with colorful sets representing the pages of a book. The audience watched the two main characters in their picaresque quest. When the Messiah comes, Senderle tells his companion: "All the poor Yids will be taken care of." Benjamin responds, "And that's why we two walk and wander."[21] Despite the religious references to a Messiah and

12. ***Where To, Benjamin?*** **(December 1938): Alfred Berliner (*left*) as Benjamin and Rudolf Müller (*right*) as Senderle. Akademie der Künste, Berlin, FWA 20.53.648, photographer unknown.**

Jerusalem, Wisten and his dramaturgical team instructed actors to make the dialogue comprehensible to the audience. This meant that the actors should not "Jewify" (*jüdeln*) the language by preventing an overinflection of the Yiddish-tinged dialogue.[22] Alfred Berliner as "Benjamin" or Mendele and the newly hired Rudolf Müller as Senderle were adept at comic timing and improvisation. Müller proved himself a superb comic foil to Berliner. Müller's affecting onstage physical and vocal presence showed his "skill, maturity, heart, and personality."[23]

With the production of *Where To, Benjamin?* Wisten appealed to audiences by focusing on the comic spirit of the play. At intermission and in the theatre house, visitors could be "one big family," as the reviewer of the *Nachrichtenblatt* described.[24] The clowns in *kippas* (skullcaps) and worn coats on the Kulturbund stage personified wandering Jews, but Wisten was careful not to caricature the East European Jew (*Ostjude*). Hinkel, however, could tout the production's shtetl ambience as a Jewish theatre performance that successfully separated Jewish culture from German art. By December 1938 Hinkel was serving as an "intermediary" between the Ministry of Propaganda and the elite national security divisions, the SS-SD (Sicherheitsstaffel and Sicherheitsdienst), whose goal was to purge the "Jewish presence" from German life.[25]

Hinkel tightened his grip on the Kulturbund. Just weeks after the theatre reopened, he informed Levie that his recent "oral directive" (16 December) would "dissolve the Reichsverband Jewish Kulturbunds e.V. and those cultural organizations in the Reich of all kinds linked to it by 31 December 1938." The sole exemption would be the Kulturbund Berlin, which—after another name change—would become the catchall organization for the newly shaped Jewish Kulturbund in Germany.[26] The dissolution of the Reich Association of Jewish Cultural Leagues further consolidated all managerial and administrative power by 1939 in the Berlin Kulturbund. It would have four main divisions: Theatre and Music, Lecture Series, Film, and Publications (including a publishing house for books and the sole newspaper).[27] Hinkel could more efficiently supervise the Jews and their cultural programs by keeping the Berlin core organization intact and responsible for all Jewish cultural activity across the Reich.

Hinkel's reorganization of the Jewish association in late December 1938 made the Kulturbund the sole centralized organization for all Jewish cultural affairs in Germany. Artists from the Cologne and Hamburg theatre branches formed a small touring troupe, based in Berlin, that would travel to Jewish communities in Cologne, Hamburg, Dresden, Leipzig, Breslau, and Frankfurt. Meanwhile, all Jewish citizens had to register with the police for the mandatory photo identification card (*Kennkarte*) by 31 December 1938. Furthermore, beginning on 1 January 1939, government restrictions officially banned all Jewish newspapers except for the *Nachrichtenblatt*, edited by Leo Kreindler. The newspaper coverage of Jewish matters appeared only within these pages, which were subjected to censorship prior to publication. Arthur Eloesser of the *Rundschau* had left Germany. Hugo Lachmanski, formerly of the *C.-V.-Zeitung*, now joined Julius Bab and Leo Hirsch, who reported on the Kulturbund for the *Nachrichtenblatt*.

Levie appealed to the cultural needs of his community as best as he could in his new capacity as artistic director and general manager of the Berlin theatre. The establishment of a film studio in the Kulturbundsaal next door to the theatre provided Jews with a new outlet for entertainment. Levie also engaged actively in public relations efforts to convince the community of the continued importance of the Kulturbund in their lives. Because the organization had fewer members, he had to promote the prospective theatre and music events. Together with Wisten, he determined to use the winter program of 1939 to lure new members, scheduling several modern plays which exploited the rags-to-riches premise of fairy tales with a magical twist. One such play opened on 9 January 1939: Ferenc Molnár's *The Good Fairy* (*Die Fee*, 1930), under the direction of the comedian and cabaret emcee Max Ehrlich. The modern fairy tale centered on a movie theatre usherette, who used a rich industrialist's money to support a poor lawyer she claimed was her husband.[28] Perhaps the early February production of Shakespeare's *The Winter's Tale* (*Das Wintermärchen*), however, best illustrated the theatre staff's desire to amuse the audience while offering an allegorical story for solace during difficult times.

"A sad tale's best for winter," the young prince Maximilius tells his mother as Shakespeare's play unfolds. The play pivots on a tyrant's paranoia and deadly jealousies, when King Leontes believes that his pregnant wife, Hermione (Jenny Schaffer-Bernstein), has committed adultery with his one-time friend Polixenes, king of Bohemia (played by Martin Brandt). Out of fear of illegitimacy Leontes throws his queen into prison, where she bears a daughter, Perdita. Hermione is then tried and condemned—and her newborn taken from her. Destruction and death mark the first three acts, culminating in a deadly storm that decimates a ship's crew on Shakespeare's imaginary Bohemian sea coast. Sixteen years later redemption rights the course of events: Leontes is absolved; his wife miraculously revives from a statue made in her likeness; the parents reunite with their lost daughter; the kings mend their friendship; and Perdita will marry the prince of Bohemia.

In production, Wisten used Bab's adaptation of Dorothea Tieck's translation to make credible such supernatural elements as the figure of Father Time; a wild bear character; a clown (played by Max Ehrlich) who spoke in riddles; and a statue of Hermione that came to life. Yet the Kulturbund's *Winter's Tale* defied classic fairy-tale expectations. Wisten did not cast his king in traditional fashion. Rudolf Müller as Leontes did not look the fairy-tale part at all. His "stocky," medium build and "heavy head on a short neck" hardly appeared kinglike.[29] But according to Leo Hirsch, the actor exhibited great energetic force and fury as he expressed the inner conflict of Leontes.[30] Bab also thought that Müller projected a powerful kingly demeanor through his "astonishing" vocal and physical range of action, which gripped the spectators' attention.[31] Jenny Schaffer-Bernstein performed her role as queen regally and with restraint. Steffi Hinzelmann (Ronau) played the role of Perdita, with Hans-Karl Rosenberg as her love, Florizel.

Wisten heightened the play's elements of levity and the fantastic in production, perhaps at the expense of the underlying concerns of illegitimacy, interbreeding, and the blending of social classes. Bab and Wisten had carefully adapted Shakespeare's scenes in the shepherd's garden to avoid altogether Perdita's banter on breeding and cross-breeding plants.[32] Overt references to foreign bastard children in *The Winter's Tale* would have been viewed by censors as an assimilatory attempt by Jews to defile the Aryan race. Significantly, the director omitted the exchange between Polixenes and Perdita about her garden's lack of cross-bred flowers (referred to as "nature's bastards": lines 80 ff.). Shakespeare's Polixenes wants the lovely shepherdess to make the garden rich in "gillyvor" flowers but not to call them bastards. He champions the skill of the gardener who can "marry / A gentler scion to the wildest stock / And make conceive a bark of a baser kind / By bud of nobler race. This is an art / Which does mend nature—change it rather—but / The art itself is nature."[33]

Wisten knew that Jewish actors must not utter such references to cross-breeding, even on the Jewish stage. Tieck's translation included the botanical allusion to breeding, with "Stamm" as "trunk" or "stock," punning on the words for "breed" and "race." But Wisten saw to it that his production would not include Perdita's refusal to cross-breed beautiful flowers with lesser stock. Gone from the production were her words about her low status and unavailability to breed with the young man (Doricles) she knows to be Prince Florizel. Her ironic speeches would mask a provocative discourse on pedigree while referring to acts of intermarriage and sex between people of unequal status. Although in Shakespeare's tale the would-be lovers turn out to be of the same class at the end of the play, directors at the Kulturbund knew that they could not even suggest assimilation on their stage. The play's allegorical plot line and its themes of physical dislocation nonetheless lent the production a timely significance for spectators.

Leo Hirsch concluded his review of the *Winter's Tale* production by alluding to the comfort and joy that an audience might take from the performance: "We must believe in the possibility of a happy ending and in the reality of the fairy tale's end," he wrote.[34] But as the Kulturbund stage crew dismantled the sets for Shakespeare's make-believe Bohemian coast, a wave of emigration from Berlin and its theatre accompanied the end of the production run. Even Bab had recognized the growing futility of his efforts at the Kulturbund. He left Germany in February 1939, continuing to file columns about the Kulturbund and its actors for the *Jüdisches Nachrichtenblatt* from Paris. Max Ehrlich scheduled several farewell cabaret performances in March before he too left Berlin for good. Werner Levie's wife and children traveled on the same boat as Ehrlich to the Netherlands, not long after German troops marched into Czechoslovakia on "this blizzardy day of spring," as William L. Shirer reported in his diary on 15 March 1939.[35] Moravia and the real Bohemia had become a protectorate of the German Reich. On 15 March the British colonial minister in Palestine proposed publicly that 75,000 Jews would be permitted to resettle in Palestine over the next five years. But the Jews and Arabs would swiftly reject his proposal.

During the spring of 1939 Wisten's penchant for the real in fairy tales and the make-believe in real life may have affected his repertoire choices. The Kulturbund had already produced the popular authors Molnár, Bus-Fekete, and Fodor and the composer Emmerich Kálmán; their romantic tales set in Vienna, Paris, and Budapest were acclaimed by audiences, who recognized familiar aspects of the milieu depicted in those plays.[36] At the theatre on Kommandantenstraße Berthold Sander directed Verdi's *Traviata* throughout March. The theatre's touring troupe took Wisten's 1937 light-hearted production of Scribe's *Duel of Love* to communities across Germany. By April 1939 the centralized Reich Association of Jews in Germany had absorbed almost all Jewish organizations within its bureaucratic domain. The Kulturbund was exempt, as was the Jewish Agency for Palestine. Yet even these organizations maintained ties to the Reich Association, which Rabbi Leo Baeck continued to lead. Laws now required Jews to notify the Reich Association in order to apply for community welfare programs; to register possessions for "de-Judaization"; and for all matters related to emigration.

Emigration remained the overwhelming concern among Jews in Berlin. Twice a week the *Nachrichtenblatt* front page headlined ongoing attempts by the British high commissioner in Palestine to increase the quota for Jews to resettle there. The Reich Association warned Jews not to bypass the proper bureaucratic channels if they wanted to cross the German border or they would be sent back to Germany. In these circumstances the Kulturbund staged a modern fable that premiered 13 April 1939. Wisten's production of J. B. Priestley's *People at Sea* (*Menschen auf See*; 1937) in Leo Hirsch's translation signaled a far bleaker undercurrent than in Wisten's production of *The Winter's Tale*. For the action in Priestley's drama unravels aboard a ship somewhere on "Middle American Seas."[37]

People at Sea opens on a wrecked drifting ship with nine passengers and three crew members who have just survived an explosion and near-disaster. The passengers include a professor of philosophy, who maintains that reality is just an illusion; the writer Valentine Avon, a drunk; and his former lover, a has-been actress, Diana Lismore. One passenger, Karl Velburg, is stateless. He has been imprisoned several times for stealing passports. He calls himself a "nothing," for he has no identity or citizenship papers.[38] In act II the ship is still adrift, but the crew has made contact with a cruiser hours ahead of them. When a sailor tries to take over the boat, hitting a passenger over the head with an iron bar, the professor shoots the sailor.

In the final act, as their predicament worsens, the passengers reveal more about themselves and their illusions. Several people have died, including Lismore's maid, Miriam. She and Velburg committed suicide by jumping off the ship. The cruiser arrives to save the remaining passengers. Valentine recognizes his ruin. Diana, who has kept her illusions intact through a narcotic haze, angrily stamps on her prescription pills. In the final stage image the professor tears up his philosophical treatise.

A new designer, Egon Marcus, constructed the shipboard settings with assistance from his young apprentice, Hanna Litten. Alfred Berliner as the professor and Jenny Schaffer-Bernstein as the histrionic Lismore led the cast. Two new performers from Hamburg and Vienna joined the ensemble in time to show off their talent in the production: Fritz Melchior as Valentine and Theophil Menu as Captain Boyne. Schaffer-Bernstein relied on her considerable range to alternate hysteria with paranoia. Fritz Grünne played the desperate romantic Velburg opposite Gerda Klein-Weissmann's Miriam.

The audience members at the performances of *People at Sea* had to draw their own allusions to real life. They could recognize in Priestley's dislocated characters their own uncertain futures. Wisten omitted from the production one potentially sensitive interchange about war. When Diana Lismore remarked to her lover, "The World War has been over for some time," Valentine quipped, "Do you know this for a fact?"[39] The war in question was World War I; but in the buildup to a second war Valentine's response could not have been spoken on the Jewish stage.[40] In late April 1939 it was unclear whether Hitler would go to war; but he had denounced a long-standing pact with Poland and made clear his desire to reclaim Danzig as German. Priestley believed that he had captured the pulse of the times in his play, claiming how relevant the content was to a "tragic period like the present."[41]

Priestley's play contrasted the outside (real) world with the interior world of his characters. The play's juxtaposition of illusion and reality may have taken on extra intensity as the Kulturbund audience members faced reality at home that spring of 1939. The Jewish newspaper regularly presented refugee reports from Jews in Asia, Australia, South America, the United States, and Palestine. The serial feature "English for Beginners" aimed to help those seeking to emigrate. These reports appeared along with reviews for the Kulturbund production of *People at Sea*. Reviewers omitted from these analyses, however, obvious parallels to the Jews, for whom life in Germany had become a limbo. Nor was reference made to the scores of Jews seeking passage from Germany. Instead the reviewers focused on Priestley's characters and their common crisis at sea.[42]

People at Sea eerily presaged the real-life circumstances of passenger ships such as the S.S. *St. Louis*, whose Jewish refugees were rejected entry at ports in Havana, Cuba, and Miami, Florida, only a month later in May 1939. Strict immigration rules would block safe haven for the refugees.[43] Since his incarceration at Sachsenhausen, Fritz Wisten had begun to think about "jumping ship" and leaving Germany. He had applied to emigrate to Britain. At the same time, he gathered papers to send to the United States as a backup option for relocation.[44] In the meantime, however, he worked with Werner Levie to keep the theatre going. This required him to choose plays that could be performed by the actors who remained at the Kulturbund. He arranged a quick repertoire substitution in May, for example, when he switched plays at the last minute so that one of his best actors, Alfred Berliner, would reenact a role that he had already performed. Wisten substituted the comedy *XYZ* by Klabund (Alfred Henschke) just five days before its opening on 10 May. Wisten also got more experience managing the theatre when Levie took a two-week trip in late May and signed over temporary control of the Kulturbund to him.[45]

During the summer season of 1939 Kulturbund audiences could choose to attend romance and light comedies. Although Wisten believed in ensemble acting, the repertoire was increasingly dominated by actors such as Berliner and Hinzelmann, who was the leading actress in romantic comedy. Now that youth audiences attended whatever the ensemble offered on the main stage, Hinzelmann took on new acting roles. She impersonated Countess Y in *XYZ* and the lower-class hat-check girl Mariette in Fodor's modern fable *Fairy Tale of Justice* (*Märchen von der Gerechtigkeit*) under Wisten's direction (premiered on 11 June 1939).[46] Fodor's play in five scenes unfolds in a Parisian night club at three o'clock in the morning as a drunken aristo-

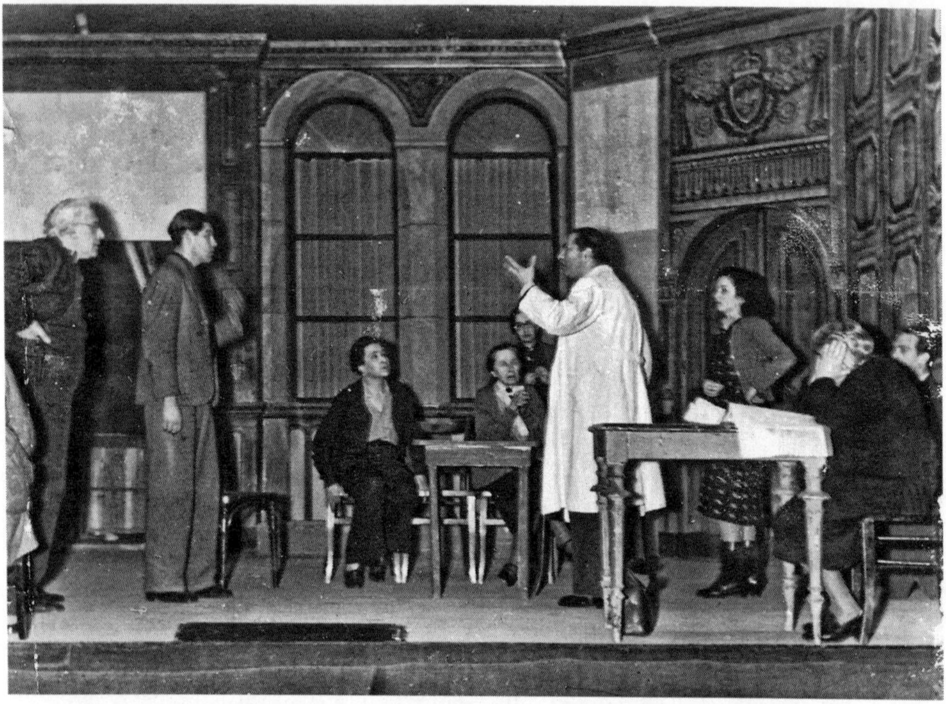

13. Fritz Wisten directs a rehearsal for Fodor, *Fairy Tale of Justice*, June 1939: Steffi Hinzelmann (Ronau) is behind Wisten on right. Akademie der Künste, Berlin, FWA 20.63.375, photographer unknown.

crat gives Mariette a costly gold cigarette case. Scene 2, set in a pawnshop later that day, shows the young woman selling the gift. The now-sober nobleman, however, has her arrested for stealing. Mariette eventually gets due justice, despite her lower status (from a high judge who is the aristocrat's father).[47] In addition to choosing plays which showcased the ensemble's strongest performers, Levie and Wisten staged Fodor's fable to provide light summer fare, albeit entertainment with a moral.

On 4 July 1939 government law transformed the Reich Association (*Reichsvertretung*) into the Reich Union of Jews in Germany, whose mission expanded to promote Jewish emigration, operate Jewish schools, and manage social welfare. The Kulturbund managing staff now answered to the Reich Union. With Max Ehrlich's departure from the theatre cabaret, Levie turned his attention to producing operettas. Three musical productions with dance, romance, and intrigue brought the season to a close in August, along with

Levie's own exit from Germany and the Kulturbund. As he prepared to join his wife in his native Holland, Levie produced Kálmán's *Countess Marizá*. Twenty thousand people saw the highly successful operetta, whose sold-out performances ran throughout July.[48]

The operetta takes place at Countess Marizá's country estate on the border between Hungary and Bulgaria. Marizá's new bailiff is really an impoverished count in disguise, Tassilo Endródy-Wittemburg, who must organize a celebration of Marizá's marriage engagement. The countess has fabricated a fiancé to dissuade suitors. But to her astonishment the fictitious Baron Zsupán appears at the dinner. Zsupán—named after a popular Johann Strauss operetta—falls in love with Tassilo's sister. Marizá falls for her steward, who goes by the name of Török; but her noble rank makes him an impossible love match. An elderly and comic suitor, Prince Moritz Dragomir Populescu, reveals Tassilo's true status and his false intentions. The operetta ends with Marizá's marriage proposal to Tassilo, who accepts. The two couples declare their love in the final musical number, "Waltz Our Worries Away." Hungarian dance (czardás) and gypsy melodies merge with the Viennese tradition of Oscar Straus and Johann Strauss II as well as Franz Lehár.

Werner Levie overcame substantial technical hurdles and organizational costs to advertise and stage Kálmán's operetta, requiring the orchestra conductor (Rudolf Schwarz) to travel to Vienna for final casting decisions. Under Wisten's direction, the cast featured thirty-nine artists, including extras and children (for a village choir), plus the orchestra. The large cast, with Berliner as Zsupán, assured many Jewish singers and actors in Germany two months of employment (including rehearsals and performances), despite special authorization to hire a leading lady from Vienna to play Marizá (Friederike Sara Frey-Waldmann) and retain a lead tenor of Hungarian nationality (Ernö Garay) to play Count Tassilo.[49] The extravagant undertaking also featured eight dancers and a choreographer from Hamburg, who brought tap dance to the stage.[50]

The musical production appeared lighthearted and fanciful with its orchestral accompaniment, waltzing aristocrats, and peasants. Behind the scenes, however, Levie and Wisten worried about securing casts and costs, while working in lockstep with their censors. Hinkel and his staff had scrutinized the libretto for what remained the most egregious affront to German purity in 1939—assimilatory impulses on the part of the writer, director, or actor. Wisten used the German-language opera libretto by Julius Brammer and Alfred Grünwald, which required substantial revision before performances could start to avoid references to nobility, ancestry, Viennese sports figures, and esteemed Nordic writers.[51]

In his review of the cheery production with "splendid music and an improbable plot," Micha Michalowitz commented on the "uninterrupted grinning contentment" in an audience that came to see something "totally improbable that would not remind them in any way of the heavy concerns of the day."[52] The excellent cast, able direction, and musical spectacle, the critic continued, provided distraction as well as "a colorful, amusing, music-filled quid pro quo," worthy of admiration.[53] The audience, of course, had not been privy to the censorship that led to revisions and ensured the operetta's production run. Wisten rephrased full sections to appease the censors. In the libretto's humorous first act, Tassilo (as steward) shows Populescu the estate. The dialogue pokes fun at Tassilo's Viennese wit and dialect and Populescu's ignorance of that dialect. For example, when Populescu comments on the castle and asks whether it was built onsite, Tassilo answers: "No, we had it brought over piece by piece in a paper bag" ("zitzerlweise in Stanizl"). Populescu responds to Tassilo's Austrian expressions, misunderstanding "Stanizl" as a geographical region and not a bag.[54] With Austria part of the Nazi Reich, Wisten had to rewrite this repartee. Wisten thus revised Populescu's question, substituting "What kind of style is that?" Tassilo answered, "Barock" (baroque). Populescu's new line, "Tarock," rhymed with "baroque."

A seemingly innocent exchange between Tassilo and Populescu about culture was revised and then thrown out altogether before performances began. Originally, Populescu pointed to a statue, asking Tassilo whether it was "Schiller or Goethe?" (Hinkel had long excluded references to these playwrights on the Jewish stage). Tassilo answered that it was the famous soccer player in Vienna, "Uridil":

P: Napoleon or Dante? T: That is Belvedere's Apollo. P: Ah, the world champion in wrestling. I think it's Nawratil.[55]	P: Schiller or Goethe? T: That is Uridil [*famous Viennese soccer player*].

For the stage production, however, Wisten omitted his own revisions, opting to remove the entire exchange from his production script.

In the operetta's final act, Wisten allowed the censors to prevail, even after he had rephrased an exchange about Germanic literary culture. The exchange between Marizá and her would-be suitor Zsupán occurred directly after a lively trio sung by Marizá, Zsupán, and Populescu, "Nut Brown Maiden from the Puszta [Prairie]." Zsupán (in love with Tassilo's sister) then tries to bring Marizá and Tassilo together:

ZSUPÁN: Lovely lady, do you know Strindberg?

MARIZÁ: Yes?

ZSUPÁN: Wedekind?

MARIZÁ: Yes!

ZSUPÁN: Do you know Ibsen? Also how to tipple? [*schnapsen*]. These three men claim that women always torment and torture us poor men!

MARIZÁ: Oho! Who says that?

ZSUPÁN: Please, it is sadistically proven! The one in question is madly in love with you![56]

Wisten first replaced the names of Nordic playwrights with the following dialogue, only to omit the clever banter entirely from production:

ZSUPÁN: Lovely lady, do you know Salomo?

MARIZÁ: I do not want to know a new man!

ZSUPÁN: But I mean S. M. King Salomo! Experience with one thousand women, S. M. has said.

MARIZÁ: All is frivolous.

ZSUPÁN: That goes without saying. But that women always torment and torture us poor men . . .

MARIZÁ: Because he had one thousand. Or is it fraud?

ZSUPÁN: Please, it is sadistically proven! The one in question is madly in love with you!

The esoteric reference to the biblical King Solomon (who married "a thousand wives") may have masked an obscure literary reference to a more contemporary "Salomo" or "S. M.": the Jewish-Austrian writer and journalist Soma Morgenstern.[57]

Wisten meticulously prepared the *Marizá* production script and struggled to reword possible offending passages before performances. By altering the performance script in advance himself, Wisten facilitated the script's successful transfer to the stage. Kálmán's operettas had been easily adapted for Austrian and German audiences. But cultural affinities between Germany and the former Austro-Hungarian Empire—now part of the greater Reich—caused great concern among censors, lest Jewish performers tried to appropriate or mimic German dialects, mention culture, or discuss ancestry.[58] Just as directors avoided such references in scripts by Fodor and Molnár, Wisten's *Countess Marizá* production had to be free of references which could be construed as attempts to assimilate Germanic culture.

Kulturbund technician Siegfried Hirsch reported from Berlin on the theatrical events of "July/August 1939" to a former colleague and recent émigré: he catalogued "twelve performances of *Maritzá* [*sic*]" and a "dance pantomime," adding that these performances were "nothing special."[59] Hannah Kroner-Segal had choreographed the ballet as part of a double feature (premiered 16 August 1939). She was aware that the performance came about because the Reich Department of Labor considered the dancers to be superfluous workers whose service could be better used elsewhere in the Reich.[60] Levie and Wisten chose to stage the pantomime as a stratagem to keep their dancers employed and thereby protected. Nineteen-year-old Kroner-Segal had just completed her debut as a dancer in the *Marizá* production, for which she choreographed a tennis dance scene. She was grateful to the Kulturbund directors for her continued employment. It did not matter that the musical dance production was a simple entertainment. Kurt Baumann wrote the plot for the pantomime, *The Kidnapping* (*Die Entführung*), which was set to music by André Ernest Modeste Grétry and Enrico Bosso. Ben Spanier directed its companion piece, a version of Goldoni's romantic comedy *Mirandolina*, costumed in rococo style.[61]

A sense of menace surrounded the Kulturbund during the late summer of 1939. Gestapo SA men guarded the theatre's doors as the dancers and singers entered and left the theatre. A non-Jewish friend of Kroner-Segal picked her up after all evening performances, personally escorting the anxious dancer to the underground train and all the way home. "That was a time when art was exercised on stage, but backstage, one was nervous and not really on task," Kroner-Segal later admitted.[62] During August the dancer knew that her fellow artists were no longer happy working at the theatre, being so preoccupied with efforts to leave Germany. Talk backstage about emigration papers and visas mirrored reports in the *Nachrichtenblatt* about Jewish life outside of Germany. The staff publicized the upcoming theatre performances, urging new members to join the theatre out of solidarity and a sense of moral obligation. The public campaign promoted the Kulturbund for those seeking distraction from the daily concern with affidavits, permits, and ship passage.[63] The Kulturbund was after all the only "institution of Jewish culture and art in Germany" — the last bastion for Jews to nurture their spirit with art.

With a glance toward the autumn, Leo Hirsch highlighted what audiences could expect to see in the 1939–1940 season: classics by Shakespeare; plays by modern authors (J. B. Priestley and Aldo de Benedetti); scripts by "Jewish virtuosos" Henri Bernstein and Ferenc Molnár; and world premieres of specifically Jewish plays from eastern Europe and Palestine, in addition to a "drama by a young Jewish author."[64] The summer pantomime performances, already scheduled through 5 September, continued during the "hot and sultry" late days of August. Werner Levie left Berlin for the Netherlands on 26 August 1939. He did not indicate how long he would be away. As tensions increased in Berlin and rumors of war floated, the correspondent William Shirer watched from his window as an antiaircraft gun was installed across the street on the roof of I. G. Farben. "It looks like war tonight," he wrote on 24 August, noting the frequency with which German bombers had flown over the Berlin skies that day.[65] The chemical cartel liaison office Berlin N.W.7 housed the Nazi military and economic espionage center. Germany's foreign minister Joachim von Ribbentrop had just signed the Soviet-German nonaggression pact the day before, pledging neutrality in case of war. Although the Germans appeared to be against the idea of war, just days later, on 30 August, Hitler announced the formation of a War Cabinet to defend the Reich. Kroner-Segal's unease about the general atmosphere in Berlin was well founded; the start of World War II would cut short her debut as a choreographer and the aspirations of other Jewish artists in the Reich capital.[66]

8 HOLDING OUT

WAR AND FANCY

1939–1940

At daybreak on Friday, 1 September 1939, Hitler's army advanced over the German border into Poland. In Berlin, clouds hung over the gray Berlin morning. Hitler addressed the Reichstag assembly at ten o'clock, justifying the heavy troop movements to the East as a "counter attack."[1] At his ministry office on Berlin's Wilhelmstraße, Goebbels worked on propaganda posters for Poland. "Excitement has reached a maximum level. . . . We are prepared," he noted in his diary.[2] The Jewish *Nachrichtenblatt* had gone to press hours before the military incursion began, so the editors made no mention of imminent war. Instead they headlined the results of the Twenty-first Zionist Congress. A preview of the Kulturbund's weekend schedule publicized performances of Carlo Goldoni's *Mirandolina* and the pantomime *Die Entführung* (The Kidnapping) for 2, 3, and 4 September. The "last performance of the August series" would take place on Tuesday, 5 September.[3] But the beginning of World War II preempted the theatre programming and "planned events."

Those Kulturbund Jews who remained in Berlin were catapulted into an off-kilter existence fraught with doubt and terror after the German push into Poland. On their first evening of war city residents experienced an air-raid drill. A government-directed blackout blanketed Berlin in darkness. By nightfall on 1 September the British and French governments had issued an ultimatum to Hitler to withdraw his troops from Poland. When the Britain government warned Germany to accept its demands on Sunday morning, 3 September, von Ribbentrop rejected the ultimatum. By noon at Berlin's central Wilhelmplatz near the Reich chancellery, loudspeakers trumpeted Britain's declaration of war on Germany. Air-raid sirens wailed as Berlin experienced a blackout for the third night in a row.

Britain and France severed their diplomatic ties to Germany, and their embassy staffs prepared to leave Berlin.

"The die is cast," Levie wrote to Fritz Wisten from Amsterdam, referring to the recent outbreak of war. Levie hoped that he could return to Berlin in a week or so when it was safer. But he had decided to stay in Holland. He wanted to tell Wisten how difficult it was for him to leave what they had accomplished at the Kulturbund. And he wrote of his deep sadness about the "end of our work."[4] On 4 September Hans Hinkel ordered Wisten to his office at the Ministry of Propaganda, to the division known as Division IIA for "Cultural Activities by Non-Aryans." At this face-to-face meeting or *Rücksprache* (literally "talking back"), Hinkel appointed Wisten as the new artistic director of the Kulturbund in Germany.[5] Later that day Wisten convened a meeting with Kulturbund theatre employees to discuss the situation. The Kulturbund was in debt, and recent events as well as the lack of leadership affected the whole enterprise and its employees.

Wisten's agenda included arranging payments for all work during August and discussion about "our deadline to quit."[6] The following day (5 September), subscribers to the Jewish newspaper read the front-page announcement: "All theatre, film, and other events of the Jewish Kulturbund in Germany e.V. are canceled until further notice. One may assume, however, that the performances will resume in the near future."[7] An additional notice "to our subscribers" cautioned Jews in the German *Reichsgebiet* to pay attention "with scrupulous exactitude" to all newly issued laws and provisions as well as general rules (*Richtlinien*) issued by public authorities (the Nazi government).[8] The revival of Ossip Dymov's *Jusik*, originally scheduled for 16 September 1939, was canceled; the projected world premiere of *Homecoming: Shabbat Fruit* (*Heimkehr: Shabbat Obst*) by Yecheskel Moscheh Neumann (Yehezkiel Moshe Neyman)—translated by Hirsch—was postponed indefinitely.[9]

Germany's declaration of war also hastened the government-led expropriation of Jews and Jewish property. At the Kulturbund a full reorganization began during the first week of September. On 7 September Hinkel called a meeting at his ministry office between Kulturbund executive board chairman Heinrich Stahl, committee members from Berlin and Vienna, and propaganda staff members Walter Owens and Erich Kochanowski. The restructuring process entailed an initial "liquidation" of the Kulturbund. This required giving up all theatre space, laying off personnel, and reshuffling some of the employees into new jobs.

Kulturbund committee member Dr. Otto Hirsch, who led Germany's Reich Association of Jews, recorded the minutes from the meeting. He detailed the discussion, which centered on the restructuring and representation of the Kulturbund in light of Werner Levie's departure from Germany. Although Hinkel had banned theatre productions, he permitted the film studio to operate and allowed occasional concerts and lectures. The publication of the *Nachrichtenblatt* would continue. Members discussed the newspaper's content, particularly whether editors could publish articles of religious import the following week for the High Holidays (beginning 13 September 1939). The meeting also focused on finances and the need to shift monies from the Reich Association of Jews to cover debts at the Kulturbund.[10] The reorganization continued over the course of the month, at the end of which the Ministry of the Interior—and by extension the Gestapo—fully controlled the Reich Association of Jews and the Kulturbund.

By late September Wisten and Kulturbund board members—often the lawyer Martin Brasch—appeared sometimes twice a week at Hinkel's office for the *Rücksprache*. The Kulturbund film division resumed its public series of international films on 24 September. The enforced blackouts and 8 P.M. evening curfews for Jews meant that films had to be shown earlier than before the war—at 3 P.M. and 5 P.M.[11] Wisten and Brasch meanwhile catalogued their needs for office and theatre staff now that their organization had been downsized. They compiled personnel lists of male employees under forty-five years old and females under thirty as well as those employees who had been fired but were over forty-five and over thirty, respectively.

The government now mandated that able Jews must support the Reich's war effort and join the Reich labor pool. Wisten tried to keep as many employees as he could at the Kulturbund, but many were let go. Even those who remained on the now stalled payroll had to seek other employment. According to one such employee, Wisten gave Hinkel a list of "*only* 40 names and to employ all the people in the film department was impossible."[12] Hinkel notified Goebbels that the early "liquidation" of the Kommandantenstraße theatre had reduced the artistic and office staff from "over 400 to 90" people by 1 November.[13] Those still employed would be paid in two monthly installments instead of one.[14]

Erich Kochanowski or Walter Owens convened regular meetings between Hinkel's staff and Wisten's executive board to restructure the Kulturbund. Except for his secretary, Ursula Framm, Hinkel's staff members belonged to the Nazi Party and were ideologically committed members of the SS. The chief of the propaganda department, Kochanowski, had studied history, while Owens, a former engineer, supervised professional estate affairs.[15] The meetings dealt with operational and financial measures such as mandatory tax payments for Jews and bureaucratic issues regarding personnel. While negotiating future work opportunities for artists and technicians, Wisten also submitted requests for cultural programs, specifically special performances, which were occasionally permitted by October. But with the theatre still officially closed, Wisten proceeded cautiously as he reported to Kochanowski his plans for the stalled theatre season of 1939–1940.[16] He promoted Sunday afternoons as good occasions for performances: instructive lectures on Jewish duties, short musical presentations, orchestral concerts, and light music and cabaret. Many performers were available, Wisten suggested: for example, the *buffo* Gerhard Pechner could sing and play piano at a Sunday afternoon event with tea and cake.

Since the government had seized the main theatre auditorium at 57 Kommandantenstraße in early September, Wisten managed to secure the Josef-Lehmann high school for lectures and performances. Besides the school auditorium, the only other available performance space available was the Kulturbundsaal on the second floor at 58–59 Kommandantenstraße, which housed the film studio. The room had a stage and could be used for concerts and cabaret.[17] Wisten added playing spaces like a synagogue and the first-floor rooms of the Central Offices for Jewish Emigration on Kurfürstenstraße.[18] Wisten reported that four lectures and recitations, eight concerts, and thirteen cabarets took place between 29 October 1939 and March 1940.[19]

The restructuring took place simultaneously within the four Kulturbund divisions: theatre, music, lecture series, and publishing. With the layoffs and the attrition of members through emigration, the orchestra had to be reorganized to include fifty members of the previous Kulturbund orchestra and members from the orchestra of the Jewish community (an orchestra that aided Jewish artists). The Kulturbund committee arranged the details for the orchestra's appearances, rehearsal and performance space, terms for monetary recompense, and the repertoire for concerts, such as one planned for 19 November 1939. The program was to feature work by Georg Friedrich Händel, Antonín Dvorák, and possibly Mendelssohn's Overture to *A Midsummer Night's Dream*.[20] Hinkel and his staff increasingly objected to program choices, as they did with Mendelssohn's Overture. He was a Jew. The Sunday symphony concert had to substitute Pyotr Tchaikovsky's fifth symphony for the Mendelssohn piece. On 1 December 1939 Hinkel forbade special events

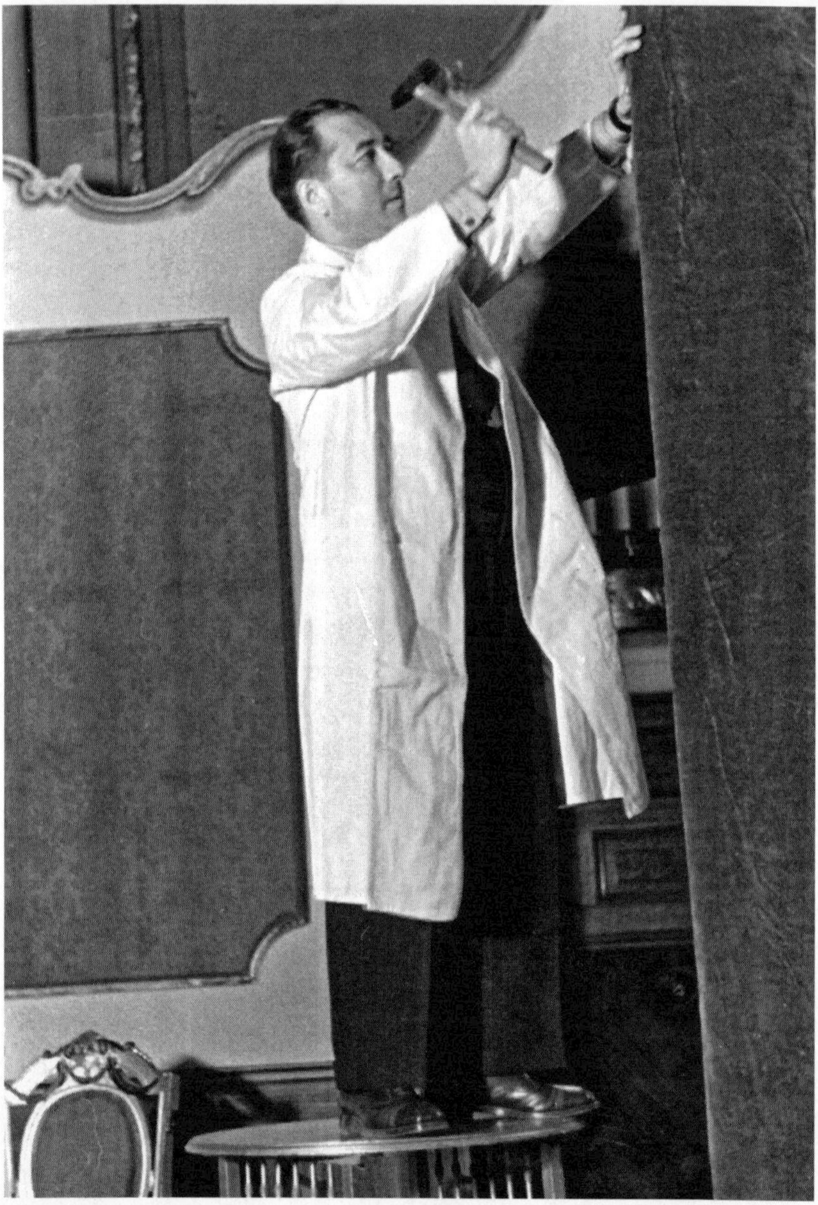

14. Fritz Wisten at work onstage, hammering set, Josef-Lehmann-Schule, 1939. Akademie der Künste, Berlin, FWA 20.63.272, photograph by Abraham Pisarek, courtesy Ruth Gross.

for Sundays, except film showings. All public lectures were banned. Formal requests for authorized events had to be submitted three weeks in advance of the event.[21]

Hinkel's Division IIA (Cultural Activities by Non-Aryans) was undergoing its own reorganization by late 1939: its transition to the "Be K A" (Besondere-Kulturaufgaben; Special Cultural Tasks) by 1940 included a new subdivision for "Troop Entertainment." Hinkel remained the director of the new department; but he delegated more responsibility for Jewish cultural matters to his staff, specifically to Erich Kochanowski.[22] General censorship powers in the Reich had expanded quickly since 1936.[23] The war "elevated the issue of cultural and intellectual conformity, as well as that of racial purity, to a question of national security."[24] None of Hinkel's staff for "special cultural tasks" had experience in the arts. If the need for conformity and purity in repertoire choice and script readings was paramount for German theatres, it was even more vital for the Jewish theatre to refrain from defiling that "racial purity."[25] Wisten's 1939–1940 playing season was beset with additional difficulty before it even started. The repertoire suffered partly because of decisions by Nazi functionaries, to whom literary matters and theatre art meant little. Instead the officials scoured the submitted scripts for perceived assimilatory characteristics, as in the case of Molnár's one-act play from 1935, *The Pastry Chef's Wife (Die Zuckerbäckerin)*.

Kochanowski banned the comedy in December 1939, although Wisten already had cast the play. Wisten submitted the one-act for approval in the autumn of 1939, but the war and the concomitant closing of the Kulturbund delayed the authorization process, making rehearsals impossible.[26] "Nothing is yet decided on the application for authorization of a production of *Zuckerbäckerin*," noted Brasch after a *Rücksprache* in early December.[27] Wisten had nonetheless projected the costs for four weeks of employment, including sums for posters, two women to check coats, a fee of 25 RM per week for Wisten as director, 20 RM for royalties, and 35–40 RM a week for the lead actors, Alfred Berliner as Edmund Kiss and Jenny Schaffer-Bernstein as his wife, Ilona the confectioner. Fritz Grünne would play Ilona's lover, Vadasz.[28]

Molnár's comedy takes place in a Budapest suburb where the husband and wife run a pastry business. The police question Ilona because she was in a taxi accident. Edmund learns that Ilona was with a lover in the taxi. In a comic twist, it turns out that she has been supporting him. After the lover reveals that he never loved her, she faints. Edmund begs Vadasz to visit the shop regularly. And the play ends with a normal day at the bakery.

Perplexed by the ban on the production, Wisten recorded his bafflement: "Herr Kochanowski . . . indicates that plays with an 'assimilatory character' must be rejected from the start. Their [Nazis'] program rejects the assimilation of the nineteenth century. I cannot see any assimilatory aims in *The Pastry Chef's Wife*; however, I will see to it in future submissions that I check against such tendencies. My will is strong; my spirit is weak."[29] Kochanowski may have considered the play's content to be "assimilatory" because the characters speak a dialect-tinged German. They refer to themselves as "bürgerlich" (commoners). They bake meringues and sell "Rosenzucker" and "Linzertorten."[30] The play included jibes at government taxation, as when Vadasz referred to the tax form as "noble printed matter on which the financial administration of our Fatherland [*Vaterland*] poses indiscreet questions to Herr Kiss."[31] Jewish actors referring to Viennese confections and jokes about the "Fatherland" could no longer be tolerated.[32]

During his meeting with Kochanowski, Wisten had broached the topic of something new as a substitute for the Molnár: "I touch on the question of the next play by suggesting an 'Oriental evening' with *Judith* by Ettinger (Act 3) and *The Language of the Birds* (*Die Sprache der Vögel*) by Adolf Paul."[33] Wisten likely had a musical evening in mind, featuring Max Ettinger's "musical tragedy" *Judith*. Adolf Paul's farce portrays a sultan, a friend in love, and a young woman who asks the king to reveal to her the language of the birds.[34] Kochanowski first wanted to review the play in advance of any submission. But the play never had a test run at the Kulturbund.

As Wisten restarted the Kulturbund's theatre season, he shuttled between gestures of appeasement to the Be K A and attempts to provide culture in the closing window of leisure time available to Jews for evening outings and Sunday matinees. In January 1940 Kochanowski informed Wisten that works by German composers—except for German Jews—would no longer be acceptable in Kulturbund performances; music by Händel was forbidden to Jewish musicians, while music by Dvorák and other foreigners could be authorized.[35] Hinkel and Kochanowski's tightening parameters, dwindling resources in the Jewish community for the cultural league, difficulties in paying royalties, and a generally dire climate for Berlin's Jews greatly hampered the Kulturbund's creativity and output.

"To sum things up, it is *no longer* nice being here: Cinema is all that is going on, except for some cabaret afternoons for the elderly at the Josef Lehmannschule and an occasional concert," wrote an unemployed Kulturbund artist to a former colleague with his New Year greetings for 1940.[36] Martin

Rosen was desperate. Referring to his situation as "tragic, without exaggeration," the performer reported how former Kulturbund members had been replaced. He wanted to work or to emigrate but had no immediate chance to do either.[37] Siegfried Hirsch experienced similar difficulties: "Except for me, all of us were confirmed. . . . I was passed over. . . . 28 Jan. On Friday (26.I) was at Kubu . . . all are getting other jobs." Referring to the government's labor requirement, the former technician continued: "None of the young ones were left at the Kubu, and they [the labor department] had to grab those of older years."[38] Wartime had brought an even greater urgency for Kulturbund Jews to emigrate, but it was increasingly difficult to secure ship passage or overseas contacts for affidavits. The Kulturbund did rehire several of those unemployed artists, eventually including Rosen.

"On principle, theatre is allowed. There are no reservations about Shakespeare. All authors of German descent or those who belong to the Reich Theatre Chamber are excluded from consideration," Wisten recorded after his first meeting of 1940 at the Ministry of Propaganda.[39] Kochanowski had given him renewed guidelines for choosing plays. Deferring to "the audience's need for cheerful entertainment of a high order," as he put it, Wisten chose Shakespeare's *The Taming of the Shrew* (*Der Widerspenstigen Zähmung*) to reopen the Kulturbund in the winter of 1940.[40] Rehearsals for the second most popular Shakespeare play in the Reich began before the production was officially confirmed.[41] In February the *Nachrichtenblatt* promoted the Kulturbund and its forthcoming production.[42] Meanwhile Wisten and Brasch negotiated financial arrangements for the actors. Once the theatre could produce an account of its expenses, Kochanowski agreed that actors who drew permanent pay would receive an honorarium for each role performed.[43] "It is anticipated that further theatre performances will be approved in the future," Brasch noted after a "conference" with Kochanowski, who asked about costs for the next production.[44]

The Taming of the Shrew opened in the 700-seat Kulturbundsaal on 2 March 1940 after the six-month hiatus in production and with a two-week delay.[45] Wisten cut Shakespeare's framing "Induction" to reduce scene changes due to the "limited spatial conditions of the stage." In order to accommodate the smaller stage, Hanna Litten designed one stationary setting in front of which multiple scenes unfolded. Translucent captions oriented the audience to each scene locale. Wisten had directed actors Steffi Hinzelmann (Kate) and Alfred Berliner (Petrucchio) to tone down the comic elements. The actors did not overplay their roles; their performances reflected the "uncomplicated simplicity of the stage setting."[46] The Kulturbund's seventh season had begun.

The morale among Germans generally was low during the bleak winter months of 1940. Freezing temperatures spoiled Berlin's supply of potatoes during late February, adding to existing food shortages. By early 1940 food rationing for Jews was stricter than for Aryans. Jews could not get most vegetables, meat, and fruit. Limited shopping venues and times for Jews also made it more difficult for them to get whatever food was available. The number of Jews wait-listed for emigration to the United States now far exceeded the permitted quota for Germans, by over 200,000 applicants.[47] Going to the theatre became logistically more difficult for Berlin's Jews: the government had issued a curfew of 8 P.M. for them by the time that *The Taming of the Shrew* premiered. The wartime curfew and citywide blackouts necessitated earlier performance times: evening curtain times were at 6 P.M., with weekend matinees at 4:30 P.M. The government also had mandated shorter shopping times for Jews by late 1939; about six months later those shopping times would be further restricted to one hour between 4 and 5 P.M.[48] The rehearsal time for Kulturbund productions had been reduced to only eight days for actors to prepare the play.[49] Because the Kulturbundsaal served as the only theatre space for all cultural events, performances and concerts could no longer be scheduled at two venues simultaneously. This led to shorter production runs. Despite these drawbacks, audiences witnessed seven performances of *The Taming of the Shrew* (once for children), with 3,900 attendees during its March run.[50]

Jewish community leaders expected Wisten to stage relevant "positive-Jewish" plays now that the Kulturbund had reopened. Even before the *Taming of the Shrew*, the former editor of the Jewish *Gemeindeblatt* and director of publishing at the Kulturbund, Leo Kreindler, renewed a public plea to feature "plays that reflected Jewish life."[51] Wisten planned to produce Jewish plays; but besides the unexpected theatre shutdown, Kochanowski imposed further limitations on the repertoire selection during the second half of 1940. The "problems with repertoire choice" for Wisten stemmed from the fact that contemporary plays by foreign authors—even Jews—were often scuttled due to difficulties with royalties. Moreover, the scripts had to be "simple," because of the small number of available actors. The limited space in the Kulturbundsaal also meant that Wisten could not choose plays with many scene changes.

Wisten knew that he had to give careful consideration to what Jewish audiences wanted to see, "given the difficult and subtle psychological effects related to the circumstances of the times," as he put it.[52] Balancing all of these factors, he looked for plays with small casts, uncomplicated technical requirements for staging, and authors whose scripts would be acceptable to censors. He hoped for low royalty fees and that living authors would waive the rights for performing their plays. Dymov and Molnár had done so in the past. Wisten and Hirsch had previewed these playwrights for the 1939–1940 playing season, with Neumann's Yiddish-language *Homecoming: Sabbath Fruit*. But that was before war broke out.[53]

Wisten placated community advocates for more Jewish stage material by rescheduling his production of Dymov's fairy tale *Jusik* for April 1940. Originally planned for a 16 September 1939 performance, Dymov's "tragicomedy in three acts" begins with a prologue. Grandmother tells her granddaughter how the howling wind personifies Jusik in his search for his heart. According to legend, the lovelorn Jusik tore out his heart and threw it at the feet of the girl he loved. As act I begins the grandmother becomes the violin-playing Jusik. The granddaughter becomes the daughter of the "good house" in which the play's action unfolds.[54] The kitchen maid had an affair with the son of the house, who spurned her. Jusik writes a love letter for the maid to the son but also writes of his own unrequited love for her. In act II the son's wealthy family offers to pay Jusik to marry the maid. She does not love him but consents to the marriage.[55] When Jusik wins the lottery, he signs his money over to the maid. The son then decides to marry her, and she agrees. When the clock strikes thirteen, Jusik rips out his heart. In the epilogue the grandmother tells her granddaughter that Jusik waits for the clock to strike thirteen so that someone may find his heart.

On 13 April the Kulturbundsaal curtain rose at 5 P.M. on a scene infused with Old World superstition and legend. Wisten's *Jusik* production relied on atmospheric lighting effects and a musical score (by Gerhardt Goldschlag) to suggest the play's dreamlike qualities and the inherent sadness of the lovelorn singer (played by Alfred Berliner).[56] Hanna Litten based her costume designs on traditional shtetl types: the mayor with a long waistcoat; the beggar as a skeleton; the water carrier with a gray beard, fur hat, and long coat; and the heartbroken musician with the fiddle.[57] Litten used lighting to make the kitchen scenes transparent. The kitchen design included the outline of a human face on the wall. Two plates suggested the eyes, with pans for the nose and mouth. As the kitchen maid (played by Steffi Hinzelmann) hung up pots and pans, the face changed during the course of the action to reflect her mood.[58] *Jusik* ran for seven performances with 2,869 attendees, 600 of whom were children.[59]

Despite their commitment to stage Jewish plays, Wisten and Leo Hirsch could not produce all of the plays they hoped to stage for the same reasons that had plagued Singer's submissions years before. In addition to pressures from the censors, the artistic staff still had to take into account the preferences of their own community. Hirsch had already prepared his translation of Neumann's Jewish folk-play *Homecoming* (*Heimkehr*) for performance during 1940.[60] Anticipating audience hostility, he tried to justify his choice by addressing what he assumed audiences would object to:

> I am fully aware of the difficulties in staging this play: the antipathy of a certain portion of the Jewish audience in Germany against Jewish themes, however, is not a factor for an enterprise that calls itself the Jewish Kulturbund. That it [the play] deals with a strange world is an objection that one must also expect with non-German plays by Shakespeare, Goldoni, or Tagore. . . .
>
> We are urgently in need of a Jewish reason and an artistic one [to stage this].[61]

Hirsch saw the play's focus on the Sabbath as universally accessible as "an ideal of human morality and culture."[62] The play, set in a nineteenth-century Polish shtetl, spanned twenty-four hours: from the start of the Friday Sabbath through the following day after sunset. The plot about a soldier's homecoming from war in Russia converges with the advent of Sabbath. The dialogue, steeped in Jewish superstition, interspersed expressions from Yiddish and Hebrew prayers and talk of the Messiah.[63] Hirsch never revised his script for a Kulturbund production of the Jewish folk play.[64] Wisten produced *Jusik* in the slot that may have been reserved for *Homecoming*.

Wisten continually sought suitable dramaturgical material for the stage, especially for the "Jewish" category. His failed attempts in December 1939 to bring Molnár's "boulevard comedy" or the musical "Oriental" evening into the repertoire did not halt his efforts. He filed several play texts among the Kulturbund's unproduced dramaturgical materials during 1940. The scripts dealt with concerns such as emigration and a burgeoning Jewish Palestine. Interest in leaving Germany peaked. The Be K A pushed to increase newspaper coverage on emigration. In March Kochanowski ordered the Kulturbund (and Kreindler) to expand the emigration-related section of the *Nach-*

richtenblatt. This included advertising by passenger ship companies for their transatlantic crossings.[65] A front-page notice from the Reich Association of Jews in Germany addressed readers: "Whoever has relatives in countries open to emigration, WARN THEM URGENTLY to press those family members still here to follow them as quickly as possible."[66] Meanwhile, by late April the Kulturbund had allocated almost half of its profits for 1939 to the Reich Association for the Advancement of Emigration.[67]

Royalties would not have been an issue for the authors of the short plays promoting emigration like one by Shulamith Batdori, whose *Trial* had already played for Kulturbund audiences. Her one-act of settlement life, *Before the Rain* (*Vor dem Regen*), might have been considered stageworthy if coupled with another play about a kibbutz, *The Little Radio Operators: A Play for Children in 3 Scenes* (*Die kleinen Funker: Ein Kinderspiel in 3 Bildern*, ca. 1940).[68] The two plays focused on protecting one's children and one's land in Palestine. Martin Rost's *Homecoming* (*Heimkehr*) describes the boat trip of Pioneers (Halutzim) to the land of their fathers and the life encountered there.[69] *Neues Land* by Bruno Israel Bendix highlights the nostalgia for Berlin of a German father and his son as they build a home in tropical South America.[70] Wisten wanted the repertoire to appeal to all (Jewish) audiences during difficult times. But none of these plays made it to the stage in 1940, although Wisten earmarked them as appropriate choices for the repertoire.[71]

After the April production of *Jusik*, Wisten deemed it "prudent to offer a comedy next, perhaps because of Jusik's inherent sadness and the very mood of the piece."[72] As he noted after a meeting with Kochanowski at the Be K A, "I boost the new play *Steadfast Business* as harmless and necessary after the heavy *Jusik*, because of its cheerful tone."[73] Kochanowski now asked for written commentaries on the plays before they were staged. Gregor Rogoff's new comedy would be an "experiment," according to Wisten and Hirsch, who praised Rogoff's youthful affirmation of spirit. New scripts were especially welcome, given the difficulty of performing "practically anything" from modern theatre literature, German or foreign. "Even most of the Jewish ones are out of the question for political, thematic, or technical reasons," Hirsch wrote. He concluded that the theatre had a "cultural duty" to produce the work of the Jewish author Rogoff, who lived and worked in Berlin.[74]

The world premiere of *Steadfast Business* (*Bob beehrt sich vorzustellen*) on 18 May 1940 took place while Germany's army stunned western Europe with its Blitzkrieg. Just a week before, German troops had invaded the Netherlands and swiftly occupied the country. A further push into Belgium followed, with troops reaching Brussels at dusk on 17 May. The Reich had extended the mandatory labor age requirements for men up to the age of fifty-five and for women up to fifty.[75] At the Kulturbund Wisten prepared for opening night of Rogoff's play, whose subject matter was at odds with the realities at the German borders.

The play begins with a prologue and the entrance of Bob Young, who threatens a theatre director with a revolver and a play script: "I am a talented, although unknown playwright. You are a well-known, but untalented theatre director." The director agrees to hear the play rather than be shot. Bob introduces the play, which unfolds with himself as a law student. Young heads an "idea factory," an ingenious business where several students sell good ideas during poor economic times. They benefit from comic scams like a spot remover soap that they sell to people in crowds, whom they have already dirtied with ink. In an epilogue the theatre director decides to produce Bob's play, convincing him to play the lead. Bob Young gets his premiere.[76]

Wisten did everything thinkable to get the "somewhat primitive gearing" of the play going.[77] Hirsch had indicated the risk of performing the play-in-progress: "It was clear to us that we did not have a patented or polished classic before us, nor a sophisticated or tightly constructed box-office hit like the French or Hungarian Boulevard plays. We are dealing with a facile play, albeit one less mechanical and stereotypical."[78] The entertaining production featured the ensemble's comic stars Alfred Berliner and Steffi Hinzelmann in the main roles, however, and an onstage jazz band for ambience. Rogoff set *Steadfast Business* in America; but curiously, Wisten removed from performance references such as "America is the land of unlimited opportunities."[79] He also cut from his production a song by a guitar-playing student, "America! America! You are the most beautiful country in the world!"[80] Kochanowski may have wanted to prevent an onstage promotion of American virtues.[81]

After only three performances the experiment failed. In the play's epilogue the audience discovers that Bob carries a revolver made of chocolate. While Alfred Berliner as the young playwright brandished his candy-coated comedy on the Kulturbund stage with gusto, German military forces outside Berlin were conducting aerial bombing strikes across continental Europe: the Wehrmacht already had invaded Denmark and Norway a month before. "Inferno in Western Europe," screamed the headlines, which stretched across the first page of the Paris-based uncensored *Jüdische Welt Rundschau* on 20 May 1940.[82] "Lille, Bruges, Ostend captured! Ypres stormed!" Shirer reported from Berlin in late May, as the rapid string of German military victories filled "incredible headlines."[83]

Editor Kreindler avoided public coverage of the growing list of events in the *Jüdisches Nachrichtenblatt*. Instead the Berlin newspaper devoted the bulk of its now-shortened editions to emigration reports, learning tips for foreign languages, information about ration cards, and taxes that Jews owed to the Reich.[84] The newspaper also previewed Kulturbund entertainments. Even as turmoil rolled across Germany's expanding borders, the shrinking Jewish community in Berlin still had some cultural opportunities.

Kochanowski had approved Wisten's summer program in the spring, when he cautioned the director to be careful in his "calculation" regarding the planned musical. The musical may have been Pietro Mascagni's *Cavalleria rusticana*, which the theatre produced on 1 June 1940 as a concert.[85] But Wisten also had reworked Molière's *The Imaginary Invalid* and incorporated a new musical score by Karl Wiener.[86] This was one of the productions that Kulturbund board members agreed to tour outside Berlin to increase box-office profits in case of a deficit.[87] Kochanowski preapproved tours of Molière's comedy to Cologne and Frankurt am Main in August and one to Breslau in October.[88] The play's small cast and minimal set requirements made the production easy to transport. Stage props could be procured on site for the Breslau performances. Although Kochanowski informed Wisten that the French classicist was "on principle accepted," the play's authorization for Berlin performances was still pending by 3 June.[89] That afternoon the Luftwaffe bombed Paris.

The *Jüdische Welt Rundschau* did not report the Nazi aerial bombing of Paris. As German troops moved toward the French capital, in Berlin Rogoff's comedy played a last time on 8 June. That day the Reich Ministry of Defense enacted a law which forbade indirect and direct correspondence with anyone in "enemy" countries abroad, including Great Britain and Ireland, France, Egypt, Sudan, and Iraq. The Reich's crackdown on communication abroad further isolated those Jews inside the Reich. Nor could they rely on the German Red Cross anymore to send letters to relatives in the Benelux countries. On 10 June Italy aligned itself with Germany and declared war on France and Britain.

"Paris has fallen. The hooked-cross flag of Hitler flutters from the Eiffel Tower," Shirer wrote in his diary on 14 June. Just weeks later the Nazis occupied the city and forced France's capitulation. By the time the Berlin

Kulturbund presented Molière's classic comedy about a hypochondriac on 13 July, France had installed Marshal Henri-Philippe Pétain to lead the collaborationist Vichy government. Wisten presented *The Imaginary Invalid* as a "Singspiel" which he streamlined for production, retaining the original plot and comic spirit. To appeal to a wider audience, Wisten and Hirsch stripped the play to its basic elements. They kept the plot intact and cut the entr'acte, which in Molière's original called for a ballet amid lavish decor to honor King Louis.[90] The Kulturbund Jews had no leader to honor. But not far from the Kommandantenstraße, morale soared at Hitler's chancellery. Later that week Hitler would stage a military victory parade through the Brandenburg Gate for the first time since 1918. A holiday spirit reigned in central Berlin as many Germans celebrated their army's might and lauded their supreme commander-in-chief.

Due to limited stage space and sparse technological means, the Kulturbund production used only one setting to depict Argan's sick-room. Wisten relied on a new scene sequence in which shadow images on a screen signaled the action: for example, an image of Argan led to a live "tyrannical" Argan onstage. This technique oriented theatregoers to the plot and characters and reduced scene changes, saving stage space. Wisten added rhyming couplets and chansons, a "filmlike" prologue, and a musical epilogue.[91] Jenny Schaffer-Bernstein played Toinette to Alfred Berliner's Argan.

Wisten's production of *The Imaginary Invalid (Der eingebildete Kranke)* pleased audiences for ten sold-out performances through July and August. Proud of his achievement, the theatre director made sure that Kochanowski knew of his success when he met him for a July conference about the repertoire:

> Herr Kochanowski expresses his satisfaction that our performances are so well attended. He regrets that he cannot come to the performance of *The Imaginary Invalid* on Thursday, the 15th of August. . . . I tried to expand our options for shaping future programs. . . . Molnár is not principally forbidden as a submission. Further, I may suggest Wilde (Bunburry) in the future.[92]

Wisten had become the primary intermediary for his staff, community organizations, and the Nazi officers to whom they were beholden. Besides reporting on recent productions in his meetings at the Be K A, he broached concerns about obstacles to securing sites for special performances.[93] He tried to strike a balance between advocating for the Kulturbund and bending

15. Molière, *The Imaginary Invalid*, summer/fall 1940: Jenny Schaffer-Bernstein and Alfred Berliner. Akademie der Künste, Berlin, FWA 0020.63.250, photograph by Abraham Pisarek, courtesy Ruth Gross.

to Kochanowski's restrictions. Wisten could not have kept the theatre going without accommodating himself to the dictates of the Nazi Be K A office. It is not surprising that a former theatre worker complained about Wisten after an August visit to the theatre: "Wisten is still there; supposedly, he is getting less and less sympathetic each day."[94]

During the second half of August Germany led air attacks on Britain. A character in *The Imaginary Invalid* questions Argan's audacity "to declare war on the whole band," a line noticeably absent from the Kulturbund production.[95] Night after night in Berlin air raid alarms sounded, even on 19 August, when the cast brought *The Imaginary Invalid* to Frankfurt and Cologne. The two final Berlin performances fell on evenings when the Luftwaffe bombed London. Only hours after the sold-out finale of 24 August, Britain bombed Berlin. The three-hour air raid on 25 August 1940 stunned Berliners, who to this point had been spared direct British bombings. Over the next days the raids on Berlin intensified. Like other Berliners, the Kulturbund Jews tried to maintain as normal a life as possible under abnormal circumstances.

As Britain's retaliatory raids increased in Berlin skies several times a week in September, Hinkel already was planning an eventual "evacuation" of Berlin's Jews to German-occupied Poland.[96] Meanwhile, at the Be K A, Kochanowski had yet to approve Wisten's annual theatre report for 1939–1940. In the Kulturbundsaal Wisten prepared Hirsch's translation of Jacob Gordin's *Mirele Efros* or *Die Mutter* (*The Mother*), the season's final production, to herald the Jewish High Holidays. Hirsch justified performing Gordin's play because, as he noted, "The selection among those generally available dramas with Jewish content in Hebrew or Yiddish is . . . limited. And the few manuscripts suitable for a production under the current circumstances are difficult to stage."[97] Gordin's "specifically Jewish play," however, fulfilled many criteria for the compromised theatre: the production would not require much in the way of scenic challenges. Importantly, it could be produced successfully by the ensemble, for the cast required only ten actors. Nor did Hirsch foresee any problem with royalties. Finally, the "patriarchal Jewish" milieu of the play would provide audiences with a familiar theme: the tragic experience of a mother in her changing relationships with her children.[98]

The "folk play," set in nineteenth-century Russia, begins with a marriage. Two families represent different sets of people: the groom's family from Grodno, where the elegant Mirele Efros reigns over her household; and the bride's family, simple folk from the provinces. In act I Mirele calls off the betrothal, because the bride's family does not match her expectations. She

16. Gordin, *The Mother*, September 1940: Jenny Schaffer-Bernstein (*right*) and Cläre Arnstein as the grandson (*left*). Akademie der Künste, Berlin, FWA 0074/86/24-II, photograph by Abraham Pisarek, courtesy Ruth Gross.

finally agrees to the marriage. Three years later conflict remains between Mirele and her daughter-in-law, who by the third act throws her mother-in-law out of the house. Ten years pass before she asks Mirele to return. The matriarch refuses. But she returns for her grandson's bar mitzvah, allowing for a familial reconciliation.[99] In his commentary to justify the production, Hirsch summed up the play's main ideas: "If one is [a] worthless [person], then inheriting nobility is worth nothing. Money does not make happiness; and honor one's father and mother."[100]

Mirele Efros opened on 28 September 1940, just days before Rosh Hashanah. Wisten directed his actors to accent their speech to draw out the contrast between the two families and their backgrounds. Hirsch retained Gordin's original expressions from Hebrew and Yiddish: "mazeltov," "chuppah," "bar mitzvah," and the prayer "mole rachmim" (oh merciful God) to enhance the linguistic authenticity of the Jewish milieu.[101] Karl Wiener's music score of old Jewish motifs underscored the play's mood. In the powerhouse title role of Mirele, Jenny Schaffer-Bernstein portrayed the "proud-willed" mother, who harbored disappointments in self-exile. Steffi Hinzelmann played her daughter-in-law with temperament; and Fritz Grünne portrayed the son as more than a weeping boy. Wisten's understated direction did not heighten the play's inherent melodrama. In the wedding scene, for example, he staged the prayer silently. In addition, he did not present the wedding dance as an expression of religious celebration but rather as a joyous family occasion.[102] Reviewer Hugo Lachmanski concluded from the applause at the premiere that no doubts remained about the Kulturbund audience's readiness to be affected by "specifically Jewish material."[103]

For the first time in seven years, the Kulturbund suspended performances during the ten-day period between Rosh Hashanah (1 October) and Yom Kippur (11 October). This decision may have been made for religious reasons or because of economic concerns. Perhaps a shortage of personnel necessitated the pause in performances.[104] The *Nachrichtenblatt* also shut down its publication during the Jewish holidays. When the newspaper resumed on 10 October, Kreindler published Lachmanski's review of the *Mother* premiere, reminding theatregoers about the play's enthusiastic reception.[105] But restrictions on shopping for Jews and evening curfews during wartime had forced Wisten to set earlier times for performances. Theatregoers arrived at the Kulturbundsaal for a 4 P.M. curtain on 19 October as weekly autumn performances resumed on Saturdays. Wisten appealed to Kochanowski on behalf of several theatre artists over the age of fifty, including Jenny

Schaffer-Bernstein, whose mandatory labor for the Reich took them away from the theatre and their work there.[106] Of these artists, Wisten especially needed Schaffer-Bernstein, who starred in *The Mother* and in the Molière play. His intervention successfully led to work exemptions for his artists. Despite the mounting difficulties surrounding Jewish life in Berlin, the demand for tickets to see the Gordin play was so great that the performances sold out quickly.

Wisten meanwhile planned the details for the upcoming tour of *The Imaginary Invalid* to Breslau.[107] He had committed himself to continue the work of the Kulturbund and to help those artists who depended on the theatre for their livelihood. After Kristallnacht, it had been difficult to justify staying in Germany. He had two affidavits for travel to the United States. His family and friends encouraged him to leave the country alone. But the war had lengthened the waiting time to more than a year. Wisten's plans to leave Berlin remained on hold indefinitely.[108]

9 DISSOLUTION

AFTERMATH

1940–1943

On Sunday morning, 20 October 1940, the cast of eleven and the set designer of *The Imaginary Invalid* boarded a train for Breslau at Berlin's Charlottenburg station. Jenny Schaffer-Bernstein, Alfred Berliner, Steffi Hinzelmann, and Cläre Arnstein had performed in Gordin's *The Mother* just the day before. Wisten's leading actors had taken a week's break to entertain Jewish audiences near the Polish border. Their successful performance run of Gordin's play extended the Kulturbund's seventh playing season into the eighth year, through late October. During their three-day tour they would present Molière's comedy in matinee and evening performances. The travelers carried costumes and wigs in their suitcases. Upon arrival they would borrow furniture, pillows, and props—a key chain, tray, glasses, and a carafe—from the Jewish community. Hanna Litten's one-room setting could be easily built and dismantled on-site.[1]

The theatregoers in Breslau's "Saal der Freunde" on the Neue Graupenstraße did not care about the makeshift stage. They applauded the Kulturbund performers, grateful for the entertainment from Berlin.[2] Seven hundred kilometers to the southwest, the Nazis expelled 6,500 Jews from the Baden and Palatinate-Saar regions. This first deportation of Jews from Germany to Vichy, France, on 22 October coincided with the second day of the performance tour.[3] Neither the Kulturbund performers nor their audiences knew about the action. But a week later a Breslau-based journalist alluded in his production review to the timely significance of the Molière play: as a theatre director, Molière had not wanted his players to go hungry. At the Kulturbund Wisten also made sure that his artists earned an income at a time when Jews could not work in their professions.

More poignantly, the critic referred to Molière's own performance as the invalid onstage and his death following the performance.[4] Hypochondria and its theatrical mockery turned ironically lethal during autumn of 1940.

Wisten remained in Berlin during the *Invalid* tour to attend to theatre business. When he and Martin Brasch met with Kochanowski on 30 October, he reported on the successful tour. But the men quickly turned to the topic of transported Jews and the immediate impact of their deportation on the Kulturbund. They asked to cancel all performances the following day, 31 October, which had been designated a "fasting day" by the Reich Association of Jews. Brasch underscored the seriousness of their requests, noting after the meeting: "In view of the fact that prayers will be said in religious services for the evacuated Jews . . . on Saturday, 2.11 [2 November], it is requested that all events also be canceled on this day." The men also discussed what position the executive board ought to take regarding possibilities for future Kulturbund activity, considering the present "situation for Jews in Germany."[5]

The deportations from southern Germany represented a grave threat, enough to instigate a collective sign of solidarity by the Reich Association of Jews and soul-searching about the Kulturbund's purpose. Yet Kochanowski made it clear that he could not cancel performances until he consulted Hinkel.[6] It is unclear whether Hinkel granted the men's public request to cancel events for a week.[7] Readers of the *Nachrichtenblatt* found no mention of cancellations or rescheduled performances in their Friday edition of the newspaper on 1 November or during the following week. Instead Gordin's *The Mother* proceeded as a scheduled matinee performance on 2 November.[8] Nor did Brasch speak again publicly about canceling events. He had received a clear warning to keep quiet. Ever the lawyer, he meticulously noted an alarming incident that he suffered at the hands of the Secret State Police. "On Saturday, 2 November 1940, 8 A.M., I was ordered to appear at Gestapo Headquarters Berlin, and meanwhile be interrogated."[9] The Gestapo agent questioned Brasch about his role in the Reich Association, the declared fasting day on 31 October, and his affiliation with the Kulturbund. The interrogation may have been intended to squelch internal protest that could have had broader appeal within the greater Jewish community: "The civil servant [interrogator] could not understand that people who were thought to have the correct personality and were on the right side [of an issue] would try to ram their skulls against a steel wall," Brasch noted. He had assured his interrogator that all recent actions taken by the Reich Association had a "strictly internal" nature and in no way represented a protest against government leadership.[10] It appears that Hinkel censured Brasch for his indirect involvement with the Reich Association of Jews. Two days later Kochanowski ordered Brasch to his office again. Hinkel had determined that Wisten alone would be responsible for the theatre's programs from then on, but Brasch would remain on the executive board to control financial and personnel-related matters.[11]

Wisten and Brasch knew that their work and the well-being of their employees depended on continued negotiations with Kochanowski and compliance with his superiors, Hinkel and Goebbels. "Herr Kochanowski emphasizes again that I should not be limited in my artistic work. He is there to advance my work; and . . . I am to come to him personally with my doubts," Wisten wrote after a meeting at the Be K A.[12] As much as the propaganda chief flattered Wisten that he "should not be constrained artistically," Kochanowski had more important matters to supervise beyond the Jewish theatre. By the end of October he still had not read Wisten's annual theatre report, which probably had been submitted two months before.[13] Nonetheless, Wisten took the initiative during November and alternated performances of the *Mother* with a "concert" version of Ruggiero Leoncavallo's *Bajazzo*.[14] He had added a final performance of *The Mother* on 30 November.[15] But Wisten also was preparing a new play production for the first time in three months: a version of Jacinto Benavente's comedy *The Virtuous Knight of Fortune* (*Der tugendhafte Glücksritter*), originally known as *The Bonds of Interest*.[16]

In the tradition of Félix Lope de Vega and Pedro Calderón de la Barca, Benavente's "masked" drama of intrigue combined elements of the commedia dell'arte with somber tones; this particular play had a cynical message: those who cheat and those who are cheated "enter into mutual bonds of interest."[17] With the eighth playing season starting two months later than in past years (on 14 December 1940), Benavente's idea about alliances and complicity reverberated with meaning. It was not purely coincidental that Kochanowki permitted productions of authors born in Spain, Italy, and Hungary. Germany now shared political and military alliances with all three Axis nations. On a more personal level, Wisten continued to work together with Kochanowski, despite the real compromises he endured as a result of his unequal alliance with the SS officer.

Restrictions continually straitjacketed Wisten. He had limited artistic freedom regarding the repertoire; he also had fewer resources to produce plays, procure materials for them, or even retain personnel. While directing his close friend Alfred Berliner as Crispin (a Harlequin commedia type) and Fritz Grünne as his sidekick Leonardo, Wisten had to rely on imaginative means to create a stage illusion. His actors played once more in a sparse stage setting almost devoid of "decor." The comedy's nonstop action took place exclusively on a narrow square podium, where audiences had to imagine the garden setting or the house interior. To highlight the play's irony, the director made simple choices. A background sound score accompanied a duel scene. A smiling moon descended during a love scene. Without enough understudies to take over roles, the designer Hanna Litten, who doubled as a stage manager, stepped in at the last moment when Steffi Hinzelmann fell ill.[18] Leo Hirsch had described Benavente's comedy as a "modern play in old dress" where laughter served a healing and restorative function.[19] Perhaps audiences sought more hopeful messages than Benavente's cynical one. The Kulturbund performed his play only four times.

"31/12: Today I was at the Kubu. One's hair stands on end to see what transpires in the offices," reported a stage technician on the eve of 1941. "Not including the film box-office and the newspaper, I counted 20 people. . . . And who of them works? Don't ask me—I don't know."[20] Wisten's surplus of clerks and secretaries had more to do with their protection from the Reich Labor department than with actual need. Until the director received an explicit request to downsize Kulturbund personnel, he supported as many employees as possible. He deliberately overstaffed the office administration, giving his workers extra needed income. The international blockade of the past year and a half had "pinched" Germany. The severe cold snap of 1939 had ruined the fruit crop and caused shortages of vitamin-rich foods in the country a year later. An early December blizzard further blighted the country's food supply during the winter of 1940. This meant especially meager food rations for Jews.[21]

With the start of 1941 German soldiers in occupied Romania began mass killings of Jews there. In Poland the Nazis deported Jews into the newly sealed Warsaw ghetto. A feeling of déjà vu loomed in Nazi-occupied Holland for German émigrés like former Kulturbund director Kurt Singer and the actor Max Ehrlich, who officially had to register themselves with the civil authorities as Jews. They remembered their gradual exclusion from civil society in Germany: "Dutch Kubu-movement underway," Singer reported from Amsterdam in December 1940. Jewish community leaders had asked him to direct a German division of a cultural league being considered for the city: "What should the Dutch Jews perform as their first play to please all sides? I recommended *Jacob's Summer Night's-Dream-Play in the Castle*," Singer wrote to a friend.[22] His irony and ambivalence, especially after his experience in Berlin, kept him only peripherally engaged with the developing Dutch theatre for Jews.[23]

An increase in anti-Jewish regulations mirrored the German model: the separation of Jews and their culture from Aryans and their formal registration as Jews.[24] The Dutch Jewish theatre that formed in the summer of 1941 at the Hollandse Schouwburg on Amsterdam's Plantage-Middenlaan provided Jewish performers with a venue for cabaret and concerts. Under the management of former Kulturbund administrator Werner Levie and Max Ehrlich, the Nazis restricted the Joodse Schouwburg to Jewish-only audiences by late 1941. A German delegation closed down the Schouwburg in July 1942 and would convert the theatre into a deportation site in October 1942.[25]

Eight years to the day after he took power in Germany, Hitler addressed adoring crowds at Berlin's Sportpalast. He outlined his plans for a New Order in a new year:

> Finally this year will help to assure the basis for understanding between the peoples, and thereby, for their reconciliation. I do not want to miss pointing out what I pointed out on 3rd of September [1940] in the German Reichstag, that if Jewry were to plunge the world into war, the role of Jewry would be finished in Europe. They may laugh about it today, as they laughed before about my prophecies. The coming months and years will prove that I prophesied rightly in this case too.[26]

Fritz Wisten may have heard parts of Hitler's broadcast speech on a borrowed radio. Jews were no longer permitted to own radios. But Wisten and his non-Jewish wife, Gertrud (née Widmann), could listen to broadcasts at their next-door neighbor's home in Berlin-Schlachtensee.[27] Trude Wisten owned the Bauhaus-style house in the exclusive lakeside neighborhood. Wisten's "privileged mixed marriage" to an Aryan gave the family relative protection. On the same street lived the head of the Reich Military Intelligence, Admiral Wilhelm Canaris, and his wife, Erika. Before 1933 Wisten's daughter Susanne played with the Canaris daughter. SS chief of security police Reinhard Heydrich and his wife, Lina, lived around the corner at Reifträgerweg. Despite Hitler's chilling prophecy about Jews, the Wisten couple, their two daughters, and Wisten's octogenarian father (Isidore) led as normal a life as possible amid almost impossible circumstances.

As a man of the theatre for much of his adult life, Wisten had developed a strong sense of himself as an actor. He was well-spoken, poised, adaptable in his theatre roles, and authoritative as a stage director. These skills afforded him advantages when it came to dealing with people in his neighborhood, within the Jewish community, and in Kochanowski's office at the Nazi ministry. Wisten had learned how to use opportunities to benefit himself and his family. And he knew how to use his influence to help other Jewish theatre artists who were less fortunate. In this way his strong ego and his ability to accommodate his needs to others aided him in keeping the theatre running.

Each morning Wisten walked from Dianastraße down the Wahrmundzeile, to the elevated railway train (S-Bahn) which brought him across the city to the central Potsdamer station. Then he took the streetcar toward Kommandantenstraße.[28] From his theatre office there, he addressed artistic questions and logistical concerns pertaining to the Kulturbund. He juggled requests from his staff, Kulturbund division leaders, and the Be K A, tackling the economic and bureaucratic realities of the enterprise: salaries had to be paid; special performances required authorization; and all events in the "provinces" had to be approved first by the Be K A and then by local Gestapo offices.[29] Because attendance and revenue were linked, programming would have to improve both. While awaiting approval to produce a comedy by Aldo de Benedetti, Wisten approached Kochanowski about the repertoire: "I spoke of the difficulty in choosing a play that must follow the not very successful *The Virtuous Knight of Fortune* [The Bonds of Interest]. I ask permission to submit Wilde's *Bunburry*. . . . I stress that Wilde is Irish and belongs to a past epoch so removed from us that the English atmosphere should not be able to cause offense."[30] The British Royal Air Force, however, caused damage enough with air strikes over Berlin. Kochanowksi would not authorize a play by an Irishman, not even one translated by a Jew.

It was becoming physically dangerous to go to the theatre. Bomb shelters, sirens, and blackouts were part of Berlin's cityscape. For several months temporary emergency shelters had been created for those homeless from bombings in Berlin's central district, where the theatre was situated.[31] Pink flyers attached to playbills alerted audience members about what they should do in case of air-raid warnings during performances: "We ask you to remain in your seats and follow instructions from theatre personnel. The Management."[32]

The topic of emigration monopolized the community's newspaper headlines and classified ad section in 1941: "Central Point of Emigration: Financial Basis"; "A Lot of Space Overseas"; "Not Enough Passages." Every issue featured reports on Jewish communities—in Asia and the Pacific Rim, the United States, and South America. Leo Kreindler published numerous articles urging Jews to leave Germany and detailed which overseas passage routes were accessible in wartime—by spring, only through Portugal or Spain.[33]

At the same time when division leaders in the Kulturbund publishing sector were promoting emigration, their own lives remained in limbo between their service to the Jewish community and their subservience to the Be K A. Kochanowski stalled the emigration plans of Kreindler and Willy Pless, head of book publishing. At a conference meeting in early March Kochanowski cautioned the two, along with Brasch and Wisten, that "the emigration of those present . . . was not possible at the present time."[34] Kochanowski needed the four men to orchestrate Kulturbund-related activities.

Kochanowski made Wisten indispensable to the organization, reemphasizing the director's right to artistic license without limitation.[35] He encouraged Wisten to describe the situation at the Kulturbund with details about audience interest and theatre attendance. Wisten knew that Kochanowski ultimately controlled the theatre agenda, whittling down the parameters of what was permissible or even open to discussion. At almost every meeting that spring he exerted pressure on Wisten to transfer personnel from the theatre staff to Reich labor units and to cut costs wherever possible. Squeezed between Kochanowski's dictates and a Jewish community increasingly unable to make additional financial commitments to the theatre, Wisten and Brasch had to replace hourly wages for theatre ushers and cloakroom attendants with a flat rate, for example. Additionally, Kochanowski demanded that the Jewish community take on more financial responsibility by partially subsidizing the Kulturbund orchestra, which by 3 April 1941 already had dwindled in size.[36] Under Rudolf Schwarz the orchestra united musicians from the Kulturbund and community help organizations. Their recent and moving rendition of Gustav Mahler's Requiem ("Resurrection") in February and March was a "miracle with such a small group," according to the oboist Kurt Michaelis, who recalled a communal sense of hope and spirit in the concert experience.[37]

Amid a gradual but definite dismantling of the Kulturbund and its diminishing resources, Wisten reduced the spring and summer's offerings to only several plays and musical events during 1941. In the publishing department, Kreindler shortened the newspaper length to four pages on Tuesdays and eight on Fridays. But critics Hirsch, Lachmanski, and Michalowitz still filed and published their theatre and music reviews. Hirsch worked closely with Wisten on scripts, including the forthcoming *Thirty Seconds of Love* (*30 Sekunden Liebe*) by Aldo de Benedetti. Kochanowski authorized the play premiere for 8 March 1941 but forbade performances on Good Friday and on Hitler's birthday (20 April).[38]

The plot of the innocuous comedy set in Rome turns on a kiss. The kiss is a plan for blackmail after a married woman causes an accident. Signora Grazia accepts the settlement of a thirty-second kiss instead of paying damages to the man she allegedly harmed. The plaintiff faked his injury to exploit the situation.[39] Grazia chooses to be alone with him instead of kissing him in front of her relatives. The man drops all charges and leaves without a kiss. Grazia tells her husband that she was kissed. The man returns for his kiss. Grazia tells her husband that she never got a kiss. The secret remains intact.

"Rousing applause" followed the Kulturbund premiere, starring Alfred Berliner and Steffi Hinzelmann. Audiences were impressed by Litten's elegant onstage house interior designs.[40] Kulturbund members could choose from ten scheduled performances of Benedetti's comedy through 10 May. Coincidentally, the *Nachrichtenblatt* editor placed the production review directly above an advice column on how to apply taxes to property that was once owned by Jews. The sale of Jewish property required legal approval, given that property "in the hand of a Jew can have less worth than in the hand of a non-Jew." To make up the balance of the total sale profit, an "Aryanizing" payment had to be levied in favor of the Reich. Wisten's wife spared him and their daughters the humiliation of transferring Jewish property. But Jews who did not have a non-Jewish partner to protect their assets paid a "flight tax" and a "Jewish atonement tax."[41] The newspaper's juxtaposition of tax tips with the play review illustrates the reality of transferring Jewish property to non-Jews. And it underscores the vacuous premise of Benedetti's onstage world, in which a man and woman barter a kiss as a commodity.

Yet the hostile realities for Jews in Germany seeped into the foreground at the Kulturbund. On orders from Hermann Göring, all able Jews could be recruited for labor in the Reich. In March 1941 Himmler expanded the network of concentration camps with the construction of a camp at Birkenau in Poland. The Nazis added a second ghetto in Krakow. Then in early April Germany invaded Yugoslavia and Greece. From his Berlin office Hinkel began to consider how to resolve the "Jewish Problem."[42] Meanwhile Kochanowski solidified power from the outside to dictate control within the Kulturbund. He mandated another reorganization of the cultural enterprise, effective 15 April 1941. This put the four department heads in charge of their divisions, with overall administrative power assigned to Brasch.

Backstage at the theatre some performers tried to flee their country. Others succumbed to daily pressures, unable to leave, as Kurt Süßmann wrote to fellow actor Martin Brandt in emigration. Süßmann had performed roles with the Youth stage, in *The Trial*, *The Mother*, and most recently *Thirty Seconds of Love*. He pointed to the proximity of death and play at the Kulturbund:

> 4/27/41. Some news in the Kulturbund. The sudden death of Wilhelm Guttman has shaken me. He sang Thursday afternoon—three days ago . . . where he collapsed as he was singing: stroke, right side-total paralysis. He died at 10 P.M. In the new play, *Señor Alan Out of Purgatory*, a modern, Spanish comedy, I have a nice, small part . . . youthful comical; Wisten plays the leading role. . . . You cannot imagine how bleak it has become there now.[43]

Even during rehearsals Süßmann could hardly contain his ongoing preoccupation with affidavits and ship passage.

Wisten had just begun rehearsals for *Señor Alan* in early May when the Gestapo detained Martin Brasch again.[44] This time they imprisoned him. The arrest of Brasch, as chairman of the Kulturbund organization, reverberated throughout the enterprise. Wisten could not focus solely on the theatre while Brasch was in prison. A day after the arrest Wisten met with Kochanowski and persuaded the SS man to look into the incident. In the meantime Kochanowski offered Wisten Brasch's position on the Kulturbund board. But he refused. Instead he requested that the departments be permitted to function independently during Brasch's absence. He asked to schedule a meeting with all department leaders for the following week in case Brasch had not been released.[45] A week later Brasch remained in detention.

Play rehearsals for Sancho López de la Puerta's comedy proceeded and ran for two weeks. With the premiere approaching on 14 June 1941, Süßmann continued his long wait for an exit visa. "Believe me, dear Martin, no

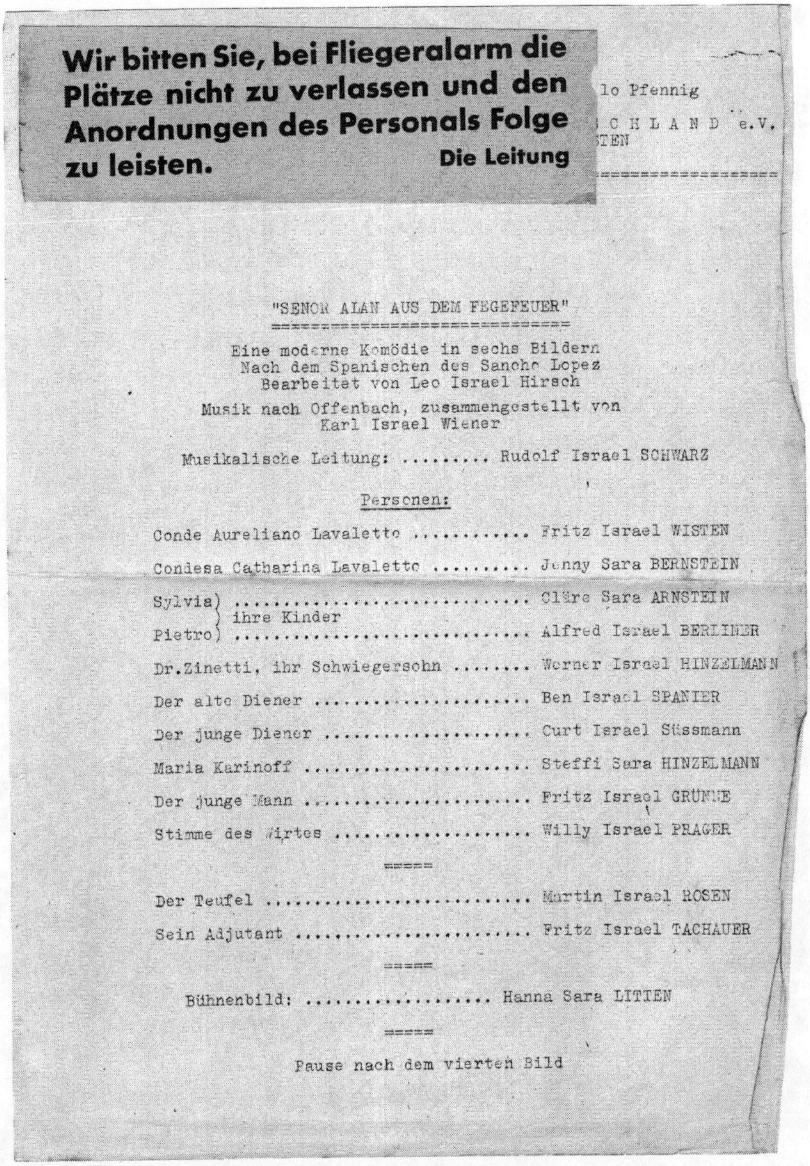

Wir bitten Sie, bei Fliegeralarm die Plätze nicht zu verlassen und den Anordnungen des Personals Folge zu leisten.

Die Leitung

10 Pfennig

...CHLAND e.V.

...TEN

"SENOR ALAN AUS DEM FEGEFEUER"

Eine moderne Komödie in sechs Bildern
Nach dem Spanischen des Sancho Lopez
Bearbeitet von Leo Israel Hirsch

Musik nach Offenbach, zusammengestellt von
Karl Israel Wiener

Musikalische Leitung: .... Rudolf Israel SCHWARZ

Personen:

Conde Aureliano Lavaletto .... Fritz Israel WISTEN

Condesa Catharina Lavaletto .... Jenny Sara BERNSTEIN

Sylvia } ihre Kinder .... Cläre Sara ARNSTEIN

Pietro } ihre Kinder .... Alfred Israel BERLINER

Dr.Zinetti, ihr Schwiegersohn .... Werner Israel HINZELMANN

Der alte Diener .... Ben Israel SPANIER

Der junge Diener .... Curt Israel Süssmann

Maria Karinoff .... Steffi Sara HINZELMANN

Der junge Mann .... Fritz Israel GRÜNNE

Stimme des Wirtes .... Willy Israel PRAGER

=====

Der Teufel .... Martin Israel ROSEN

Sein Adjutant .... Fritz Israel TACHAUER

=====

Bühnenbild: .... Hanna Sara LITTEN

=====

Pause nach dem vierten Bild

17. ***Señor Alan Out of Purgatory*****, playbill with flyer on air raid, June 1941. Akademie der Künste, Berlin, FWA 74/86/53.81, photograph by Akademie der Künste.**

18. ***Señor Alan Out of Purgatory***, June 1941: Fritz Wisten (*left*) and Alfred Berliner (*right*). Akademie der Künste, Berlin, FWA 74/86/24_60, photographer unknown.

day may be lost, and with every day that passes, everything is in limbo."[46] The actor reported on the too-slow progress of his emigration and his first dress rehearsal for *Señor Alan*: "Prager [Willy] thinks I'm very good. Nevertheless, I don't feel comfortable in the general atmosphere."[47]

Martin Brasch lay in the hospital with severe blood poisoning. Wisten finally received word that his friend had been sent there from the forced labor camp Wuhlheide. "Herr Kochanowski shows deep interest and hopes along with me that the patient's youth . . . will be in his favor," Wisten noted. But Brasch died within a week.[48] By that time the Reich Cultural Chamber had undergone an internal restructuring. Hinkel earned a promotion to general secretary and oversaw a management center that encompassed five departments. The Be K A had been reintegrated into the new organization, which would be renamed the RMVP (Reichsministerium für Volksaufklärung und Propaganda) in August 1941.[49] Wisten now reported to Kochanowski at his new Division C for Propaganda. "Tremendous reduction measures" must be taken, Wisten learned, as his summer meetings with the SS officer focused less on aspects of programming and more on dismantling offices. Kochanowski called the "whole cultural undertaking" into question as he pushed the Jewish Kulturbund toward the denouement of its active life.[50]

Dismantling procedures loomed for the entire organization. Yet when the Ministry of Propaganda took something away from the Kulturbund, Wisten strategically negotiated a temporary gain. Although Kochanowski did not foresee subvention funds from the Jewish community for the theatre, Wisten persuaded him to set up financial bonuses for artists who contributed extra work. He specifically named Martin Rosen and Karl Wiener (essential to the ongoing production of *Señor Alan*), whose "artistic versatility" it was "urgently necessary" to boost.[51] Wisten's temporary victory was soon countered by a loss. Kochanowski announced that the Jewish newspaper would shut down, which meant a blow to the Kulturbund's publishing sector and its employees. Kreindler already had condensed the newspaper to a four-page edition on Fridays only.[52] By late June, with *Señor Alan* in production, it was "looking worse and worse to leave Germany," Süßmann wrote between his performances as a Spanish servant.[53]

Señor Alan Out of Purgatory opens in an underground room—ostensibly Hell—where a verse-speaking Devil sits on a throne before a red curtain. His consul tells him of new developments in the planetary system and about Hell's new arrivals. The residents from earth cannot adjust. One is causing trouble, says the consul: "Instead of behaving meanly, he is melancholy and sits on a stone, swinging his legs, and sings love songs."[54] After interrogating the rabble-rouser, the newly dead Lavaletto, the Devil sends him to earth for two days. Lavaletto's yearning for goodness could ruin Hell. Lavaletto hopes to make amends for his adulterous behavior. He returns "home" for his own funeral as a friend of the "dead" man Antonio Alan. He wants his family to know the real Lavaletto's flaws and ensure that his girlfriend and illegitimate daughter profit from his inheritance.

The scenes alternate between "Antonio" at home and in Hell, as the Devil watches in horror. As "Antonio," Lavaletto convinces his son of the father's flaws, provides for his former girlfriend, gains forgiveness from his wife, and falls in love with her. When the "living dead man" returns to "Hell," it is cold with blue skies: "This guy is going to ruin us with his decency; throw him out!" the consul advises the Devil. "We've let him torment us enough. Let Heaven deal with him," he says as the curtain falls.[55]

Wisten directed *Señor Alan Out of Purgatory* and played the double role of Condé Aureliano Lavaletto and Señor Antonio Alan. López de la Puerta's script about goodness trumping evil underwent various changes before the Kulturbund debut. It is possible that Wisten and Hirsch fabricated the author to bypass the censor. And they succeeded. They reworked *Señor Alan* into a fantasy in six scenes, with a score based on Offenbach's operettas (by Karl Wiener).[56] Seated at the piano, Rudolf Schwarz conducted an orchestra of fourteen, whose musical accompaniment underscored the action with melodramatic tones. Wisten chose his most trusted actors to lend a mix of sentimentality and comic timing to the play. Martin Rosen played the Devil to Fritz Tachauer's consul and Wisten's title role. Wisten cast Alfred Berliner in a role atypical for the actor—as his son. Jenny Schaffer-Bernstein played the jilted wife and mother, countered by Steffi Hinzelmann as the ex-girlfriend and mother of his child (Cläre Arnstein). Werner Hinzelmann and Fritz Grünne took on roles as the son-in-law and a suitor. Despite "primitive" furnishings, Litten's sparse scene settings showed a well-defined perspective to accommodate the limited stage space.[57]

It is ironic that Wisten directed himself in the Spanish allegory about a man too good to stay in Hell. The play's metaphor of a man's goodness that physically transforms Hell evokes a surreal world that inverts Heaven and Hell. During June 1941 art and life or illusion and reality eerily merged at the Kulturbund. Wisten's multiple roles as director, negotiator, and Jewish actor came together in his double stage-role as a "living dead man" who moves between the Devil and Hell and his family on earth. One cannot ignore the significance of the director's offstage function as artistic manager of the Jewish Kulturbund in Germany. During the same period when he was embodying his double character onstage in *Señor Alan*, offstage he met with Nazis like Kochanowski to keep the theatre alive, even as it was being dismantled.

"How can you explain the strangeness—you just go on living. If someone hits you, you get up again," explained Michaelis about his ability to perform music amid ominous threats to his existence.[58] By 1 July 1941 the forced disbanding of the orchestra was complete, leaving only one quartet intact. Kochanowski requested a list of the musicians' names to send to the Reich Labor department.[59] Even while the Kulturbund and its orchestra were being disbanded, Wisten pushed forward, scheduling two more productions of *Señor Alan* in July. He still had access to Ministry of Propaganda officers. And he continued to advocate for his employees in Berlin and for his former theatre colleagues in Dutch exile who were developing the all-Jewish theatre in Amsterdam.

"There must be a way to subsume this [Dutch] group within the Kulturbund," noted Wisten after returning from meeting with Kochanowski in early August. Theatre performances by Jewish-born German émigrés took place in Amsterdam's Jewish community.[60] The cabaret troupe at the Hollandse Schouwburg under the direction of Levie and Ehrlich had performed Molnár's *The Play's the Thing* (*Spiel im Schloß*) in June 1941—once for general admission and then for Jews only.[61] But Wisten's good intentions did not bring the Dutch-based acting ensemble into the Kulturbund theatre network. Nor could Wisten turn Hell into Heaven. The hellish atmosphere for Jews in Berlin intensified. By the end of July 1941 the SS held a monopoly on all Jewish policy.[62] Hermann Göring issued an order to Heydrich (chief of the Reich Main Security Office) to initiate a "solution" to the "Jewish Question" that plagued Europe. The date was 31 July 1941. The Nazi policy for annihilating Jews was in place.[63]

At the Kulturbund, however, Wisten prepared yet another play production. Following the example of his colleagues in Holland, he readied a revival of Molnár's play-within-a-play, *The Play's the Thing*, for its premiere. In the play two seasoned librettists, a young, inexperienced composer, his prima donna fiancée, and an actor gather in an Italian castle with thin walls. The composer overhears his actress-girlfriend rehearsing a love scene, which he mistakes for a seduction. With his companions, he crafts the overheard dialogue into a play to catch the actress and her would-be lover in their liaison.

19. Molnár, *The Play's the Thing*, August 1935: (*left to right*) Max Ehrlich, Fritz Wisten, Liselotte Rosen. Akademie der Künste, Berlin, FWA 74/86/18_92, photograph by Abraham Pisarek, courtesy Ruth Gross.

The play is a hit; the writer-composer's girlfriend's loyalty is assured; and misunderstandings are resolved.[64]

"It was an excellent performance under Ben Israel Spanier," a reviewer wrote about the Kulturbund production of *The Play's the Thing* on 9 August 1941. Hanna Litten rendered an effective stage setting for the farce that suited the very limited stage space.[65] Spanier cast himself in the play's on-stage theatre ensemble. He played the actor in the "seduction" scene, with Steffi Hinzelmann as the "Diva of Kitsch and love."[66] Fritz Grünne played the "green" composer, while Alfred Berliner and Fritz Tachauer's flair for comedy enhanced their roles as the two librettists.

Five years earlier, in August 1935, *The Play's the Thing* marked the Kulturbund's final production at the theatre on Charlottenstraße, with Fritz Wisten as a librettist and Max Ehrlich as the actor. A reviewer pointed to the frivolity of the play choice for the times: "The Molnaresque anecdote . . . is an unmistakable summer play that requires only a happy theatre spectator to enjoy the play—one who doesn't want to be bothered by problems. This August perspective explains the choice of this play. . . . The audience amused itself. And now to new deeds in the winter season at the Kulturbund's new venue—on Kommandantenstraße!"[67] The late summer of 1935 held promise for the Kulturbund as its third playing season approached. Yet at that time Nazi policies already poisoned Berlin's atmosphere. During August 1941 the conditions for Jews in Europe were outright deadly. Jewish theatregoers in Berlin may not have wanted to be "bothered by problems," but they could not ignore increasing impediments to their liberty.[68]

Kurt Süßmann remained in Berlin, looking for borders that he could afford to cross that had not been blocked.[69] Across the Atlantic in the United States, Martin Brandt wrote letters on behalf of his fellow actor. As the summer passed, however, immigration policies became increasingly restrictive: "The Department of State, D.C. . . . advises that no affidavits will be accepted on behalf of persons in occupied countries. We quite understand the desperate plight of Mr. Süssman [*sic*], however."[70] On 23 August Himmler announced a directive to stop emigration of Jews from Reich territory.[71] Singer urgently sought passage from Europe, having secured a Cuban and Spanish transit visa and an exit permit.[72] As autumn neared, American consulates closed. Meanwhile the Nazi government issued a police ordinance on 1 September 1941, mandating that all Jews in the Reich and Protectorate, except those in mixed marriages and families, identify themselves by wearing a yellow Star of David visible on the left breast of their outermost clothing, effective 19 September.[73]

Despite the alarming signals for Jews in Germany, Wisten pushed ahead in the narrowing space he controlled at the Kulturbund. Kulturbund audiences in Berlin had witnessed six performances of *The Play's the Thing* by the second week in September. The next performance was scheduled for 11 September, with guest tours in Hamburg (7–8 September) and Breslau (14–15 September). Wisten also had prepared a new production using Leo Hirsch's translation of Mosche Lipshitz's *Were I Not a Fool: A Whimsical Story with Hershel Ostropoler* (*Wenn der Narr nicht mein wär: Eine wunderliche Geschichte mit Hershel Ostropoler*).[74] The Yiddish-language comedy would star Ben Spanier and Steffi Hinzelmann. Even during these difficult last months, the director remained committed to carrying on business, producing Jewish plays from the East as well as popular drama. He began rehearsals for the new play on 10 September.

The Gestapo headquarters contacted Moritz Henschel of Berlin's Jewish community Kultusvereinigung on Thursday, 11 September. "I am dissolving the Jewish Kulturbund in Germany e.V. Berlin as of today": so began the drily worded police directive. Henschel served on the Kulturbund executive board. The news delivered to his Oranienburgerstraße office was based on "paragraph #1 of the Reich President's law to protect the people and the state."[75] The ruling effectively shut down the Kulturbund except for the publishing division. "I forbid any activity that attempts to continue or reorganize the association with the same or similar goals," warned Gestapo officer Dr. Kunz.[76] Nonetheless, the seventh Berlin performance of *The Play's the Thing* took place that evening.[77] Henschel did not receive an official copy of the dissolution directive until the next morning, Friday, 12 September 1941, when he forwarded it to Wisten.[78]

Steffi Hinzelmann approached the theatre on Kommandantenstraße for morning rehearsals. She was five months pregnant. The production run of Molnár's play-within-a-play was nearly over. The next production would be the "Russian-Jewish" comedy in which she played a main role. She especially looked forward to wearing her character's wide peasant skirt to hide her growing pregnancy.[79] A crowd of people stood gathered in front of the theatre: Hinzelmann saw SS men, automobiles, and workers. Gestapo men were removing "everything that could be taken away" from the building.[80]

When the Secret State Police officers swept through the theatre, they seized Kulturbund property and assets and sealed off all theatre offices. Before shuttering the organization for good, however, a Gestapo official allowed all employees to receive compensation for their work through 15 September. But personnel were ordered to be available to the Gestapo throughout the month. Performers and staff would be forced to assist in the "liquidation" of their Kulturbund and clear out stockrooms at the Jewish Book Publishers.[81] A Gestapo officer gave Wisten a deadline by which to oversee the disbanding process of the Kulturbund, which included removing his personal property.[82]

The raid by Gestapo officers cut short the September production run of *The Play's the Thing*. Besides the Breslau tour, Wisten had added a performance for 4 October.[83] This performance never took place. Nor did rehearsals proceed for Wisten's production about the legendary prankster Ostropoler. Wisten had planned the premiere of Lipschitz's comedy to coincide with the High Holidays (21–30 September 1941), edging the Kulturbund theatre into its ninth year.[84] "My father was, as grotesque as it sounds, a notorious optimist," Susanne Wisten-Weyl has stated.[85] Wisten probably wanted to keep the theatre going as long as he could, protecting his employees from Reich labor laws or worse. His attempt to produce the Yiddish-language script suggests something about his character. His savvy as a theatre professional allowed him to take advantage of his position at the helm of the theatre. He remained committed to his theatre and his personnel. In the new play Ostropoler the itinerant rascal always profits, duping the most pious community members. Ostropoler trades places with a rabbi. Their division of labor works well until Ostropoler cuckolds the rabbi and impregnates his once-barren wife, Rebbezin Sorele. The moral of the play is that a fool knows more than a holy man.

The play's carefree—albeit cynical—ending belies the reality of what was happening in Germany as Wisten marked stage entrances and exits and anticipated which Hebrew expressions Kulturbund audiences might know besides a prayer for the dead.[86] Wisten knew from his meetings with Kochanowski that the Nazis could shut down the theatre at any time. Yet the director plotted scenes and calculated production costs for a play whose future on the stage was highly uncertain. The Gestapo raid cannot have come as a surprise to the shrewd manager. Perhaps he anticipated that the longer he could keep the theatre enterprise operational, the better it would be for his employees. At the same time, as a longtime performer and director, Wisten probably thought of his own posterity as an artist. He already may have begun to take stock of his office files, gathering his papers. We know that sometime during the month of September, little by little, he brought important materials home to keep them safe. On his commute from the theatre in the city center, Wisten transported in his briefcase and bags play scripts, newspaper clippings, correspondence, and photographs.[87]

■ The Jewish Kulturbund did not—indeed could not—simply end with a Nazi government order. With the immediate closure of the theatre, Fritz Wisten began to write its history. "On 12 September 1941 the Gestapo dissolved the Jewish Kulturbund in Germany e.V.," he informed a director at the Reich Association of Jews.[88] Wisten had spent September dealing with the aftermath of his shuttered theatre. The liquidation of all Kulturbund holdings was ongoing. His employees gravely needed financial assistance. Wisten sent to the Reich Association a list of employees still on the payroll, stipulating that their salaries be paid by 30 September 1941.[89] The list numbered thirty-eight, plus five who worked for hourly wages; six employees, among them Steffi Hinzelmann and Jenny Schaffer-Bernstein, had not been paid in September.[90] Their employment records remained sealed in a Kulturbund office.

The theatre artists faced oppressive worries with the dissolution of the Kulturbund: "What depresses me most is my concern for the people who acknowledge my authority," Wisten wrote to Max Ehrlich in Amsterdam. "The majority will find work. But what will become of the old people, whom we brought along with us all these years?"[91] The High Holidays provided Jews with an opportune time to contact friends and commiserate. The Hinzelmanns expressed their gratitude to Wisten: "In this time of emptiness that lies before us . . . we especially will miss your personality and your electrifying optimism."[92] Yet Wisten's optimistic spirit had waned: "One cannot imagine Jewish life without this institution," he conceded to Ehrlich.[93] The fallout from the Kulturbund's breakup spread to Holland, where Ehrlich and Kurt Singer pondered the news. Recalling his role in shaping the organization, Singer reflected on the theatre: "It has moved me deeply that the 'Ku-Bünde' are closed. Almost symbolic, coming together with my imminent emigration. A piece of life's work sinks with it."[94] Singer's emigration from Holland had stalled temporarily, as had Kurt Süßmann's plan to leave Germany.

Unable to travel through occupied Reich territory, Süßmann hoped to escape Germany via Ecuador; but the ship passage was too costly. Still optimistic in October, he informed Brandt that "thousands are worse off" than he was.[95] Yet one week later, on 14 October 1941, the Nazis began to transport Jews from Germany to the Łódź Ghetto.[96] The following week the head of the Gestapo, Heinrich Müller, banned the emigration of all Jews from the Reich (23 October). Süßmann's brother soon confirmed the futility of helping Kurt.[97] Just two days later, on 4 November, Kurt Singer discovered that his visa was eight days too late for him to leave the Netherlands.[98] The two men from different generations of Berlin's Jewish theatre waited to leave Berlin and Amsterdam. They held out hope—their lives connected to the Kulturbund stage and its demise.

It was impossible to get an affidavit to escape Germany. Steffi Hinzelmann and her husband wanted to leave illegally for Italy. But they were barred from emigration, and the SS confiscated their puppet theatre. By November 1941 Nazi law required all Jews in the Reich to work in factories and construction firms, with a substantial portion of their salaries automatically taxed and paid to the Reich.[99] Fritz Wisten helped former Kulturbund employees, including the Hinzelmanns, to find temporary employment at the Reich Association of Jews. Their names appeared among the sixteen colleagues whom he recommended two years in a row as "indispensable employees," along with actors Ben Spanier, Fritz Tachauer, Cläre Arnstein; designer Hanna Litten; and conductor Rudolf Schwarz.[100] The artists thus avoided labor shifts in factories by working in Jewish community offices. As part of his work assignment, Werner Hinzelmann listed vacant apartments and registered Jews for the transports until his heart attack later that summer.[101] In February 1942 Steffi Hinzelmann gave birth to their child, a "blonde angel with big blue eyes . . . but I wore the star," she would remember.[102] Her Kulturbund connection and subsequent work in the Jewish welfare office afforded her the privilege of visiting her mother at Berlin's central deportation site and averting the same fate.

Wisten worked at the Reich Association office as a librarian late into 1941. His privileged marriage status made everyday life much easier. Neither he nor his daughters had to wear the star.[103] Wisten could not have known that his former neighbor Reichsführer-SS Heydrich had returned briefly to Berlin to convene the 20 January Wannsee Conference, which sanctioned plans for mass extermination in the "Final Solution" to the "Jewish Problem." The 1942 conference proceedings gave the Nazi government license to accelerate its plans to deport Jews to the East and exploit their forced labor.

When Adolf Eichmann ordered the dissolution of Berlin's Reich Association book publishing office in mid April 1942, Wisten had recently celebrated his fifty-second birthday. In his next job assignment at a factory (where he wore the star), he delivered boxes all day. His daily absences from the work site protected him from the factory roundups and arrests of Jews. Nor was he at home on the June day in 1942 when Gestapo men raided his house and arrested his wife. A household helper had denounced the Wistens for boarding Isidore Wisten. Fortuitously, the aged father had died a month before, sparing him deportation. But the police arrested Fritz Wisten. He and his wife spent three weeks in prison until their daughter Susanne "went sobbing down the street" to their neighbor Erika Canaris. Evidently Admiral Canaris arranged for the Wistens' release from prison, saving the family.[104] Their survival turned on a set of fortunate circumstances. Trude Widmann Wisten kept the family together by fiercely guarding her marriage. She owned property and had children, which also protected the family. Yet she was not immune to Nazi interrogations. The Gestapo did not free her from prison until six weeks after Wisten's release.

"It is hopeless," Singer wrote about leaving the Netherlands for Cuba; "to emigrate is no longer a topic. . . I have buried this hope. Maybe it is just as well. I would not have had another visa." Jews in Holland had worn a Star of David since early May 1942.[105] Singer served as an honorary member to the Jewish Council (Joodse Raad), which exempted him from mandatory labor. He resigned himself to his work, gave lectures, and wrote a book on opera. He had mostly ignored the cabaret revues and concerts at the Joodse Schouwburg for Jewish-only audiences that summer. In July 1942 a German delegation led by Hauptsturmführer Ferdinand aus der Fünten closed the theatre down. The cabaret artists found clerical work assignments at the Jewish Council in Amsterdam, facilitating the dissolution of Holland's Jewish community. On 14 October 1942 the Nazis turned the Schouwburg building into a deportation site.[106]

"If God exists, he will not honor you as he did me so that 8 days should decide my destiny: the 8 days that my visa was missing, while my passage was there. I will not allow myself to think about it."[107] Four days after Singer mourned his missed chance to emigrate in March 1943, he sent his book manuscript to a publisher. On 20 April 1943 the Nazis deported Singer from the Schouwburg building to Terezín (Theresienstadt), where he would engage musically in the ghetto's organized "leisure time" activities (*Freizeitgestaltung*).[108] Werner Levie's transport left a month later for the Westerbork transit camp. Many of the Jewish Schouwburg actors were deported from their former theatre on a September 1943 transport to Westerbork; some subsequently went on to Theresienstadt and Auschwitz-Birkenau.[109]

By 1943 the Nazis had deported most of the Berlin artists Wisten deemed "indispensable employees."[110] Werner Hinzelmann was dead. Steffi Hinzelmann, however, saved not only herself from deportation but also her sister and two children. The Gestapo man in charge of transport numbers recognized Hinzelmann from a performance he had seen at the Kulturbund. In a macabre parody of her role in Benedetti's *Thirty Seconds of Love*, Hinzelmann told the clerk who crossed out her sister's name from his master list, "Ach, Herr Dobberke, if it were not forbidden, I would kiss you." The actress recalled the Gestapo officer's "exact" words: "Aww, go on home now," he called after her: "Take your identification with you; or else you'll never get away from here!"[111] Hinzelmann and her baby would survive the war by hiding in a Berlin brothel.

The final issue of the *Jüdisches Nachrichtenblatt* appeared on 4 June 1943 and made public all regulations for Jewish readers left in Berlin.[112] Deportations left German Jewry a "scattering of individuals" without support institutions. Nazi authorities dissolved all Jewish community organizations, including the Reich Association.[113] In Berlin-Schlachtensee, at great risk to her family's safety, Trude Wisten agreed to hide Steffi Hinzelmann's leading man and Wisten's close friend and fellow actor Alfred Berliner. He would remain with the family for two years from 1943 through 1945. Wisten's daughters remembered how "Uncle Fredy" shared their house (and ration cards) in rough times. During air raids Berliner stayed hidden in the house. When the family returned from the bomb shelter in their yard, they found him in the kitchen, trying out new recipes. He wanted to be a chef after the war. But because food rations were limited, he used only flour and water.[114]

At the end of 1943 the former Kulturbund theatre on Kommandantenstraße housed an "alternative" theatre for troop entertainment.[115] Hans Hinkel no longer concerned himself with the Kulturbund Jews. Goebbels had given him a new assignment to prepare the German cultural establishment for total war. He supervised an extensive entertainment program for German soldiers, including a "Front" Theatre. On the Eastern Front, meanwhile, the Red Army made progress throughout the winter of 1943 and 1944. Allied forces, backed by the United States military, pressed on against the Axis powers. Bombs fell on Berlin with increasing frequency. The Wistens lived in terror, simultaneously euphoric at the allied victories but fearful that bombing strikes might kill them before they could witness the liberation of their city. Eva and Susanne Wisten have attributed their family's survival to their father's positive attitude and their mother's courage.[116]

■ Wisten's first role at the Kulturbund had been the congenial and witty Dervish in *Nathan the Wise*, with its ominously prophetic ending. Just months after the Soviets liberated Berlin, Wisten directed Lessing's *Nathan* as the first production in postwar Germany. On 7 September 1945, the Deutsches Theater opened with a production that scene designer Willi Schmidt described as an "Oriental fairy-tale with Talmudic cleverness and melancholy" but without pathos. Wisten and his cast (Paul Wegener as Nathan and Alfred Berliner as the Dervish) allowed the script's inclusive spirit to emerge. But as in 1933, the director avoided the final stage tableau of an "all around" embrace of world religions. It would take years for Germans to come to terms with the enormity of the war's devastation on their country. In 1945, critics approved of Wisten's caution to proclaim a happy end for Nathan. What most distinguished the post-war production from the pre-war one, however, was its endorsement of human solidarity, suggesting the hopeful "utopia of the reconciliation of ideology."[117]

CONCLUSION

BEYOND THE ABYSS

Fritz Wisten survived, but Kurt Singer did not. Word of his death in February 1944 at Theresienstadt did not reach his family and friends until six months after the fact.[1] It took until August for them to spread the news of his fate. Vera Simon asked Singer's former secretary: "Do you happen to have any old Ku-bu-play programs which you don't want? Do you know that I haven't anything here with me which has to do with his Ku-bu-work (except, of course, from his letters)."[2] Their personal exchange in 1944 was the first attempt to acknowledge Singer's contribution to theatre history. The beginning of the end neared—in the war and in an evaluation of the Kulturbund which is still developing.

How do we gauge the significance of the Kulturbund and its theatre decades later? What can we make of the admirable mission that a small group of Jewish artists set in motion within a dictatorship that adversely affected Jews in Germany? The all-Jewish theatre's leadership under Kurt Singer, and later Fritz Wisten, cultivated the artistic and scholarly interests of Jews, providing work for unemployed artists. Although Singer and Wisten were men of different temperament and backgrounds, they shared an obstinate belief in the need for the all-Jewish cultural institution. Their Berlin-based theatre gave many Jewish artists an economic boost and practical experience, enabling them to pursue their craft. And the theatre enterprise made it possible for Jews regularly to attend plays, concerts, and lectures of quality year after year under conditions of duress. It is remarkable that a Jewish theatre could survive in the Nazi regime at all, let alone for eight years, from 1933 to 1941.

The way the two artistic managers of the Kulturbund developed the theatre repertoire suggests something about the kind of compromises that the men made in balancing the competing demands of the Ministry of Propaganda, the Jewish community, and their own ideals. In 1933 and 1934 Singer tried to establish programs to reflect the German and Jewish heritage of the players and the audiences. He and his creative team Julius Bab (dramaturgy), Kurt Baumann (artistic programs), Heinz Condell (design), and indirectly Fritz Jessner (directing) and Fritz Wisten (acting), appealed to Jewish sensibilities across the ideological and religious spectrum, addressing the concerns of community groups that sponsored the theatre. As the Nazi government solidified its laws against Jews between 1936 and 1938, the managers increasingly made concessions to Hinkel's dictates. Assisted by Werner Levie, Bab, and Wisten, Singer adjusted his tone to account for Nazi racial and cultural policies; and he more readily obliged Zionist critics who demanded that play productions by Jewish authors convey a distinct Jewish quality.

"You don't have to collaborate with the Nazis the way that Singer did," Ruth Anselm-Herzog made clear decades after she emigrated.[3] She faulted the Kulturbund leadership for having been out of touch with the reality of the times. Singer had grossly misunderstood the extent of Hitler's politics and neglected to look at fascism as a political system, she suggested. She claimed that Singer only focused on the persecution of the Jews, believing that it must stop and that then the Nazis would see that Jews were really "decent" people. Their "Jewish" theatre thus would be able to withstand the torture of the Third Reich.[4] But Anselm never acknowledged Singer's change of heart regarding the Kulturbund and its place in Nazi Germany.

As the Nazi government increased the number of obstacles to Jewish life, Singer realized that the theatre could not attain the top quality he once envisaged. He traveled to the United States to see about transferring the Kulturbund enterprise to American soil. His decision to emigrate came directly after a temporary two-month absence from the theatre. Did he gain objective distance while in the United States to reflect on the future of the theatre under dictatorship? Perhaps from afar he could see more clearly the difficulty of keeping the theatre company intact. His departure from the Kulturbund in November 1938 pointed to his gradual recognition that insurmountable problems beset the theatre.

The events of Reichskristallnacht sparked Singer's allegiance to Germany and spurred his return to the Kulturbund. Not until he reached European soil, however, did he palpably understand the severe impact of the German pogroms on Jewish life and the futility of sustaining the all-Jewish theatre. "The fate of my Kulturbund colleagues in Berlin and elsewhere will be before my eyes and in my heart in all that I do or achieve," Singer wrote in 1938 after he left the Kulturbund.[5] Although he identified with his colleagues, he could not deceive himself about the desperate situation for Jews in Germany and the uncertain future for the Kulturbund. He never returned to Germany, opting to stay in the Netherlands. It is bitterly ironic that he ended up trapped in war-bound Europe with his only exit under Nazi command to the Jewish Schouwburg deportation site and to Terezín. The Nazi ploy to lure prominent German-born Jews to Terezín ensnared Singer, who believed that his privileged resettlement in the "Spa" Theresienstadt would allow him to prove his unflagging service to the arts. At the Nazis' showcase ghetto for culture, he contributed to the organized cultural programs. But he died amid deteriorating conditions for the inmates.

Unlike Singer, Fritz Wisten remained in Nazi Germany from 1933 to 1945. After leaving his native Vienna in 1919 for a performance career in Germany, Wisten's immersion in the theatre, his marriage to a non-Jew (1923), and his early ties to the Berlin Kulturbund (1933) may have insulated him somewhat from reflecting on the all-Jewish theatre and its future. Wisten's strong sense of himself as a performer and director led to his many promotions within the theatre leadership, strengthening his commitment to the institution. The jolt of Kristallnacht and his incarceration shocked him enough to seek emigration. But he immediately got caught up in the everyday business of the Kulturbund when Singer and Werner Levie emigrated, leaving the theatre leaderless. Wisten took over the theatre management even as he awaited his emigration visa. But world war erupted. Unable to leave the country and solely in charge of a faltering institution, Wisten may have thought that only he possessed the strength, the knowledge, and the skills to shore up the theatre organization, keep it solvent, and negotiate with Nazi authorities on behalf of his artists. In the two years he led the organization, despite daily problems, he established a film studio and duly noted "record numbers in the final year of 130,000 people attending 420 events." As for his employees, the musicians and theatre artists worked during the day in factories. But at night they performed at the Kulturbund, providing their fellow Jews with mental balance, solace, and inspiration through art.[6]

Wisten performed in the theatre, worked closely with Kurt Singer and Bab, and led the acting and directing divisions. As the organization's artistic director from September 1939 to the theatre's official end, he shepherded the Kulturbund theatre through some of its roughest years. He faced a Sisyphean challenge to manage a theatre in an impasse, where all structures for producing programs were being dismantled. And yet, within the liberating area of their ever-narrowing stage space, he and his artists created theatre, even while arrangements for their eventual extinction were being discussed.

Riding elevated above the war-wracked city on his S-Bahn commute to the lakeside district of Schlachtensee, Wisten may have sensed a deep devastation at the closing of his theatre in September 1941. But even in the emptiness of the moment he preserved a sense of mission. It is his own assessment of the Kulturbund—as told to Herbert Freeden after the war—that captures how the performers could continue to make art amid circumstances that had become artistically and existentially impossible: "Evening after evening we proved that art does not stop affecting people, not even under the Gestapo's thumb. Today that sounds pathetic, but that's how it was. . . . We could not protest. But that we continued in spite of it all—that was our protest. To see the abyss, and nevertheless to play [theatre]."[7]

The Kulturbund performers have iterated their need and passion to be onstage under the spotlight, breathing in theatre air, and engaged in what they did best: "It may have been a ghetto theatre, but the actors were acting. We were happy to work in our profession," Steffi Hinzelmann would concede.[8] Whether for distraction or for art's sake, this sentiment about the theatre recurs among those voices preserved in interviews and on audiotape and videotape. It is only in hindsight that the Kulturbund artists and their critics become skeptical about the theatre enterprise as a "devilish plan" by the Nazis to block emigration, a propaganda ploy to fool the outside world, or, as the actress Camilla Spira Eisner acknowledged, an environment in which people lived in illusions without believing the extent of the "Jewish Question."[9]

But perhaps a better Jewish question is whether the tenacious strength of spirit shown by the Kulturbund artists amid persecution suggests a uniquely Jewish trait that has existed for thousands of years. Or is our instinct to maintain a sense of dignity and hope under duress what keeps us human? It has been shown again and again that in situations of severe deprivation, in ghettos and concentration camps, incarcerated artists risked their lives to make art. And the very act of making art and performing theatre gave them a sense of humanity, dignity, and hope, often even prolonging their lives.

Mascha Benya-Matz told me that in the prayer book for the High Holidays it is already decided who will live and who will die. People go to the synagogue to pray that the decision will be postponed. Some of the people do not know that they are doomed. And they go home to eat and break their fast. As Benya-Matz put it, "A people doomed, but they go home to eat Zimmes and Kugel. That's why the German Jews who went to the Kulturbund were singing, enjoying themselves; but they were doomed."[10] Yet not all of the

20. Mascha Benyakonsky as Nemea in Adam's *If I Were King* (with Richard Dresdner as Zephoris), spring 1937. Private collection, photographer unknown, courtesy Dov Matz.

21. Ruth Anselm in a costume, Kulturbund production photograph. Private collection, photographer unknown, courtesy Joan Durham.

Kulturbund Jews were ill-fated. Many of them, like Fritz Wisten, Heinz Condell, Steffi Hinzelmann, Alfred Berliner, Ruth Anselm, and Benya-Matz herself, were not doomed. They were blessed.[11]

Benya-Matz closely linked her pursuit of art in the Nazi dictatorship to her identity as a Jew and a Zionist. Yet she encountered resistance when she tried to develop a Yiddish and Hebrew singing repertoire. At the theatre on Kommandantenstraße she performed a strictly classical repertoire. She only sang once in Hebrew for the Kulturbund's *The Pioneers* (1938). As a foreign-born Jew in Germany, Benya-Matz had maintained an outside perspective, later stating that the German Jews were betrayed "because they were more German than Jewish."[12] In 1936 Singer and Levie appointed German-born Herbert Freeden to further the theatre's "Jewish" direction. Did they hire him out of true conviction or as a conciliatory gesture to Hinkel and to community Zionists? Freeden viewed his pedagogical and dramaturgical tasks as a way to intensify the repertoire's Jewish focus. He directed the Kulturbund's only contemporary production of a play from Palestine, but it is highly questionable whether he successfully projected his own Zionist bent onto the Kulturbund programs.

My history of the Kulturbund raises questions about the fluidity of cultural identity and ideology under duress. Over its eight-year existence, the organization's leadership did not really want to create a solely Jewish culture. Self-preservation, however, compelled the theatre artists to find a means that allowed them to keep working. For the most part Singer, Wisten, Berliner, Hinzelmann, Brandt, and Anselm, to name just a few, pursued their craft for art's sake rather than for the sake of their Jewish identity. Their self-protective instinct reveals something about the restorative nature of performance, especially under extreme conditions. How could Kulturbund artistic managers best preserve the longevity of their institution within the narrowing restrictions that the Nazis imposed on the theatre and its community?

My study begins to address such questions, while tracing the evolution of a repertoire which was often at cross-purposes with the policies on which it was founded. Any extended inquiry into how the Jewish theatre operated in the Third Reich calls for additional exploration into the mechanisms by which victim-artists negotiated terms with their oppressors. Further analysis of the Nazi Theatre Chamber, in turn, may provide scholars with new insight into the complex interplay between collaboration and state censorship within Germany and in its occupied lands.

AFTERWORD

NEW ROOTS

It is natural to wonder what happened to the Kulturbund players after the war. It enhances our understanding of the organization's legacy if we can create a record for former employees of the theatre. What kind of lives did they lead? How did the émigrés transfer their skills to a new culture? Many of the artists who survived the Shoah were surprisingly resilient and resourceful. What follows is an account of some of the figures from the Kulturbund theatre and their whereabouts after 1945.

■ "We are alive. Our house is still standing; and I am engaged in the general theatre business again," Fritz Wisten reported to Camilla Spira Eisner in 1946 upon hearing of her wartime travails.[1] Of the Kulturbund actors who performed at Westerbork, only Spira Eisner survived.[2] Still reeling from the events of the war, Wisten wanted to help in the rebuilding of Berlin's cultural landscape. But the rubble of the recent past haunted him. "I already had heard your news about Max Ehrlich, Singer, Gerron [Kurt], Wallburg, Willy Rosen," he wrote to Spira Eisner, verifying the ill fate of former Kulturbund colleagues. Accounting for his former lost and found artists, the director added to the growing list of the dead Grünne, Spanier, Arnstein, Sander, and Doris Wilamowska, while cataloguing the lucky ones: "Saved as if by miracle are Rudolf Schwarz, who is in Göteborg, the little Martin Rosen, Friedländer [Adolf], and the violinist Heinz Meyer. Freddy [Alfred Berliner] lived hidden with us for two years; also in hiding and saved are Max Michailow and Steffi Hinzelmann with her child."[3]

During 1945–1946 Wisten worked as a freelance director in occupied Berlin until the Soviet cultural officer for the city's Eastern Sector granted him a license to manage the Theater am Schiffbauerdamm.[4] Alfred Berliner did not become a chef. He joined Wisten's new theatre ensemble that united Kulturbund performers. Steffi Hinzelmann emerged from hiding to take her place on the Berlin stage with Berliner and Spira Eisner. Herbert Grünbaum returned from Palestine to join the ensemble; and Martin Rosen, who survived the camps, rejoined his former colleagues onstage. From 1954 to 1961 Wisten served as artistic director at the newly reconstructed Volksbühne on Rosa-Luxemburg Platz. It is fitting that politics and the Holocaust defined his final stage production. The construction of the Berlin Wall in 1961 overshadowed rehearsals for the premiere of Hedda Zinner's *The Ballad of Ravensbrück*.[5] Wisten retired after the 1961–1962 season and died on 12 December 1962.[6]

While Spira Eisner, Grünbaum, Rosen, and Ronau-Hinzelmann (Walter) stayed in Germany to perform, other uprooted artists resumed their lives in emigration.[7] Martin Brandt's acting credits at the Kulturbund spanned almost eight years. After his emigration to the United States in 1941, he played Nazi characters in anti-Nazi films and television movies. Yet he returned to Germany to continue his theatre career.[8] Brandt's good friend Kurt Süßmann was not so lucky. He perished in the camps, along with Jenny Schaffer-Bernstein, dramaturg Leo Hirsch, and Werner Levie, who died of typhus directly after liberation. Ben Spanier's deportation to Theresienstadt thrust him along with Kurt Singer into the *Freizeitgestaltung*.[9] He died at Auschwitz-Birkenau, along with many of his fellow actors and audience members.

The oboist and French horn player for the Kulturbund, Kurt Michaelis, never performed again after 1945; but his musical instrument is on permanent loan at the United States Memorial Holocaust Museum in Washington, D.C. Michaelis made a career in music publishing, translating biographies of composers into German. His conductor from the Kulturbund orchestra, Rudolf Schwarz, survived three concentration camps, eventually settling in England, where he became the musical director for the British Broadcasting Corporation. Some of their colleagues from the Kulturbund recommenced their lives in England.[10] Others traveled to the United States to put down new roots: of the original members of the Kulturbund in 1933, Kurt Baumann, Julius Bab, Heinz Condell, and Ruth Anselm resettled in New York state.

When I asked the actress Mira Rostovsky (Rostova) how the Kulturbund and emigration affected her career, she told me: "It ruined my life the way I expected it to be: it is easier to do something that comes to you than something that you fight for."[11] Rostova performed only one season at the Kulturbund, 1934–1935. She waited four years in England to emigrate to the United States under the Russian quota. At New York's Actor's Studio she met Montgomery Clift and became his personal acting coach, accompanying him on his film shoots. Her training and Hollywood connections made her a popular acting coach. She has worked with Roddy McDowall, Joseph Chaikin, Alec Baldwin, and Jessica Lange.[12] Reflecting on her life, she claimed that if she had been German-born she would have left Europe for Israel.

Herbert Freeden (Friedenthal) did emigrate to Palestine in the summer of 1939 to work as a journalist. He must be credited with writing the first theatre history of the Kulturbund: *Jüdisches Theater in Nazideutschland* (Jewish Theatre in Nazi Germany, 1964). His experience as a drama critic and an assistant stage director at the Kulturbund gave him insight into the onstage and offstage workings of the theatre. Skeptical about the Kulturbund, he maintained an unchanged position on the theatre until his death in Jerusalem in 2003: the Kulturbund provided economic opportunities for unemployed Jews and offered audiences a distraction from their ghettoization; but ultimately the enterprise failed, because it facilitated the German plan to hinder Jewish emigration.[13]

Ruth Anselm (Herzog) knew all about emigration. She had helped others to flee Germany. "Where should I have gone as a young person?" she countered when Freeden publicly indicted the Kulturbund during a reunion of former artists in 1992.[14] Anselm-Herzog possessed more firsthand knowledge of the organization's earliest years than anyone else convened for the roundtable discussion. She developed her talents at the Kulturbund. But her acting ambition and her political cause clashed, prompting her flight from theatre and Germany. Anselm's longtime resistance partner referred to her as "a dancer between dreams and death that frightens you, as in Balinese dance."[15] Unable to resume a performance career after she left her country, Anselm remained committed to social and political causes. She did not return to Germany until 1959. She feared that people wanted to kill her—perhaps a psychological remnant from her clandestine life in Berlin as a Jew and as part of the underground. She remarried, as had her first husband, Heinz Condell. Condell worked as a costume and set designer for the New York City Opera, the Maurice Schwarz Yiddish Art Theater, and the Arbeter Teater Farband (Workers' Theater Alliance, known as ARTEF) until his death in 1951. Anselm died on 5 January 2005.

The young dancer from *Countess Marizá*, Hannah Kroner-Segal (born 1920), never invested in the Kulturbund the way Anselm had. Fortunate to secure her ship passage to America within two months in 1939, Kroner-Segal developed a career based on her ballet training and the two Kulturbund seasons in

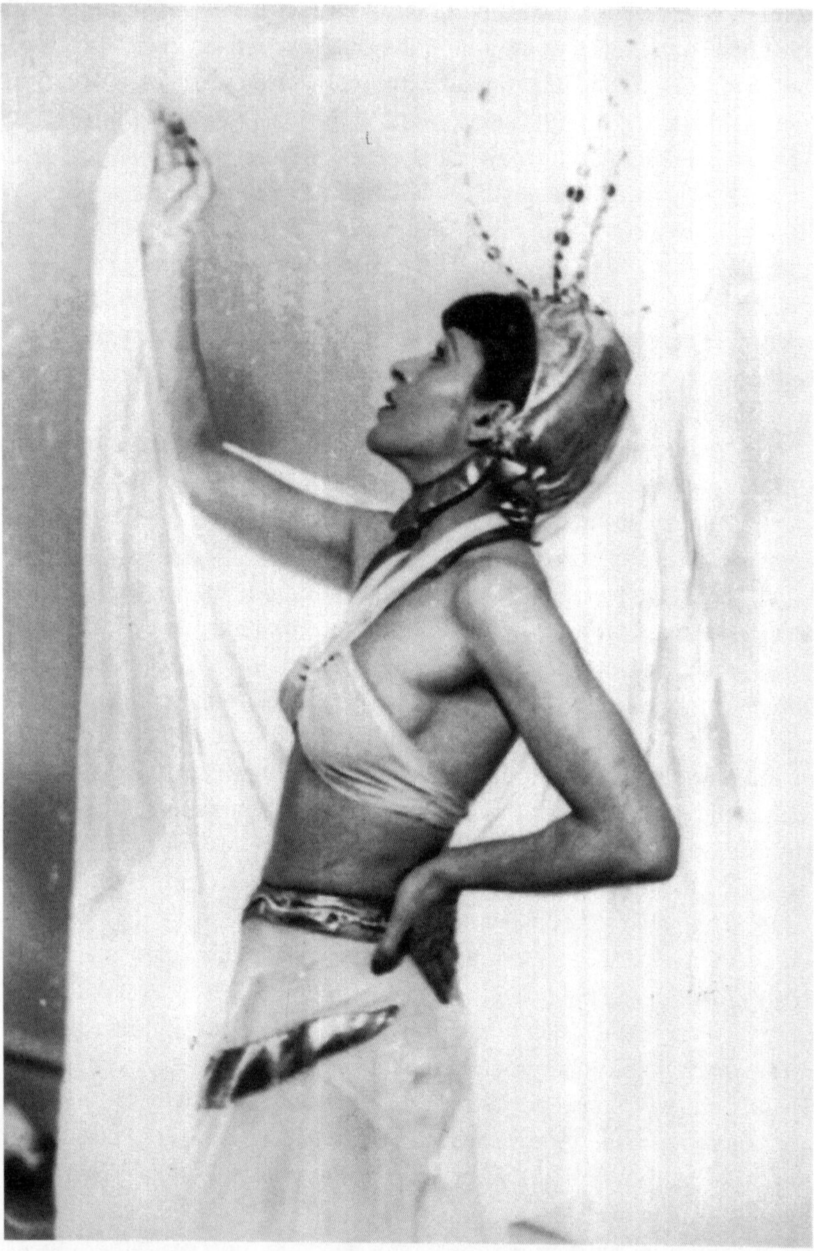

22. Ruth Anselm in a costume, Kulturbund production photograph. Private collection, photographer unknown, courtesy Joan Durham.

which she performed. As a dancer, Kroner-Segal could transfer her performance skills more easily to a new culture than could those artists who relied on their speaking and singing voices. Nor did she need to consider whether her artform incorporated German or Jewish-based performance repertoires. Mascha Benya-Matz (Benykonsky), by contrast, devoted her career exclusively to Jewish music when the horrors and the truth about the Shoah emerged. In the 1950s and 1960s she performed Jewish songs across the United States, Central America, and Israel. The coloratura soprano retired from teaching at the Hebrew Arts School of the Elaine Kaufman Cultural Center for Music and Dance in 1995. She coached singers and cantors in secular and sacred music until her death in November 2007. Kroner-Segal's dance studio in New York's borough of Queens is not far from where Mascha Benya-Matz resettled.

Most of the main participants of the Kulturbund theatre have died. We are left to fill in the rich details of personal stories for those artists who fled and survived the Third Reich. I hope that by weaving together the particulars of their lives and presenting their voices my re-creation of the theatre and its protagonists reveals the evolving historiography of an extraordinary Jewish artistic venture in Nazi Germany.

NOTES

ABBREVIATIONS

AdK: Stiftung Archiv der Akademie der Künste, Berlin

BA III: Bundesarchiv III, Berlin-Zehlendorf (formerly Berlin Document Center)

C.-V.-Zeitung: *Centralverein Zeitung der deutscher Staatsbürger jüdischen Glaubens* (Central Association for German Citizens of the Jewish Faith)

EG: Eike Geisel Private Collection of Kurt Singer Correspondence, Berlin

FWA: Fritz-Wisten Archive, Akademie der Künste (AdK), Berlin

IFB: *Israelitisches Familienblatt*

JN: *Jüdisches Nachrichtenblatt*

JR: *Die Jüdische Rundschau*

LBI: Leo Baeck Institute, New York

SJK: Sammlung Jüdischer Kulturbund (individual Kulturbund artists), AdK, Berlin

WL: Wiener Library, London

WL Binder: Wiener Library Binder (duplicated materials from the Wiener Library, London and Tel Aviv), AdK, Berlin

INTRODUCTION: OUSTED

1. Jeanette R. Malkin, "Introduction," in Jeanette R. Malkin and Freddie Rokem, eds., *Jews and the Making of Modern German Theatre*, 6.

2. Dr. Hugo Lachmanski, "Die Premiere des Kulturbundes: *Nathan der Weise* im Berliner Theater," *C.-V.-Zeitung* 38, 4 October 1933, 6.

3. "*Nathan der Weise*: Die Premiere des 'Kulturbundes,'" JR 79/80, 4 October 1933, 624.

4. Ibid. (Hinkel quoted by anonymous reviewer).

5. Ibid. The production showed a historical "understanding" of Jewish tragedy.

6. The appointment in August 1933 led to a dramaturg's position for Schlösser by May 1934. See Barbara Panse, "Censorship in Nazi Germany"; Alan E. Steinweis, *Art, Ideology, and Economics in Nazi Germany*, 48.

7. Steinweis, *Art, Ideology, and Economics in Nazi Germany*, 106.

8. Hinkel to Laubinger, 15 June 1933, WL Binder 2.53.20 (also at WL).

9. Singer to Hinkel, 29 June 1933, requesting July 6 meeting; report from Baron von Holthoff on Singer's behalf to Hinkel, 23 June 1933; letter from von Holthoff to Singer, 3 June 1933, WL Binder 2.53.20.

10. Many scholars have situated the Kulturbund in music studies. See Lily E. Hirsch,

A Jewish Orchestra in Nazi Germany; Horst J. P. Bergmeier, Ejal Jakob Eisler, and Rainer E. Lotz, eds., *Vorbei . . . Beyond Recall* (including recordings from the Lukraphon label); Martin Goldsmith, *The Inextinguishable Symphony*. See http://www.judischekulturbund.com/, a website launched by Gail Prensky (Washington, D.C.).

11. Michael Brenner examines the Jewish community in Wilhelmine Germany and the Weimar Republic in *The Renaissance of Jewish Culture in Weimar Germany*. See the essays in Malkin and Rokem, *Jews and the Making of Modern German Theatre*: Bernhard Greiner's "German-Jewish 'Theatromania,'" on German-cultured Jews and the theatre (99–115); and Anat Feinberg's "Stagestruck," on Wilhelmine attitudes toward theatre by Jews in Germany (59–76).

12. *Geschlossene Vorstellung*, documents 5–9, especially letters from 16 January 1934 and 9 July 1934, 223–230.

13. Henry Bloch interview by author, 10 November 1995.

14. Rebecca Rovit and Alvin Goldfarb, eds., *Theatrical Performance during the Holocaust*, 74.

15. Kurt Michaelis, 1995–1996 correspondence and interview by author, 12 August 1996.

16. Raul Hilberg describes Holocaust history as identification, deportation, and annihilation in *The Destruction of the European Jews*. See my essay "Cultural Ghettoization and Theater during the Holocaust."

17. Saul Friedländer, *Nazi Germany and the Jews, Vol. 1*, 66, calls the Kulturbund a ploy to subordinate Jewish culture to the Nazis, creating a "pretence of internal autonomy" for Jews; Jörg W. Gronius, "Klarheit, Leichtigkeit, und Melodie," in *Geschlossene Vorstellung*, 67–94.

18. See my book co-edited with Alvin Goldfarb: *Theatrical Performance during the Holocaust*.

19. Victor Klemperer, *I Will Bear Witness, 1933–1945*, 8 October 1935, 134.

20. Herbert Freeden, *The Jewish Press in Nazi Germany*, 161. Jewish newspapers between 1933 and 1938 were subject to government and self-enforced censorship.

21. Steffi Ronau's memories allowed me to amend a date related to the theatre's closure in September 1941. Her recollection of a role for which she wore a peasant costume to hide her pregnancy helped me to identify the play that was in rehearsals when the Gestapo cleared the theatre. I modified the record of the repertoire by registering the play and its production date. See Steffi Ronau Hinzelmann in E. Geisel and H. M. Broder, eds., *Premiere und Pogrom*, 151 ff. She wrote that rehearsals for the play were on 9 September, but she probably meant 12 September. The play was Mosche Lipshitz, *Were I Not a Fool: A Whimsical Story with Herschel Ostropoler (Wenn der Narr nicht mein wär: Eine wunderliche Geschichte mit Hershel Ostropoler)*, FWA 74/86/56, 54, cast list and rehearsal schedule, 27.

22. Dr. Martha Sara Wertheimer, "Jüdisches Publikum: Zu den Gastspielen des jüdischen Kulturbundes," JN 79/80, 1 October 1940, 8–9.

1. A CULTURAL COMMUNITY: THE JEWISH KULTURBUND THEATRE EMERGES, 1933

1. Berlin had been the destination for an influx of East European Jews (*Ostjuden*) since the nineteenth century. In the 1920s they preserved their Yiddish language and maintained Orthodox rituals and Yiddish theatre traditions in the central eastern district (the Scheunenviertel). Peter Sprengel, *Scheunenviertel-Theater: Jüdische Schauspieltruppen und jiddische Dramatik in Berlin (1900–1918)*; Peter Sprengel, *Populäres jüdisches Theater in Berlin von 1877 bis 1933*. See John Willett, *The Theatre of the Weimar Republic*.

2. Shachar Pinsker, "Spaces of Hebrew and Yiddish Modernism: The Urban Café of Berlin," in *Transit und Transformation Osteuropäisch-jüdische Migranten in Berlin 1918–1939*, 61–62, on the Romanisches Café, targeted by the Nazis as a hub for Jewish intellectuals.

3. The Jewish-born poet Mascha Kaléko (born Golda Malka Aufen in Galicia) joined Berlin's intellectual enclave after World War I. The actors Shimon Finkel and Alexander Granach left Lemberg to study at Max Reinhardt's acting school. See Shelly Zer-Zion, "The Shaping of the Ostjude," in Jeannette R. Malkin and Freddie Rokem, eds., *Jews and the Making of Modern German Theatre*, 184–185. Kurt Katsch (born Isser Katch) left Grodno for Germany to pursue theatre, while Slatan Dudow left Bulgaria in 1922 for Berlin, where he collaborated with Bertolt Brecht, Günther Weisenborn, and Hanns Eisler, all transplants to Berlin's arts scene.

4. Ruth Anselm (Herzog), interview by author, 24 May 1995. Anselm (1909–2005) engaged in leftist resistance activities in the early 1930. See Anselm, "I Was Kicked Out of the Kulturbund," in E. Geisel and H. M. Broder, eds., *Premiere und Pogrom*, 77–86.

5. Anselm interview. Grüning, who emigrated to the United States in 1934, played Mrs. Leuchtag in *Casablanca* (1942). She directed an acting school with Lucie Höflich.

6. In my interview with Anselm, she called Brecht a "Salon-Mensch" (the kind of person who advantageously mingled with intellectuals to exchange ideas). Anselm suggested, however, that his tastes were higher than his political ideas about egalitarianism—he sewed patches on his clothes to appear lower class; see Geisel and Broder, *Premiere und Pogrom*, 84. The Nazis blacklisted writings by Brecht and Weisenborn, who were politically active Communists. Brecht, Weigel, and Eisler went into exile. Weisenborn published under the pseudonyms W. Bohr, Christian Munk, and Eberhard Förster.

7. Mascha Benya-Matz (Benyakonsky), interview by author, 9 November 1995, reproduced in Rebecca Rovit and Alvin Goldfarb, eds., *Theatrical Performance during the Holocaust*, 62. Benya-Matz, personal communications to author, 1995–2007. Benyakonsky was born 15 October 1908 and died on 4 November 2007.

8. Benya-Matz interview by author. She tutored the president of the Berlin Zionist

Organization and the wife of Robert Weltsch, editor of Berlin's Zionist newspaper. Kaléko published *The Lyric Stenogramm* (1933); but when the Nazis found out that she was Jewish, they burned her books in May 1933.

9. Contrary to the assertion by Alan Steinweis that Singer lost his job at the opera in March 1933, Lily E. Hirsch in *A Jewish Orchestra in Nazi Germany* notes that Singer's leadership officially ended in 1931 (10, citing Fred Prieberg, *Musik in NS-Staat* [Frankfurt: Fischer, 1982], 80). The archivist for the Akademie der Künste, Stephan Dörschel, told me that Singer likely worked under Ebert as a deputy director; but it was unclear when he stopped. Personal correspondence with author, 4 January 2011.

10. Kurt Baumann, "The Kulturbund: Ghetto and Home," 120. This response sounds naïve and out of sync with Bab's character.

11. Anselm interview; also roundtable discussion on audiotape, 2 April 1992, AdK.

12. Anselm interview. The performers Fritzi Jokl and Lilly Kann lived with Anselm for a while.

13. Benya-Matz interview, partially cited in Rovit and Goldfarb, *Theatrical Performance during the Holocaust*, 63. Benyakonsky did not audition for the Kulturbund until 1937. The clerk, unimpressed by her Yiddish repertoire, said, "No one could possibly understand it. Who needs that stuff?"

14. Anselm was one of the first artists to join the Kulturbund as a dancer, choreographer, and actress. Benyakonsky performed at the Kulturbund for Dr. Anneliese Landau's lectures on music in the early years and formally joined the opera troupe in 1936.

15. Anselm interview. Anselm and Günther Weisenborn (1902–1969) worked together in antifascist groups. Weisenborn, dramaturg of Brecht's *The Mother*, joined the "Red Orchestra" resistance group and survived incarceration from 1942 to 1945.

16. Ibid. Anselm decided to emigrate to the United States. When she told Singer of her plan in 1938, he asked her to leave the Kulturbund, insisting that someone with her "view of duty" did not belong there. It is curious that Singer would keep her from performing because she wanted to emigrate, because he himself would emigrate. SJK, Anselm 1.53.646, 1.53.641.

17. They shared the Kulturbund stage in 1938: in Adolphe Adam's opera *If I Were King* (February) and Shulamith Batdori's *The Trial* (May).

18. Anselm in Geisel and Broder, *Premiere und Pogrom*, 83.

19. This audition took place in 1936. Benya-Matz interview, quoted in Rovit and Goldfarb, *Theatrical Performance during the Holocaust*, 65.

20. Kulturbund member Shabtai Petrushka (Siegfried Friedmann) founded a music group to support Zionism that had to register all meetings with the Gestapo. See SJK, Petruschka.

21. George L. Mosse, "Jewish Emancipation: Between Bildung and Respectability," in *The Jewish Response to German Culture*, ed. Jehuda Reinharz and Walter Schatzberg, 2–5. Amos Elon refers to a moment of "paradox" during the Depression in Germany: the

number of "anti-Semitic outrages" rose, while Jews got recognized in the arts (*The Pity of It All*, 239, 386).

22. Elon, *The Pity of It All*, 377–378.

23. Michael Brenner, *The Renaissance of Jewish Culture in Weimar Germany*. Acting troupes from eastern Europe exposed Berlin audiences to plays based on Hebrew and Yiddish lore, staged in a nonrealistic presentational style. Joseph Roth describes a performance during the 1920s (*The Wandering Jews*, 74–79).

24. Shulamit Volkov views growing anti-Semitism and assimilation as vital to accelerating dissimilatory trends within Weimar Germany. She describes the "dialectical process" in "The Dynamics of Dissimilation: Ostjuden and German Jews," in Reinharz and Schatzberg, *The Jewish Response to German Culture*, 195–211.

25. See Brenner, *The Renaissance of Jewish Culture in Weimar Germany*, 53; also H. I. Bach, *The German Jew*.

26. See Jacob Katz, "German Culture and the Jews," in *The Jewish Response to German Culture*, ed. Jehuda Reinharz and Walter Schatzberg, 92–94.

27. Shulamith Volkov, Keynote Address, "Fulfillment and Disillusion: German Jews between Empire and Republic." Conference on German Jewry in Weimar, Indiana University, Bloomington, Indiana, 17 March 1996. See essays on this issue in Jeanette R. Malkin and Freddy Rokem, eds., *Jews and the Making of Modern German Theatre*.

28. See Avraham Barkai, *From Boycott to Annihilation*, 1, who relies on U. O. Schmelz, "Die demographische Entwicklung der Juden in Deutschland von der Mitte des 19. Jahrhunderts bis 1933," *Zeitschrift für Bevölkerungswissenschaft* 8 (1982): 31–72.

29. George L. Mosse, "Jewish Emancipation: Between Bildung and Respectability," in *The Jewish Response to German Culture*, ed. Jehuda Reinharz and Walter Schatzberg, 2–5.

30. Kurt Michaelis, personal communication to author, 29 January 1996.

31. Ibid. This is part of an interview on 12 August 1996 reproduced in Rovit and Goldfarb, *Theatrical Performance during the Holocaust*, 69.

32. Fritz Wisten to Julius Bab, 17 May 1933, FWA 74/86/995, translated in Rovit and Goldfarb, *Theatrical Performance during the Holocaust*, 72–73.

33. Bab to Wisten, 19 May 1933, FWA 74/86/996.

34. Ibid.

35. Julius Bab to Fritz Wisten, 30 May 1933, FWA 74/86/999. Baumann states erroneously that all was authorized for the Kulturbund by 20 May 1933 ("The Kulturbund: Ghetto and Home," 127).

36. *Geschlossene Vorstellung*, 217; cited from Kurt Baumann archives, LBI. By August 1938 the monthly fee was 2.85 Reichsmark. Members chose two events a month: a play and a concert or an opera and a lecture.

37. *A Midsummer Night's Dream* and Ibsen's *Ghosts* were produced in 1936 and 1938.

38. Hinkel to Laubinger, 15 June 1933, WL Binder 2.53.20 (also on microfilm at WL).

39. According to my interview with Anselm, Singer met Hinkel regularly for drinks.

40. Singer to Hinkel, 29 June 1933, for July meeting; report from von Holthoff to Hinkel, 23 June 1933; letter from von Holthoff to Singer, 3 June 1933. WL Binder 2.53.20.

41. Bab to Wisten, 7 July 1933, FWA 74/86/1002.

42. FWA 74/86/5002. This is part of Singer's proposed plan as stipulated in the bylaws for the Kulturbund.

43. Hinkel to Singer, 15 July 1933, Berlin, FWA 74/86/5000.

44. Kurt Singer describes what led to the premiere: *C.-V.-Zeitung* 3, 28 September 1933, 5–6.

45. See Herbert Freeden's informative study, *The Jewish Press in Nazi Germany*.

46. The newspaper retained its independence even when it relocated to Berlin in 1935.

47. In 1926 the Centralverein was one of the most influential Jewish organizations in Germany, with a membership of 60,000.

48. Brenner, *The Renaissance of Jewish Culture in Weimar Germany*, 142.

49. Mira Rostovsky (Rostova) performed during the first two seasons. Interview by author, 23 May 1995.

50. Ibid.

51. Anselm interview.

52. Benya-Matz interview.

53. Heinz Condell, "Stilprobleme des jüdischen Theaters," *Monatsblätter* (Jüdische Kulturbund Berlin), October 1936, 27–29.

54. Ibid. Condell would design costumes and the sets for *Nathan the Wise*. He explained that his budget necessitated a minimalist approach, *Kulturbundbühne* 4, no. 4 (April 1935): 7–10. He depicted a biblical townscape with stairs to a Jerusalem temple for Stefan Zweig's *Jeremiah* (1934), columns and projections for Giuseppe Verdi's opera *Nabucco* (1935), and a dream "montage" influenced by Marc Chagall for Ossip Dymov's *Bronx Express* (1935).

55. Kurt Singer, "Für Hilfe und Aufbau," *C.-V.-Zeitung* 29, 20 July 1933, 285.

56. Bab to Wisten, 11 August 1933, FWA 75/86/1012. Bab anticipated that actor contracts would be ready by late August: 10 August 1933, FWA 75/86/1013.

57. Anonymous, "Warum *Nathan der Weise*?" JR 53, 25 July 1933, 365.

58. Singer letter, 31 August 1933, JR 63, 8 August 1933, 405 (with afterword).

59. Ibid.

60. Hinkel to Secret Police (Geheime Staatspolizeiamt), 31 August 1933, WL Binder, 2.53.20. It is unclear whether this was a draft or an actual note sent.

61. Singer on 1 October 1933 premiere, *C.-V.-Zeitung* 31, 28 September 1933, 1.

62. See Gerwin Strobl, *The Swastika and the Stage*, 8, on *Reichsdramaturg* Dr. Schlösser.

63. Johann Wolfgang von Goethe's one-act play *The Siblings* (*Die Geschwister*) was per-

formed in November 1934. The Youth troupe performed Heinrich von Kleist's *The Broken Jug* in January 1937.

64. Wernie Levie, JR 74, 15 September 1933, 532.

65. Letter dictated by Hinkel, 16 September 1933, signed by Ursula Framm, WL Binder 2.53.20.

66. Hinkel cited in interview (no author) with Conti-Nachrichten Büro (propagandist news organization), JR 78, 29 September, 1933, 588.

67. K. L., "Assimilation und Dissimilation," JR 78, 29 September 1933, 590.

68. "Die Reichsvertretung an die Öffentlichkeit," *C.-V.-Zeitung* 37, 28 September 1933, front page.

69. Kurt Singer on premiere, *C.-V.-Zeitung* 37, 28 September 1933, 5.

2. UPROOTED: THE KULTURBUND AND THE FIRST PLAYING SEASON, 1933–1934

1. Heinz Condell, *Monatsblätter*, October 1936, 28.

2. Kurt Katsch, *Zurück ins Ghetto*, n.d., 191, LBI, ME 419.

3. "Der Aufbau des Theaters," *Frankfurter Zeitung*, 1 October 1933, WL Binder 575, 2.53.20.

4. Lauber to Hinkel, 1 October 1933, WL Binder, 575.2.53.20 (WL, microfilm reel 2, 29, 575).

5. See my discussion in "An Artistic Mission in Berlin."

6. Herbert Freeden cited in "Jüdischer Kulturbund: Geschlossene Gesellschaft," *Der Spiegel* 33, 11 August 1965, 73. Freeden was hired at the Kulturbund in 1936.

7. Anselm in E. Geisel and H. M. Broder, eds. *Premiere und Pogrom*, 81.

8. "Die Premiere des Kulturbundes," JR 79/80, 4 October 1933, 624. The critic may have been Arthur Eloesser, who wrote for the JR.

9. Hugo Lachmanski, review of *Nathan the Wise*, *C.-V.-Zeitung* 38, 4 October 1933, no pagination; www.compactmemory.de/librarye (accessed 12 February 2010).

10. "Die Premiere des Kulturbundes," JR 79/80, 4 October 1933, 624.

11. "Die Reichsvertretung an die Öffentlichkeit," *C.-V.-Zeitung* 31, 28 September 1933, 1.

12. Singer, open letter in *Israelitisches Familienblatt*, 22 March 1934. Corina L. Petrescu refers to the Jewish Kulturbund in Berlin as a "subversive" space in which Jews practiced resistance to the regime. She addresses the theatre's opening, stating that *Nathan* was the "most appropriate choice" that the theatre could perform, given that the protagonist was a humanist par excellence and the play a celebration of tolerance (*Against the Odds: Subversive Spaces in National Socialist Germany* [Peter Lang, 2010], 28, 31). The author cites my 1995 essay, where I write that the *Nathan* performance may have been "a calculated attempt to please all the segments of the prospective audience" (Rebecca

Rovit, "Collaboration or Survival: Reassessing the Role of the Kulturbund, 1933–1938," in Glen Gadberry, ed., *Theatre in the Third Reich*, 144).

13. Singer and Hinkel correspondence: see 19 October 1933. WL Binder, 2.53.20.

14. The Kulturbund Rhein-Ruhr (Cologne base) evolved first in December 1933.

15. Bab to Wisten, 24 October 1933, FWA 74/86/1021.

16. Werner Levie to Hinkel, 9 October 1933, WL Binder, 2.53.20.

17. BA III, Reichskulturkammer, Box 041, File 01, Schlösser, 26 October 1933 to Hinkel (included in WL Binder 2.53.20). Joseph Wulf reproduced this in *Theater und Film im Dritten Reich*, 102–103. Saul Friedländer refers to Wulf in *Nazi Germany and the Jews, Vol. 1*, 67, n. 115. A letter from Bab to Wisten, 24 October 1933, mentions lack of permission: FWA 74/86/1021. See my essay "Jewish Theatre," 193–194.

18. Emil Bernhard Cohn, *Die Jagd Gottes* (Berlin: Volksbühnen Verlags- und Vertriebe GmbH, 1925).

19. On 6 January proofs were sent back for February publication. WL microfilm reel 2, 29, 575; see Alan E. Steinweis, *Art, Ideology, and Economics in Nazi Germany*, 63.

20. Ibid.

21. Hinkel to Singer, 20 October 1933. This answers Werner Levie's letter of 9 October 1933; WL Binder 2.53.20.

22. See an informative report about the theatre behind the scenes in the *Almanach Kulturbund Deutscher Juden, 1934/1935* (Berlin: Kulturbund, 1935), 64–73.

23. Hinkel to Singer, 22 November 1933; Singer to Hinkel, 28 November 1933; WL Binder, 2.53.20.

24. Ibid. Hinkel wrote on Singer's letter "precisely the first act" as a reason for the ban.

25. "Sabbatfeierfrohen, Lösungsjauchzendefreien Juden streiten über den Trummer": script for I. L. Peretz, *The Golden Chain: The Drama of a Hasidic Family* (*Die goldene Kette: Das Drama einer chassidischen Familie*), trans. Siegfried Schmitz (Vienna and Berlin: R. Lowit Verlag, 1920), FWA 8°-27.261.

26. Schlösser forbade Hugo von Hofmannsthal's *The Incorruptible* at the Rhein-Ruhr Kulturbund because he thought a performance by Jews encouraged "tendentious generalization" with roles played as "Aryan caricatures" (by Jews). Schlösser to Hinkel, 5 December 1933, WL, 500 series, microfilm reel 1.

27. Hugo Lachmanski, "Kulturbund und Othello," *C.-V.-Zeitung* 43, 14 December 1933, 2; Beilage, 8; Singer to Wisten, 12 December 1934, reproduced in *Drei Leben für das Theater*, 73.

28. Stehr report, WL Binder, 2.53.20; Hinkel to Singer, 27 November 1933, WL Binder.

29. Jessner left the Kulturbund in 1936 to manage the Staatstheater Bern. He emigrated to the United States, where he died in 1946.

30. Bab refers to the production of *Sonkin der Haupttreffer* in *IFB*, 11 January 1934, no pagination. The original *Sonkin* is lost.

31. Bab wrote in the privately owned *IFB*, 11 January 1934, no pagination.

32. Dr. Ludwig Davidsohn, *Jüdisch-Liberale Zeitung* (later called the *Jüdisch Allgemeine Zeitung*), 13 February 1934; review, *Gemeindeblatt*, 9 February 1934.

33. Herbert Freeden, *The Jewish Press in the Third Reich*, 21–28, 49–53, 57–59.

34. Singer's open letter, *Jüdisch-Liberale Zeitung*, 20 February 1934; editorial, *Jüdisch-Liberale Zeitung*, 6 March 1934.

35. Singer, "Offener Brief an Dr. Ludwig Davidsohn," *Jüdische-Liberale Zeitung*, 20 February 1934. The director was Fritz Jessner.

36. Singer-Hinkel correspondence, WL Binder, 2.53.20. Hinkel approved *Esther* on 31 January 1934.

37. A Czech-language folk version was staged at Terezín in 1943. See Zdenka Fantlová-Ehrlich, "The Czech Theatre in Terezín," in Rebecca Rovit and Alvin Goldfarb, eds., *Theatrical Performance during the Holocaust*, 243–248.

38. Arthur Eloesser, on the Purim program, *JR* 19, 6 March 1934; Ludwig Altmann, *C.-V.-Zeitung* 10, 8 March 1934, 9–10.

39. Franz Grillparzer, *Esther*, in *Sämtliche Werke*, vol. 4, ed. Albert Zipper (Leipzig: Philipp Reklam, 1902), 16–44. Steinberg worked at the Berlin Kulturbund through May 1934.

40. Arthur Eloesser, *JR* 19, 6 March 1934; Dr. Hugo Lachmanski, *C.-V.-Zeitung* 10, 8 March 1934, 9–10.

41. "Bund der Kultur," *Jüdisch-Liberale Zeitung*, 6 March 1934.

42. "Was sie unter jüdischer Kultur verstehen," *IFB*, 15 March 1934, 2.

43. Kurt Singer, "Jüdische oder deutsch-jüdische Kultur?" *IFB*, 22 March 1934 (newspaper clippings, 16/58), AdK.

44. "Was sie unter jüdischen Kultur verstehen," *IFB*, 15 March 1934, 2.

45. Singer response to 15 March article in "Jüdische oder deutsch-jüdische Kultur?" *IFB*, 22 March 1934.

46. Ibid.

47. Lutz Weltmann, "Spielplan im Berliner Kulturbund-Theater," *IFB*, 12 April 1934.

48. Singer to Hinkel, 25 April 1934; Hinkel to Singer, 2 May 1934 (approved play); WL Binder, 575.2.53.20. The Kulturbund produced the play in February 1935.

49. 28 April 1934 typewritten statement of Kulturbund artistic personnel, FWA 74/86/5077, reproduced in *Geschlossene Vorstellung*, 244–245.

50. K.L., "Dissimilation?" *JR* 34, 27 April 1934, front page. The author cites Lutz Lenders verbatim from the *Völkischer Beobachter*.

51. Ibid.

52. "Dissimilation oder Assimilation," *C.-V.-Zeitung* 18, 3 May 1934, front page.

53. Ibid.

54. Ibid.

55. Lutz Weltmann, "Ein Jahr jüdische Kulturarbeit," *IFB*, 18 August 1934.

56. Hanns Brodnitz, "Wo steht der Kulturbund?" *Jüdische-Liberale Zeitung*, May 1934.

57. JR 38, 10 May 1934, 5; WL, microfilm reel 2, 29.575; Hinkel to Singer, 20 June 1935, authorized Valetti's appearance in Shaw's *Mrs. Warren's Profession*, which never took place.

58. *Gemeindeblatt der jüdischen Gemeinde zu Berlin* 29, 11 August 1934, 1–2. Herbert Freeden, *The Jewish Press in the Third Reich*, 99, refers to this newspaper as the "official organ of the whole [Jewish] community" in Berlin.

59. Hinkel to Singer, 30 August 1934, WL 500 series, microfilm reel 2, 29, 575.

60. WL, 500 series, microfilm reel 2, 575 (request, 21 September 1934).

61. Ibid., 24 September 1934.

62. Ibid., Singer to Hinkel, 25 September 1934.

3. GROUNDED: ESTABLISHING A REPERTOIRE, 1934–1935

1. Arthur Eloesser, "Jeremias im Kulturbund," JR 81, 9 October 1934, 3.

2. Justizrat Julius Brodnitz, "Aufstatt zum Hilfswerk" (preperformance address), *C.-V.-Zeitung* 41, 11 October 1934, 14.

3. Ibid.

4. Hugo Lachmanski, "Die künstlerische Leistung," *C.-V.-Zeitung* 41, 11 October 1934, 14; Arthur Eloesser, JR 81, 9 October 1934, 9.

5. Singer response to Hinkel, 29 October 1934, WL 500 series, microfilm reel 2.

6. Stefan Zweig, *Jeremiah*, 152 (compare the original director's script [*Regiebuch*] for *Jeremias*; Fritz Jessner), FWA 8°-27.265; Stefan Zweig, *Jeremias* (Leipzig: Insel Verlag, 1928), 111–112.

7. Director's script for *Jeremias*, 115–119, FWA 8°-27.265.

8. Zweig, *Jeremiah*, 152; compare director's script for *Jeremias*, FWA 8°-27.265.

9. Zweig, *Jeremiah*, 163–164.

10. Dr. Hugo Lachmanski, "*Jeremiah* in the Berliner Kulturbund," *C.-V.-Zeitung* 41, 11 October 1934, 14.

11. Zweig, *Jeremiah*, 255.

12. Ibid., 256–257. "JEREMIAH: [In ecstasy, stretching out his arms as if on the cross]: 'Let God's will be done. / Nail my limbs to the cross, pierce my side with the spear.'"

13. Jessner cut lines after Jeremiah praised the vanquished: "Kings who mastered us have vanished like smoke; nations which enslaved us have been scattered and their seed has been destroyed." (The transposed scene in the director's *Regiebuch* for *Jeremias* is on 176–181, then back to 176; compare English translation, Zweig, *Jeremiah*, 317.)

14. Director's note in director's script for *Jeremias*, 176–177, 183; Zweig, *Jeremiah*, 319.

15. Director's script for *Jeremias*, 180, 186; Zweig, *Jeremiah*, 323–324.

16. Director's script for *Jeremias*, 186–187, FWA 8°-27.265; compare Zweig, *Jeremiah*, 330.

17. Director's script for *Jeremias*, 189 (Third Chorus), FWA 8°-27.265; compare Zweig, *Jeremiah*, 332.

18. Director's script for *Jeremias*, 184–189, 8°-27.265; compare Zweig, *Jeremiah*, 335–336.

19. Arthur Eloesser on *Jeremiah*, JR 81, 9 October 1934, 3.

20. Proposal 1552, Sammlung Jüdische Kulturbund 1258; WL Binder, 2.53.25, Forbidden Texts. On 10 October 1934 Singer sent Hinkel the excerpt with text by Bab. Hinkel approved it on 7 November.

21. Julius Bab, introduction to Zweig's *Jeremiah*, in ibid. (underlining in the original); compare director's script, FWA 8°-27.265.

22. Director's script for *Jeremias*, 176; Zweig, *Jeremiah*, 317; Hinkel barred script allusions to Jews "chosen" for a special destiny. Bab's program notes in the October 1934 *Monatsblätter Kulturbundbühne* duplicate the material, but the notes do not reflect censorship. The underlined passages in his remarks are intact in his published program notes.

23. Walter Hertner performed excerpts from scene 9, where the prophet led his people beyond their destroyed city. 7 November 1934, WL Binder, 2.53.27.

24. Ibid.; authorized on 19 January 1935.

25. Director's script for *Jeremias*, 175–176, FWA 8°-27.265; lecture proposal for performance by Walter Herz, #1557, SJ 1258, 317. The abbreviation "SJ" appearing in several notes on pages 229–239 is embedded in papers from the Nazi Office for Jewish Affairs (Forbidden Texts) but is not explained further. An excerpt from scene 9 appears in Forbidden Texts (7–8) from 1936 (WL Binder, 500 series, microfilm reel 2).

26. Director's script for *Jeremias*, 216.

27. Rabbi Dr. Löwenstamm, "Jüdischer Lebensstil," *Gemeindeblatt für die jüdischen Gemeinden Preussens: Verwaltungsblatt der Preussischen Landesverbandes jüdischer Gemeinden*, 1 November 1934.

28. WL, microfilm reel 2, 29, 575, on 11 February 1935 performance. Compare to permission granted in March 1934 for "performances for school pupils" of Hofmannsthal's *Death and the Fool* (requested on 22 March 1934).

29. Singer to Fritz Wisten, 9 July 1935, FWA 74/86/207,2.

30. Arthur Eloesser (n.d., review, probably from JR) in Kurt Singer's Scrapbook, "Drei Jahre Kulturbund 1934–1937 und Kritiken der Aufführungen des *Jeremias* bis zu *Stützen der Gesellschaft*," Singer 1.55.35, AdK.

31. German Workers' Party Propaganda Office to Parteigenosse Hickethder, 19 November 1934, WL, 500 series, microfilm reel 1. The complaint deals with a theatre publication.

32. Schlösser to Hinkel, 5 December 1933, WL, 500 series, microfilm reel 1. Curiously, Hinkel authorized performances at the Kulturbund Rhein-Ruhr of Hauptmann's *Michael Kramer* and Schiller's *Kabale und Liebe* (Cabal and Love), although Schlösser rejected an all-Jewish performance of Kleist's work there in 1933.

33. This was regarding Arthur Eloesser, "Jacob Wassermann und sein jüdischer Schicksal," 19 January 1935. On 29 June 1935 Hinkel warned Singer about following the guidelines. WL, 500 series, microfilm reel 2.29, 575.

34. Chronos Verlag, Stuttgart, to Hinkel, 8 April 1935, on request of 21 March. Singer's request for *Jettchen*, 4 April 1935, was approved on 15 April; WL, 500 series, microfilm reel 2.29, 575.

35. Martin Bunzl, "The Poetics of Politics and the Politics of Poetics: Richard Beer-Hofmann and Theodor Herzl Reconsidered," *German Quarterly* 69, no. 3 (1996): 277–304.

36. See editorial on Eloesser's report on production, JR 12, 8 February 1935, 9.

37. Singer to Hinkel, 27 January 1935. The submission of the new prologue came two days after Hinkel authorized the production (25 January). On 25 April 1934 Singer sent Hinkel Beer-Hoffman's *Jaákobs Traum: Ein Vorspiel*. Hinkel okayed authorization for performance of *Jacob* on 2 May 1934. On 23 January 1935 Singer announced the premiere of *Jacob's Dream* for February 5 (1935). WL, 500 series, microfilm reel 2, (2) B2–13766/291.

38. Compare Genesis 32:28, after Jacob wrestled with a stranger, who said, "Thy name shall be called no more Jacob, but Israel: for as a prince hast thou power with God and with men, and hast prevailed."

39. Julius Bab, "*Jaakobs Traum*: Zur Erstaufführung am 5. Februar," *Gemeindeblatt*, 3 February 1935.

40. Arthur Eloesser, "*Jaakobs Traum* im Kulturbund," JR 12, 8 February 1935, 9; WL Binder, 2.53.25, 651.

41. Hugo Lachmanski, "*Jaakobs Traum* zur Erstaufführung im Berliner Kulturbund," *C.-V.-Zeitung* 7, 14 February 1935, 5.

42. WL, 500 series, microfilm reel 2, 575. There is no other information on the actress.

43. Ibid. See Eloesser, "*Jaakobs Traum* im Kulturbund," 9.

44. WL Binder, 2.53.21.

45. Hinkel cut the dream portion of the play from public recitation. Barbara Müller-Wesemann refers to censors in her study of the Hamburg Kulturbund: *Theater als geistiger Widerstand*, 329.

46. Hugo Lachmanski, "Jaakobs Traum zur Erstaufführung im Berliner Kulturbund," *C.-V.-Zeitung* 6, 7 February 1935, 5; review in *Schild*, 8 February 1935.

47. Eloesser, "*Jaakobs Traum* im Kulturbund," 9.

48. Richard Beer-Hofmann, *Jacob's Dream*, 59, 60–61; Richard Beer-Hofmann, *Jaákobs Traum*.

49. Dr. Otto Hirsch to Kurt Singer (with copy for Wisten), 12 February 1935, FWA 74/86/1083.

50. Lachmanski, "*Jaakobs Traum* zur Erstaufführung im Berliner Kulturbund," *C.-V.-Zeitung* 7, 14 February 1935, 5.

51. Ibid.; WL Binder 2.53.25 (651), Forbidden Texts, *Jacob's Dream* (application submission #2281, SJ 2048), lines 1369–1383; Beer-Hofmann, *Jacob's Dream*, 163–164.

52. Müller-Wesemann, *Theater als geistiger Widerstand*, 329, verifies that Hamburg produced the play on 15 September 1935. But "Das Hamburger Kulturbundprogramm," *Jüdische Allgemeine Zeitung*, 4 September 1935, states that the Kulturbund planned *Jacob's Dream* for the winter 1936 season; WL Binder, 2.53.25, 651. The original script no longer exists. Scene excerpts are among Hinkel's undated Kulturbund Banned Text files, under proposal #2278; SJ 2059.

53. WL and WL Binder 2.53.25 (651), Forbidden Texts, *Jacob's Dream* (application submission 2281, SJ 2048); Beer-Hofmann, *Jacob's Dream*, 161: excised section where Archangel Michael predicted the downfall of all but the Jews (lines 1328–1331).

54. Hinkel's remark on the general ban on the play refers to proposal 2281, SJ 2048, whereas the proposal number is 2278, SJ 2028, on play excerpts from act II of *Jacob* which belong to the same period; WL Binder 2.53.25, Proposal #2281. See also Müller-Wesemann, *Theater als geistiger Widerstand*, 329.

55. Alice Levie, "Wer ist die blonde Frau? Das ist ja keine Jüdin!" (on her husband), in E. Geisel and H. M. Broder, eds., *Premiere und Pogrom*, 157.

56. Hinkel barred a 1935 production of Grillparzer's *Esther* for the Frankfurt Kulturbund. He authorized the Hamburg branch to produce *Jacob's Dream* in September 1935.

57. 22 February 1935, Hinkel to Singer, response to Singer letter dated 21 February 1935. On 25 February 1935 Singer wrote again to Hinkel.

58. Wisten to Singer, 31 March 1935, FWA 74/86/1201.

59. Singer to Wisten, 9 July 1935, FWA 74/86/1207, 2. Instead of directing Molnár, Wisten would direct Shaw's *You Never Can Tell*.

60. WL Binder, 2.53.21, 12 April 1935; Hinkel okayed the production on 15 April 1935. On 4 April 1935 Singer requested *Jettchen Gebert* to substitute for the play by Kästner (Neuner). Hermann was an honorary board member of the Kulturbund.

61. *Jettchen Gebert* (Berlin: Oesterheld, 1928); Martin Brandt actor rolebook for Jason Gebert, FWA 74/86/1571, 78 ff.

62. Kurt Baumann and Friedrich Brodnitz, "Exposé zur Durchführungen einer Reichsgemeinschaft des jüdischen Jugendbühne zur Erweckung des Interesses an Theater und Drama innerhalb der jüdischen Jugend," 25 June 1935, FWA 86/5078.

63. *Jettchen Gebert* (Berlin: Oesterheld, 1928); Martin Brandt actor rolebook for Jason Gebert, FWA 74/86/1571, act I, 39.

64. Brandt rolebook, 48.

65. Ibid., 47.

66. Hermann Sinsheimer, "*Jettchen Gebert* in Kulturbund," *Gemeindeblatt*, 7 July 1935, 3.

67. Hilde Cohn, "*Jettchen Gebert* von Georg Hermann," *Frauenbund* (August 1935).

68. Sinsheimer, "*Jettchen Gebert* in Kulturbund," 3.

69. Werner Levie to Wisten, 6 August 1936, FWA 74/86/1112.

70. Kurt Jutrosinki to Gerhard Lehmann, 21 October 1935 (Jutrosinki worked at the Kulturbund); SJK 1.53.133.

71. Ossip Dymov, *Bronx Express*, in Nahma Sandrow, trans. and ed., *God, Man, and Devil*, 294–295. The Kulturbund script, translated by Georg Ritter, is unavailable. See Bab on *Bronx Express*, September 1935 program, 3–4; FWA 74/86/19.

72. Hinkel to Singer, WL, series 500, microfilm reel 2-28.

73. Letter from Hinkel's office to Singer, 2 January 1934, requesting Singer's presence for 4 January at 2:30 P.M. Hinkel requests Singer's presence for a meeting in spring 1934 (24 April request for 2 May meeting); WL, 500 series, microfilm reel 2, 1B2-13766/291.

74. Mascha Benya-Matz interview by author, 9 November 1995.

75. Levie, "Wer ist die blonde Frau? Das ist ja keine Jüdin!" 157.

76. Singer to Hinkel, 28 March 1935; WL, 500 series, microfilm reel 2.29, 575. Singer sent Hinkel tickets on 4 April 1935.

77. Hinkel to Singer, 14 February 1935; WL, 500 series, microfilm reel 2.29, 575.

78. Singer to Hinkel, 9 July 1935, WL, 500 series, microfilm reel 2-28.

79. WL Binder, 2.53.16, FWA Kulturbund-Dokumente, 13; Hinkel to Singer, 5 August 1935, AdK.

80. See Jeanette R. Malkin and Freddie Rokem, eds., *Jews and the Making of Modern German Theatre*.

81. Singer detailed these numbers in a report on the Kulturbund on 17 August 1935 (WL Binder), reproduced as document 31 in *Geschlossene Vorstellung*, 250.

4. SOLIDARITY: A NAME CHANGE FOR A NEW THEATRE, 1935–1936

1. I relied on Ian Kershaw's *Hitler: A Biography*, 339–345, for information on anti-Semitic actions in Berlin and Hitler's order to halt them prior to the Nuremberg Laws. For historical weather in Berlin during August 1935, I accessed data on 28 July 2010: www.tutiempo.net/en/Climate/Berlin-Tempelhof/08–1935/103840.htm. See letter from Police President to Executive Board of the Kulturbund Deutscher Juden, 7 August 1935, FWA 74/86/5020, 17, reproduced in *Geschlossene Vorstellung* as document 18, 230.

2. Letter in *Geschlossene Vorstellung*. See the decision made by the Prussian Court on the Kulturbund, 9 July 1934, FWA 74/86/5017, document 9. Letters are reproduced as documents 5–9, 223–230.

3. Singer to Hinkel, 11 March 1935; Hinkel to Singer, 12 March 1935, reproduced in *Geschlossene Vorstellung* as documents 13 and 14, 228.

4. See Heidelore Riss, *Ansätze zu einer Geschichte des jüdischen Theaters in Berlin 1889–1936*, 213. See also Peter Sprengel, *Populäres Jüdisches Theater in Berlin von 1877 bis 1933*; Marline Otte, *Jewish Identities in German Popular Entertainment, 1890–1933*.

5. Diplom. Ing. Gusti Hecht, "Vorhang auf im neuem Haus," *C.-V.-Zeitung* 40, 3 October 1935, 40, 3–4.

6. *The New Jerusalem Bible* Standard Edition (New York: Doubleday, 1998) includes *Judith*.

7. Friedrich Hebbel, *Judith*, 3–4.

8. Ibid., 8.

9. Ibid., 21–22.

10. Ibid., 72. The Apocrypha narrative leaves ambiguous the question of consummation: Judith 13:2. See Edgar J. Goodspeed, trans., *Apocrypha: An American Translation*, 157; http://etext.virginia.edu/toc/modeng/public/KjvJudi.html (accessed 4 December 2011).

11. Cited by Lutz Weltmann, "Hebbels *Judith*," *Schild*, 11 October 1935, Newspaper Compilation, FWA 74/86/19, 7.

12. *Jüdische Allgemeine Zeitung*, 9 October 1935; FWA 74/86/19, 16.

13. Julius Bab, "Im neuem Hause," *Kulturbühne* (1935): 4.

14. Fritz Wisten "scrapbook" for 1935–1936, FWA 74/86/19, 7: praise for Condell in *Jüdische Allgemeine Zeitung*, 9 October 1935, 16.

15. Ibid.

16. Hugo Lachmanski, "*Judith* im Berliner Kulturbund." *C.-V.-Zeitung* 41, 10 October 1935, 3.

17. Weltmann, "Hebbels *Judith*."

18. Ibid.

19. Arthur Eloesser, "Im neuen Kulturbund-Haus: Hebbels *Judith*," JR 80, 4 October 1935, 13.

20. Arthur Eloesser, review of *You Never Can Tell*, JR 98, 6 December 1935, 5.

21. Ordinance announced in *C.-V.-Zeitung* 48, 28 November 1935, 2.

22. Hinkel to Singer, 14 February 1935, WL Binder, 2.53.20. The Kulturbund presented *Candida* in April 1935.

23. This arrangement was made in 1937. For sources on the Nazi reception of Shaw, see John London, "Non-German Drama in the Third Reich," in *Theatre under the Nazis*, 256–257, notes 37–39. Glenn R. Cuomo cites Schlösser's view of Shaw as a "semi-classic of the Third Reich," in "'Saint Joan before the Cannibals': George Bernard Shaw in the Third Reich," *German Studies Review* (1993): 256–257.

24. Boguslaw Drewniak, *Das Theater im NS-Staat*, 269–272.

25. Eloesser, "Im neuen Kulturbund-Haus: Hebbels *Judith*," 13.

26. Director's script of Shaw's *You Never Can Tell* (*Man kann nie wissen*), trans. Siegfried Trebitsch, 8°-27.299 (Berlin: S. Fischer, 3rd ed., 1924), act IV, 374. The line puns

in German: "clever children—clear-headed, well brought up children" ("kluge, hellköpfige, gut erzogene Kinder"). Compare to George Bernard Shaw, *You Never Can Tell*, act I substitution, 265; act IV cut, 329.

27. Director's script, *Man kann nie wissen*, 8°-27.299, act II, 291–292; Shaw, *You Never Can Tell*, act II, 254.

28. Shaw, *You Never Can Tell*, 208; director's script, *Man kann nie wissen*, 8°-27.299, 339–340. This is in act III.

29. Introduction to *Green Fields* (1916), in Sandrow, *God, Man, and Devil*, 96–98, introduction to play, 99–138.

30. Heinz Condell, "Stilprobleme der Jüdischen Theaters," *Jüdischer Kulturbund, Monatsblätter* 10 (October 1936): 27–29.

31. Hugo Lachmanski, review of *Green Fields* in *C.-V.-Zeitung* 6, 6 February 1936, 1.

32. Ibid.

33. Hinkel to Singer, 6 February 1936, WL Binder 2.53.16; Kulturbund documents SJ 193, SJ 315 #48, Hinkel to Singer, 9 March 1936, lifting ban for 15 March.

34. Singer to orchestra committee and actors in the *Antigone* production, 7 March 1936: microfiche, FWA 74/84/1220.

35. Ibid.

36. Ludwig Altmann in *C.-V.-Zeitung* 12, 19 March 1936 (press material archives, AdK, 9/74).

37. WL Binder 2.53.16, also part of FWA 74/86/5000, #48. Only serious drama could be performed on Hitler's birthday.

38. Hugo Lachmanski in *C.-V.-Zeitung* 12, 19 March 1936 (press material archives, AdK, 9/74); Kurt Pinthus in *Schild* 20 March 1936 (press material archives of the AdK, 9/74–9/75); FWA 8°-27.264, actor's rolebook for Sophocles, *Antigone*, trans. Georg Thudicum (Leipzig: Reklam, n.d.), stage directions, 42: "Tiresias from below, built over orchestra."

39. Hermann Sinsheimer in *Gemeindeblatt*, 22 March 1936 (press material archives, AdK, 9/75).

40. Altmann in *C.-V.-Zeitung* 12, 19 March 1936. Music by Werner Seelig-Bass.

41. William Niven, "The Birth of Nazi Drama? Thing Plays," in London, *Theatre under the Nazis*, 83; on banning the *Sprechchor*, 93, n. 49; Franz Moraller, "Der Sprechchor in der nationalsozialististischen Feiergestaltung," *Unser Wille und Weg* 6 (1936): 118–121.

42. Review in *C.-V.-Zeitung* 12, 19 March 1936.

43. Actor's rolebook for *Antigone*, FWA 8°-27.264.

44. Ibid., 13 (lines 178, 181–183); and modern translation by Robert Fagles: Sophocles, *Antigone*, 49 (lines 198–204). Fagles uses italics.

45. Actor's rolebook for *Antigone*; Sophocles, *Antigone*, line 288.

46. Sophocles, *Antigone*, lines 330–332; actor's rolebook for *Antigone*, cut lines 291–292. The bracketed lines indicate Wisten's deletions in his rolebook.

47. Actor's rolebook for *Antigone*; Sophocles, *Antigone*, lines 335–345.

48. Actor's rolebook for *Antigone*, lines 1320–1322 on 54; Sophocles, *Antigone*, lines 1445–1446 on 108.

49. Actor's rolebook for *Antigone*, transposition of chorus leader's lines, line 1270; Creon's speech, lines 1272–1276 on 52–55; Sophocles, *Antigone*, chorus leader, lines 1400–1401; Creon, lines 1402 ff. on 106.

50. Hermann Sinsheimer review, *Gemeindeblatt*, 22 March 1936 (newspaper clipping compilation, AdK). Antigone's sentence to be buried alive would transgress Jewish burial customs.

51. Sophocles, *Antigone*, lines 715–722 on 75; actor's rolebook for *Antigone*, 30, lines 641–648 deleted. See my essay "Jewish Theatre," 207–211.

52. Sophocles, *Antigone*, lines 734–736 on 76; actor's rolebook for *Antigone*, lines 658–659 on 30: "Lass sie um Rache stehn vor Zeus, / Der Blutverwandschaft!" was changed to "Lass sie um Rache stehn vor Zeus / Dem Gott des Blutbanns!" Blood jurisdiction gives a ruler the power to order executions.

53. Sophocles, *Antigone*, lines 751 ff. on 76; actor's rolebook for *Antigone*, 30–31.

54. Sophocles, *Antigone*, lines 800–803 on 78; actor's rolebook for *Antigone*, deleted lines 715–717 on 32.

55. Sophocles, *Antigone*, line 826; actor's rolebook for *Antigone*, line 739 on 32.

56. Sophocles, *Antigone*, lines 743–748 on 33; actor's rolebook script for *Antigone*.

57. Arthur Eloesser, "Aufführung im Kulturbund: *Antigone*," JR 22, 17 March 1936; Sinsheimer criticized Wisten in his review in *Gemeindeblatt*, 22 March 1936 (press material archives, AdK, 9/75). But Eugen Roth's review in *Jüdische Allgemeine Zeitung*, 18 March 1936, commended Wisten's skills (press material archives, AdK, 9/74).

58. Hugo Lachmanski in *C.-V.-Zeitung* 12, 19 March 1936.

59. Eloesser, "Aufführung im Kulturbund: *Antigone*."

60. Sinsheimer review in *Gemeindeblatt*, 22 March 1936.

61. Kurt Pinthus in *Schild*, 20 March 1936; *Gemeindeblatt*, 22 March 1936.

62. Hugo Lachmanski in *C.-V.-Zeitung* 12, 19 March 1936.

63. Eloesser, "Aufführung im Kulturbund: *Antigone*," 6.

64. Pinthus in *Schild*, 20 March 1936.

65. Sinsheimer review in *Gemeindeblatt*, 22 March 1936.

66. Eloesser, "Aufführung im Kulturbund: *Antigone*." Eloesser found Klein-Weissmann's black robe perfect for attending an afternoon tea.

67. Actor's rolebook for *Antigone*, across from 44–45, lines 1075, 1084–1086, for example.

68. Pinthus in *Schild*, 20 March 1936.

69. See my discussion on censorship in "Jewish Theatre," 209–210. Hinkel may have accepted the Kulturbund *Antigone* because Goebbels undoubtedly sanctioned Hegel's interpretation of *Antigone*, which emphasized Creon's authoritarianism. Inter-

estingly, Jean Anouilh's version of *Antigone* in Nazi-occupied Paris eight years later (1944) would characterize Creon as a dictator.

70. These regulations were made public through Jewish newspapers in Berlin. The R-Karte ordinance appears in *C.-V.-Zeitung* 13, 26 March 1936.

71. Cited in "Kulturbund Dämmerung?" *Jüdische Allgemeine Zeitung*, 16 June 1936 (press material archives, AdK, 11/114).

72. Ibid.; among the spate of articles, see also *IFB*, 18 June 1936; and *Jüdische Allgemeine Zeitung*, 17 June 1936.

73. "Jüdisches Theater in Deutschland," *IFB*, 18 June 1936 (press materials, AdK, 11/115–116).

74. "Kulturbund Dämmerung?" *Jüdische Allgemeine Zeitung*, 17 June 1936 (press materials, AdK, 11/114).

75. As quoted in ibid.

76. Ibid. Successful Jewish collectives existed in Prague and in Palestine.

77. Ibid.

78. Hans Hinkel, "Juden können Eigenleben führen," *Berliner Illustrierte* (evening edition), 18 July 1936 (press material archives, AdK, 11/124).

79. Ibid.

80. Alice Levie, in E. Geisel and H. M. Broder, eds., *Premiere und Program*, 157–158, claims that Jews went to theatres "every night" during the Olympics.

81. This article was in a German newspaper for non-Jews: "In der Jüdischen Kulturbund: Ein Besuch Berliner Schriftleiter," *Der Morgenpost*, 26 August 1936.

82. "Jüdisches Theater Spielt, v.d.D.," *Berliner Zeitung*, 25 August 1936.

83. Hinkel, "Juden können Eigenleben führen." The "outside" culture referred to German culture.

84. FWA 74/86/78, notes for Molnár's *Grosse Liebe*. Comments on cuts: "top of page 36; isn't the preparation for Margot's love for H. important!?" Notes refer to a "shame" about cuts on 11 by the "civil servant."

85. Heinz Condell to Fritz Wisten, 26 June 1936, FWA 74/86/1048.

86. Werner Levie to Fritz Wisten, 6 August 1936, FWA 74/86/1112.

87. "Ein Besuch Berliner Schriftleiter," *Der Morgenpost*, 26 August 1936 (written by "lhk").

5. DIDACTICISM: FALSE MESSIAHS, 1936–1937

1. "Die Kulturtagung," JR 72, 8 September 1936, 3–4.

2. Kurt Singer, "Die Arbeit der Jüdischen Kulturbünde—Rückschau und Vorschau," Berlin [5 July 1936], FWA 74/86/5032, reproduced in *Geschlossene Vorstellung* as document 37, 267.

3. "Eröffnungsrede zu Beginn der Kulturtagung," FWA 74/86/5032, reproduced in *Geschlossene Vorstellung* as document 36, 266.

4. Singer, FWA 74/86/5032, reproduced in *Geschlossene Vorstellung* as document 37, 267–268.

5. "Die Kulturtagung," JR 72, 8 September 1936, 3–4; Prinz speech, FWA 74/86/5032, reproduced in *Geschlossene Vorstellung* as document 39, 273–279.

6. Werner Levie, "Jüdisches Theater in Deutschland," JR 71, 4 September 1936.

7. Werner Levie to Fritz Wisten, 6 August 1936, FWA 74/86/1112.

8. I. L. Peretz, *The Golden Chain: The Drama of a Hasidic Family* (*Die goldene Kette: Das Drama einer chassidischen Familie*), premiere on 1 September 1936.

9. Fritz Wisten, conference presentation, 6 September 1936: "Das Bildungsprobleme des jüdischen Schauspielers"; "Die Kulturtagung," JR 72, 8 September 1936, 3–4, FWA 74/86/5032, reproduced in *Geschlossene Vorstellung* as document 40, 282.

10. Two actresses resisted the notion of special training in performing "Jewish" roles. Rostova (Rostovsky) emigrated before 1936. Anselm performed many Jewish roles but did not see the theatre as Jewish. Mira Rostovsky interview by author, 23 May 1995; Ruth Anselm interview by author, 24 May 1995. The commission recommended Wisten's ideas. "Die Kulturtagung," 4.

11. See Julius Bab, "Die nächste Kulturbundpremiere: *Die goldene Kette*," *Gemeindeblatt*, 30 August 1936 (press archives, AdK, 11/129); I. L. Peretz, *The Golden Chain: The Drama of a Hasidic Family: Die goldene Kette: Das Drama einer chassidischen Familie*, trans. Siegfried Schmitz (Vienna and Berlin: R. Lowit Verlag, 1920), FWA, 8°-27.261.

12. Ibid. The director's production script has stage directions and prologue preceding and following the cast list.

13. Ibid. The supplementary prologue is handwritten into the script.

14. Ibid.

15. Ibid., instruction on blank page across from 14.

16. Ibid., 14.

17. Ibid., 16.

18. Ibid., 21–22 (described on 21). Jenny Schaffer-Bernstein played the daughter-in-law.

19. Ibid., stage direction, 22. Miriam's words play on the original psalm: "Let him kiss me with the kisses of his mouth: for thy love is better than wine."

20. Ibid., 54.

21. Ibid., original pencil drawing of the set design between 42 and 43.

22. Ibid., 60.

23. *IFB*, 3 September, 1936; remarks based on dress rehearsal.

24. Hugo Lachmanski, "*Die Goldene Kette*: Zur Erstaufführung im Berliner Kulturbund," *C.-V.-Zeitung* 36, 2. Beiblatt, 3 September 1936, 3; also see Lachmanski's "Bilanz des Schauspiels," *C.-V.-Zeitung* 38, 3. Beiblatt, 16 September 1936, 7.

25. Arthur Eloesser, "*Die goldene Kette*: Aufführung im Kulturbund," JR 74, 4 September 1936, 5. A note in the script's introductory pages reads: "Hasidic dance per-

formed with permission of the *Jüdische Rundschau* press, song text compiled by Chemjo Winaver."

26. Ibid.

27. Dr. Max Nussbaum's notes accompany the script; *Die Goldene Kette*, FWA 8.27.261, first page of two-page description. On Havdalah, see Nicholas de Lange's *An Introduction to Judaism*, 96–97.

28. Dr. Oscar Liskow, "Jüdisches Theater von heute," *Nordische Rundschau Kiel*, 14 October 1936, press archives, AdK, 22/116. The reference is to Spain and points to partisan fighters against Gen. Francisco Franco's factions.

29. Werner Levie, "Jüdisches Theater in Deutschland," JR 71, 4 September 1936.

30. This would occur on a level higher than that of the *zaddik* (spiritual leader of a Hasidic community), who deemed that everyday things—not just sacred ones—radiated holy sparks.

31. Joseph Dan, *Kabbalah*, 86–88. Sabbatai Zevi was popular in eastern Europe, where Jews suffered. Kabbalistic belief dominated religious Jewish culture in the seventeenth century; interest in messianic prophecy led people to take Nathan of Gaza's claims seriously. Sabbatai Zevi converted to Islam to escape death (1666), and the movement collapsed.

32. De Lange, *An Introduction to Judaism*, 97, 99. Early writings discouraged messianic fervor among Jews under Roman rule. Medieval philosophers linked the idea of redemption with a Messianic Age.

33. Isaac Luria (1534–1572) saw himself as a prophet. He believed that worshippers influenced redemption through their deeds. Performing good deeds released sparks of divine light. The collective power of holy sparks hastened the Messiah's coming through the process of tikkun. See de Lange, *An Introduction to Judaism*, 203; Dan, *Kabbalah*, chapter 6, 71–79.

34. De Lange, *An Introduction to Judaism*, 205–207. See also Michael O. Wise on "crisis cults" in "Messiahs and Myth Dreams," in *The First Messiah: Investigating the Savior before Christ* (New York: HarperCollins, 1999), 29.

35. Bertha Badt-Strauss, "The False Messiah," JR 88, 3 November 1936, 5.

36. Kurt Pinthus in *Gemeindeblatt*, 8 November 1936. See Condell on his designs: "Stilprobleme des Jüdischen Theaters," *Monatsblätter* 10 (October 1936): 29, FWA 8°-27.241.

37. Meier Broser, "Probleme der Übersetzung dramatischer Werke aus dem Hebräischen: Einige Bemerkungen zur Übersetzung das Dramas *Schabbathai Zwi*," WL Binder, 2.53.25, Forbidden Texts, Antrag 70, SJ 1310, galleys, 737–738.

38. Ibid. (underlining by censor). Hinkel banned the article. The censor took umbrage at Broser's merging of Jewish and German "components" in his writing.

39. Ibid., 2. The censor underlined "beautiful German" in the text.

40. Rabbi Nussbaum's lecture notes are among the collected "forbidden texts" from

Hinkel's office. See "Wer war Schabbatai Zwi?" exposé of lecture, 4 (of six pages), WL, 500 series, microfilm reel 2, SJ 1337, Antrag 162.

41. Hinkel's underlining in original banned text by Nussbaum, "Wer war Schabbatai Zwi?" 4, WL, 500 series, microfilm reel 2, Forbidden Materials, SJ 1337, Antrag 162. Nussbaum forbidden lecture text as marked by Hinkel: "Grund zum Verbot" (reason for ban).

42. Kurt Pinthus in *Gemeindeblatt*, 8 November 1936. The play had been written for the Ohel workers' theatre in Tel Aviv.

43. Martha Wertheimer review, *IFB*, 5 November 1936.

44. Ibid.

45. Arthur Eloesser, "*Sabbatai Z'wi* im Kulturbund," *JR* 89, 6 November 1936, 6.

46. Wertheimer review.

47. Condell on style: "Stilprobleme des Jüdischen Theaters," *Monatsblätter* 10 (October 1936): 29, FWA 8°-27.241.

48. Pinthus in *Gemeindeblatt*, 8 November 1936.

49. Eloesser, "*Sabbatai Z'wi* im Kulturbund." He refers to the film *The Cabinet of Dr. Caligari*.

50. Excerpted scene, act III from translation of *Sabbatai Zevi* by C. Z. Klötzel, n.d., "Drei Jahre Kulturbund," Kurt Singer Archiv, Szènen aus Sabbathai Zwi von Nathan Bistritzki, 1.53.35, AdK.

51. Broser did not translate this. Wertheimer refers to Broser's translation in her review.

52. Ibid.; Pinthus review in *Schild*, 13 November 1936.

53. See Jonathan Petropoulos, *Art and Politics in the Third Reich*, 53.

54. Actor Werner Hinzelmann was in charge. The first recorded play was Molière's *The Imaginary Invalid* (February 1936), which did not take place due to a performance ban.

55. Herbert Freeden worked in this branch of the Kulturbund. See his description on the Jewish Schools' troupe in *Jüdisches Theater in Nazideutschland*, 120–121.

56. Mascha Benyakonsky tutored Hebrew. Mascha Benya-Matz interview by author, 9 November 1995.

57. See John London, "Non-German Drama in the Third Reich," in *Theatre under the Nazis*, 243–244.

58. Stage Manager's Book (*Inspirizenbuch*, 1936), FWA 74/86/5094.

59. Kurt Singer, "Der Jüdische Kulturbund wirbt, Berlin," 6 April 1937, FWA 74/86/5032, also reproduced in *Geschlossene Vorstellung*, 309.

60. Director's script for Shakespeare, *A Midsummer Night's Dream* (*Ein Sommernachtstraum*), trans. A. W. Schlegel, FWA 8°-27.72; Vera Cramer, "Gut gebrüllt, Löwe!" *C.-V.-Zeitung* 48, 26 November 1936, on rehearsals for the play.

61. Ruth Anselm interview by author, 24 May 1995. Wisten wanted her to play Puck, but she did not want the role.

62. Director's script, *Ein Sommernachtstraum*, FWA 8°-27.72, across from 18; William Shakespeare, *A Midsummer Night's Dream*, 153.

63. Director's script, *Ein Sommernachtstraum*, across from 20, segue to Wisten's scene 3 (originally II.1).

64. Ibid., 59–60; Wisten's notations and drawings are across from these pages.

65. Arthur Eloesser on *Ein Sommernachtstraum*, JR, 4 December 1936, 5.

66. Ibid.; Hugo Lachmanski in *C.-V.-Zeitung* 50, 10 December 1936; Kurt Pinthus in *Gemeindeblatt*, 13 December 1936.

67. Shakespeare, *A Midsummer Night's Dream*, lines 414–417.

68. Hinkel to Singer, 18 February 1937, WL, 500 series, microfilm reel 2, 29.575.

69. A copy of the 1934 script is in Wisten's archives; but he reused the script in 1946, making it hard to know when the changes were made. See Kingsley, *Men in White* (New York: Covici, Friede Publishers, 1933).

70. Preface to the 1937 ed. of Joseph Roth, *The Wandering Jews*. Roth was an Austrian novelist and journalist. See Joseph Roth, *The Wandering Jews* (no preface in the 1927 ed.).

71. Ibid., 131.

72. Ibid., 130. Roth's Austrian citizenship insulated him from what he criticized. He died in Parisian exile in 1939.

73. Freeden cited in "Geschlossene Gesellschaft," *Der Spiegel* 33, 11 August 1965, 74.

74. Director's script for Hofmannsthal, *Die Hochzeit der Sobeide*, FWA 8°-27.292; Hugo von Hofmannsthal, *Die Hochzeit der Sobeide: Ein dramatisches Gedicht* (Berlin: S. Fischer Verlag, 1922).

75. Rabindranath Tagore, *The Post Office* (*Das Postamt*), trans. Hedwig Lachman and Gustav Landauer (Munich: Karl Wolff Verlag, 1921), FWA 8°-27.290, 27.

76. Ibid.; Hofmannsthal, *Die Hochzeit der Sobeide*. According to Arthur Eloesser, "Kulturbundtheater, Rabindranath Tagore und Hugo von Hofmannsthal," JR 10, 5 February 1937, 15, the actress's delivery cooled down the effect of Sobeide's outbursts.

77. Hofmannsthal, *Die Hochzeit der Sobeide*, 116, FWA 8°-27.292.

78. Director's script for Tagore, *Das Postamt*, FWA 8°-27.290.

79. Ibid.; Kurt Pinthus review, *Gemeindeblatt*, 7 February 1937.

80. Wertheimer emphasized Wisten's directing failure in her review: IFB, 7 February 1937; Pinthus in *Gemeindeblatt*, 7 February 1937; Eloesser, "Kulturbundtheater, Rabindranath Tagore und Hugo von Hofmannsthal."

81. Pinthus in *Gemeindeblatt*, 7 February 1937. See Hofmannsthal, *Die Hochzeit der Sobeide*, FWA 8°-27.292, especially scene 1, 39–43.

82. The play *Der Hauptreffer* (The Big Win) was reworked by M. M. Amwrossjew from German, translated from Hebrew by M. [Meir] Broser, FWA 74/86/232.

83. Kurt Singer Archiv, AdK, 1.55.35, *Kritiken der Aufführungen*; Meir Broser, "Zur Übertragung der Komödie *Amcha*." The German verb was "jiddeln."

84. Arthur Eloesser, review of *Amcha* in JR 28, 9 April 1937.

85. Ibid.

86. Anselm interview; Benya-Matz interview. The opera took place in May 1937.

87. The report was published in July 1937. Walter Laqueur, *A History of Zionism*, 509, 513 ff.

88. Kurt Singer, "Der Jüdische Kulturbund wirbt, Berlin," 6 April 1937, FWA 74/86/5032, also reproduced in *Geschlossene Vorstellung*, 308.

89. London, "Non-German Drama in the Third Reich," 222, cites addresses by Schlösser and Goebbels in 1934 and 1935; see n. 2 on 252.

90. Ladislaus Bus-Fekete (1896–1971) Americanized his name to Leslie Bush-Fekete.

6. PROTECTION: COMMUNITY VALUES, 1937–1938

1. Arthur Eloesser, "Der Kulturbund ruft!" JR 70/71, 3 September 1937, 18.

2. Henrik Ibsen, *Pillars of Society*, 118. See actor's rolebook script for Ibsen, *Die Stützen der Gesellschaft*, trans. Wilhelm Lange (Leipzig: Reclam, n.d.), 92, FWA, 8°-27.284.

3. Actor's rolebook for *Die Stützen der Gesellschaft*. This was Wisten's rolebook for Consul Bernick.

4. Ibid., 58; Ibsen *Pillars of Society*, act III, 78–79.

5. Actor's rolebook for *Die Stützen der Gesellschaft*, 65–67; Ibsen, *Pillars of Society*, 86–88.

6. Lutz Weltmann, 1937 Wisten clipping, Konvolut, FWA 74/86/212/33.

7. Ibid. See Arthur Eloesser's review, JR 72, 10 September 1937, 6.

8. Bernick's line to the ship repairman Aune in act II was also cut: "The particular must be sacrificed to the general good." See actor's rolebook for *Die Stützen der Gesellschaft*, 31.

9. Bogoslaw Drewniak, *Das Theater im NS-Staat* 269, 272n.; Rebecca Rovit, "Jewish Theatre," 234.

10. Actor's rolebook for *Die Stützen der Gesellschaft*, act IV, 88; Ibsen, *Pillars of Society*, act III to the end of act IV, 110–111.

11. Actor's rolebook for *Die Stützen der Gesellschaft*, 59; Ibsen, *Pillars of Society*, 79.

12. Ibsen, *Pillars of Society*, 80; actor's rolebook for *Die Stützen der Gesellschaft* cut, 60.

13. Raul Hilberg, *The Destruction of the European Jews*, section on expropriation, 60.

14. Actor's rolebook for *Die Stützen der Gesellschaft*, act IV, 85–86; Ibsen, *Pillars of Society*, 110.

15. Actor's rolebook for *Die Stützen der Gesellschaft*, act I, 6–7; Ibsen, *Pillars of Society*, 17.

16. Levie uses 15 September 1937 as his baseline date in *Mitteilungen des Reichsverbandes des Jüdischen Kulturbünde in Deutschland* 6 (January 1938), FWA 74/86/5093, reproduced in *Geschlossene Vorstellung*, 315–319. Strengthened resistance among Arabs in Palestine against the Peel land partition created new unrest.

17. "Ein Werbefilm der 'Jüdischen Rundschau,'" *JR* 81, 12 October 1937, 3.

18. In Hebrew "Golem" refers to shapeless matter. Joseph Dan, *Kabbalah*, 107–108. MaHaRal comes from "Moreinu Ha Rav Rabbi Liva." See Nicolas de Lange, *An Introduction to Judaism*, 230, for a description of "kavanah."

19. Leivick (1888–1962), born in Belorussia, wrote the play in 1921. Imprisoned for trying to overthrow the tsar, he wrote *Chains of the Messiah* in solitary confinement. He fled to the United States in 1913.

20. A production promptbook (*Soufflierbuch*) in seven scenes provides insight into the production. Promptbook of *Der Golem*, FWA 74/86/51a; see H. Leivick, *The Golem*, 121–254. In the English translation scene 7 ("In the Cave") is followed by the eighth scene, "The Last Mission."

21. Leivick, *The Golem*, 175.

22. Ibid., 247–248; promptbook for *Der Golem*, FWA 74/86/51a, 97.

23. Leivick, *The Golem*, 248; promptbook for *Der Golem*, FWA 74/86/51a, 97–98.

24. A second scene 7 ("In the Cave") version exists among the Kulturbund Golem-related pages. This alternate script reverses the order of Leivick's scenes 7 and 8, but both scenes are labeled "7." An additional photocopy of the script exists with different markings and an extra scene 7, "In the Cave," is the last scene. FWA 74/86/51b, 105 ff.

25. Promptbook for *Der Golem*; see Leivick, *The Golem*, particularly "In the Cave," 210–234.

26. Promptbook for *Der Golem*; Leivick, *The Golem* (descriptions as Golem enters scenes 2 and 3, respectively), 132, 143.

27. Martha Wertheimer, "Kampf mit dem Golem," *IFB*, 14 October 1937.

28. Arthur Eloesser, "*Der Golem*: Aufführung im Berliner Kulturbund," *JR* 81, 12 October 1937, 3.

29. Ibid.

30. Wertheimer, "Kampf mit dem Golem."

31. Leivick, *The Golem*, 185.

32. Ibid., 182.

33. Review (by "t."), "Komödienabend im Kulturbund: *Zweikampf der Liebe*," *JR* 90, 12 November 1937, 18.

34. The novel was published posthumously in 1905. F. Jöhlinger wrote on the premiere at the Kulturbund Rhein-Ruhr, *JR* 5, 19 January 1937, 8–9. Ben Spanier directed.

35. Director's script for *Der Pojaz*, FWA 74/86/130, 25.

36. Ibid. 32, end of scene 3. Galicia belonged to the Austrian-Hungarian Empire. German was spoken in Christian and secular enclaves. Yiddish was the language of the shtetl.

37. Ibid., 48.

38. Ibid., 56.

39. Ibid., 59, 61.

40. Ibid., 2, stage directions.

41. Review of *The Pojaz* by "N," JR 94, 16 November 1937, 13.

42. In January 1938 Herbert Freeden directed Karl Gutzkow's tragedy about another rebel, Uriel Acosta. Acosta had been excommunicated for criticizing rabbinical authority.

43. Director's script for William Shakespeare, *Much Ado about Nothing* (*Viel Lärm um nichts*), trans. Wolf Heinrich Graf Baudissin (Leipzig: Reklam, n.d.), FWA 8°-27.287. Wisten changed five acts into eleven scenes. Don Pedro's line on 29 ff. in William Shakespeare, *Much Ado about Nothing*, 290. Leonato's reference to "shame" derived of "unknown loins" in act IV, scene 1 (295) is deleted in the director's script for *Viel Lärm um nichts*, lines 132–133, no pagination.

44. Walter Laqueur, *A History of Zionism*, 29–30.

45. Hinkel to Singer, 26 February 1938, WL, microfiche FWA 74/86/5000, 37.

46. Director's script with notations for Ladislaus Bus-Fekete, *Kap der guten Hoffnung* (Cape of Good Hope), FWA 74/86/59, act III, 49; premiere 2 February 1938.

47. Ibid., 96.

48. Dr. Jacob Schönberg, "Kulturbund Opera Performance: Adolphe Adam, *Wenn ich König wäre*," JR 17, March 1938, 25.

49. E. R.-J., "Neue Einwanderungsquote für Palästina," *C.-V.-Zeitung* 11, 17 March 1938, 1; 2.8 percent of the Austrian population was Jewish.

50. Freeden quoted in E. Geisel and H. M. Broder, eds., *Premiere und Pogrom*, 262.

51. The report was published in July 1937. Laqueur, *A History of Zionism*, 509, 513 ff.

52. Lutz Weltmann, "*Das Gericht*," IFB, 12 May 1938, 3.

53. Ibid.

54. Promptbook for *Das Gericht*, reworked by Herbert Freeden, FWA 74/86/48, scene 1, 3.

55. Ibid., scene 3, 19 (underlining in original).

56. Ibid., 24.

57. Ibid., 48–60.

58. Weltmann, "*Das Gericht*," 3. Also see Leo Hirsch, "Zeitgenössisches Palästina: Weltpremiere im Jüdischen Kulturbund," *Jüdische Gemeindeblatt für Berlin*, 15 May 1938, 5.

59. Promptbook for *Das Gericht*, scene 7, 64. This was changed from the Narrator's "the three there are still very young and the future is in their hands"; Weltmann, "*Das Gericht*."

60. Laqueur, *A History of Zionism*, 518.

61. Leo Hirsch, *Jüdische Gemeindeblatt für Berlin*, 15 May 1938, 5; also Micha Michalowitz, JR, 10 May 1938, 3.

62. Two letters from Batdori to Wisten, 14 June 1938, FWA 74/86/1042, 1043, requesting production photographs. In the second (undated letter), Batdori awaited a response.

63. Letter from Singer to Wisten, 18 May 1938, FWA 74/86/1271. Wisten's summer salary, June–September 1938, was reduced to 560 Marks.

64. See Hilberg, *The Destruction of the European Jews*, specifically chapter 6, 118–119, on the "identification system."

65. Director's script for Henrik Ibsen, *Ghosts* (*Gespenster*), trans. M. von Borch (Leipzig: Reklam, n.d.), FWA 8°-27.269. See Henrik Ibsen, *Ghosts*, 276.

66. Micha Michalowitz, "Ibsens *Gespenster*," JR 71, 6 September 1938; Leo Hirsch, *Jüdisches Gemeindeblatt für Berlin*, 11 September 1938; Bab to Wisten, 19 July 1938, FWA 74/85/1028.

67. Singer to Wisten, 13 September 1938, FWA 74/86/1273. Even the Nazis banned *Ghosts* from all stages after the war began because the play was too depressing. Drewniak cited in John London, ed., *Theatre under the Nazis*, 234, n. 33.

68. Singer to Wisten, 6 September 1938, FWA 74/86/1272.

69. It is not clear when Anselm left Germany, although it was after May 1938, as indicated by a farewell letter. "We experienced seven years together, Ruth. Go to a great future," wrote her resistance cell partner as she prepared for a new life. Weisenborn to Anselm, 27 May 1938, SJK. In my interview, Anselm told me that she witnessed Kristallnacht.

70. Benya-Matz (Benyakonsky) interview by author, in Rebecca Rovit and Alvin Goldfarb, eds., *Theatrical Performance during the Holocaust*, 63. Vinaver emigrated to New York in late 1938.

71. Dr. Jacob Schönberg, "Eine Palästina-Oper: Die Aufführung von Jacob Weinbergs Oper *Die Chaluzim*," JR 71, 6 September 1938, 3.

72. Benyakonsky played Gilda in her final Kulturbund leading role. She had her visa for the United States but wanted opera reviews for her career.

73. Singer to Wisten, 1 October 1938, FWA 74/86/1274.

74. Copy of Singer, "Jüdisches Kulturbundtheater" (1938), Kurt Singer Archives, AdK, unnumbered. The original is at the LBI. This was an annual publication by the Reich Association of Jewish Cultural Leagues: 2–3.

75. Ibid., 4.

76. Singer to Wisten, 1 October 1938, FWA 74/86/1275. A Singer letter (from Amsterdam) to the Kulturbund executive committee, FWA 74/86/1276, 8 December 1938, suggests that he heard about Kristallnacht while still in the United States.

7. ASSAULT: THE VISE TIGHTENS, 1938–1939

1. Hinkel's general performance bans, WL Binder 2.25.21, (underlining in the original).

2. Hodge (1903–1958) was a medical doctor and playwright from New Zealand. His play was performed in New York in the 1930s. The title alluded to Shakespeare's *Twelfth*

Night: "When that I was and a little tiny boy, / With hey, ho, the wind and the rain" (act V, lines 378–379).

3. Micha Michalowitz, review, JR 88, 4 November 1938, 14. There is conflicting information on when some of these performers emigrated. In a report from 1938–1939 Levie notes that Borodin, Herz, and Segall emigrated in October 1938, although they actually emigrated later than that: 9 July 1939, FWA 74/86/5042.

4. Kurt Singer was abroad when he heard the news. He wrote the Kulturbund executive committee about his decision to leave Germany on 8 December 1939, FWA 74/86/1276.

5. Reich Ministry for Enlightenment and Propaganda to Werner Levie via Reichsverband der Jüdischen Kulturbünde in Deutschland, 8 November 1938: "I hereby inform you that in accordance with the telephone warning that I received today at 12:10 [P.M.], I have (1) notified all Kulturbund branches that with immediate effect the publication of the *Kulturbundblätter* is forbidden until further notice." WL, 500 series, microfilm 56; Herbert Freeden, "Begegnungen mit Fritz Wisten," in *Drei Leben für das Theatre*, 48–49.

6. Berthold Segall in E. Geisel and H. M. Broder, eds., *Premiere und Pogrom*, 289–290; Kurt Michaelis interview by author in Rebecca Rovit and Alvin Goldfarb, eds., *Theatrical Performance during the Holocaust*, 68.

7. Protective custody (*Schutzhaft*) was a euphemism for arrest and imprisonment.

8. Hinkel to Levie, 14 November 1938, WL, 500 series, microfilm 59: Lifting the Ban on Jewish Cultural Events (the ban on lectures in the Jewish cultural realm remains).

9. Werner Levie refers to the date 15 September in his "Work Report" (*Arbeitsbericht*, 12 July 1939, outlining the events from the Kulturbund between 1 October 1938 and 30 June 1939). The report is reproduced as document 64 in *Geschlossene Vorstellung*, 322. The original is FWA 74/86/5042. See Susanne Wisten, "Momente, die Sternstunden waren," in Geisel and Broder, *Premiere und Pogrom*, 115–116.

10. Levie, "Work Report"; Levie report in *Geschlossene Vorstellung*, 334. Membership in the Kulturbund in Germany peaked during the 1936/1937 season at 58,000 people.

11. Herbert Freeden in Geisel and Broder, *Premiere und Pogrom*, 266–268, recalls a letter of "protection" from 17 November, requesting that he report to the theatre the following day to resume rehearsals.

12. Merton Hodge, *The Wind and the Rain* (*Regen und Wind*) arranged for the German stage by Detlef Sierck (Berlin: Vertriebsstelle und Verlag deutscher Bühnenschriftsteller und Bühnenkomponisten GmbH), FWA 74/86/77, act I, John and Gilbert, 13.

13. Besides Mascha Benyakonsky and Ruth Anselm, Camilla Spira emigrated to Holland.

14. "Die jüdischen Kulturbünde," JN 1, 23 November 1938, 1, 1.

15. Singer to Hinkel, 8 December 1938 (original in R561/113Bl.7. Bundesarchiv Koblenz); reproduced in *Geschlossene Vorstellung* as document 65, 341.

16. Singer to executive committee, 8 December 1939, FWA 74/86/1276.

17. Singer to Hinkel, 8 December 1938; reproduced in *Geschlossene Vorstellung*, 341.

18. Levie, Work Report, 12 July 1939, FWA 74/86/5042; reproduced in *Geschlossene Vorstellung* as document 64, 323. Levie began work on 1 January 1939.

19. Singer letter to Kulturbund executive committee, FWA 74/86/1276, 8.

20. Sholem-Yankev Abramovitsh (also known as Broido; 1836–1917), a Yiddish storyteller from Russia, was known as "Mendele the book peddler." *The Travels of Benjamin III* may have been the source for the adaptation. Director's script and second half of the promptbook for *Where To, Benjamin?* (*Benjamin, wohin?*), FWA 74/86/70. The heavily revised script was condensed for production.

21. Director's script for *Benjamin, wohin?* 22, 71 (epilogue); "Premiere im Kulturbund: Aufführung der Komödie *Benjamin, wohin?*" JN 8, 20 December 1938, 1.

22. Director's script for *Benjamin, wohin?* (preface), 1; photo of Miller, FWA 20.53.646.

23. Julius Bab on the replacement for Siegmund Nunberg, "Jüdische Schauspieler: Rudolf Israel Müller," JN 14, 17 February 1939, 9. Müller changed his name to Martin Miller upon emigration to Britain.

24. "Premiere im Kulturbund: Aufführung der Komödie *Benjamin, wohin?*" 1.

25. See Alan E. Steinweis, *Art, Ideology, and Economics in Nazi Germany*, chapter 5, 124.

26. Hinkel to Reichsverband der Jüdischen Kulturbünde e.V., attention Dr. Levie, 19 December 1938, WL Binder, 2.25.21; also Hinkel to Levie, 4 March 1939.

27. See an article on the formal changes: "Konzentrierte Kulturbund-Arbeit," JN 11, 30 December 1938, 1.

28. Steffi Hinzelmann played a "good fairy." Leo Hirsch in JN 4, 13 January 1939, 3.

29. Bab, "Jüdische Schauspieler: Rudolf Israel Müller," 9.

30. Leo Hirsch, "Die Premiere der Kulturbund-Bühne: *Das Wintermärchen*," JN 12, 10 February 1939, 9.

31. Bab, "Jüdische Schauspieler: Rudolf Israel Müller," 9.

32. Director's script for William Shakespeare, *The Winter's Tale: A Play in Five Acts* (*Das Wintermärchen*), trans. Dorothea Tieck (Leipzig: Philipp Reclam, n.d.), 57–62, FWA 8°-27.285; compare William Shakespeare, *The Winter's Tale*, 1337–1368 (act IV, scene 4, 1354–1362).

33. Shakespeare, *The Winter's Tale*, lines 80–104, 1355; director's script for *Das Wintermärchen*, act IV.iv (scene 9), 59–60. "Scion" refers to "heir" and to a woody plant used in grafting.

34. Hirsch, "Die Premiere der Kulturbund-Bühne: *Das Wintermärchen*," 9.

35. William L. Shirer, 15 March 1939, in *Berlin Diary*, 160.

36. Hungarian writers were connected to Austrian culture; see Boguslaw Drewniak, *Das Theatre im NS-Staat*, 278.

37. J. B. Priestley, *People at Sea (Menschen auf See)*, rolebook for Diana Lismore, adapted and translated by Leo Hirsch, FWA 74/86/47b.

38. Ibid., 14.

39. Ibid., act II, 43–44.

40. Priestley's line reading is more explicit: Val responds to the "Great War": "It's never stopped. And for all we know, the still Greater War might have started now." See my analysis in "Jewish Theatre," 206. For Priestley's original, see *People at Sea* (London: Samuel French, 1938), 36.

41. Priestley to Wisten, 25 April 1939, on premiere and his play *Time and the Conways*, FWA 74/86/1156, 1157.

42. Leo Hirsch, "*Menschen auf See*: Zu der Aufführung im Jüdischen Kulturbund in Berlin," JN 29/30, 14 April 1939, 9; Hugo Lachmanski, "*Menschen auf See*: Erstaufführung im Jüdischen Kulturbund in Berlin," JN 32, 21 April 1939, 9–10.

43. This was a propaganda stunt on the part of Goebbels. For more on the S.S. *St. Louis*, see Robert N. Rosen, *Saving the Jews*, chapter 5. Belgium, France, and Britain issued quotas for Jews. See "Die Passagiere der St. Louis," JN 51, 27 June 1939, 1.

44. Wisten to Bab in Paris, 1 May 1939, FWA 74/86/1030.

45. On 24 May 1939 Werner Levie signed over management duties to Wisten temporarily, from 26 May to 9 June 1939, FWA 74/86/1123. Werner Hinzelmann's duties were related to correspondence with the Ministry of Propaganda.

46. Hugo Lachmanski review of *XYZ*, JN 39, 16 May 1939, 4.

47. Hugo Lachmanski review of *Fairy Tale of Justice*, JN 48, 16 June 1939, 10; director's script for Ladislaus Fodor, *Fairy Tale of Justice (Märchen von der Gerechtigkeit)*, FWA 77/86/62.

48. Herbert Freeden emigrated before the *Marizá* success but refers to the high number of attendees and the successful operetta in *Drei Leben für das Theater*, 49.

49. Werner Levie, "Arbeitsbericht des Jüdischen Kulturbundes in Deutschland e.V. vom 1.10.38–30.6.1939," submitted 12 July 1939, FWA 74/6/5042; reproduced in *Geschlossene Vorstellung* as document 64, 327–328. The Reich had collaborated with Hungary since 1938 on territorial issues. Garay performed in 1938 with the Kulturbund opera.

50. Hannah Kroner-Segal, "Tap Dance at the Kulturbund," in Geisel and Broder, *Premiere und Pogrom*, 92–93.

51. Director's script for Emmerich Kálmán's *Countess Marizá: Operetta in 3 Acts (Gräfin Marizá*; libretto by Julius Brammer and Alfred Grünwald), FWA 74/86/74. The premiere was in Vienna in 1924.

52. Micha Israel Michalowitz, review of *Countess Marizá*, JN 55, 11 July 1939, 4.

53. Ibid.

54. Director's script for *Countess Marizá*, 12, act I, scene 4.

55. Ibid. Josef Uridil was a well-known soccer player in Vienna. The script shows Wisten's double cuts written in red pencil.

56. Ibid., act III, scene 3, 59. Ibsen, Strindberg, and Wedekind created strong female characters who tormented men. Zsupán puns on the words "statistically" and "sadistically."

57. Ibid., act III, scene 3, 59. Soma Morgenstern (1890–1976) fled Vienna in 1938 for the United States.

58. Ibid., act II (scene 12), 46, 48, 51. Tassilo uses "Ahnen" for ancestors, a word used by the Nazis when referring to Aryan lineage. Deleted lines include references to Tassilo's fabricated family tree and his father's occupation as a teacher.

59. Siegfried Israel Hirsch to Hanne (John and Harriet) Isaak (Shanghai), 24 January 1940, SJK, 1.53.110, 1.

60. Kroner-Segal, "Tap Dance at the Kulturbund," 92.

61. Hugo Lachmanski on premiere of *Mirandolina* and Micha Michalowitz on premiere of *Entführung*, JN 68, 25 August 1939, 8–9.

62. Kroner-Segal, "Tap Dance at the Kulturbund," 92.

63. See Leo Hirsch, "Jetzt kommt es darauf an! Was man außer Permit und Passage braucht," JN 64, 11 July 1939, 10. The full-page ad praises six years of achievement.

64. Leo Hirsch, JN 68, 25 August 1939, 8, 9; see the newspaper edition prepared in advance of its release date: JN 70, 1 September 1939, 9. Wisten kept this clipping in his scrapbook for the season 1939–1940, FWA 74/86/22.

65. Shirer's *Berlin Diary* suggests the growing certainty of war (24 August 1939, 181). See 27 August 1939: "Hot and sultry today which makes for an increase in tension," 186.

66. Hannah Kroner-Segal, personal correspondence with author, June 1994.

8. HOLDING OUT: WAR AND FANCY, 1939–1940

1. William L. Shirer, *Berlin Diary*, entries 1–3 September, 1939, 197–200. I have relied on William Shirer's eyewitness reports to capture the general atmosphere in Berlin leading up to the outbreak of war.

2. Joseph Goebbels, *The Goebbels Diaries*, 1939–1941, entry, 1 September 1939.

3. "Die nächsten Veranstaltungen," JN 70, 1 September 1939, 9.

4. Werner Levie (Amsterdam) to Wisten on 4 September 1939, FWA 74/86/1126.

5. The *Rücksprache* is a dialogue among civil servants and their superiors and between co-workers. It may be seen as a euphemism for meetings between SS officers and representatives from the Kulturbund.

6. Letter from Siegfried Israel Hirsch to Hanne (John and Harriet) Isaak, 24 January 1940, SJK, 1.53.110, 1. Siegfried Hirsch says the meeting was on 4 September, when he found out that he lost his job to Werner Hinzelmann. See Wisten's Work Report, 1 September 1939–31 August 1940, FWA 7/86/5054, folder 12.

7. Announcement, "Jüdischer Kulturbund," JN 71, 5 September 1939, 1.

8. Ibid.

9. *Jusik* was announced in the *Jüdischer Kulturbund Monatsblätter* 8 (August 1939): 5–6.

10. 7 September 1939, Dr. Otto Hirsch, Aktenvermerk, 86–89 from Bundesarchiv Potsdam, archived under FWA 74/86/5001.

11. "Neue Verordnungen," JN 76, 22 September 1939, 1, on film showings and "blackouts." See also 1 November 1939: Hinkel to Reichsminister Goebbels refers to a curfew for Jews, 8 P.M. (4), WL, 500 series. In summer 1940 the curfew would be 9 P.M.

12. Siegfried Hirsch to Hanne (John and Harriet) Isaak, 24 January 1940, SJK, 1.53.110, 1 (underlining in the original). See Wisten's minutes from two meetings: *Rücksprache* from 25 September 1939, item 9 on personnel; minutes from 28 September 1939, item 4 includes lists of names for staff positions of those men and women who were replaceable (1–2); FWA 74/86/5001, series of protocols compiled in WL Binder, 2.53.22; also on microfilm at WL.

13. Copy of a draft from Hinkel to Goebbels, 1 November 1939, WL Binder 2.53.22, 2 (reference to new labor laws is on 3).

14. Martin Brasch, *Rücksprache*, 20 October 1939, FWA 74/86/5001, 12.

15. See Alan E. Steinweis, *Art, Ideology, and Economics in Nazi Germany*, 63, on Hinkel's staff members: Ursula Framm, Walter Owens, Erich Kochwanowski, and Lock (no first name known). Two protocols from October 1939 show Wisten's case for special matinee performances on Sundays. The minutes from 13 October 1939 and from 20 October 1939 (#2) show that performances were permitted. See FWA 74/86/5001, 11 and FWA 74/86/5001,12, WL Binder 2.53.11. These are also at the WL.

16. Wisten Report to Kochanowski, FWA 74/86/5045, folder 12, from November 1939.

17. Inaugurated in November 1937, the space accommodated 700, with a stage 6.5 meters deep. See Herbert Freeden, *Jüdisches Theatre in Nazideutschland*, 96.

18. Ibid.; Wisten Report to Kochanowski, FWA 74/86/5045, 2; see *Rücksprache* (with Brasch) 1 December 1939, items 1 and 5, FWA 74/86/5001, 30.

19. Wisten Report to Reich Ministry, 1 February 1940, FWA 74/86/5053, folder 11.

20. Brasch, Committee Minutes of Kulturbund board, 25 October 1939, FWA 74/86/5001,14; Minutes, 1 November 1939, FWA 74/86/5001, 16. See "Die nächsten Veranstaltungen des jüdischen Kulturbundes im Deutschland," JN 92, 17 November 1939, 1–2.

21. Brasch, Minutes, 1 December 1939, items 2, 1, and 3, FWA 74/86/5001, 20.

22. Website for the Archives of Federal Republic of Germany: www.bundesarchiv.de (accessed on 29 July 2010) for details on the Reichskulturkammer and the Be K A ("Special Cultural Tasks"). Kochanowski led the propaganda department by 1941.

23. Henning Rischbieter, ed., *Theatre im "Dritten Reich."*

24. Steinweis, *Art, Ideology, and Economics in Nazi Germany*, 157.

25. Kurt Baumann was appointed "self-censor" or "reader" in 1935 to vet the programs in advance of Hinkel's censors. After Baumann emigrated in 1939, Wisten and Hirsch took over the "Jewish precensorship." Kurt Baumann's 1977 account in Monika Richarz, ed., *Jewish Life in Germany*, 382.

26. The ban on Molnár's play coincided with his emigration to the United States.

27. Brasch *Rücksprache*, 1 December 1939: #4, FWA 74/86/5001, 20.

28. FWA 74/86/5080, 1,2,3.

29. Wisten *Rücksprache*, 14 December 1939, FWA 74/86/5001, 21. Also translated for Rebecca Rovit and Alvin Goldfarb, eds., *Theatrical Performance during the Holocaust*, 76.

30. Director's script for Franz Molnár, *Die Zuckerbäckerin: Kömodie in 5 Episoden* (Vienna: Georg Marton, 1935), FWA 8°-50.302, AdK.

31. Ibid., scene 5, Vadasz, 54.

32. See my chapter "Jewish Theatre," in John London, ed., *Theatre under the Nazis*, 187–221. See also see Saul Friedländer, *Nazi Germany and the Jews, Vol.* 2, 97–98, where he reached a similar conclusion.

33. Wisten, minutes, 14 December 1939, FWA, 74/86/5001, 21; translated in Rovit and Goldfarb, *Theatrical Performance during the Holocaust*, 76–77.

34. Script for Adolf Paul, *Die Sprache der Vögel* (comedy in three acts), FWA 74/86/131.

35. Minutes, *Rücksprache*, 5 January 1940, translated in Rovit and Goldfarb, *Theatrical Performance during the Holocaust*, 76.

36. Martin Rosen to Hans Isaack (Shanghai), 4 January 1940, SJK 1.53.111, 1 (underlining in the original). The Josef-Lehmann high school was the venue for these events.

37. Ibid. He wanted to join his family in Shanghai, but he was still in Berlin in June 1941.

38. Siegfried Israel Hirsch to Hanne (John and Harriet) Isaak, 24 January 1940 (written over time through 18 February), SJK, 1.53.110,1.

39. Wisten *Rücksprache* on meeting with Kochanowski, 5 January 1940, microfiche, part I, FWA 74/86/5001; in Rovit and Goldfarb, *Theatrical Performance during the Holocaust*, 77.

40. Wisten Report, 1 September 1939–31 August 1940, 4, FWA 74/86/5054, folder 12.

41. John London, ed., *Theatre under the Nazis*, 244; Gerwin Strobl, *The Swastika and the Stage*. See letter from Siegfried Israel Hirsch to Hanne Isaak, SJK, 1.53.110,1.

42. "Der Jüdische Kulturbund arbeitet," JN 12, 9 February 1940, 5; the 11 February issue reports on the premiere for the following week, 17 February.

43. Brasch *Rücksprache*, 12 February 1940, item 8, the amount of which would be determined by the theatre, FWA 86/5001, 32.

44. 12 February 1940 minutes: from "conference" in ministry: Brasch and Kochanowski, FWA 86/5001, 32, item 8. Shakespeare's *Taming of the Shrew* was the production.

45. Wisten Report to Reich Ministry, 1 February 1940. A choral concert was the first of twenty-five events (29 October 1939); FWA 74/86/5053, folder 11.

46. Hugo Lachmanski, review of *The Taming of the Shrew*, JN 20, 8 March 1940, 3. On the same page Mischa Michalowitz reviews Karl Wiener's score for a string quartet, which used music from the seventeenth and eighteenth centuries.

47. Shirer, *Berlin Diary*, entries of 23 and 27 February 1940, 200, 292.

48. Marion A. Kaplan, *Between Dignity and Despair*, 150; on shopping curfews, 151–152. Shopping was reduced to one hour, 4 July 1940. See Friedländer, *Nazi Germany and the Jews, Vol. 2*.

49. FWA 74/86/145, 1.2; rehearsals ran from 9 to 16 February 1940. This included two dress rehearsals and a final run-through with music.

50. Wisten Report, 1 September 1939–31 August 1940, 4, FWA 74/86/5054, folder 12.

51. Leo (Israel) Kreindler ("LIK"), "Jüdisches Theater," JN 14, 16 February 1940, 1.

52. Wisten Report on work at the theatre from 1 September 1939 to 31 August 1940 (first draft), FWA 74/86/5074, folder 10.

53. "Der jüdische Kulturbund: geplante Veranstaltungen," JN 54, 7 July 1939, 10; also *Jüdischer Kulturbund Berlin Monatsblätter* 7, no. 8 (August 1939): 5, preview of *Jusik*.

54. Director's script for Ossip Dymov, *Jusik*, *Der Sänger seiner Trauer*, German by Erich Boehme, FWA 74/86.55a–55i. This version was used for the April 1940 production.

55. Ibid., FWA 74/86.55a, 30.

56. See review by Hugo Lachmanski, JN 32, 19 April 1940, 3; see also Dr. Ludwig Misch on Goldschlag's music for the *Jusik* production, on the same page.

57. Costume designs by Hanna Litten, 1940, FWA 10.63, 69–73.

58. Director's script for Dymov, *Jusik*, *Der Sänger seiner Trauer*. The script includes a cast list, prop list, ground plan, and one line change from "pastor" to "rabbi."

59. FWA 74/86/5095.

60. The playwright Yecheskel Moscheh Neumann (1893–1956) wrote for the Warsaw-based Yiddish-language daily *Haynt* (Today).

61. Afterword of Neumann's *Heimkehr: Shabbat Obst* by translator Hirsch, n.d., FWA 74/86/63, 2.

62. Ibid.

63. Yecheskel Moscheh Neumann, *Heimkehr: Shabbat Obst* (folk play in three acts), translated from Yiddish by Leo Israel Hirsch, was among the unperformed plays; FWA 74/86/63.

64. See Wisten, minutes from *Rücksprache*, 14 December 1939, FWA 74/86/5001, 21, item 1; Wisten referred to the "layoff of our dramaturgical adviser, Leo Hirsch"; quoted in Rovit and Goldfarb, eds., *Theatrical Performance during the Holocaust*, 76. In spring 1940 Hirsch was reappointed as dramaturg and head of the lecture division. See minutes from Brasch meeting with Owens and Kochanowski, 6 May 1940, item 8, FWA 74/86/5001, 56.

65. Brasch *Rücksprache*, 18 March 1940, items 6 and 1; FWA 74/86/5001, 43.

66. JN 23, 19 March 1940, 23, 1 (capitalized in the original). See Friedländer, *Nazi*

Germany and the Jews, Vol. 2, 83, on Heydrich's call to intensify emigration for Reich Jews in April 1940.

67. Minutes by Brasch, item 6, 24 April 1940, Kulturbund executive committee meeting, FWA 74/86/5001, 54. The Jewish offices worked closely with the community to promote emigration. After 1940 these offices became complicit in the Nazi plan for deportation. See Raul Hilberg, *The Destruction of the European Jews*, 260.

68. Shulamith Batdori, *Vor dem Regen*, FWA 74/86/86; *Die kleinen Funker: Ein Kinderspiel in 3 Bildern* by Jemimah Czernowitz, FWA 74/86/85.

69. Martin Rost, *Heimkehr* (Tel Aviv: Ramat-Gan, 1938), FWA 74/86/84.

70. Bruno Israel Bendix, *Neues Land*, FWA 74/86/87. The play was submitted after 1939. Bendix performed in Kulturbund variety shows in 1940.

71. Among the unproduced scripts is Halper Leiwik's preface to his *Redemption Comedy*, the second half of the Golem drama; FWA 74/86/129.

72. Wisten Report on the theatre from 1 September 1939 to 31 August 1940 (first draft), FWA 74/86/5074, folder 10.

73. Wisten *Rücksprache* (with Kochanowski), 17 April 1940, FWA 74/86/5001/51.

74. Leo Hirsch, rationale for production of Gregor Rogoff, *Steadfast Business* (*Bob beehrt sich vorzustellen*), FWA 74/86/5102, translated in Rovit and Goldfarb, *Theatrical Performance during the Holocaust*, 82.

75. *Rücksprache*, 16 October 1940, FWA 74/86/5001, 88. See Kaplan, *Between Dignity and Despair*, 173–174.

76. Director's script for Gregor Rogoff, *Bob beehrt sich vorzustellen*, FWA 74/86/81.

77. Hugo Lachmanski, "Ein heiteres Spiel von Gregor Israel Rogoff: Weltpremiere," JN 42, 24 May 1940, 4. The curtain was at 6 P.M.

78. Hirsch rationale for production of Rogoff, *Steadfast Business*, FWA 74/86/ 5102, in Rovit and Goldfarb, *Theatrical Performance during the Holocaust*, 82–83.

79. Director's script for Rogoff, *Bob beehrt sich vorzustellen*, FWA 74/86/81, 22.

80. Ibid., 30.

81. Lachmanski, "Ein heiteres Spiel von Gregor Israel Rogoff: Weltpremiere," 4. The review refers to a "student of American origin."

82. *Jüdische Welt Rundschau* 11, no. 20 (20 May 1940): 1. The lead article details the occupation of Holland and Belgium.

83. Shirer, *Berlin Diary*, 29 May 1940, 384.

84. Kaplan, *Between Dignity and Despair*, 151–152.

85. Wisten *Rücksprache* (with Kochanowski), FWA 74/86/5001, 17 April 1940, item 2.

86. Partitur (musical score), Molière, *Der eingebildete Kranke*, 74/86/1531. Wiener updated the music by a century with French and Italian masters of the Rococo. See "*Der eingebildete Kranke*," JN 56, 12 July 1940, 5.

87. Brasch minutes to Kulturbund board committee meeting on 24 April 1940, item 4, FWA 74/74/86/5001, 54.

88. Brasch minutes, 17 April 1940, FWA 74/74/86/5001; Wisten *Rücksprache*, FWA 74/86/5001,51, item 3 for tour permission.

89. Wisten minutes, 3 June 1940, FWA 74/66/5001, 64.

90. Shirer, *Berlin Diary*, 14 June 1940, 403; Molière, *Der eingebildete Kranke*, 31–33 in revised script by Leo Hirsch, FWA 74/86/49. Also cut were scenes 10 and 11 (with Argan and Beline; with Argan and Louison).

91. Wisten Report (1 September 1939 to 31 August 1940) under "Theatre Work" (first draft), FWA 74/86/5074, folder 10, 7–8. See Hugo Lachmanski on *Der eingebildete Kranke*, JN 59, 19 July 1940, 5.

92. Wisten *Rücksprache*, 31 July 1940, in Rovit and Goldfarb, *Theatrical Performance during the Holocaust*, 78. "Bunburry" is from Oscar Wilde's *The Importance of Being Earnest.*

93. *Rücksprache*, 9 September 1940, FWA 74/86/5001, 81, item 3, 1.

94. Siegfried Israel Hirsch to Hanne (John and Harriet) Isaak, 11 August 1940, SJK 1.53.110, 4.

95. FWA 74/86/49, Molière, *The Imaginary Invalid*, 40: the first half of the query is "How dare he ridicule consultations and prescriptions" ("Wie kann der sich unterstehen, über Konsultationen und Rezepte zu spotten, der ganzen Zunft den Krieg zu erkläre").

96. Steinweis, *Art, Ideology and Economics in Nazi Germany*, 125, on Hinkel's interest in the Madagascar Plan for Jews; Himmler promoted Hinkel on 16 September 1940 to SS Brigadeführer; see Steinweis, 205 n. 103.

97. Rationale and commentary on Gordin's play *Mirele Efros*, FWA 74/86/5081.

98. Ibid.

99. Director's script for Jacob Gordin, *Mirele Efros*, translated by Leo Hirsch, FWA 74/86/67, 11.

100. Ibid.; Hirsch on *Mirele Efros*, FWA 74/86/5081.

101. Hirsch on *Mirele Efros*.

102. Hugo Lachmanski, "*Die Mutter*, Schauspiel von Jacob Gordin: zur Erstaufführung im jüdischen Kulturbund in Berlin," JN 82, 10 October 1940, 4.

103. Ibid.

104. Wisten scheduled the play once a week on Saturdays. There may have been a shortage of technical personnel and audiences on the first Sabbath in October before Yom Kippur.

105. Lachmanski, "*Die Mutter*, Schauspiel von Jacob Gordin: zur Erstaufführung im jüdischen Kulturbund in Berlin," 4.

106. *Rücksprache*, 16 October 1940, FWA 74/86/5001, 88.

107. Wisten's notes from 11 October on the tour, props, and payment for actors are attached to the production script for Molière, *The Imaginary Invalid*, FWA 74/86/49.

108. Stephan Dörschel, *Fritz Wisten*, 58. See also Susanne Wisten-Weyl and Eva Wisten interviews by author, 7 June 2010.

9. DISSOLUTION: AFTERMATH, 1940–1943

1. The script and notes for Molière, *The Imaginary Invalid* (*Der eingebildete Kranke*; 11 October 1940) attest to tour dates (20–23 October). Wisten lists props and payment for actors. FWA 74/86/49.

2. Dr. Martin Israel Baeck, "Zur Aufführung *Der eingebildete Kranke* von Molière im Jüdischen Kulturbund," JN 87, 29 October 1940, 2 (regional report from Breslau).

3. Saul Friedländer, *Nazi Germany and the Jews, Vol.* 2, chapter 11, 65; Molière, *Der eingebildete Kranke*, FWA 74/86/49. The Jews were deported to Gurs.

4. Baeck, "Zur Aufführung *Der eingebildete Kranke* von Molière im Jüdischen Kulturbund," 2.

5. Brasch *Rücksprache*, 30 October 1940, item 2, FWA 74/86/5001, 90.

6. Ibid. The Kulturbund board was to telephone later that afternoon.

7. Friedländer, *Nazi Germany and the Jews, Vol.* 2, 103–104, mentions the meek response to Nazi proclamations by the Reich Association. He writes that cultural events were canceled for one week.

8. "Die Nächsten Verantstaltungen des Jüdischen Kulturbundes in Deutschland," JN 88, 1 November 1940, 4; 89, 5 November 1940, 2. The Stage Manager's Book skips all performances between summer 1940 and spring 1941.

9. Martin Brasch, 2 November 1940, 2, report on interrogation, FWA 74/86/5001/92.

10. Ibid.

11. Ibid.; *Rücksprache*, 2 November 1940, item 8, FWA 74/86/5001, 91.

12. Wisten *Rücksprache*, 14 November 1940 (item 1 refers to rehearsals for Benavente, item 4 to artistic license), FWA 74/86/5001, 97.

13. Brasch *Rücksprache*, 30 October 1940, item 9, FWA 74/86/5001, 90.

14. Wisten *Rücksprache*, 11 November 1940, item 5, FWA 74/86/5001, 27; Dr. Ludwig Misch, "Opern-Aufführung im Kulturbundsaal," JN 92, 15 November 1940, 3, on *Bajazzo*.

15. "Die Nächsten Verantstaltungen des Jüdischen Kulturbundes in Deutschland," JN 94, 22 November 1940, 5.

16. Wisten *Rücksprache*, 14 November 1940, item 5, 1, on *Crispin*, FWA 74/86/5001, 87.

17. Hugo Lachmanski, "*Der tugendhafte Glücksritter: Ein Maskenspiel in 3 Bildern*," JN 102, 20 December 1940, 3.

18. Ibid.

19. Leo Hirsch, "Ein neues Spiel: Zur Aufführung des *Tugendhaften Glücksritters* im Jüdischen Kulturbund," JN 96, 29 November 1940, 4.

20. Siegfried Israel Hirsch to Hanne (John and Harriet) Isaak, 31 December 1940, 2, SJK 1.53.110, 4.

21. See William L. Shirer, *Berlin Diary*, 1 December and 5 December 1940, 576, 596.

22. Singer to Vera Simon, 15 December 1940, Eike Geisel private collection. Singer gave a former friend, Vera Simon (Cohn), executive power of attorney in January 1939.

23. February developments included the new Association of Jews, Joosche Raad. The only newspaper permitted to Jews was the *Weekblad*.

24. For background on occupied Holland and Jews, see Jacob Presser, *Ashes in the Wind*. The deportation of Jews from the Netherlands did not occur until 1942–1943.

25. The Schouwburg (Theatre) became the city's main deportation site for the transport of Jews to Westerbork, Theresienstadt, and Auschwitz-Birkenau.

26. Adolf Hitler, excerpted speech 30 January 1941 at Berlin's Sportspalast, www.jewishvirtuallibrary.org/jsource/Holocaust/hitler013041.html (accessed 28 July 2010).

27. Eva Wisten and Susanne Wisten-Weyl interviews by author, 7 June 2010; telephone conversation with Eva Wisten, 11 July 2010.

28. http://www.schroederniko.de/schlachtensee.htm (accessed 28 July 2010).

29. Wisten *Rücksprache*, 3 February 1941, item 3, 5, FWA 74/86/5001, 110.

30. Wisten *Rücksprache*, 3 January 1941, item 2, FWA 74/86/5001/ 102, translated in Rebecca Rovit and Alvin Goldfarb, eds., *Theatrical Performance during the Holocaust*, 79–80. Oscar Wilde's plays were banned in 1939.

31. "Schaffung von Notunterkünften für Personen, die infolge von Luftangriffen vorübergehend obdachlos werden," JN 88, November 1940, 3; "Schaffung von Notunterkünften für Personen, die infolge von Luftangriffen vorübergehend obdachlos werden," JN 1, 3 January 1941, 3.

32. Such flyers are attached to the playbill for the opening night of *The Mother* (28 September 1940), in Wisten Clipping Compilation, 1940–1941, FWA 74/86/24. See program for *Señor Alan Out of Purgatory* (*Señor Alan aus dem Fegefeuer*), FWA 74/86/53, script with notes and playbill.

33. JN 1, 7, and 31, first-page headlines from 3 January, 24 January, and 18 April 1941; references to passage via Lisbon and Spain in JN 105, 31 December 1940, 1; 17 and 28 February 1941, 2.

34. File Notice, *Rücksprache*, 3 March 1941, item 4, FWA 74/86/5001, 115.

35. Brasch *Rücksprache*, 17 March 1941, item 2, FWA 74/86/5001.

36. Wisten *Rücksprache*, 3 April 1941, item 4, FWA 74/86/5001, 122.

37. Kurt Michaelis interview by author, 12 August 1996, in Rovit and Goldfarb, *Theatrical Performance during the Holocaust*, 71; letter from Michaelis to author, 8 December 1995, 2.

38. Brasch *Rücksprache*, 3 March 1941, item 4 (no performances were permitted on 11 April and 20 April 1941), FWA 74/86/ 5001/115.

39. Director's script for Aldo de Benedetti, *Thirty Seconds of Love* (*30 Sekunden Liebe*), act II, 42–43, FWA 74/86/52, 93.

40. Hugo Lachmanski, "*30 Sekunden Liebe*: Erst-Aufführung im Jüdischen Kulturbund," JN 21, 14 March 1941, 5.

41. "Arisierungsabgabe," JN, 14 March 1941. Lachmanski's review is above this col-

umn on this page. Raul Hilberg, *The Destruction of the European Jews*, 93, details the expropriation of Jewish property: table 19 on "flight tax" and "Jewish atonement payment."

42. Alan E. Steinweis, *Art, Ideology, and Economics in Nazi Germany*, 62 (by 30 April 1941).

43. Süßmann to Martin Brandt, 26–27 April 1941, SJK (Brandt) 1.53.66, 1; translated in Rovit and Goldfarb, *Theatrical Performance*, 86. Brandt left for America in March 1941.

44. Wisten actor's script, Sancho López de la Puerta, *Señor Alan Out of Purgatory* (*Señor Alan aus dem Fegefeuer*), revised by Leo Hirsch, FWA 74/86/53, rehearsal schedule.

45. *Rücksprache*, 5 May 1941, FWA 74/86/5001, 126 (no item numbers).

46. Süßmann to Brandt, 18 May 1941, SJK, 1.56.67.

47. Süßmann to Brandt, 10 June 1941, 2, SJK (Brandt), 1.56.68; Süßmann refers to Willy Prager, known for his comic roles.

48. Wisten *Rücksprache*, 18 June 1941, item 1, FWA, 74/501/138. Wisten reports to Kochanowski and calls Wühlheide a "labor educational camp." *Rücksprache* (all divisions), 26 June 1941, minutes by Leo Kreindler referring to Brasch obituary, item 12, FWA 74/86/ 5001, 141, 2.

49. On the organization of the Reichskulturkammer, see www.bundesarchiv.de, 3 (accessed 28 July 2010).

50. Wisten *Rücksprache*, 18 June 1941, item 5, FWA 74/86/5001/138 (WL microfilm).

51. Ibid., 18 June 1941, item 2. Wiener was a composer.

52. Ibid., item 5. The SS officer held out the possibility that it might function as a newsletter. On 22 June the Nazis attacked Soviet territories. See Hilberg, *The Destruction of the European Jews*, 177, 257. On the 1941 massacres, see Friedländer, *Nazi Germany and the Jews, Vol. 2*, 282.

53. Süßmann to Martin Brandt, 26 June 1941, SJK (Brandt), 1.56.70.

54. Wisten actor's script, *Señor Alan aus dem Fegefeuer*, FWA 74/86/53, 2–3.

55. Ibid., 73.

56. Leo Hirsch on *Señor Alan aus dem Fegefeuer*, JN 46, 10 June 1941, 3. Hirsch wrote that the author had borrowed from a Jewish contemporary of Calderón, Enríquez Gómez. Susanne Wisten-Weyl and Eva Wisten have suggested that the author was a fabrication; interviews by author, 7 June 2010.

57. Hugo Lachmanski, review of *Señor Alan aus dem Fegefeuer*, JN 49, 20 June 1941, 2.

58. Michaelis interview by author in Rovit and Goldfarb, *Theatrical Performance during the Holocaust*, 71; letter to author from Michaelis, 8 December 1995, 2.

59. Wisten *Rücksprache*, 26 June 1941, item 6, FWA 74/86/5001, 141, 2; see Lily E. Hirsch, *A Jewish Orchestra in Nazi Germany*.

60. Wisten *Rücksprache*, 5 August 1941; EG, Kurt Singer correspondence to Vera Consuelo Hirsch. On 8 May 1941 Wisten asked Kochanowski about sending plays on tour to Prague and to Holland.

61. EG; see also Geisel interview with Camilla Spira in E. Geisel and H. M. Broder, eds., *Premiere und Pogrom*, 101–102; Volker Kühn, "Laughter at the Edge of the Abyss," translated in Rovit and Goldfarb, *Theatrical Performance during the Holocaust*, 40–57.

62. Steinweis, *Art, Ideology, and Economics in Nazi Germany*, 125. By May 1944 Hinkel was vice president of the RKK.

63. See Hilberg, *The Destruction of the European Jews*, 261–262. By the spring jockeying in Berlin led to the declaration that Reich Jews were "stateless" or "protectees" of the state, weakening their potential claims to full citizenship; David S. Wyman, *The Abandonment of the Jews*, 4. Heydrich was appointed deputy protector of Moravia and Bohemia on 27 September 1941 but returned to chair the 20 January 1942 Wannsee conference. He was assassinated in 1942.

64. See Ferenc (Franz) Molnár, *The Play's the Thing*, adapted by P. G. Wodehouse, in *All the Plays of Molnár* (New York: Garden City Pub. Co., 1937), 728–777.

65. Micha Michalowitz, review of Molnár's *Spiel im Schloß*, JN 57, 15 August 1941, 2. This is the last published review of a Kulturbund performance.

66. Ibid.

67. Hilde Cohn, "Premiere im Kulturbund, *Spiel im Schloß*," JR 65, 13 August 1935, 14.

68. Of the 1935 cast for Molnár's play only Wisten remained at the Kulturbund. Ehrlich was engaged by the Joodse Schouwburg in Amsterdam.

69. In July 1941 America limited its quota for Jewish refugees, making it nearly impossible to emigrate to the United States. Wyman, *The Abandonment of the Jews*, 5–6. See Friedländer, *Nazi Germany and the Jews, Vol.* 2, 86, 90, on the difficulty of getting transit visas to travel through the territory of fascist regimes in Spain and Portugal.

70. Letter from a representative of the State Department to Brandt, 25 August 1941, SJK (Brandt), 1.56.15.

71. Leni Yahil, *The Holocaust: The Fate of European Jewry, 1932–1945* (Oxford: Oxford University Press, 1991), 293, refers to Himmler's directive and Adolf Eichmann's August 1941 rally against permitting Jewish emigrants to cross the Reich on their way to access ports on the Atlantic.

72. Singer to Vera Hirsch, undated, August 1941; refers to progress on attaining the visa. Singer's sister, Erna Nitke (New York), informed Ruth Abeldorff née Falkenstein (London) on 23 November 1941; letters, EG.

73. JN 61, 12 September 1941, 1, for ordinance. See Hilberg, *The Destruction of the European Jews*, 268–277, on the status of mixed Jewish-German citizens (*Mischlinge*).

74. Mosche Lipshitz, *Were I Not a Fool: A Whimsical Story with Herschel Ostropoler (Wenn der Narr nicht mein wär: Eine wunderliche Geschichte mit Hershel Ostropoler)*, FWA 74/86/56; 74/86/51, 52 (groundplan); 74/86/56, 54, rehearsal schedule; glossary of Yiddish and Hebrew expressions, FWA 74/86/56, 48, 49, 50.

75. Gestapo headquarters (Dr. Kunz) to Moritz Henschel, 11 September 1941, FWA 74/86/5074. This is reproduced in *Geschlossene Vorstellung* as document 78, 370–371.

76. Ibid.

77. Stage Manager's Book, 1940/1941, FWA 74/86/5095, 397. The performance began at 5:40 P.M. and ended at 7:46 P.M. Discrepancies exist between dates published and those in the Stage Manager's Book.

78. Delivery was made by registered mail from Moritz Israel Henschel to Wisten et al., 12 September 1941, FWA 74/86/5074; reproduced in *Geschlossene Vorstellung* as document 80, 372.

79. See Steffi Ronau Hinzelmann in Geisel and Broder, *Premiere und Pogrom*, 151 ff., on her roles in 1941. She may have miscalculated the date, noted as 9 September; it was probably 12 September. Lipshitz, *Wenn der Narr nicht mein wär: Eine wunderliche Geschichte mit Hershel Ostropoler*, FWA 74/86/56, 54, rehearsal schedule, 27.

80. Ronau Hinzelmann in Geisel and Broder, *Premiere und Pogrom*, 151.

81. Wisten to Paul Eppstein, 27 September 1941, FWA 74/86/5074, folder 10.

82. Telephone conversation with Eva Wisten, 11 July 2010. Wisten likely removed most of his papers directly after the theatre was shut down. But it cannot be ruled out that he had begun to take his belongings home even earlier.

83. "Spielplan des Jüdischen Kulturbundes," JN 61, 12 September 1941, 4, Kulturbund classified ads.

84. Historians have not identified this play as part of the Kulturbund repertoire at all. Lipshitz, *Wenn der Narr nicht mein wär: Eine wunderliche Geschichte mit Hershel Ostropoler*. FWA 74/86/56; FWA 74/86/51, 52.

85. Susanne Wisten, "Momente, die Sternstunden waren," in Geisel and Broder, *Premiere und Pogrom*, 118; Susanne Wisten, telephone conversation with author, 10 July 2010.

86. Hirsch anticipated that audiences might not understand words: "gabbai," "mezuzah," "rav," "borscht," "schikkur," and "Hasidim." Some expressions are crossed out, including "Rebbezin," "Koscher," "Jom Kippur," and "Streimel."

87. Wisten and Wisten-Weyl interviews by author.

88. Wisten to Paul Eppstein, 27 September 1941, FWA 74/86/5074, folder 10.

89. Ibid. Wisten asked for all paperwork to be complete by 15 October. These employees were still in Berlin, unable to emigrate. Some awaited emigration visas.

90. Ibid.

91. Wisten to Max Ehrlich, 7 October 1941, translated in Rovit and Goldfarb, *Theatrical Performance during the Holocaust*, 88–89. FWA 74/86/053.

92. Hinzelmanns to Wisten, 21 September 1941, FWA 74/86/1082.

93. Wisten to Max Ehrlich, 7 October 1941, in Rovit and Goldfarb, *Theatrical Performance during the Holocaust*, 88–89. FWA 74/86/053.

94. Singer to Vera Consuelo Hirsch (Buenos Aires), from occupied Holland, September 1941, 21, EG. Hirsch emigrated in January 1942.

95. Kurt Süßmann to Brandt, 8 October 1941, SJK (Brandt), 1.56.75.

96. Steinweis, *Art, Ideology, and Economics in Nazi Germany*, 125–126.

97. Hans Süßmann to Brandt, 2 November 1941, SJK (Brandt), 1.56.76. The RSHA ban is in the Yad Vashem Archives, TR-3/1209, http://www1.yadvashem.org/about_holocaust/documents/part_one.html (accessed on 28 July 2010).

98. Singer (Amsterdam) to Vera Hirsch, 4 November 1941, EG.

99. Friedländer, *Nazi Germany and the Jews, Vol. 2*, 289, on law of 4 November 1941. See Hinkel draft to Goebbels, 1 November 1939, WL Binder, 2.53.22, 3.

100. WL Binder, 2.53.28, #19, 1942, from Central Archives of Potsdam, May 1942–July 1943, papers from the Reichsvereinigung der Juden in Deutschland, on personnel from the Jewish Kulturbund, 8/9 June 1942 and 19 October 1942.

101. Ibid. Hinzelmann died in August 1942.

102. Hinzelmann interview in Geisel and Broder, *Premiere und Pogrom*, 151–152; Ronau remarried as Ronau-Walter. She describes 1942–1943 in her 1986 interview with Marion Neiss, Zentrum für Antisemitismusforschung, Berlin (private collection), reproduced in *Geschlossene Vorstellung* as document 76, 356. Ronau-Walter died on 11 January 1995 in Berlin.

103. See Hilberg, *The Destruction of the European Jews*, 268–277, on the complex status of *Mischlinge* or Jews in mixed marriages.

104. Canaris lived on the same street as the Wistens. Although he led military intelligence for the Reich, he was in on the plot to assassinate Hitler and was hanged. See Eva Wisten's comments on her father in *Drei Leben für das Theater*, 40–45; Wisten and Wisten-Weyl interviews.

105. Singer to Vera Hirsch, 26 April and 23 May 1942, EG; Star of David decree on 29 April 1942, effective 5 May.

106. Eike Geisel, "Da Capo in Holland," in *Geschlossene Vorstellung*, 207–208.

107. Singer to Vera Hirsch, 3 March 1943, EG.

108. See Rovit and Goldfarb, *Theatrical Performance during the Holocaust*, 208; Kurt Singer Archives, AdK, 1.55.36, 2. Singer died in February 1944 at Terezín.

109. Camilla Spira, Max Ehrlich, and Willy Rosen played in the camps. On Westerbork and Theresienstadt cabarets, see Rebecca Rovit, "Cultural Ghettoization and Theatre during the Holocaust"; H. G. Adler, *Theresienstadt 1941–1945*; Rovit and Goldfarb, *Theatrical Performance during the Holocaust*, part 3.

110. WL Binder, 2.53.28, #19, 1942, Central Archives of Potsdam, May 1942–July 1943, papers from the Reichsvereinigung der Juden in Deutschland, on personnel from the Jewish Kulturbund, 8/9 June 1942 and 19 October 1942.

111. Ronau-Walter interview by Neiss, in *Geschlossene Vorstellung*, 357.

112. "Aus den Verordnungen: 'Jüdischer Wohnraum in Berlin,'" JN 20, 4 June 1943, 1–2. Jews registered apartments with the Reich Association.

113. Friedländer, *Nazi Germany and the Jews, Vol. 2*, 518. This was by July 1943.

114. Wisten and Wisten-Weyl interviews.

115. Reich Theatre Division, 2 December 1943, to Goebbels, WL 2.53.28, 75 C Re1 (Reichsvereinigung der Juden Kunstlerkriegeinsatz, 1941–1944), WL Microfilm; Alan Steinweis, "Hans Hinkel and German Jewry, 1933–1941," in Rovit and Goldfarb, *Theatrical Performance during the Holocaust*, 26.

116. Wisten, "Momente, die Sternstunden waren," 119; Wisten and Wisten-Weyl interviews.

117. Willi Schmidt, "Rückkehr zu Nathan, dem Weisen: Fragmentarische Erinnerungen," in *Drei Leben für das Theater*, 112. Also see Paul Wiegler, "Nathan in Reinhardt's Haus," *Allgemeine Zeitung*, 9 September 1945; Paul Rilla, "Das Hohelied der Humanität," *Berliner Zeitung*, nr. 101, 9 September 1945.

CONCLUSION: BEYOND THE ABYSS

1. Erna Nitke (New York) to Vera Simon, 30 July 1944, on Kurt's condition at the ghetto; Vera Simon to Ruth Abelsdorff on the news of Singer's death; EG.

2. Vera Simon to Ruth Abelsdorff, 17 August 1944 (English original), EG. Her own Kulturbund-related papers were en route to America.

3. Ruth Anselm (Herzog) interview by author, 24 May 1995.

4. Anselm interview in E. Geisel and H. M. Broder, eds., *Premiere und Pogrom*, 84.

5. Kurt Singer to Ruth Falkenstein-Abelsdorff, 8 December 1938, EG.

6. Wisten to Dr. Paul Eppstein, Reichsvereinigung der Juden, 20 September 1941, FWA 74/86/1424, 1425.

7. Wisten to Freeden on Berlin visit in *Leben zur falschen Zeit* (Berlin: Transit Verlag, 1991), 130–131. Freeden notes the meeting date (1946) but refers to the passage of eight years between his emigration and meeting Wisten (1947). See "Begegungen mit Fritz Wisten," in *Drei Leben für das Theater*, 51.

8. Hinzelmann interview in E. Geisel and H. M. Broder, eds., *Premiere und Pogrom*. "We had blinders on," recalled Martin Brandt about the insulated space of the Kulturbund stage, in Geisel and Broder, *Premiere und Pogrom*, 150.

9. Former actor Bert Bernd, "Eine kranke Idee, ein teuflischer Plan," in Geisel and Broder, *Premiere und Pogrom*, 292; Camilla Spira, "So etwas machen die Deutschen doch nicht," in Geisel and Broder, *Premiere und Pogrom*, 102.

10. Mascha Benya-Matz interview by author, 9 November 1995, in Rebecca Rovit and Alvin Goldfarb, eds., *Theatrical Performance during the Holocaust*, 66.

11. Mascha Benya-Matz, telephone conversation with author, 2 October 2007.

12. Benya-Matz interview in Rovit and Goldfarb, *Theatrical Performance during the Holocaust*, 63.

AFTERWORD: NEW ROOTS

1. Wisten to Camilla Spira Eisner, March 1946, FWA 74/86/434 (copy).

2. See the work of Sybil H. Milton, whose term "cultural heritage" refers to artistic

production during the Holocaust years. See also http://holocaustmusic.ort.org/ (theatre art); Rebecca Rovit, "Cultural Ghettoization and Theatre during the Holocaust," 459–486.

3. Ibid.

4. Stephan Dörschel, *Fritz Wisten*, 87. Alexander Dymschitz granted Wisten the license in August 1946. Wisten led the theatre until 1954.

5. See *Drei Leben für das Theater*, 189, on the October 1961 premiere. The theatre at 57 Kommandantenstraße suffered damage from Allied bombs. It was rebuilt in the German Democratic Republic as a residential block. A commemorative plaque indicates the site of the theatre.

6. A telephone conversation on 6 December 2007 with Eva Wisten (Berlin) revealed that her father had suffered from cancer.

7. Alfred Berliner (Balthoff) left Berlin to perform at Vienna's Burgtheater. He died in Vienna in 1989.

8. Brandt, born in 1903, emigrated in 1941. In 1965 he returned to Germany, where he died in 1989. See his interview "Das Theatre war unser Rettung," in E. Geisel and H. M. Broder, eds., *Premiere und Pogrom*, 121–127. Broder credits Brandt with aiding the search for former Kulturbund artists, leading to the 1992 exhibition catalogue.

9. H. G. Adler, *Theresienstadt 1941–1945*, 590. In 1943 Spanier directed Molnár's *The Play's the Thing* for fellow inmates.

10. Cabaret artist Edith Elmer (Eisenheimer) and actor Martin Miller revived their careers in London. Herbert Freeden lived in London before going to Palestine.

11. Mira Rostovsky (Rostova) interview with author, 23 May 1995. Rostova was born in St. Petersburg, Russia, in 1909.

12. Chaikin refers to Rostova's method at Berghof Studios in the 1950s. See Toby Cole and Helen Krich Chinoy, eds., *Actors on Acting* (New York: Crown, 1970), 664, 668.

13. Herbert Freeden (born Friedenthal) interview in Geisel and Broder, *Premiere und Pogrom*, 269. Because they could prolong their careers at the Kulturbund, some artists stayed in Germany. But the Nazi government actively encouraged Jewish emigration, especially between 1936 and 1938.

14. The roundtable discussion (moderated by Henryk Broder) took place at the Akademie der Künste, Berlin. See Miriam Niroumand, "Freiheitshauch und tödliche Illusion: Ehemalige Mitglieder des Jüdischen Kulturbundes im Disput," *Die Berliner Zeitung*, 4/5 April 1992, 66.

15. Günther Weisenborn to Ruth Anselm, 27 May 1938, SJK (Anselm), 1.52.640, 2.

BIBLIOGRAPHY

ARCHIVAL COLLECTIONS

Bundesarchiv III, Berlin-Zehlendorf (formerly Berlin Document Center)

Eike Geisel Private Collection of Kurt Singer correspondence, Berlin

Leo Baeck Institute, New York

Stiftung Archiv der Akademie der Künste, Berlin:

Fritz-Wisten Archive (includes Regiebücher and actor rolebooks)

Kurt Singer Archive

Sammlung Jüdischer Kulturbund (individual Kulturbund artists)

Wiener Library Binder (duplicated materials from the Wiener Library, London and Tel Aviv)

INTERVIEWS AND PERSONAL CORRESPONDENCE

Anselm, Ruth (Herzog), 24 May 1995, New York

Benya-Matz, Mascha, 9 November 1995, New York

Bloch, Henry, 10 November 1995, New York

Geisel, Eike, April 1995, Berlin

Kroner-Segal, Hannah, New York (personal correspondence)

Michaelis, Kurt, 12 August 1996, New York

Rostovsky (Rostova), Mira, 23 May 1995, New York

Singer, Kurt, private correspondence, courtesy of Eike Geisel (received in 1995)

Wisten, Eva, December 2007, 7 June 2010, Berlin

Wisten-Weyl, Susanne, 7 June 2010, Berlin

NEWSPAPERS AND PERIODICALS

(Some of these are electronically available at http://www.compactmemory.de/ and http://deposit.d-nb.de/online/jued/jued.htm; others are available at the Akademie der Künste, Berlin)

Centralverein Zeitung der deutschen Staatsbürger jüdischen Glaubens (drama critic: Dr. Hugo Lachmanski)

Frauenbund

Gemeindeblatt

Israelitisches Familenblatt

Jüdische Gemeindeblatt für Berlin

Jüdischer Kulturbund Berlin Monatsblätter

Die Jüdische Rundschau (drama critic: Dr. Arthur Eloesser)
Jüdisches Nachrichtenblatt
Jüdische Welt Rundschau
Jüdisch-Liberale Zeitung (in 1935 known as *Jüdische Allgemeine Zeitung*)
Monatsblätter Kulturbundbühne (1933–1939)
Der Schild (drama critic: Kurt Pinthus)

PUBLISHED SOURCES

Adler, H. G. *Theresienstadt 1941–1945: Das Antlitz Einer Zwangsgemeinschaft*. Tübingen: J. C. B. Mohr, 1960.

Bach, H. I. *The German Jew*. London: Oxford University Press, 1984.

Barkai, Avraham. *From Boycott to Annihilation: The Economic Struggle of German Jews, 1933–1943*. Trans. William Templer. Hanover, N.H.: University Press of New England, 1989.

Baumann, Kurt. "The Kulturbund: Ghetto and Home." In *Germans No More: Accounts of Jewish Everyday Life, 1933–1938*, ed. Margarete Limburg and Hubert Rübsaat, 119–123. Providence, RI: Berghahn Books, 2006.

Beer-Hoffman, Richard. *Jaákobs Traum: Ein Vorspiel*. Berlin: S. Fischer Verlag, 1918.

———. *Jacob's Dream: A Prologue*. Trans. Ida Bension Wynn. Philadelphia: Jewish Publication Society of America, 1946.

Bergmeier, Horst J. P., Ejal Jakob Eisler, and Rainer E. Lotz, eds. *Vorbei . . . Beyond Recall: Dokumentation jüdischen Musiklebens in Berlin, 1933–1938*. Hambergen: Bear Family Records, 2001.

Bernard, Emil (Cohn). *Die Jagd Gottes*. Berlin: Volksbühnen Verlags- und Vertriebe-GmbH, 1925.

Blatter, Janet, and Sybil H. Milton, eds. *Art of the Holocaust*. New York: Routledge, 1981.

Brenner, Michael. *The Renaissance of Jewish Culture in Weimar Germany*. New Haven: Yale University Press, 1996.

Dan, Joseph. *Kabbalah: A Very Short Introduction*. Oxford: Oxford University Press, 2006.

de Lange, Nicholas. *An Introduction to Judaism*. Cambridge: Cambridge University Press, 2000.

Dohrn, Verena, and Gertrud Pickhan, eds. *Transit und Transformation Osteuropäisch-jüdische Migranten in Berlin 1918–1939*. Göttingen: Wallstein Verlag GmbH, 2010.

Dörschel, Stephan. *Fritz Wisten: Bis zum letzten Augenblick—ein Jüdisches Theaterleben*. Berlin: Hentrich and Hentrich, 2009.

Drei Leben für das Theater: Fritz Wisten (1919–1962). Ed. Akademie der Künste. Berlin: Edition Hentrich, 1990.

Drewniak, Boguslaw. *Das Theater im NS-Staat: Szenarium deutscher Zeitgeschichte 1933–1945*. Düsseldorf: Droste, 1983.

Dutlinger, Anne, ed. *Art, Music, and Education as Strategies for Survival: Theresienstadt, 1941–1944*. New York: Herodias, 2001.

Elon, Amos. *The Pity of It All: A Portrait of the German-Jewish Epoch, 1743–1933*. New York: Henry Holt and Co., 2002.

Es waren wirklich Sternstunden. Film by Henryk M. Broder and Eike Geisel. Berlin. Akademie der Künste, 1989, 33.63.443/1–2 (interviews with former Kulturbund artists).

Fackler, Guido. *"Des Lagers Stimme": Musik im KZ. Alltag und Häftlingskultur in den Konzentrationslagern, 1933–1936 (mit einer Darstellung der weiteren Entwicklung bis 1945 und einer Biblio-/Mediographie DIZ-Schriften)*. Bremen: Temmen, 2000.

Fantlová, Zdenka. *My Lucky Star*. Trans. Deryk Viney. New York: Herodias, 2001.

———. *The Tin Ring: How I Cheated Death*. Northumbria (UK): Northumbria Press, 2010.

Freeden, Herbert. *The Jewish Press in the Third Reich*. Trans. William Templer. Providence, R.I.: Berg, 1993.

———. *Jüdisches Theater in Nazideutschland*. Tübingen: J. C. B. Mohr, 1964. Rpt. Frankfurt/M: Ullstein, 1985.

———. *Leben zur falschen Zeit*. Berlin: Transit, 1991.

Friedlander, Henry. *Origins of the Nazi Genocide: From Euthanasia to the Final Solution*. Chapel Hill: University of North Carolina Press, 1995.

Friedländer, Saul. *Nazi Germany and the Jews, Vol. 1: The Years of Persecution. 1933–1939*. New York: HarperCollins, 1997.

———. *Nazi Germany and the Jews, Vol. 2: The Years of Extermination, 1939–1945*. New York: HarperCollins, 2007.

Gadberry, W. Glen. "Nazi Germany's Jewish Theatre." *Theatre Studies* 22.1 (1980), 15–32.

———, ed. *Theatre in the Third Reich, the Prewar Years: Essays on Theater in Nazi Germany, 1933–1939*. Westport, Conn.: Greenwood, 1995.

Garcia, Max Rodrigues. *As Long As I Remain Alive*. Tuscaloosa, Ala.: Portals Press, 1979. Reprinted as *Auschwitz, Auschwitz . . . I Cannot Forget You: As Long as I Remain Alive*. San Jose, CA: Think Social Publishing, 2008.

Geisel, E., and H. M. Broder, eds. *Premiere und Pogrom: Der Jüdische Kulturbund, 1933–1941, Texte und Bilder*. Berlin: Siedler Verlag, 1992.

Geschlossene Vorstellung: Der Jüdische Kulturbund, 1933–1941. Ed. Akademie der Künste. Berlin: Edition Hentrich, 1992.

Gilbert, Shirli. *Music in the Holocaust: Confronting Life in the Nazi Ghettos and Camps*. Oxford: Oxford University Press, 2005.

Goebbels, Joseph. *The Goebbels Diaries, 1939–1941*. Trans. Fred Taylor. London: H. Hamilton, 1982.

Goldsmith, Martin. *The Inextinguishable Symphony: A True Story of Music and Love in Nazi Germany*. New York: John Wiley, 2000.

Hebbel, Friedrich. *Judith: Eine Tragödie in 5 Akten*. Frankfurt am Main: Wolter Ed., 1966.

Hilberg, Raul. *The Destruction of the European Jews*. Chicago: Quadrangle Books, 1961.

Hirsch, Lily E. *A Jewish Orchestra in Nazi Germany: Musical Politics and the Berlin Jewish Cultural League*. Ann Arbor: University of Michigan Press, 2010.

Ibsen, Henrik. *Ghosts*. In *The Complete Major Prose Plays*. Trans. and intro. Rolf Fjelde. New York: New American Library, 1978.

———. *Pillars of Society*. In *The Complete Major Prose Plays*. Trans. and intro. Rolf Fjelde. New York: New American Library, 1978.

Kaplan, Marion A. *Between Dignity and Despair: Jewish Life in Nazi Germany*. New York: Oxford University Press, 1998.

Kershaw, Ian. *Hitler: A Biography*. New York: W. W. Norton and Co., 2008.

Klemperer, Victor. *I Will Bear Witness, 1933–1945*. Trans. Martin Chalmers. New York: Modern Library, 1998.

Laqueur, Walter. *A History of Zionism* (1973). New York: Schocken Books, 2003.

Lause, Beate, and Renate Wiens, eds. *Theaterleben: Schauspieler erzählen von Exil und Rückkehr*. Frankfurt am Main: Verlag Anton Hain, 1991.

Leivick, H. *The Golem*. In *Three Great Jewish Plays*. Ed. and trans. Joseph C. Landis. New York: Applause Books, 1986.

London, John, ed. *Theatre under the Nazis*. Manchester: Manchester University Press, 2000.

Malkin, Jeanette R., and Freddie Rokem, eds. *Jews and the Making of Modern German Theatre*. Iowa City: University of Iowa Press, 2010.

Mickenberg, David, and Corinne Granof, eds. *The Last Expression: Art and Auschwitz*. Evanston, Ill.: Northwestern University Press, 2003.

Migdal, Ulrike, ed. *Und die Musik spiel dazu: Chansons und Satiren aus dem KZ Theresienstadt*. Munich: Piper, 1986.

Milton, Sybil H. "Postscript: The Remnants of Culture under Duress." In *Theatrical Performance during the Holocaust: Texts, Documents, Memoirs*, ed. Rebecca Rovit and Alvin Goldfarb, 287–291. Baltimore: Johns Hopkins University Press, 1999.

Müller-Wesemann, Barbara. *Theater als geistiger Widerstand: Der Jüdischer Kulturbund in Hamburg, 1934–1941*. Stuttgart: M and P Verlag, 1996.

Musikerinnen und Musiker in Frankfurt, 1933–1942. Compiled by Judith Freise and Joachim Martini. Frankfurt/Main: Verlag Dr. Otto Lembeck, 1990.

Otte, Marline. *Jewish Identities in German Popular Entertainment, 1890–1933*. Cambridge: Cambridge University Press, 2006.

Panse, Barbara. "Censorship in Nazi Germany." In *Fascism and Theatre: Comparative Studies on the Aesthetics and Politics of Performance in Europe, 1925–1945*, ed. Günter Berghaus, 140–156. Providence, R.I.: Berghahn, 1996.

Paucker, Arnold, Sylvia Gilchrist, and Barbara Suchy, eds. *Die Juden im Nationalsozialistischen Deutschland, 1933–1943*. Tübingen: J. C. B. Mohr, 1986.

Petropoulos, Jonathan. *Art and Politics in the Third Reich*. Chapel Hill: University of North Carolina Press, 1999.

Presser, Jacob. *Ashes in the Wind: The Destruction of Dutch Jewry*. Trans. Arnold Pomerans. London: Souvenir Press, 1968.

Reinharz, Jehuda, and Walter Schatzberg, eds. *The Jewish Response to German Culture*. Hanover, N.H.: University Press of New England, 1985.

Richarz, Monika, ed. *Jewish Life in Germany: Memoirs from Three Centuries*. Trans. S. Rosenfeld. Bloomington: Indiana University Press, 1980.

Rischbieter, Henning, ed. *Theater im "Dritten Reich": Theaterpolitik, Spielplanstruktur, NS-Dramatik*. Seelze-Velber: Kallmeyer, 2000.

Riss, Heidelore. *Ansätze zu einer Geschichte des jüdischen Theaters in Berlin 1889–1936*. Frankfurt am Main: Peter Lang, 2000.

Rosen, Robert N. *Saving the Jews: Franklin D. Roosevelt and the Holocaust*. New York: Avalon Publishing Group, 2006.

Roth, Joseph. *The Wandering Jews*. Trans. Michael Hoffmann. New York: W. W. Norton and Co., 2000.

Rovit, Rebecca. "An Artistic Mission in Berlin: The Jewish Kulturbund Theatre as Sanctuary." *Theatre Survey* 135, no. 2 (1994): 5–17.

———. "A Carousel of Theatrical Performance." In *Art, Music, and Education as Strategies for Survival: Theresienstadt, 1941–45*, ed. Anne Dutlinger, 122–143. New York: Herodias, 2001.

———. "A Concert of Words: Theatrical Performance at Auschwitz." In *The Last Expression: Art and Auschwitz*, ed. David Mickenberg and Corinne Granof, 105–113, notes on 259–262. Evanston, Ill.: Northwestern University Press, 2003.

———. "Cultural Ghettoization and Theater during the Holocaust: Performance as a Link to Community." *Journal of Holocaust and Genocide Studies* 19, no. 3 (Winter 2005): 459–486.

———. "Jewish Theatre: Repertory and Censorship in the Jüdischer Kulturbund." In *Theater under the Nazis*, ed. John London, 187–221. Manchester: Manchester University Press, 2000.

Rovit, Rebecca, and Alvin Goldfarb, eds. *Theatrical Performance during the Holocaust: Texts, Documents, Memoirs*. Baltimore: Johns Hopkins University Press, 1999.

Sandrow, Nahma, trans. and ed. *God, Man, and Devil: Yiddish Plays in Translation*. New York: Syracuse University Press, 1999.

Shakespeare, William. *A Midsummer Night's Dream*. In *The Complete Pelican Shakespeare*. New York: Viking, 1977.

———. *The Winter's Tale*. In *The Complete Pelican Shakespeare*. New York: Viking, 1977.

Shaw, George Bernard. *You Never Can Tell*. In *Plays: Pleasant and Unpleasant*. New York: Brentano's, 1905.

Shirer, William L. *Berlin Diary: The Journal of a Foreign Correspondent, 1934–1941* (1941). Baltimore: Johns Hopkins University Press, 2002.

———. *The Rise and Fall of Third Reich: A History of Nazi Germany*. New York: Simon and Schuster, 1960.

Sophocles. *Antigone*. Trans. Robert Fagles. In *Sophocles: The Three Theban Plays*. New York: Viking, 1982.

Sprengel, Peter. *Populäres jüdisches Theater in Berlin von 1877 bis 1933*. Berlin: Haude and Spener, 1997.

———. *Scheunenviertel-Theater: Jüdische Schauspieltruppen und jiddische Dramatik in Berlin (1900–1918)*. Berlin: Gesellschaft für Theatergeschichte, 1995.

Steinweis, Alan E. *Art, Ideology, and Economics in Nazi Germany: The Reich Chambers of Music, Theater, and the Visual Arts*. Chapel Hill: University of North Carolina Press, 1993.

Strobl, Gerwin. *The Swastika and the Stage: German Theatre and Society, 1933–1945*. Cambridge: Cambridge University Press, 2009.

Willett, John. *The Theatre of the Weimar Republic*. New York: Holmes and Meier, 1988.

Wulf, Joseph, ed. *Theater und Film im Dritten Reich: Eine Dokumentation*. Gütersloh: Sigbert Mohn, 1964.

Wyman, David S. *The Abandonment of the Jews: America and the Holocaust, 1941–1945*. New York: W. W. Norton and Co., 1984.

Zweig, Stefan. *Jeremiah: A Drama in Nine Scenes*. Trans. Eden Paul and Cedar Paul. New York: Thomas Seltzer, 1922.

INDEX

STUDIES IN THEATRE HISTORY AND CULTURE

Actors and American Culture, 1880–1920
By Benjamin McArthur

The Age and Stage of George L. Fox, 1825–1877: An Expanded Edition
By Laurence Senelick

American Theater in the Culture of the Cold War: Producing and Contesting Containment
By Bruce McConachie

Classical Greek Theatre: New Views of an Old Subject
By Clifford Ashby

Czech Theatre Design in the Twentieth Century: Metaphor and Irony Revisited
Edited by Joseph Brandesky

Embodied Memory: The Theatre of George Tabori
By Anat Feinberg

Fangs of Malice: Hypocrisy, Sincerity, and Acting
By Matthew H. Wikander

Fantasies of Empire: The Empire Theatre of Varieties and the Licensing Controversy of 1894
By Joseph Donohue

French Theatre Today: The View from New York, Paris, and Avignon
By Edward Baron Turk

The Jewish Kulturbund Theatre Company in Nazi Berlin
By Rebecca Rovit

Jews and the Making of Modern German Theatre
Edited by Jeanette R. Malkin and Freddie Rokem

The Making of Theatrical Reputations: Studies from the Modern London Theatre
By Yael Zarhy-Levo

Marginal Sights: Staging the Chinese in America
By James S. Moy

Melodramatic Formations: American Theatre and Society, 1820–1870
By Bruce A. McConachie

Meyerhold: A Revolution in Theatre
By Edward Braun

Modern Czech Theatre: Reflector and Conscience of a Nation
By Jarka M. Burian

Modern Hamlets and Their Soliloquies: An Expanded Edition
By Mary Z. Maher

Molière, the French Revolution, and the Theatrical Afterlife
By Mechele Leon

The Most American Thing in America: Circuit Chautauqua as Performance
By Charlotte M. Canning

Othello and Interpretive Traditions
By Edward Pechter

Our Moonlight Revels: *A Midsummer Night's Dream* in the Theatre
By Gary Jay Williams

The Performance of Power: Theatrical Discourse and Politics
Edited by Sue-Ellen Case and Janelle Reinelt

Performing History: Theatrical Representations of the Past in Contemporary Theatre
By Freddie Rokem

The Recurrence of Fate: Theatre and Memory in Twentieth-Century Russia
By Spencer Golub

Reflecting the Audience: London Theatregoing, 1840–1880
By Jim Davis and Victor Emeljanow

Representing the Past: Essays in Performance Historiography
Edited by Charlotte M. Canning and Thomas Postlewait

The Roots of Theatre: Rethinking Ritual and Other Theories of Origin
By Eli Rozik

Shakespeare and Chekhov in Production: Theatrical Events and Their Audiences
By John Tulloch

Shakespeare on the American Yiddish Stage
By Joel Berkowitz

The Show and the Gaze of Theatre: A European Perspective
By Erika Fischer-Lichte

Stagestruck Filmmaker: D. W. Griffith and the American Theatre
By David Mayer

Strange Duets: Impresarios and Actresses in the American Theatre, 1865–1914
By Kim Marra

Textual and Theatrical Shakespeare: Questions of Evidence
Edited by Edward Pechter

Theatre and Identity in Imperial Russia
By Catherine A. Schuler

Theatre, Community, and Civic Engagement in Jacobean London
By Mark Bayer

Theatre Is More Beautiful Than War: German Stage Directing in the Late Twentieth Century
By Marvin Carlson

Theatres of Independence: Drama, Theory, and Urban Performance in India since 1947
By Aparna Bhargava Dharwadker

The Theatrical Event: Dynamics of Performance and Perception
By Willmar Sauter

The Trick of Singularity: *Twelfth Night* and the Performance Editions
By Laurie E. Osborne

The Victorian Marionette Theatre
By John McCormick

Wandering Stars: Russian Emigré Theatre, 1905–1940
Edited by Laurence Senelick

Writing and Rewriting National Theatre Histories
Edited by S. E. Wilmer